The Karaoke Singer's Guide to Self-Defense

featherproof BOOKS

The Karaoke Singer's Guide to Self-Defense

Tim Kinsella

For AC/CT

Extracting wasps from stings in flight...

—Bauhaus

Part 1

prologue

HAPPY HOUR AT THE LEGENDARY SHHH...

Norman had to reach into the toilet to grab the drowned mouse. Wallace crumpled his starched work shirt on the bar, checked his wristwatch against the bar clock. The clock set twelve minutes fast, he arrived at The Shhh... earlier than he'd left the forest preserve.

The dark room swelled into focus. A wide mirror propped up against the far wall, its top coming up waist high, doubled the bottom rungs of a steel ladder set on a plastic throw leaning against it. The room's dimensions difficult to gauge, assorted purples over black, Wallace momentarily mistook the thin-coils-of-glue swirling bare-wood board above the mirror as a window looking out over a sand-blown parking lot.

Wiping his hands dry on his suit pants, Norman stepped behind the bar, sighed, nodded hello. He leaned his substantial girth forward, nodded again. Wallace ordered just a ginger ale, please. The piece of pink paper left sitting on the bar, Norman picked it up and folded it, stuck it in his coat pocket. He set the ginger ale down in front of Wallace, reached for his cigar.

Wallace took a sip of his ginger ale, took out his wallet. He dropped a dollar on the bar, hoisted a leg outward to scoot up onto a stool.

At the bend at the end of the bar, Norman sat perpendicular to Wallace, lit his cigar.

With some effort, Wallace managed a pained squint-into-the-sun sort of grin. Silent, he bobbed his head back and forth, rolled his eyes.

Norman shook his head, stood up, took a few steps and poured himself a bourbon while standing. He lifted the bottle to Wallace to offer a drink. Wallace shook his head. "I don't really party," he said.

Norman nodded, spun back around the bar to his stool. He took a sip from his bourbon.

Attempting to hide it, Wallace sniffed both of his hands with a quick gesture. The two men, who had never seen each other before, sat together, alone, said nothing.

Wallace stood up, moved around the perimeter of the room in straight-legged, purposefully loping steps. Decorative steel moldings, sculpted sperms chasing eggs, sat stacked, un-hung next to a pile of large bolts. Norman watched Wallace as long as he could without turning his head, sipped from his bourbon.

Wallace sauntered over to the stage. Hand on hip, sipping his ginger ale, he admired the karaoke machine left set up from the night before. He nodded. He grinned and snorted, dropped his head. Norman spun his stool, did not hide watching him. Wallace smirked and waved, embarrassed to have drawn attention to himself. He cleared his throat.

1

The last to arrive at the funeral, Kent strut in solo, still lean and knotty as a robot, toothy grin handsome as a newscaster. His pockmarked cheeks tempered the dazzle and breezy blue chill of his eyes. He had always held his body at strange angles, tilting his head back to speak like an old-fashioned actor playing Robin Hood or the most cavalier of the Three Musketeers. With crisp articulation through a half-sneer, half-smile, he cocked his weight dramatically from one hip to the other to differentiate between speaking and listening, giving all his conversations a rhythmic bump.

Everyone else, having already assembled over the last hour and said their hellos, surrounded Kent and greeted him all at once at the back of the room. He made every greeting awkward, always offering his left hand to shake.

Mel, first time he'd seen his sister in some years, kissed him on the cheek. She looked good, still skinny as scarves draped over piping. Her black hair, wavy in a way many women envied even in passing or from afar, never needed more than a shake to fall in place. From textured freckling, like sand had been thrown at her when her thick skin was wet once and stuck, her blanched blue eyes burst.

Mel's friend Gus slapped Kent on the back. Ronnie stood a few feet away, smiling with her lips pursed, shy about Kent seeing her teeth. Breaking from her constant scratching, she waved but didn't approach.

Will greeted him with a nod and after a balked approach, a hearty left-handed handshake. Kent pulled him close, not letting go of his hand, to bump shoulders and approximate a hug. Will recoiled from the embrace, but stood close. Kent looked Will's face over carefully. Will submitted to the inspection.

"Boy oh boy, what have you been through, huh?" Kent sighed, layering on his ChapStick. Will turned away, shrugged, was ready to get back home. The small group standing around them dissipated, returned to clusters of hushed small talk. Will pulled a marshmallow bar from the inside pocket of his coat, bit the wrapper open, gripping the candy awkwardly with his mangled hand. It was earlier than he expected to need it, but he had packed a couple extra.

Glancing around the room, Kent stuck the wad of Nicorette he'd been smacking on like a wood block on his extended fingertip, took a steep pull from a pint of Crown in his pocket. Grimaced, gave Will a nod.

"Shit gives me such heartburn," Kent said.

"Crown?" Will responded with a nervous fist-clench knuckle crack, declining a slug before Kent tucked the bottle away.

"No, no." Kent shook his head. "Nicotine gum shit."

Will nodded. "You're running a little late today, huh?" he said.

Kent shrugged.

Kent had already had a shit day by the time he got there. Got behind leaving town that morning because he'd waited until after his son's football game to go. Stupid asshole Coach wouldn't even put his kid in. Kent had a long drive ahead of him, four hours, put it off for the game. Game time just early enough that with the time change he gained an hour, so he could justify sticking around. And the stupid asshole didn't even put his kid in.

The green field a glare, reflected bright white. Gave Kent a goddamn headache to watch even. The other idiot parents, drunks, deadbeats, cuckolds, and everyone knew that that one woman slept with her best friend's husband, the Coach. Wouldn't put Kent's kid in to play, even though he was the quickest one out there, because Kent didn't condescend to their small talk. Petty assholes took it out on the kids. Cost the team the game.

Wrapped up in their flirting, planning for ice cream and

nachos after the game, failed to give the boys the cheering they needed. Kent clapped alone on the sideline and jackass wouldn't even put his kid in. The heart those kids put into it, least the parents could have done, kept up the energy on the sidelines. Fed their spirits, down by ten in the fourth, not impossible.

Even Kent's own goddamn kid couldn't keep up the enthusiasm. He unbuttoned his chinstrap and Kent strode right over there, grabbed him by the arm. "You want to embarrass me? Button up, you gotta be ready to play."

Standing around like a floppy rag doll and what did he expect? The boys ran the field after a punt. Defense went on. The other boys lined up to give their teammates five, a slap on the rear, something, a little team spirit. But Kent's kid, brooding, stuck to himself, kicked at the dirt.

But Kent would not let those kids on the field down, just because everyone else had given up. "Come on, Killer Bees! Let's hold them!"

But that one kid in the backfield, they were trying to run the clock down, and that kid piled right over the Killer Bees. Straight up the middle, hit hard with his head down. The Killer Bees looked tired out there, embarrassing.

"Come on defense! Let's hold them here! Turn this game around now!"

And Kent's excuse for a son gave him a look? Kent had the team spirit his kid and his entire team lacked and he was gonna look at Kent? Kent should have left him there. Made him walk home.

The teams for the next game warmed up behind the far side of the field. The parents of those teams assembled, doubling the crowd. Kids with cleats on the concrete, what should Kent have expected with parents like that?

Other team scored, that one goddamn kid. Without him they'd have been nothing. He ran straight up the middle. Same play over and over, hand it to the big kid, plow straight over everyone. After a quick series of eight-yard runs, clock never stopping, he broke away up the middle. Those kids the Coach played, they didn't even try to catch him from behind.

The kid looked over his shoulder with ten yards to go still before the end zone, saw no one chasing him, and slowed down to a trot.

Time to look over his shoulder? Well, Kent had enough. "Come on, Defense! The game's not over! Look alive out there!"

Same play for the extra point. Down by seventeen with five minutes to go. Coach put Kent's kid in. Finally, ready to turn that thing around. Kent rooted hard, but he wasn't gonna let the Coach think he was getting away with that shit, blowing the game, not playing Kent's kid until the final minutes. Kent was on to him. "Alright, Coach! About time, We're gonna turn this around!"

Will caught a whiff of the Crown on Kent's swallowed belch.

"You're just getting here, to town?" Will asked.

"Yeah, just pulled in," Kent replied, plunking the small wad of Nicorette on his fingertip back into his mouth, chomping firmly to soften it.

"But I think I'm going to try to make it back tonight," Kent continued, noticing two large plastic grocery bags, stuffed close to tearing open, leaned against a wall.

"Really?" Will asked.

Kent shrugged. Two women, familiar, Nana's neighbors maybe, stood a few feet away. One whispered, pointed to Will. Mel approached the women with a light touch to one woman's elbow.

"Won't leave you much time in town," Will said.

Kent shrugged again, exaggerating the depth of his shrug. Duh. That was the idea, not much time in town. Shot a glance at the two women whispering. They pivoted, considered the wallpaper, one running her fingers along its tightly striped gold texture. Mel smirked at Kent.

"You could always stay at Nana's," Will suggested, flicking a lighter a few times to light a cigarette gripped low beneath his middle knuckles, close to his palm.

Kent really did love something about Nana's guest room. The quilt and draperies matched, pastoral scenes. He'd sniff at dust hung in sunbeams and smell fresh laundry.

Portraits of the three of them, Will, Mel, and him, captured at awkward ages, fixed in in-between states, tiled the walls, the most recent photos at least twenty years old. The meticulous hanging of three long rows above the dresser, standardized mismatched frames, but no system organized the sequence.

In the narrow area between the closet and the television, high up on a wooden stand, shingled jumbles of more photos hung no higher than Nana's furthest vertical extension.

Kent grabbed the lighter from Will's hand, shook it, flicked it a couple times quick until it sparked. Leaned in close to Will. Inhaling, Will nodded thanks.

"Yeah, I just got to town late last night," Will said.

Kent knocked his balance to his other hip, furrowed his brow.

"But I do understand you don't want to stick around," Will continued. "It's good to see you, man. But I've had just about enough of Michigan myself."

Kent looked over Will's shoulder and offered a pithy smirk to Nana's neighbor who poked at the plastic bags leaned against the wall. Fearing what Kent might say to them, Mel led the two women to the snack room. Kent looked back to Will, confused.

"Yep," Will said, dragging a toe along the edge of the plastic mat on the carpet. "I really am about ready to get home already." Nothing he had to do at home, probably just settle in with his videotape compilations of old television commercials. Just not being seen, relief from the gaze, all Will desired.

Kent shook his head. "What do you mean?" he said.

"What do you mean 'What do I mean?'" Will asked.

"I mean, what do you mean you 'just got to town?'"

Will didn't understand. He got to town the night before and he was ready to get out of there. Nothing he had to do, just wanted to be home.

"I got here last night, took the bus," Will said.

"You got here last night? From where? You don't live here?" Kent asked.

Will chuckled. "No, man. I left five years ago. Haven't been back since. Not even once."

"Really?" Kent said, nodding. "Oh."

"Yeah."

"I haven't seen you in five years then?" Kent asked.

"I don't know," Will shrugged. "I don't know. Guess not," he said.

Kent nodded. Guess that accounted for his shock, Will's transformation.

Kent had taken the half-hour-longer route to avoid a toll, but wasn't sure if the gas ended up negating the saved toll money. "How much did the bus cost?" he asked.

Carving through the fields outside of town, the October corn green and yellow in the rain-slashed beams and flat before the endless miles of black beyond, Will leaned into the bus's tilt around each curve.

1. He admitted he was powerless over fighting—that his life had become unmanageable.
2. Came to believe that a Power greater than him could restore him to sanity.

Since he'd left town, a new water park had been built among the old houses close to the road. Its marquee slide had two symmetrical inclines equally steep, a wide V of metallic tubing. Will couldn't imagine the glide down from either direction would propel one with enough momentum to launch up the other side.

3. Made a decision to turn his will and his life over to the care of this higher power as he understood It.

That first house past the park's last fence had always been painted a faint aquamarine, probably a subconscious prompt for the construction of the water park. The house at the apex of a curve in the road had curtains pinched into diamonds in four windows across the front, offering the household's life on display as if a purposely constructed diorama, any movement past a window appearing as a taut one-second drama composed for the audience whizzing by. The next house, with its collapsed front porch under crunched screens, was a canary yellow.

The only one awake on the bus, maybe. It was maybe eight-thirty, but seemed late. People leaning upright against crumpled coats for pillows were outlined by the dim dotting of low orange lights along each side of the bus, everyone silent in the hiss of the rain.

4. Made a searching and fearless moral inventory of himself.

5. Admitted to God, to himself, and to another human being the exact nature of his wrongs: fighting.

The bus swerved and returned in a dark fluid hurl. A graveyard for propane tanks behind a tall fence flashed past. Will's overstuffed plastic bags crowded his foot space. He kept one on his lap.

The driver kept the bus at a hurried, bumping speed for a two-lane highway in the rain at night. His shadow stretched and turned back toward Will when they occasionally crossed another vehicle's lights. Will looked through rain like scuttling amoeba, magnetized and vibrating, transparent except for its motion on the cold pane at his nose.

6. Was entirely ready to have God remove all these defects of character.

The real shock of coming home was in having survived to return. Whatever, not even necessarily any daunting trials or epic journeys, just time passed. In returning, he could feel for the first time that he truly had been gone. Leaving, he had brought his continuous awareness with him; leaving never felt disruptive, but continuous. The continuous-self greeted the new place, unfamiliar people, and that continuous-self carried home along with it.

But returning home, he set this memory of home he had been unaware of bringing everywhere with him up against the place itself. Doing so revealed how faded the impression of home he'd been carrying had become. This was the real jolt, the necessary modifications. Which was to be trusted— the home he had been living with for five years since having been there or the home that flashed by him now, altered in innumerable tiny ways?

After some hypnotizing minutes—maybe a minute or fifteen—Will took a marshmallow bar from his bag. The road straightened. The homes retreated from crowding the road and pulled together, back to the far side of small yards. The gravel shoulder melted into the burping mud of the lawns in the rain.

All those missing years lost to addiction of some kind, always something taken too far, always a new thing until the fighting finally stuck. He kept straight by picking up where he left off, a 33-year-old teenager coming home after having started over some place new, had never been at home without some form of addiction before. Keeping straight was a pattern maintained—a fruit cup for breakfast, eleven grapes, six pieces of melon, a dry bologna sandwich with crackers same time every day. Same time every day, go running.

That one brown house still had that hole in its garage door splintering like a chewed cookie smile, the hole the exact size and height of the car parked on the driveway in front of it. Streets shot off and hid around bends under thick trees.

7. Humbly asked Him to remove his shortcomings.
8. Made a list of all persons he had harmed, and became willing to make amends to them all, willing, yes, in theory, all of them.

Slowing from a long way back, the bus came to a halt at a stoplight. Everyone on board woke in stretches and moans. With a volleyball net in a deep sand puddle and a grill left to plink in the rain, one of the three churches at this corner, hardly bigger than its sign, was a trailer made of aluminum siding.

The Cherry Vale Community Center appeared to be built with a kindergartener's big blocks. A mile of tall barbed-wire fencing locked in piles of garbage, kept out the garbage thieves. Birds sat on the barbed-wire.

The bar without a name, hardly bigger than a car, stood alone among enough warped pavement for a mall parking lot. It displayed an *OPEN* sign behind bars in its window, but it was dark. Will remembered it further toward downtown than it was.

9. Hadn't made direct amends to such people wherever possible, but he will, sure will.
10. Continued to take personal inventory and when he was wrong promptly admitted it.

The salon, speckled brick against vanilla brick, was closed. Thin steel beams like torn braces along its slanted roof revealed where the sign once was. Passed Ronnie's house, overgrown. Would she have any teeth left? Can't stare. The Chinese House of Buffet closed down.

11. Sought through prayer and meditation to improve his conscious contact with God as he understood Him, praying only for knowledge of His will for him and the power to carry that out.

Handwritten signage was still in the window: "Pam and John's Place" in shaky red paint. A swirling single line graphic of a cappuccino was scratched through and left in pulses. Blinds half-pulled open at an angle, the restaurant had been filled with scattered office furniture, high-back padded chairs with shopping cart wheels.

Of course The Shhh... was bustling. Will wouldn't know Mel's car. The cartoon woman on the sign with a finger up to her lips to say 'shhh...' was three wide swooshes of color, yellow hair blowing, red lips and blue eyes on blankness. The neon name fried in the rain, shhh.

12. Having had a spiritual awakening as the result of these steps, he hid for five years in his small room above the Saigon Restaurant in southeast Ohio, practicing these principles in all his affairs.

Five years above the Saigon Restaurant, that small room, chipped paint and soiled wallpaper, not enough light to make out the cracked tile's stains. Three steps from the toilet to the stove and the bed one step from either, Will never got sick of waking up and thinking to himself, "Saigon, shit. I'm still only in Saigon." He really thought that was funny in a sort of spiritual-warrior kind of way.

He'd scoot the bed from the wall to make room to do his sit-ups, his Tai Chi. He could stay in shape even if he quit fighting. Sore all the time, he could never stretch enough, felt his muscles slowly liquefy as his last gashes weaved themselves closed under his final fading bruises. Quit drinking, not because he had a drinking problem, but because of the slippery slope it might trigger. He could no longer allow himself to relax, drink a beer, think, Eh, what's the big deal, throw just this one punch this one time. Required vigilance.

He shadowboxed, removed the lampshade, balanced the bare-bulbed lamp on the throw rug, stepped in between the lamp and the wall. Thrown upward, his shadow bent at the ceiling. He scooted the lamp back, stepped closer to the wall, back toward the lamp to flatten his shadow on the screen, the wall of his small room. His shadow still looked the same as it ever had, no disfiguration.

Though careful, he cracked small dimples in the plaster where the wood screws held, removing the mirror upon moving in. He pushed the dresser aside, blocking the closet to clear the screen for projection. Uppercut, uppercut, turn sideways to see the jabs. Dancing feet planted, slick with sweat and panting, an indulgence to leave one's self open with a wide sideways swing. He'd even drop himself backwards on the bed when he first got there, stave off the body slam withdrawal.

He'd been fine five years out of Stone Claw Grove. It was always within him. No one could ever take away from him whatever idealized, beautiful ways in which he chose to remember it, even if it was only idealized by association as the grounds of that idealized, beautiful youth of his, ha!

Sometimes Will was glad Dell left not only for his own sake, but for Dell's sake too. Dell never had to see this mess Will had made of himself. Who wouldn't have left? Probably saw it coming.

And things were simpler somewhere new, even if moving hadn't been his own choice. People he met could just assume he'd always been that way, disfigured. No one judged him. No one knew that gangly olive-skinned blond kid. Will wouldn't have to worry, turn a corner in the grocery store and run into that kid's aunt.

His personal mandate, the thirteenth step, the important one—

13. Do not, under any circumstances, ever, no matter what: never set foot in Stone Claw Grove again.

That was the deal.

But returning, a quick visit even, a prohibited visit, associations threatened to awaken the urges he kept buried. Being away and staying away, he kept the appetites squashed. Returning, he'd have to remain doubly aware, constantly, keep the appetites squashed. Only takes one second of weakness.

In the front window of an empty grocery store, twisted butcher paper taped on one side hung like a crinkled curtain, a kite frozen mid-swoop. Cardboard leaned up to different heights in the window from the floor inside. The marshmallow bar melted in his mouth.

You'll pull it together. That's really the only confidence one needs. When the time comes, no choice, when it matters and it alone matters and nothing else can be done, action alone, then yes, it, I, you can, will, must pull it all together. You'll pull it all together because how else? What choice? Confidence doesn't ask when. And home, first time in five years, no fights. Been five years, it'll be fine, no fighting. Remember the steps, no fighting. And they'll all be looking at you, watching you, fine.

But that thing he always carried, never needed, but always carried in case he needed it, break-glass-in-case-of-emergency, that thing, call it rage; he needed it exactly because what if he forgot to carry it with him one day? Not actually needing it, but the worry that he may need it required him to carry it with him everywhere, always.

Everyone on the bus was as quiet awake as they had been asleep. Wet, crimped brick in the streetlights brought out the broad brush-strokes of white on white.

Kent deemed the funeral an occasion to wear his favorite silky shirt, covered cuff to collar in a royal blue and white, continuous print. He wore it like a parachute spun out of egg whites. An armored dragon coiled up the sleeve, its underbelly shell patterned and cinching around his bicep, opened up into the dragon's wild smile. Its teeth covered the curve of his shoulder.

If Kent had not always worn it so, the dragon's spiked hair would have appeared to motivate his own hair, impossibly thick and beginning to gray in a perfect frosting pattern. Kent's cowlicks frolicked like the curls of breaking waves. His spiked top and shaved sides too short to be pulled back into his ponytail, no larger than a small thumb.

Even the riotous look he had always carried in his eyes as carefully as a bucket of water matched that of the dragon. The shirt's print opened up across the left side of his chest into a sunset through a brewing cloud-scape, that wide breath of sky heightening the dense sense of the dragon as a mountain. The identical scene was illustrated from behind across his back.

How was he supposed to know Will no longer lived in town? He never saw that coming. No one ever told him anything.

At the game that morning the big ape asshole Coach looked sideways at Kent, thought he could stare him down. The starting lineup had their helmets off. They didn't even care.

They were talking with their mommies about which pricey ice cream place to go to. They wanted to celebrate being losers?

"Let's turn this around now!" Kent shouted, his hands cupped over his mouth. The kids on the sideline who had been in the game until that point, rolled their eyes at Kent.

Running to the outside, Kent's kid was pitched the ball. Moving toward the sideline, come on, stop the clock, but his fullback, the oaf, didn't help him out. Clobbered, the linebackers let straight through before Kent's kid could make it out of bounds. They brought him down hard. The clock ticked. Their laughter audible, the linebackers did a stupid, choreographed dance as they got up.

Coach gave Kent a look. Fuck him. Kent could outshout those little linebacker, little shits, threw his arms up, "Gaaah!" Coach shook his head, looked at Kent as he whispered in the end's ear, sent him out to the huddle with a pat. Kent layered on the ChapStick.

And again the same play, a pitch to Kent's kid heading toward the sideline. Same play as last, but he pulled back, turned to throw. He looked downfield. No one out there, the linebackers on him again. Spinning to stay on his feet, unprotected out there. Darted back toward the center of the field.

"Throw the ball!" Kent shouted. "Stop the clock!"

Dazed, Kent's kid was wobbly-kneed out there. That linebacker boosted himself up to crash down hard on him and Kent saw it, but he couldn't believe it. Turning from the blow, his kid just extended his arm, handed the ball to the linebacker. The linebacker didn't even break his stride, grabbed it and off down the field, no one between him and the end zone.

Parents shook their heads, groaned. Coach looked to the parking lot. But Kent wouldn't let him go so easy. His kid sauntered over to the sideline and Kent called him over. He pretended not to hear Kent, but no way. He was not getting away with this. This was our team. Kent would not show him any favoritism.

"Get over here! What was that?" He stood over his kid, grabbed him by his facemask when he refused to look up at him.

"What was that?"

The kid shrugged. Shrugs!

"What? You don't know?"

His kid pivoted to head over toward the team, but no way.

"No way. Look at me. Look at me. What was that?" Kent had him by the facemask again. "You afraid to get hit?"

Coach called him over. "Hey, come here."

Coach's wife and her best friend, the one the Coach fucks, stood behind him, looking at Kent. One whispered to the other.

"No. You stay right here," Kent said.

"Dad, Coach is calling me."

"I don't care," Kent said, jerked his facemask. "You stay right here. Listen to me. What was that?"

"I don't know."

Hands on hips, the Coach approached.

"You don't know? You afraid to get hit?" Kent went on. "Are you?"

"I don't know." He wouldn't look up.

The Coach interjected. "Alright, Kent. It's been a long day. We're all frustrated."

Kent turned to that son of a bitch. The big ape thought he scared him? "Oh, long day for all of us, huh?"

"Come on, Kent. Let's all calm down now."

"Long day? I got a four-hour drive today. You don't think I would've liked a head start on it. But I waited to leave for this?"

Coach pleaded, "Well, go easy Kent. It's only a game."

The big ape son of a bitch put his hand on Kent's shoulder and Kent jerked out from under it.

"Okay Kent, whatever."

The big oaf walked off, his stupid windbreaker crackling. Looked over to his wife and her best friend—they rolled their eyes to him and he shook his head, dropped his head and sighed as he walked.

"Well, what's that Coach?" Kent called out. "I guess you don't care if we lose."

Kent glanced around, waited to make sure people were listening. "You get fucked anyway, whether we win or lose."

The Coach stopped, turned around and looked at Kent confused.

"Which one do you fuck after a loss, Coach? The wife or the mistress?"

Other parents looked, and the kids, but fuck him. Kent didn't care. The Coach stepped back to him in long, deliberate steps. Another kick-off was returned behind them.

"Look, Kent, I don't know what you're talking about. But I am really gonna have to insist you quit cursing on my sideline, alright?" He smacked and chomped on his wad of gum, stared hard at Kent. Kent knocked his weight to his left, set his left foot back. He lifted his sunglasses to his hair, wanted to smile, faked a smile awkwardly. Lots of people standing around, Coach glanced back to his sideline, the breeze.

"Now beat it, alright? You guys both go ahead." Coach turned to Kent's kid. "I'll see you at practice Monday, alright? Rest up."

Kent's kid headed toward the car. Two backs turned to Kent, headed off in different directions, cleats on concrete and the Coach, calling out to the defense. "Look alive. Let's hold them!"

Coach picked through the kids in a loose swarm around him, spun a couple around by their shoulder pads. "Who hasn't been in yet?"

The whistle blew. The next game's teams warming up beyond the end zone grunted in unison. The ice cream man's jingle looped. Kent's kid stood at the car, his uniform not even dirty.

"Nice shirt, asshole," a Killer Bee bumping past Kent said to his friend's amusement.

Football—hardly Kent's idea—every Saturday morning chasing all over with these illiterate slobs, arguing Reality TV and sports radio feuds. Teaching the kids to run into each other and act all big, the pretenses of sophisticated strategy. Okay, not Kent's thing, at all.

But you wanna do it, come on, you gotta do your best, right? These fucking apes, the barbarian Coach, my god, his sluts...

Collect yourself, Kent. A piece of Nicorette, lower your shades from your hair. Knock mud clumps from gym shoes stepping into the lot. Goddamn mud stain on white shoes. Like Kent would have time to coach, but didn't seem it'd ever get done right otherwise. Look at them, eating their gross orange slices with their dirty paws, the citrus another sticky layer over the dirt. Fuck them. This was what Kent's kid wanted him to spend his money on, his time. Did he even care? Did he even take it seriously?

March to the car in long steps, Kent. Don't turn back, head up.

"Don't you want me to throw my jersey and pads in the trunk?"

"Oh, I'm sorry. I must've missed it." Kent smiled, unlocking his own door. "Did you break a sweat today?"

From across the room, Ronnie watched poor Will, heavy plastic bags at his feet, struggle to make conversation with Kent. Kent just so unfriendly, scanning the room to tally how many family members, how many acquaintances, strategize how he'd position himself away from most of them. No problem for Will, most people afraid to even approach him. Catching Ronnie's eye a second, Kent sighed, Joe next to her with the hiccups, scratching at himself. Will offered Kent a bite of his marshmallow bar. Kent thought he was sneaky with a pull from the bottle of Crown tucked in his pocket.

Greeting Will earlier, Ronnie clasped her hands behind his back and leaned her head on his shoulder, held it there, lowered her head and heard his heartbeat. Joe grimaced looking Will over, lit a cigarette and shivered. But when Kent arrived Ronnie had remained a step away, never really said hello.

Ronnie still had all her teeth when she first met Joe in 1987, giving in to a predisposition for drink she didn't know she had until then. Worked as a cashier at the hospital cafeteria. Joe thought he'd maybe had a heart attack or a collapsed lung, but no test could determine anything wrong. The pain persisted for over a week. Finally, on his third visit, someone thought to give him an X-ray. A broken rib. He didn't remember anything happening, but he often woke up on the floor without remembering falling asleep. Must've maybe fallen and cracked it.

Ronnie fancied herself qualified as at least a nurse, if not a doctor, simply by proximity. But she never calloused as the doctors and nurses had to. Instead she was known to hold up her line to hear someone's story through. Eating a rib sandwich while still standing in line, rib sandwiches being a Tuesday special and Tuesday being the high traffic "Open Clinic Day" had become a punch line among hospital staff.

Joe never set foot in the cafeteria until a follow-up visit some weeks later. His bones were brittle, malnourished. When he went through Ronnie's line, tears streaked her hot cheeks. But she remained unshaken from her task, ringing people up with a smile and friendly small talk.

He asked her what was wrong. He felt terrible seeing her cry. She explained a young kid, early twenties, had come through her line that morning, had driven all night to say goodbye to his dying grandma who passed away just minutes before he arrived.

They went to the casino that night. She brought him luck. At six AM, in line for breakfast at the casino cafeteria, Joe sprung for the breakfast of a young man in front of them. The young man protested, "No really, thanks, but I'm fine. I swear."

But Joe insisted, "Fine? In those rags boy say fine? Those rags, fine?"

Ronnie liked that Joe was immediately so comfortable with her. There was no shyness, no getting to know you. He was immediately distracted when she spoke, immediately impatient with her kids, like he'd been around all along.

He fell asleep on his back on the couch with wide peals of snoring, the first night she stayed at his motel room.

Losing interest in Kent and Mel's expanded and polite hello, Will kneeled next to a plant for a while holding his mini-fan up to his face. Leaned against some walls, gummed clumsy on a sandwich, time for dry bologna on damp bread. Nana used to give him cold green bean omelettes as a snack, hardboiled eggs in spaghetti, juice cut with water. She had witnessed the beginnings of his decay, but she had no idea what he'd eventually become.

She was solid, remained so. No wonder she made a prized Depression bride, tall and strong, skin powder soft, smooth along her broad white back. Muscled like a horse, strong and broad, rippling.

She kept her robe on as he ran the bath. It was tough for her to bend down to touch the water. She leaned against him and, pressed together like that, he lowered her, spreading his knees wide so she had space to bend. He hated the touching. Stretching fingertips toward the water, she moaned, Can't extend so low, need to wait.

"C'mon Nana. You can do it," he said.

It would be more difficult to keep her still and balanced and wait for the water to rise to her fingertips than it would be to lift her and lower her again. A catcher's-squat cramp crept over him.

He knew how slim this temperature range was. It had to be exactly right. She was not picky. She was sensitive. She was old. He'd hate a bath not hot enough. He'd hate a bath too hot. The least he could do was get this right. But he didn't want to wait.

He didn't know what the fuck he was doing. He felt sick. He felt like he'd drunk too much coffee. He knew he didn't want her to think it was her body made him sick. He knew however hard it was for him it was worse for her. He knew he had to be cool, no big deal, get it done. He knew that, accepted it.

He insisted, "No, come on Nana. Let me know if it's okay." A degree too hot or a degree too cold, she'd flip. He'd have to start over.

She wouldn't flip. She'd be really sweet about it, "Oh honey," always drawing any one syllable out into two. "That's just too hot. I can't do it."

He didn't want one extra second balancing her over the slick tub. He didn't need one extra second of her getting a chill or one extra second of her pressing up against him, one extra second of this deep-rooted nauseating awareness of his sexuality.

So he lowered her and her weight was dropped dead weight in his arms. And he tried to keep his back straight and bend with his knees but he felt her robe open and the soft flesh of her breast press up against his chest. And he looked straight up and ahead over her shoulder because he got a peek and that was enough for him. And she couldn't be a more modest woman, this woman he'd known to hide her newest set of plates when the neighbors came over because she didn't want to appear as if gloating over her new plate set. So he knew she was no happier about this situation than he was.

His feet slipped. His shoes left rubber sole track patterns in the sweat of the tiles. He lowered her. She grunted. "Oh sweetie."

"C'mon Nana."

"Oh."

"C'mon."

She dunked two fingertips up to the first knuckles and recoiled upward.

"That's good honey, that's good."

It was a relief to pick her up. She stood before him and straightened herself up, pulling her robe closed.

"I can take it a wee bit hotter."

"You sure?"

"Yeah, yeah. Turn it up a little bit."

"Yeah?"

"Yes please."

"Okay." He creaked the hot water faucet open a smidge more.

"I'd like to sit down on the toilet there honey."

"Okay."

"Rest my feet a minute."

"Yep."

He grabbed her again, throwing her arm over his shoulder. Lowering her was easier this time. He'd plunk her down into place in one motion. She could slip at any moment. He could drop her. Everything was slick and sweat. Her eyes popped from tired animality. He scooted her into place on the toilet. Her flour white curls were so thin. He'd never before noticed the swatches of peach baldness from which her curls twisted up into each other.

He leaned back against the sink alongside her, better than hovering above her. Lit a cigarette.

The events were long dissipated, but he knew the photos of her bathing him as an infant, a toddler, pulling his hair up into coiling spirals of shampoo foam, both of them smiling easily. Him with a rubber ducky and a plastic red bobbing boat. She looked not dissimilar to now, simply not yet faded.

His last night before leaving town, shriveled and shivering, having fallen asleep in a draining tub alone at The Carroll Motel, Will woke not knowing where he was, unable to determine how long he'd been out for. Attempting to unfold himself and stand, his battle hangover knocked him back down quick. His knees reached the faucet. He could reach his knees. To warm up, turned the shower on, the shock of its sudden gust over him enough to accept the lukewarm water like needling static on his chill, a makeshift blanket.

Maybe twice a year, maybe four times one year and then not even once the next, Will found himself sitting down in a shower. Maybe it was only once a year and felt like more. Sitting down in a shower, the faucet pouring over him from up high, he knew, Man, dark times. Never decided, okay now I'm going to sit down in the shower. Just happened. Maybe he was drunk. Maybe he got his ass kicked, probably drunk and got his ass kicked. Something would trigger it, the inability to not do it even, and he would sit down and let it rain down on him, Dark times man, ugh. But like an alarm, the shock woke him up to his circumstances, bad momentum and had to deal, so it was good in that way.

And it always brought Dell back. And Dell, honestly, he never really even knew the man. Of course he remembered Dell's presence, this presence, a giant penis drinking a beer in the shower. That's what he remembered about Dell.

Not like he showered with him all the time. He didn't think he did. He couldn't imagine that would've been the case for any reason. Dell was gone by the time he was two, three years old. Even memories a couple years after that, Will couldn't distinguish the memories from the photos he'd seen a million times. He could remember the experiences, but all he remembered of them was the photographs, like some afternoon had been compressed to three by five inches, browns and oranges saturated. That was the seventies, after all.

But by that time, Dell was gone. Must not have been much taking of pictures when Dell was actually around. Or those pictures were all thrown away or burned in a little bonfire ceremony. All Will knew were the stories. And in that same way that he couldn't know the photos from the memories, he couldn't know the legend of Dell from the experience of Dell. He remembered some ache through the house. Or he thought he did.

But Will did know he did remember that giant penis in the shower drinking a can of beer. The bitter smell of beer poured over his head with a chuckle, his hair lathered up in sweet shampoo. Other than that, only the general sense of mania Dell set off in everyone, or if not mania, some sort of concentrated repression, potential mania.

Will should have known, don't sit down in the shower. It's guaranteed. Might take days to get up, shake off. That's the one thing he just really, really had to remember, whatever else, anything, whatever, just don't sit down in the goddamn shower.

Sometimes when it rained even, in one second, he'd be transformed. He's a two-, three-year-old, however old kids are when they can first stand up. Will became that two-, three-year-old kid getting rained down on in the shower. Dell's penis, that lopping flesh, a thick soft snake with its Cyclops eye peeking out, its helmet, staring down on him. Dangling just above Will's forehead and if he tried to look up into the stream of the shower for a second, beating down on him constantly, it'd always be there, Dell's penis. It'd be there, looking down on him, popping out from the steam. He could never really look for long. Just the second one can look up into a stream of water pouring down onto one's face, like sharp shards, like static.

And Dell would pour his beer over Will's head. Rub the bitter beer into his hair and laugh. And Will knew that that part that hung with its own weight from Dell was like that little sprig attached to himself.

That night at The Carroll Motel, sunrise still a long ways off, he could sense it. The night felt endless. Will couldn't sit up enough to reach the faucet, too beat up to bend. The prickling of the shower pinned him. Rolling over on his side, his own weight heavy on his sore shoulder against the tub. At least the shower's stream could sting his profile for a while, give his face a break.

He drifted off, not sleeping, but drifted through and beyond the thick pulse of his body, scorching above his shoulders in the constant blast of biting droplets, goosebumps below his chest.

And if there were two of him, he considered, somehow two Wills, Will #1 and Will #2, one would undoubtedly get around to asking the other, "So when you get stuck in the rain, the clouds all came together when you were inside somewhere, you weren't expecting it and you get stuck walking, when you get stuck walking through the rain, are you really always feeling like your dad's penis is hanging down from the clouds? Really?"

And the other Will, Will #2 would think a minute sadly, gosh, maybe, before knowing just what he meant, how he really did feel. And he'd answer "No," smiling. He'd say, "No, if you are really also me, then you know that no, it's not actually like that. Not unless it's raining beer."

Nana's legs bulged in odd spots, melted fists behind her knees, a shape fighting outward finding form in compromise, her ankles like tents filled with rain. Jagged blue veins webbed her legs. Her porcelain skin tone had shattered and yet she remained upright as much as she did, the give in her step, the slip between cracked plates.

This webbing, without central roots, apparently no center at all, surprised Will. He'd expect exploded veins to look like veins and he didn't know what veins looked like but he'd expect them to have major thoroughfares and branches like snaking, two-lane highways off an interstate. But no major roads were drawn out in double thickness. Instead, it was all equal shattering without a point of primary convergence, without a connecting narrative running through them. Without a map of the body projected onto the screen of its own soft parchment shell like flaked filo dough, no center, no beginning, no end, no momentum, no path traced, no map laid, no landscape, simply flatness.

Nana looked up at Will unblinkingly, mouth tight, nostrils flared. Her chest heaved heavily. He returned her stare, nodding. She asked something of him. Something, did he mind? Did he understand this from her perspective? Did he get it? Could he stomach this? All in this look he'd never seen before from her, the look of a hunted squirrel cornered. Her large glasses amplified her gaze.

"Gimme your glasses, Nana."

"Oh, really?"

She cleared her throat and reached thumb and index finger to her glasses, but once gripping paused.

"I don't know. I'm really blind without them."

"I know."

With a bend and hard pull he quieted the faucet. Turning back to face her, again standing over her, he found her paused. Pinching still at the watch-screws of her glasses, nostrils open, she looked beyond him, concentrating on the grout of the seam of tub and tile.

"Nana."

She snapped from her gaze and sucked a hard breath into her sudden mouth.

"It's just..."

Her shoulders collapsed. He spread his fingers, stepped toward her with open palms.

"I know, come on."

"I just..."

"I know."

Slipping his arms under hers, he pulled her up against him. She helped as she could with a lean. Once up, she moved for her glasses again, around his back, but had trouble reaching. She let out a deep breath, gave up on the glasses and glanced a fingertip to the pearl edge of the sink.

"Okay?"

"Okay."

They moved one foot of their four at a time in heavy clomps. The full weight of both of them combined dropped on each single heel. This is how they turned. The bathroom spun in starts, off-white shining tiles, each framed by interlocking matte grout, graphed the wall behind the toilet. A bowl of sweet chipped-bark potpourri and a book of inspirational Bible quotes sat on the back of the toilet. A towel plush enough to have been cut from the carpet of a luxury hotel, had a tight knit monogram, unfamiliar initials curling across its bottom, folded tightly perfect. Sculpted soap to look like sea shells from pink to rose, pale aquamarine to muted sea foam.

Star, *Globe*, and *Enquirer* were stacked in a wicker basket. The thin page of the top issue was dimpled by drips of water, warping a familiar face. Burned by love and eating to cope, the star had been served up for public sacrifice before, won't flinch. The wet page pinched the star's familiar face in toward its middle, furrowing his brow and collapsing his nose, his chin like a diffused watercolor of a robot's jaw made of a bucket clamping upward.

Will looked up in the mirror as they spun, saw himself straining, his head on her shoulder as if her back was his torso and his head was set off-center. He looked away from himself quick. He looked down at the swoop of her robe. Her panting breath on his neck low at his collar rippled through him stiffening his skin like a brisk breeze and tingle. His ass clenched, pulled up toward his waist. He passed himself in the mirror in three heavy clomps of their slow spin. What's worse, what am I more afraid to look at; the thing itself I'm repulsed by, or—is it even worse—to see myself repulsed?

He looked down and away from both his own reflection and Nana.

"C'mon Nana."

"Okay."

Blinds were cracked under the thin curtain. The curtain hung, leaving the bottom third of the window visible.

Finally they stood sideways next to the bathtub's lip. He pulled away from her enough that she could lower her robe, but not so far away that he could see her. As she looked down to her robe falling to her feet, he compounded the surprise of the chill on her spread skin with a single, jerking gesture, lowering her glasses from her nose.

2

Taking Kent's leather jacket for him, Will noticed that the coat's Arabic inseam, quilted to imply some timeless regal air, was indistinguishable from Mel's jacket. Always in their crisp black jeans and crisp black leather jackets, Will's siblings had both adopted this uniform to imply some agreed upon idea of seriousness. Mel and Kent both always looked as if they might never wear an article of clothing a second time.

Mel was there already when Will arrived, limping a little. She had greeted him in the doorway with a prolonged silent collapse into his brute hug. He'd maybe never seen her leather jacket over a dress before. A cousin, no more than an acquaintance, pulled her away to mutter formalities, a polite embrace, but offered Will no more than a glancing, affected grin, eyes lowered.

Turning back to Will, her palms to his cheeks, Mel looked him over closely. One eye socket reconstructed a little lopsided, that eye faded milky white. With her fingertip she traced a scar thick and round as an earthworm across his forehead above the other eye. One side of his bottom lip completely gone, gave him a silly drunken look, a perpetual duh. The top half of one ear looked chewed off, and his crooked hairline next to it looked clawed off. Another splotch toward the crown of his head: hair didn't grow over scar tissue. Seemed happy enough, maybe. Hadn't said a word, but smiled relaxed enough. No raw wounds or bruises, no icepack's flush under his eye.

The stupid dents in the carpet at Nana's that morning had made her nervous, provoked her distrust. Will could've been back to visit Nana any time without Nana or anyone else mentioning it to her. Mel resented him for never visiting, but maybe she should've been resenting him for never getting in touch when he did visit.

Mel had been by Nana's place a lot in the last few days, sorting stuff. Met Ronnie and Joe there earlier that morning even, soon as they pulled into town.

Hands above it but not touching, as if she possessed some powers of magnetizing balance, Ronnie willed the stack of thick sweaters in Nana's guest room not to teeter, but it toppled. To clear the bed she'd hoisted the armload, dropped it on that strange piece of furniture, some crossbreed of exercise bike and giraffe made of leather and wood. Leaving the sweaters in a pile on the floor, she stepped to the bathroom, ran a washcloth under hot water, wrung it out.

In the living room, Nana's collections, pulled from shelves and drawers, stacked together in kind. Snowglobes in a square-based pyramid, painted plate sets and candy dishes in towers, a mass grave of ceramic figurines. In a large folded piece of cardboard, Nana had kept the world's ultimate collection of Mel's paintings, early dramatic figure studies evolving into the thick, dark smears of her teenage years.

Wobbly, Joe grabbed for the detailed ledger Mel held written out in Nana's neat penmanship. Mel's dress—worn over oversized flannel pajama pants—lifted when she spun away from him. She bumped her head on the chandelier, which, with the table having been moved, hung low in the middle of the room.

She poked at the list, irritated. "This thing, it exists?"

Joe swiped for the list again, stumbled to keep his balance between the stacks. "I'll let me see," in that high, shredded-throat, whistling voice of his.

"Goddamn it, Joe, hold on," she said, extending a step over a small Styrofoam snowman and a spice rack, a pang in her sore ankle. "What's she even talking about, this, Grandpa's red toy car? I've never seen that."

Joe rattled against the glass bookcase pulled from the wall.

"Here, why come on now, why not let Joe here have a look see, why not?" he hiccupped. "When a boy that's exactly,

41

exactly the kind of toy I appreciate real. Not kids now trash, got so much stuff of everything don't appreciate."

Mel twisted away from him, explained that the ledger clearly stated he was to get Grandpa's lighters and that was it, Grandpa's lighters. But he kept talking about Indian Statue Man. "All years, that old woman she knew all the years I loved Indian Statue Man."

"Yeah well, sorry," she said. "That says Kent."

Joe snorted and stepping to the end table to down the bottom of his cold coffee in a gulp, knocked over some short stacks of poker chips. He looked around the room slow, squinting, the whistle of his breath through his nose. Looking, where is Indian Statue Man?

"Why don't you take a break, Joe? Get some air, maybe go TCB at the OTB."

He smiled, repeated it with his own bump, "T—C—B—O —T—B."

Crouching, Mel smirked with effort. Figures, she'd been stuck alone with the slow details of death, every ten minutes repeating plans for Nana's ride to the doctor, remember to add water to the can of soup. Of course Mel alone would be stuck with Joe, grabby in the aftermath.

"I'm gone to more coffee," he said, apparently all at once relaxed. He offered her a cup. She stretched her back, hands to floor behind her, sat up to rub her sore ankle. "Oh, I think I'm good, thanks."

"Good warm up?" Joe said, picking up her cup as he stepped away. "Hot delicious hot coffee."

Distracted by the ledger, Mel said, "Sure, thanks, why not?" to get him out of there.

"Cream, no sugar?" Joe asked.

"Yeah, thanks."

Walking off Joe bumped his head on the chandelier, paused to steady its swing. He peeked in on Ronnie as he passed the bedroom. Flat on her back on the bed, shoes on, the folded rag masked her eyes. She scratched her side.

Surveying the stacks, Mel couldn't believe anyone might actually argue for anything there. Coffee table books of famous paintings, bathroom books of aphorisms, other books one could flip open and begin reading anywhere. The screen of a big, old calculator looked like it had been sneezed on.

She wasn't hungry, but had a taste for peas and eggs like Nana made them. Fry up the peas with onions, crack a couple eggs over them. She popped a pill, lit a cigarette.

Returning to the living room with a smile, Joe held her coffee out to her. Mel inspected two snowglobes in an attempt to determine the difference between them. "Thanks. Can you just set it on the table?"

He set her cup down and sipped from his own. He was watching her thoughtfully when she finally looked up at him and he smiled, nodded "Coffee."

Mel nodded.

"How it is going?" he asked.

"Good, fine." Mel sighed. "Where's Mom?"

"Laid down."

Mel couldn't distinguish the Christmas house snowglobe from the Santa's house snowglobe. One was worth a lot more. Joe tested the stability of every surface within his reach, considering a lean. Mel looked up. "She feeling okay?"

"Tired only." Joe slurped his coffee.

Mel stood and stretched, started toward the guest room to check on her. "Think I will do go to T-C-B-O-T-B," Joe said.

"Yeah?" Mel said.

He nodded. "Yeah."

"Yeah, sure," she said, stepping back. "Guess you do have an hour."

"Lots of time," Joe said.

She told him be sure to be back in an hour. He downed his coffee in one swallow, grimaced from the heat. "Or I can drive Mom?" she offered, sipping from her coffee.

"No, no, be fine," he said, picking up his keys. "I come back. No problem." He nodded goodbye and tilted toward the door, careful crossing the room through the piles, almost kicking over the bundle of Mel's old paintings.

Mel returned to the guest room. On her back, already dressed up in her slacks and boxy blouse, the bed made, Ronnie breathed slow and deep. Mel leaned close over her, didn't touch her.

Muted light limited the guest room's palette to pastels. Mel crossed a threshold every time. Often, maybe twice a year, she would cross town, stay for a pajama weekend. The state in between wake and sleep took expanded form for her in this room.

No one knew which yearbook photos, which years. All three of them betrayed: Mel, Will, and Kent, they were all always high as noon. Nana thought their stoned eyes, flaming pools couched between soft bruised cushions, simply a faint family resemblance that adulthood had faded. Without reservation she displayed their compulsions toward heightened dullness, her grandkids' search for the spiritual slow motion hidden in every thickly painted angle of their schools.

Kent's experiment gone orange with a bottled tan at twelve—Will smiled tight lipped with a torn-up mouth, having finally removed his braces with pliers in the garage one night two, three years after ignoring his final orthodontist appointment. In seventh or eighth grade Will wore the same paisley red, sperm shirt they used to call it, that Kent wore in tenth or eleventh grade.

Bent down to restack the sweaters Ronnie had spilled, hard on her ankle, Mel saw the dents in the carpet. The bed had been scooted a foot. A modification all at once, an event, a conscious effort on someone's part, all at once.

Maybe Nana scooted the bed to hang something, but nothing new on the wall. Or Nana might've scooted the bed all on her own for no other reason than to prove her strength, unwavering even at the end.

No, Will must've visited sometime, in and out quick enough between Mel's checkups for her to even notice. And maybe one can do sit-ups as ends in themselves, simply for the love of doing sit-ups. Will wouldn't fight again, not again after so long, so much effort not fighting, becoming a child again, returning to pre-addiction life. But maybe he never really stopped fighting, only moved away so he could carry on without criticism.

No way to tell how long the dents had been there. Dents lingered in a carpet and if they did fade, were fading, happened too slow to know if it was happening or if it was imagined. The dents themselves had no agenda. Just passive consequences unaware of their own power, they never faded, but set the torque of Mel's suspicions spinning. The alarm clock, its cord pulled tight along the headboard, was on the other nightstand, same side as the phone. Simple, Kent brought his fight for the rights of the left-handed everywhere. And Mel had never heard of Kent visiting.

And what, Mel should've noticed the dents in the carpet sometime before when visiting Nana, called Will sometime last year, whenever she noticed the dents, asked "How are you, how you feeling?" Or that morning at the funeral home when he came in, said, "Couldn't help but notice sometime in the last year maybe, it appears perhaps the bed has been scooted a foot in Nana's guest room and I suspect you're doing sit ups again which makes me worried, this fixation of yours, whatever you've been chasing to understand about your own body, however it is you've been trying to master the world by what's most immediately within your reach, well, I think you're fighting again."

Five years since she'd seen him. Even accepting the conditions one had to in expecting anything from Will, never not being let down, any simple thing, Mel had never really forgiven him for not at least saying goodbye.

She pressed down on his cheek with a fingertip. He didn't flinch. She nodded without a word, looking him in his white eye, then quickly the other. He turned, lowered his chin, wiping drool from under his missing lip with the back of his hand, just wanted to leave. Go home, relief from other peoples' concern for him. Had nothing to do at home, just wanted to be at home. The dullness and social graces, people staring, couldn't not talk to these people he hadn't seen in so long, but hard to make conversation in an otherwise quiet room, few appropriate subjects to talk about in the same room as a corpse.

"So, you making any of your art projects?" he asked.

"Good to see you, Willow. You look good," she said, pulling tight against his chest again.

He had always hated her stupid old nickname for him. She could only say it with a certain hushed pretense. With a deep breath, he patted her back, signaling his desire to be released. She lit a cigarette. The baby would've been due this week. So much she could tell him, wanted to.

She returned to her mannered remembrances but kept an eye on him. He shook a pill from its bottle.

3

THE LEGENDARY SHHH...

Only the night before, first time in a long time, Mel had been asked about Will. It was the beginning of a long night.

With no choice but to accept her voice, low and throaty, hard to hear over the bar, Mel won the right to speak very little at work. She rarely condescended to more than a passing syllable to the other girls, but to a few regulars she acted friendly. She cultivated a sense of mystery, knew she did so. People projected the impression of thoughtfulness on her utilitarian manner of communicating. Trusting herself dull, she knew better than to let on. Silence is power. In the din of classic rock treble and bass-throb clattering glassware, the volume imposed shouting or silence, no space for subtlety, no dynamics. She felt friendly enough to the regulars, giving them glimpses of half-hearted grins.

A stray—he looked familiar—called out, "Mel."

She looked around to see if anyone had heard him. A few regulars sitting close were quiet, didn't let on if they'd heard or not. She approached him. Corrected him, "Sabina."

"Sabina?" the man repeated. She nodded and he nodded with a smile, looked practiced, pinched in the corners of his mouth. He had braces.

"Okay, Sabina," the smartass asshole said. "Can I get a Lite please?"

She stepped off to get his beer, felt the weight of her step on her ankle. She took his money quick and dropped his change quick and kept on the move to avoid his attempts at sustaining a conversation, squared stacks of coasters, lined the condiments straight. Drinking alone, he kept looking at her, watching her. She had to pass near him to grab a beer from the cooler and he said "Sabina." He smiled, flashing his braces at her. "I've been meaning to ask you out for a very long time."

She shook her head, squinted. Apologized, popping the top off the beer and moving to serve it in one fluid move, explained she doesn't go out with customers.

"A coffee?" He called out.

"Sorry, busy, can't," she said.

"And what, if I may ask, do you got going on that keeps you so busy?" The jerk thought himself charming.

She turned, moved three glasses in each hand from the sink to their shelves, said, "You may not ask."

His type, rugged but sensitive, ice-blue eyes and sandy blond, perfect messed-up hair, funny and laidback, smart and interested in things, can't stand it.

"Come on," he said, a pleading put on. "You know I didn't mean that like that."

"Hmm." She didn't even look at him.

"But really," he kept at it. "Why won't you just get a cup of coffee with me?"

So perfect looking, couldn't stand him, everything about him put together and perfect, braces. The kind of guy for whom school meant no issue of self-improvement, but only confirmation of his privilege.

Then he asked, he said, "Haven't seen your brother in years. How is he, Will?" and that's when she realized how she knew him. A prompt, this guy knew something? Heard the rumors, local folklore, Will in solitary, bit a man's throat out, a string of strongarm bank robberies?

She remembered him, Beau. His big happy family with lots of money had adopted Will when they were teenagers, took him along on family vacations. Will spent holidays with them. So many kids in that big happy family, maybe they didn't even notice they'd picked up one more. Lived outside of town next to the resort, in a tasteful, modern mansion overlooking the resort's wooded acres. Justified each kid needed a new car on turning sixteen, all the best new sporting gear, the father co-signed deeds. Had it all and still insecure enough to emulate Will, of all people, in any manner possible.

"Really, how is he, Will? You talk to him?"

"I don't know," she said. She stepped away to count her tips, eighteen. Scanned the bar, no two bills to grab.

HOW WILL'S HABIT STARTED

Strange, so quickly after dangling in the light a second, broken glass lies still as if it always had been. Beau looked confused mostly, pathetic begging.

Will paused to smile, the break in his pounding to imply consideration. His fingers gripped the crown of Beau's head tight, pulled against the slip of short, gelled hair.

Will had been feeling a drag in his gait or he'd become aware of the drag in his gait that had always been there. He wanted to be silly. Was this silly, Beau pleading on his knees? The room flapping around them in heat, Will's heavy fist crashed down hard. Beau's nose popped. Will's stomach flipped.

Silliness was impossible. Hands pulled at Will from behind, around his waist, scratched under his eye. Serving this sentence in Stone Claw Grove, every night with Beau, sometimes whoever, The Carroll Motel bar off the interstate, their early evening hideout, central command to strategize Sluggo's or The Cave, sometimes The Shhh..., then their last call retreat for debriefing.

Freedom in the middle of a tornado, toppling, Will's foot came down hard on a pint glass. There was screaming. Steadying himself, he threw off the weight.

Every night in rooms too loud to talk, sportscasts, classic rock, high fives and whooping. The collective din of monosyllabic conversations leaned in closely fixed into a low sum roar, every night in pursuit of some unattainable potential, some cold light, a lift or a luminescent step.

Butt high up in the air, his palms on glass pebbles in slick beer on the floor, Beau attempted to stand. Will kicked him over, pounced and pinned him, knees on his chest. Beau gasped.

Sluggo's spread out before him in rippled tin, Will had watched Beau, dressed identically to himself, talk to two young girls. Beau's lean and jut dripped exactly how cocky he was that the girls were eating it up. Beau glanced away. The girls rolled their eyes to each other. Beau returned to lay the biddable-guy eyes on thick, the girls snapped into straight faced listening. Beau scanned the room coolly. The girls stuck out their tongues and crossed their eyes. Will walked around to the other side of the table, poured Beau's beer over his head, sang out, "It's raining beer!"

His fingers spread around the curve of Beau's head. Will pressed his thumbs deep into Beau's eyes. Same seashell necklace Will himself had taken to wearing only the week before, had not yet gotten comfortable in. Will spit in his face, all over his own thumbs in smeared blood. Beau gurgled and wretched, commotion surrounding them. Against Beau's head to the floor Will pushed. A sudden crumble, Beau stopped sputtering. A leaping knee from the side into Will's jaw forced his release.

Piled on, couldn't tell how many men, people crying, shouting in scolding tones.

"What the fuck, Will? What the fuck?" Tammy hysterical. "You animal! Animal!" Her friend quieted her.

His breathing slowly slowed. He should've slapped Beau. Silliness is not unlike happiness.

Mel had always told Will that the standard of a good bar was one could leave a good bar—Sluggo's, The Cave—not return for years, and find everything and everyone, neon logos on dark walls, framed posters and the same bulb noses tilting on stools, exactly where one left them. The kids would have rolled over a couple times, so the bulk of the faces would be new. And these new kids each year might have thought of the space as their own. But those who had put their time in, lingering in the background, knowing these kids didn't even see them when they checked out the room each night to tally who they might try to sidle up next to, the real community, the lifers who depended on each other, acknowledging each other with either a silent shrug or a big hug depending on how lit each one was, rarely a conversation, these people, they knew each other were the point of the bars. The walls stood for their sakes, even if it was these kids cycling through, their dollars keeping the low lights and jukeboxes on.

Unsure exactly how, Will pulled off the uncommon graduation to this tier of credibility among the lifers at an early age. He knew he could leave for some years without a word and return to nods all around, simple as if everyone had seen him the day before.

No one ever asked Will to expand on his often brusque talk. And if for some reason someone he didn't know spoke to him, it never registered that he had an obligation to acknowledge it. This made some uncomfortable. He was fine with that. How such discomfort was dealt with determined the outcome. If the person was sensible enough to squirm away, that was it. But so rarely with dumb kids could anything be so simple. They're still taking shape, everything becomes an issue of "I'm not gonna be the type of person who..." Nothing could simply be as it is.

After the Beau thing, much as Will had always recoiled from human touch in any other context, he was hooked. He never provoked anyone in any active sense. He had nothing to stand up for or defend. But most people's idea of an ordered world never lined up with his own. And he never backed down. The greater the tolerance he built up for pain, in an inverse ratio, the less his tolerance for others.

There were nights at the beginning, sometimes he'd stay in, couldn't afford to go out. He'd get so irritable until finally giving in to the inner command, the observance of his devotion, he'd always scrape a couple bucks together somehow. And he really was much easier to get along with after a fight. Every night he fought come closing time, if he made it to closing time without already having fought.

He preferred it early. He could move on elsewhere, unwind

with a drink instead of wondering where the trouble was going to come from. As a night went on, alone, elbows on the bar, his vision blurring at the edges, his periphery slimming toward the center with each drink, it began to weigh on him, knowing it would be coming from somewhere. But who was it going to be that night? He'd sense the menace drop a fraction of a second later, lose that reflexive advantage as the night progressed. But in return, the focus, the abandon. He let himself free. The more tightly coiled, the greater the snap of his triggered release, a snake in a prank can of peanuts, silly.

At first, he only lost sometimes, kept it interesting. In the high blur ritual of battle courtship he'd be surprised to find his fingers wrapping up in somebody's collar, some guy's voice vibrating against his eyes. Snapping awake with the rush of a crunch of his skull, his brain throbbing, hot tickling blood always did the trick. All at once his primal ideal self, all pretence stripped, no success, no failure beyond his reach, his clasp, his grip, and his slap, floating, suspended and graceful.

He surprised barking fools with open-palmed slaps. Stunning them, more psychological impact than physical. Put them in their place, they weren't worthy of his drawn-together fist. It humiliated them, fixed their responses in his terms.

All this was simple, simple and fun until the manslaughter charge, that gangly olive-skinned blond kid, and later the deal with Norman. Get out of town free. Norman cashed in some political capital, used Mel's livelihood to leverage his threat against Will. Will was free to go but never return under any circumstances, never, or the buried charges would be pressed. Brawling was simple and fun until it led to manslaughter. Parking lot combat was simple and fun until it led to the factory-church and Will's addiction to getting his ass kicked.

Mel looked back to Will's old friend, Beau, the familiar nerd smiling big with his braces shining. Bet he frequented the gym, gym body. Probably mountain biked or hiked, maybe rock-climbing. Gets his teeth cleaned twice a year beyond the monthly orthodontist visit. Bet all his brothers and sisters have grown up to be lawyers or pilots or good listeners, maybe married into idle wealth. He must work in advertising, web-based creative blah-blah, the last single one. And a coffee, even the way he asked, that coffee would lead quick enough to subtle efforts, mold her into his perfect idea of a perfect girlfriend.

Like everyone probably, Mel had always assumed— passively, as it had never been an option—money was attractive. Who wouldn't want money, to marry into it? She could be perfectly on display as his perfect wife. She could look up a recipe for every meal she cooked. Make a special trip to the store for the ingredients for that one meal. She'd probably eat out a lot, whenever she didn't feel like cooking. Shower every day. Keep up with the laundry.

Beau smiled, the rubber bands between his braces like strings of spit.

"Slumming it, huh?" she asked.

And of course he took the ribbing with perfect charm and perfect grace, shrugged. Entitlement meant the feeling of belonging anywhere. One of her regulars waved a bill at her. She turned to pour a beer and Beau planted his hand on hers, pinned it to the bar, perfect aggression.

"Mel, you know what a crush I had on you when we were kids?"

She tugged her hand back, rolled her eyes, suppressed a gag.

"No, really," he said.

"Yeah sure, best friend's sister. Why not?"

"I'd say I've come quite a long ways from that geek you once knew," he smiled. "And you, to me, when I was just a kid and—"

"And I looked just like my brother with longer hair."

He shook his head.

53

"I did," Mel said. "Your hormones were raging. Maybe you liked him. You queer?"

Smirking, the pointy-faced, tiny-eyed regular sitting nearby called out, "Oh Mel."

She stepped over to pour the man a beer. Tried to not even look at him, but gave him a look. He'd called her Mel. Any poking could burst the bubble of the illusion, enough to force her into retirement.

The tap open, she glanced to Beau, leaning back on his stool for a steep pull from his bottle. He smiled big, winked. She handed off the beer, took the money. Looked around, but no task to save her. She popped one of her pills, decided not to worry.

"So, your brother?"

"Yeah, I don't know. Haven't talked to him in a while."

Turning her back to him, she wiped down the bar. She turned back around quick to explain, before any questions, what he's heard over the years or whatever. "I mean, it's fine. He's fine and there's nothing going on. Just haven't talked in a while."

He nodded. "And you left town right after graduation, like the next day?"

Mel shrugged. Goddamn slow night, people really somehow think it's okay to ask each other to explain themselves?

"But here you are. How long you been back?"

He even smiled. He thought pushing like this he was being friendly. He expected to hear about ending up with the wrong guy, the wrong habits, maybe starting over was some variation of a happy ending. She could give him a thrill. Tell him exactly how wrong things got, class politics pornography for this guy. Her loving husband knocked up some young hussy and suggested Mel raise the baby with him. Her fault? Sold her jewelry, 4 AM one night she watched him walk out, couldn't stop him. And where does one take jewelry to sell at 4 AM? Tell this guy about how now, back home, now she had had the opportunity to be a mother, now, but circumstances. Baby would've been due this week. Thirty-eight years old, she will never be a mother and that's a thing she thinks about. She will never be a mother.

Mel shook her head, grimaced. "I don't know, long time."

"And you had no idea? You never knew how I felt?"

She scanned the bar for any task as salvation, refolded a rag. "No, I knew. Of course I could tell."

She leaned toward him and smiled, drawing out breathy syllables. "My little brother's best friend."

This guy thought buying a subscription to *Men's Health* made him a different man?

"God I feel like such a fool. You knew?" he said, his bashful pose smug.

"Best friend's older sister."

"Yeah."

"Yeah, sure I knew. I just didn't give a shit," she said, standing up straight again, dropping the tone of voice. "I just really, really didn't give a shit."

She stepped away to serve a sour-breathed customer tilting in close to shout his order. Beau sat low in his seat, watched her. Fuck him and his self-righteous savior act. Condescending, his implied, 'This is never how I imagined you'd end up.' Fuck him and his perfection. She remembered him, knew him before his *Men's Health* subscription.

Friday, hadn't changed clothes or showered since Sunday. Couldn't do that with him around. She liked macaroni and cheese. Let it sit in the pot on the stove and coagulate, rubberize, eat it in passing for a couple days at a time. It got better as it sat. Stupid perfect asshole, would his perfect girlfriend do that? She'd have to hear about his office politics and his thinking-outside-the-box creative problem-solving and his perfectly justified just-looking-out-for-number-one attitude. Imagine him at one of his sporty Colorado brewery-style restaurants he must prefer, keeping the busy waitress to repeat the specials. She remembered him, the real Beau, not the Beau he thought he'd become.

A third of his beer left, a couple bucks tucked under the bottle, he waved. "Well, say hello to your brother when... if you talk to him."

She smiled and gave him a big, fake friendly, fuck-off

wave. Have to remember what's-his-name Mr. Perfect with his gym body and braces says hello.

He'd be perfectly generous and perfectly understanding and remember everybody's name the first time he's introduced and never be shy and always fit in just perfectly anywhere, fuck him. He'd make her a better her. He'd be confident, comfortable naked, perfectly cool sexual technique, and if she only played along with his perfect script, needed only to plug some actress into it, well then she'd have a perfect fucking boyfriend, then a fucking perfect husband. Well, fuck him.

Maybe she would go see the original drummer's Foghat Sunday after all. She'd probably know a Foghat song when she heard one.

She could have afforded to have the baby if she could have kept dancing. But if she continued to dance then she couldn't have had the baby. Pregnant dancers, it turns out, don't bring home tips enough to live on. And thirty-eight, she's going to meet someone now, get to know them, decide, Yeah, let's do it?

Baby would've been due this week. Could explain this to Will in the simple terms he might understand, he'd been gone so long, standing in the doorway of the funeral home. Norman didn't want to hire her back. He wanted her to get her tits done even just to bartend. Actually, be really nice if Will would pound Norman.

Then, half hour before last call, The Russians came in with a woman their own age, a shared date. The three, all tilts, shouted monosyllables, bleary. A round of groans through the room, eyes darting, slow enough night, the patrons and the girls equally on display. Mel set her bare elbow to the bar to lean but shot up, surprised to have set it down in stickiness.

Norman had just gotten back. He was surprised and pleased to find the young girl that had come in earlier still hanging around. Told her he was going out, come back tomorrow afternoon for an interview. Feel free to hang around, get a feel for the place, he had to go out. She was still around that much later. Maybe she'd be fun. Fun!

Norman had gone out every night in the nine months since he had taken over The Shhh... He'd pop in each potential spot, strut in and look around, shift from cool lean to full throttle dirty dancing with no transition. He danced, only time his constant babble would cease, with the grace of a man half his weight, his ponytail whipping from the back of his giant head like an eel. His head, big as he was, was huge even in proportion to his body, had a baby's body ratio. His head probably weighed a hundred pounds itself. His eyes pinched into slim slits by the weight of his forehead, a cut of meat over his eyes.

But when he danced, and he danced as often as he could, pepper spray keychain bouncing on his belt, oblivious of the threat he posed to other dancers throwing his girth around with such abandon. He sweat, eyes closed, swinging his jacket over his head in wide windmills, other hand on his hip. Grabbing any woman that came near him, whether he knew her or not, around the waist, pulled her tight against him. A lot of women thought it charming, wild grace in a man so huge, a comedic trope, Chris Farley or ballet-dancing hippos. So some women ate it up. He represented no potential threat. They'd never really get with him, let alone be with him. He knew that, right? He must. It was just playing. It was fun.

A clammy giant put together with meticulous precision to look like Steven Seagal, dancing like Patrick Swayze, smart to be a wild man. He was smart, would enjoy what he could. He knew to be wild in a harmless way.

He capitalized on every opportunity to lecture anyone who'd listen on his subtle and sophisticated sensuality, the perfect baklava at the Middle Eastern bakery. One needed to know to ask, they didn't leave it out there for just anyone to buy. One needed to be in, have access. Afternoons dedicated, straining wrists, to making his own ginger syrup. Kept it in an eyedropper, gave an Old Fashioned a perfect zing. His own pool cue he left in the trunk of the Viper. Always had enough coke on him to go around. Cheeses researched and paired, olives stuffed by hand. Countless hours plotting exactly how perfect things will be when he finds the party.

But on a dance floor, absent but for blind pulse and momentum, in turns eyes closed tight, lost, you know, in the beat of the rhythm of the night, then a wide stare taking in the wonder of the throngs and the lights. Get out of his way. Whether with him or at him, people laughed, no one didn't notice him.

Arrived alone, knew some people. Knew where to find some people he knows, which night where. Attached to a group with sweat, spin, swear and shout, bought rounds of shots to pass around, badgered anyone near him into drinking one. Picking people up, boosted them over his head, thrilled by their surprise. Anyone who couldn't match his volume, everyone, he nagged, uptight, come on, loosen up and have fun.

He talked a lot about fun, about having fun. A standard of value plenty of people threw around, but few invested quite so much in. Of his long series of friends, many had been drawn in, found him when going through a break up or jobless, but none had ever been able to keep up, maintain any frequency. So, he was thrilled to greet The Russians, having gotten back to The Shhh... and finding it dead.

He'd taken to going out every night since taking over because he couldn't stand to stand around and wait for the room to fill up or not. And it never did anymore. He'd go out through the hours it potentially might fill up and then come back, every night as disappointing as the night before. He never did get used to it. It never did get easier. Hoping to find the place hopping, he'd return each night to a new, bleak shock, the room deader than what they used to call dead.

Mel and Gus suspected all his going out, his habit of public obnoxiousness, actually worked against The Shhh.... People who might otherwise stop in without thinking about it had to be reminded whenever they went out anywhere, they wouldn't want to go anywhere they were too likely to run into Norman. Gus always said to Mel, "When Norman isn't manic, he's lugubrious."

And it was all on Norman now, his place. He'd made a lot of changes, structural, conceptual. Even made his old room into his office. Never even cracked the door to his dad's office once since the bar had become his.

ABOUT NINE MONTHS BEFORE THE FUNERAL

Smoke-soaked wood-layered tone over layered tone—apricot wood, chocolate wood, barbecue wood, oak. It was a small office, a shortcut between even the idea of distance, door to far wall. A faint moan of a space tight in on itself, the woods flattened and expanded in a splatter-work on the walls. Each layer unraveled its own swirl and wave.

Rich bumped something with every flex or flutter, but did so with swimming fluidity. The office, his office of nineteen years, grew in toward him from its exoskeleton shelves with mugs, atlases, calendars, beer koozies, baseball hats, commemorative pennants, flower necklaces, beads, binders of past tax years, faded framed photos behind a globe atop a ukulele, and lost boxes of girl scout cookies. And he too, big as he ever had been, never did stop growing. The walls warped to accommodate his every slow spin. When he stood he peaked through the low chandelier of smoke like a regal mountaintop, its crown of clouds slipping down.

They all—the girls, Gus—had become accustomed to finding him sitting in a dazed silence before he himself ever came to accept these lost or found moments he was always surprised to awaken from. Chain-smoking kept him present when paperwork demanded he be so, but that tick of his had dwindled and he'd come to live longer and longer in between the inhales and exhales.

He buried his wife a lifetime ago, prompting him to leave Hawaii with a grip on nine-year-old Norman's wrist. With his head in the clouds of smoke in this windowless little room, his wife returned to him more and more often. In a quick aside within himself he once glimpsed her aged to maintain his pace. He lost hours, days, weeks a second at a time, attempting unsuccessfully to capture again a glimmer of that image, his ultimate riddle, without even hope of success. Sometimes he purposefully transposed the years on her profile from a familiar sandy afternoon long ago, compressed in his memory to only one photo wide, the sun behind her reducing her to more of an essence than even a shape. That struck enough of a compromise for him to settle into his lingering stares. But he never suspected any reason to question the value of remembering the her-at-twenty-seven he once knew until this peek at the potential-her-that-he-never-got-to-know made him feel cheated, taunted by the memories of the her-he-did-know.

Remembering is nothing. He came to trust *that* as the fundamental lesson of a life in loud laughter through vodka afternoons, card games and Nascar. The laughing always ended in coughing, the coughing always pointed back at the necessity for laughter, the laughter for forgetting for a moment. Remembering is nothing. Finding one's own effective means for forgetting was the cornerstone of a life worth making oneself cozy within. And after the substantial sum of a life lived out in its attendant habits, slowly Rich forgot how to forget. That blank state he fell into more often, the means and ends of coping deferred.

Norman approached the office and though the girls all knew to not knock, snapping his dad from his blank state with a quick knuckle to the open door always pleased Norman. But the depth of Rich's stillness that time forced even Norman to pause and watch his dad from the door for a moment.

Rich invested everything he had into opening The Legendary Shhh... as soon as they arrived in Michigan from Hawaii. The same age as his mother when she died, a little older than most of the girls, Norman assumed his acute attitude toward the girls his right, playing it out daily in the most obtuse of manners, spankings in passing, casual demands and graphic propositions. He unbuttoned one more button under his shiny suit so his shirt was open to just above his deep navel. Rich always told him to button up. Norman's cocked elbows each glanced a side of the doorframe.

Were Rich's eyes open or closed? His chest rose and fell glacial—slowly and glacial—deeply. His chest hair charcoal and ash spit out from the sausage-purple skin at his collar. His neck inflated, his face small on his head, his eyes a low center, his wire glasses low on his nose, his gray kinked straw ponytail pulled back, expanding his forehead into a screen to display his sweat. One of his countless University of Hawaii Athletic Department t-shirts, this one with some kind of Greek wreath, intoned athleticism in its Platonic form.

Kicking a hip out heavy to one side, Norman knocked. Coming to with a quick sniffle and throaty guffaw, Rich saw him and blinked himself to.

Norman announced, "Mel's here."

"Mmm-hmm." Rich sat up, pushing his massive center of gravity back in his chair. Scanning each corner of his office and taking stock of his desktop, the $2500 cash under his right hand surprised him. "Yeah, uh, sorry."

Norman stared at him, shook his head slowly, holding his gaze until Rich returned it.

My god, Rich thought, this life of mine. Even in their loose sweats and especially without their make up on or hair done, these are beautiful women. And to have this access, not in the caveman, body-longing manner their livelihoods impose on the lonely, but in trust and confidence, to have this with them, with all of them—this life. How could this thick-skulled, unappreciative asshole be my son?

Norman knew that face Rich made, the shock of waking from a nap, the disappointment without restraint.

"Hey!" Norman called out.

"Yeah."

"You here now?"

"Yeah. Yep." Rich stretched. "You, uh, been standing there?"

Brightening his eyes in mockery, Norman nodded.

Rich wiggled, "I don't know."

Norman shrugged an exaggerated playful shrug. Rich breathed in to full capacity and held it a moment, cocked his head and let his breath slip in a soft whistle between his teeth. He offered his upturned palms in explanation. Norman's patronizing smile provoked a fun moan from Rich, which sustained until punctuating in a silent shallow chuckle. He broke his pose by magnifying its components. "I don't know..." was all he could say.

Norman spun around. "I'll get her for you?"

Rich scrunched his brow.

"Mel," Norman reminded him.

"Oh yeah, yeah."

"You wanted to see her?"

"Yeah, yeah. Great. Send her up."

Norman glided his hands back along the slick of his hair. He held his look sideways back over his shoulder. Pulling his thick chin down, he gave his father a look over the horizon of his glasses. Rich reached for his cigarettes then caught Norman's look, waved him away while lighting his cigarette.

"Just go get Mel."

Norman walked off. At first, for years even, he resented Mel's flat throaty tone through both joy or grief, the impossibility of reading her connotations through such lack of inflection. But after a while, Norman picked up on the muted affection bubbling under Mel's every mutter and subtle mannerism.

The long hallway was painted flat black, ceiling, floor, over doorknobs and molding and even painted over old posters. This approach to painting was done first by some bum passing through years ago, and when Rich checked in on the job to find it completed as such, he flew through the roof. His rage scared the young man away before anyone could begin to conceptualize how to correct the job.

In testament to Rich's truly adaptive spirit, by that same afternoon's end, he gushed about the brilliance and efficiency of that painter's strategy. Painting another coat over the black matte 360° became integrated into the monthly chores of janitor after janitor, each suffering Rich's ever widening spirals of metaphysical and cosmological associations as explanation. Rich insisted on staving off the speckling minuscule margins of error, the shining dinks left from a keg knocked against a wall or the sum dandruff floated from all the girls, as if each minute star in the universe were a nick compromising the flawlessness of a night sky's otherwise perfect deep void. The universe itself could be corrected with a paint roller's broad strokes.

Norman always knew that hallway would be the first thing he would change around there. Having always found the hallway particularly migraine-inducing, he raced the pull of his eyes in toward each other to the hall's end. By the last few steps he felt that he was making it just in time before the optic cords holding his entire visual system in balance snapped and each of his eyes would finally spin out of control, the wheels and weights in a mousetrap of pulleys finally releasing the tension, each eye free-falling immediately once the stress and counter-stress went limp from exhaustion.

One single, clamped construction lamp was the only lighting in the entire hall. Norman suspected someone had scooted this light some. This happened from time to time with an accidental bump. The singular glare without margin of error, grayscale, or feathering, blasted a step or two off from the steps he expected to take before hitting its apex, threw the hallway's center off, disrupted his sense of distance.

No one's going to like this, Norman thought, secretly pleased and not breaking his stride to set the light back to its usual position. The effect would be felt especially by those unable to name exactly what they suffered from. Halfway down the hall, the walker eclipsed the clamp construction light then watched the long collapse of his or her shadow return by the hall's dark end. For Norman, this reunification of shadow into form expressed the fundamental conflict and resolution of all steps away from that office.

Yeah, Mel and him were tight. Mel's eyes, wax blue and backlit bright, sang from behind lids that lived at half-mast.

When, for expressive purposes, she widened them even slightly, the icy glow meant more. Norman devoted some energy each day, all the years he'd known her, attempting to get Mel to make that face for him, widen her eyes.

THE RUSSIAN INVASION OF THE LEGENDARY SHHH...

The more gregarious Russian, wide as Norman but shorter, small hands on arms so short and thick they couldn't possibly bend. The quieter Russian, each part of his face moved independent of each other part, each eyebrow cocking nonstop without pulling even an eyelid with it. Had been a slow enough night, goddamn Beau with his stupid braces earlier, and then The Russians had to show up. The girls all saw it coming, one cheek, then the other, wet kisses with scratchy chapped lips, on the lips with strong palms pressing cheeks into a pucker, punctuated by a squeeze from each of them.

Both of The Russians stunk of fish. Both pleaded for understanding, pulling a girl close, "I take two days, no work. I shower fifty times. I throw a whole box of fabric softener in the wash, no matter. This smell, it doesn't go away."

That whole southwest side of town no one went into, the rank smell of burning plastic and fish, the rot of fishgut piles in the sun no fence could contain. Wild dogs ran the streets with fishtails hanging from their snouts. The workers there, always seemed to Mel, couldn't help but pick up the cloudy dead fish gaze and sticky fish oil glaze. In their uniforms, red one-pieces, some worn with pegged legs, pegged short sleeves rolled up to show off a soft bicep, some with a top button undone, not what you wear but how you wear it. These guys brought their smell in with them. Didn't need the uniform to know them. Will fought these guys, Kent left town to avoid becoming one of them.

Both of The Russians drove refrigerated trucks and their

schedules overlapped, both in town with the night off, once every other week. Daring each other's thirst and tastelessness always killed the first bottle. Appeals, the lonely life of the road, granted rights.

The more gregarious one always showed off pictures of his daughter, his beautiful princess angel sweetheart pride, every time. "Beautiful girl," he always said, "Juts the age of you beauties here, but never would she dance, never." Make-up caked on thick and shelved bangs shot stiff, she looked like a little girl dressed up to look her actual age.

The two of them commandeered the sparse room, pushed tables aside to clear the floor. Sniffling and shuffling in place, their shared date, the woman their own age, laughed a quiet hyperventilation. The red men, already sweaty when they entered, began to bounce. Up and down in place, fists to waists as little teapots. First one ran the date across the floor, then back, delivered her to the other. Retracing the route, the second Russian ran her across the room and back. Back and forth, the men delivered their shared date across the room and back to the other. And she twirled, dipped, raced Red-Rover style, panted through an open mouthed smile, eyes glassy and drifting.

As annoyed as everyone else in the room, the thick, milky-skinned girl on stage stopped her dance to watch. From one far side of the room to the other, crisscross and return in itself somehow a dance. Cartoon tangos, heads thrown back and a leg kick, jitterbugs in gallop. The quieter Russian put on sunglasses, crossed his arms for a casual flex, offered a shallow nod with a pout, bounced with one slight knee-bend waiting his turn.

The club a sudden romper room, Mel behind the bar leaned, her ankle sore. The more gregarious Russian broke away to approach her, gray chest and back hair sprouting from his collar, asked for a water, darling sweetheart. She poured a pint. He chugged it.

"Oh how I miss to see you dance," he lamented. Mel nodded. "Sabina, Sabina, you no dance no more?"

Mel wiped the bar in a long stroke. She could have

afforded to have the baby if she could have kept dancing, but if she continued to dance then she couldn't have had the baby. Never occurred to her she might want to be a mom until after she had decided not to be. Toyed with the idea, despite circumstances, but it wasn't realistic. So little had ever happened as she hoped it would, the whirlpool of opportunities she'd failed to grasp quickly enough, always a moment too late, never able to accept that things happen as they should and the only way they can.

When she somehow ended up with neither the job nor the baby, having survived Norman's no-stretch-marks-on-anyone-but-himself policy, she tried to regain the one thing that she potentially could—return to dancing. Norman's re-branding of the club having failed, he liked this idea of Mel dancing, a return to the classic Shhh...

WHEN MEL ATTEMPTED TO RETURN TO DANCING

People eat while the girls dance—tater tots, beef stew, pulled pork in the dark. Mel forgot about that part, at least from the perspective of the stage. Most of being on stage came back easy enough. Maybe a slight lag between will and dexterity. Not bad after some months.

She swore Dell, behind the lights slurping gin, gummed and gnawed a steak. Forgot about that part too. Frequent repetition of being on display immunized her against always being convinced she saw him silhouetted out there. But no defense this time. This was the inoculation for future dances, Sabina's big comeback from retirement. A lot of money quick, no feminist theories executed. A hard-on is an easy target. Go blank, work. No baby anymore, no problem.

New blue curtain, never hemmed, bunched at the bottom at the back of the stage. New televisions hung up above in the corners, Norman's improvements. The lights flickered off the pole. In spins, her shadow expanded and angled across the curtain's folds. Her shadow, her partner in bump and crawl, the lights synched in a way but the beat triggered the lights and did so with an off-time mechanical lurch. The pole glared in a flash for a splintered second. If she hit her upbeat and her downbeat she knew she was free to crawl anywhere between them. Upbeat and down, she couldn't help but hit them, a jungle gym she could swing through, and in that flashing instant, the undefined nanosecond between kick and snare without obligation, all the breathing room she needed, freedom.

Gus insisted that that money from Rich belonged to her, and Norman had no right to withhold it. But she figured the money was just to get her through the pregnancy until she could start dancing again and she was no longer pregnant, so what's the big deal, she could dance again. It was fine.

The men sat and ate. She saw them. Chatter in the back, she worked for them—strain, kick, bend low, and ply. They appreciated it, faces floating with mouths hung open, blank gazes, hypnotized, and all stillness, lumps, flesh-piles like cookie-dough dollops dropped on a sheet, shoulders just above the backs of the seats, heads scattered through the room, eyes wide playing it cool, concentrated breaths, attempting to remain unshaken on the exterior.

The regulars were the only ones comfortable enough to joke about being uncomfortable. Everyone else, the creeps and the sweeties indistinguishable, flattened their expressions to respectful dullness. A cap dropped in a lap, a look away when eyes from the stage beamed. A klutz historically, in the tradition of masterful orators with pasts as stutterers, no one ever had to explain to Mel, no choice but to integrate her clumsiness into Sabina's numbers. That was her style. Grace wasn't an option for her.

But Gus said no, that money was hers. And she did trust Gus. Ronnie had three kids, one done with high school, when she was Mel's age. Nana would've been a grandmother next year already. It was okay.

Pole flash, kick drum thump, pole chill between her thighs, Norman's smile, he thought her red wig looked so funny cut short, hysterical, surprised. Curtains blue, shadow collapse, football on television, sweat chills under hot lights. Norman, side-stage, never took his eyes off Mel, Sabina, even while he felt up the girl with the pin-up style's new tits. The pole in Mel's hand, Sabina's hand, the tackiness of her grip, sudden drop into a backbend, feet planted and hunger stare. The other girls, cliquey, sizing her up, Gus in the kitchen door leaning, watching, kick drum thump, fist pump, they didn't think she could see them, they thought in the dark, invisible. Thought she was on a screen, like the football game.

But set apart, she looked back at them, eating or wadding napkins on an otherwise empty dish, salad forks clink, Dell, flash of light, white blindness, shadows darker blue on the royal blue curtain. Leapt backwards and up, always a collective whoop, caught herself on the pole, feet above her head, back arched, that's Dell, she knew it and a twist, this zombie in the front row staring at the football game on television, indifferent, strobe flash and shadow, Gus in the kitchen door, the fair-skinned serious girl that couldn't make eye contact and had a boy at home rolling her eyes, this creep in the front doesn't even see Mel, Sabina, he cheers at the television, cheers, she twisted and passed her ass-crack over his nose. Norman leapt to the stage no longer smiling, sting and chill and flash, blue curtain and shadow-tumble, motherfucker.

Dell, back over there behind the action, and she couldn't pull away from the sticky stage. Palms to stage floor, the kick drum thump she had internalized went on ahead of her, left her behind. Alarm through the room, her red wig cut short on the floor, men standing and half-standing, some sprinting toward the stage, the girl with the pin-up style shaking her head, laughing. Mel's ass cheek pressed to the cold stage floor, the TV zombie-creep's head pressed between the bouncer's big hands, smiling, "What are you talking about? I was watching my game. She tripped." Dell back there, Gus hurrying up along the side wiping his hands on his apron, lights still strobing to kick drum thump, her ankle twisted under her hard.

She, Mel, was stunned to find Sabina a pile. Dell's face

among the others saw it. The joy of thinking she'd never step on a stage again and then stepping on a stage again and ending up a pile on stage, her ankle fucked, the TV zombie-creep pinned to the stage, Def Leppard loud and Dell had seen her before walking off, finishing his salad, Ranch dressing, as he stood and turned.

Standing behind the bar, Mel asked the more gregarious Russian "How are you? You seem well. You doing good?"

"Dance with me, Sabina," he said. "Tonight it's slow business."

The Russian grabbed her wrists and pulled hard, attempting to pull her through the bar between them. She tugged back.

"No, I prefer it back here, thanks."

Smashing her wrists together in his giant grip, he pulled again. Her bony waist banged glassware tucked below the bar. A glance, yeah, Norman watching, he smiled.

"Goddamn it." She set her sore ankle to the cooler, her entire body weight pulling away. "My name is Mel now."

The Russian snorted, offended for a moment, confused. He let go.

"I don't dance anymore. I'm just the bartender." She stood up straight, tucked her hair behind her ear. "Just call me Mel."

He nodded thoughtfully a moment. Looked at her closely, squinting. What could he possibly care, Sabina or Mel? So what, a minor rupture in the bubble. She's not going to dance again. Backing up from the bar, he looked her in the eye, "Mmm, Mel," drawing out his 'm.'

He blew her a kiss, a playful gesture of heartbreak, hand to heart and begging eyes. The quieter Russian halted his straight-faced twist, grabbed his friend. They backed slow and deliberate toward the middle of the room, where their shared date, left unattended a moment and exhausted from being run back and forth across the room, had dropped her hands to her knees gasping. The quieter Russian aimed a little shoulder wiggle and pursed lips at Mel. He looked at her over the top of his sunglasses dropped to the tip of his nose. She shook her head and turned. With a leap, the quiet Russian grabbed a bar rag set out on the rail folded in neat rectangular eighths. Wringing its sticky mix of spills out over his face, he wiped his forehead with a dramatic gasp.

"Last call," Mel shouted, looking to the clock a few minutes early. Norman squeezed behind the bar.

"Sorry, a little early."

Norman flipped through the CD wallet next to the register. "No sweat. Be good to get people out of here."

Mel nodded, surprised and pleased Norman was agreeable. Bending best he could, Norman reached back behind the top shelf, where he kept his own bottle hidden. Then she understood. "Oh no, no Norman."

His tone remained flat. "Yep."

"No. No way, I'm pooped. No way."

"Overtime."

"No way. It's been a shit night. Fuck those guys. No."

Standing, bottle in hand, Norman stretched. "I'm not asking."

"I've been on my feet all day, now all night it's dead. I'm just standing here. No."

"I told you Mel. I ain't asking." He stepped away.

Mel dumped one half-filled Tupperware of cut limes into another, grabbed the juice bottles from the ice bins, spun ice cubes in the coffee pot to wash it.

Moving to wipe down the taps, she watched Norman trudge toward the back room. Unlocking it, he looked back at her. "Yeah go ahead, wipe them," he said loudly. "You know our guests will be drinking vodka."

Norman ducked into the back room and emerged hugging the karaoke machine balanced against his belly. Gasping, he crossed the floor. The girls done dancing at last call, he hoisted the machine up onstage, lumbered up behind to set it up. Called out, to no one in particular, "Turn the stage-lights back on."

THE LAST OF MEL'S KARAOKE BIRTHDAYS

Mel had thrown herself a string of twenty-ninth birthday parties, took it quite personal if anyone couldn't make it. Virgos, you know. Norman, however much no one wanted him along, came with to that last one. Loved it so much, bought his own karaoke machine after that. Gus always content, they didn't live together yet, but he went wherever Mel went. Will, things were just starting to get bad for him then, his addiction. He felt obligated.

They drove the black, country road half-an-hour over the state line to the karaoke bar. Lots of Koreans in that town, middle-aged Korean women and lots of half-Korean younger people, big military town, used to be a base there.

Mel had given Will a stern, two-part lecture. Number one, simple: he could not possibly skip her birthday. *It was her birthday.* She didn't like the things she'd been hearing about him, hadn't seen him much, and she wanted him along. So there he was, simple. And number two: under no conceivable circumstances, however provoked or challenged he might feel, no matter what, he would not, could not, brawl. The brawling had begun to emerge as a habit but not yet a compulsion.

My god, Will thought, so bored. I give and give. He doubled up on his chill pills, the tickling itch tingling by the time they arrived to the karaoke bar. He stretched a lot.

Norman insisted it was pronounced like "croaky," not "care-ee-oh-key." He corrected Mel and Gus a few times each on the drive. Silent in the backseat, moonlight glimmered through the trees across Will's face. Mel and Gus acquiesced just to not have to hear about it.

"So please do not embarrass me," Norman said, as they approached the murmur of the shack from across the lot. "Karaoke." He pronounced it purposefully.

"Oh my god," Will groaned. "Who gives a shit? No one cares."

"I care," Norman said, dignified and serious. "I would hate for you to appear ignorant."

Will drew a deep breath, shook his head. Mel smiled at him, widened her eyes. As Norman opened the door and walked in, Mel grabbed Will by the sleeve, whispered a reminder of his promise. "You promised."

No brawling. Will nodded and walked in.

Deep cushioned booths lined the karaoke bar's mirrored walls, swirls of purple and black, the sparse, but spirited crowd reflecting back on themselves. Gold disco ball snowflakes floating and laser-beam sequences cut the room in kinetic geometry and dazzle. There was a dartboard hung at the back of the stage, the drop ceiling of an insurance office. Tiny, the security cameras mounted in the corners blinked red dots.

As they entered, a man, eyes pinched tight and knees bent, hit the final high trills of Harry Nilsson's "One," swung his fannypack over his head before a shallow bow. He set the microphone, its red foam windscreen like a clown's nose, next to its twin on the stage table. A curt curl of feedback echoed the swoop of his final wordless lines.

Gus leaned between a couple people at the bar to order, waited, hands in pockets. Will and Mel, a step away, took in the room. Before even ordering a drink, Norman lifted the heavy binder from a couple's table, blowing cigar smoke in their faces without noticing, and flipped through it while standing there.

Gus turned to Mel, a third glass balanced between the glass he held in each hand. He told her that the bartender said Jammin' Josh retired. Taking the glasses from him one at a time, Mel squinted. "The MC guy," Gus clarified. "That guy you like."

Mel nodded. That sucked. He was fun. Gus shrugged. "Self-service tonight."

Mel nudged Will's elbow to hand him his beer. A longhaired

man in his thirties, t-shirt tucked in his jeans, picked up the microphone. Will nodded a thanks to Gus. The opening bars of Skid Row's "18 and Life." One thumb through a belt loop, the man swung his hair forward, bending at the waist. He stared at the monitor, its back to the front of the stage, through the mumbled verses. A few beer bottles lifted high at the chorus.

Having handed his slip in, Norman approached, suggested a round of shots. Two young women, secretaries, Mel guessed, in gym shoes and ironed dresses with wide solid swatches of color, couldn't stop laughing long enough to complete a single line of "Baby Got Back." Didn't even try, by the end of the song. When either of them heard herself or the other amplified for even a second, she'd laugh so hard, pull the microphone away as if her friend required defending from amplification. This repression, by the second half of the song, turned to desperate hamminess as a means to conceal their shared excessive bashfulness. One bent over, hands on knees, and shook her "back" at the audience while the other bent over, hands on knees, occasionally attempted to quell her laughter long enough to stand up and slap the other. Gus, Norman, Mel, and Will all shook their heads to each other regretfully. Everyone in the room felt that only feeling worse than shame: shame for another who doesn't know well enough to be ashamed.

"That's sad," Norman shouted over the music.

Mel nodded. Gus raised an eyebrow. Will looked at his toes.

"Bitches are bad enough," Norman said. "But wannabe bitches?" He shook his head and pinched his lips. "That's really just sad."

Mel rolled her eyes at Gus. Will nodded.

"You should go show them how it's done, Mel," Norman said.

She slapped his shoulder. "Excuse me?" she said.

"You should, you know, Mel," he smiled. "You should go show them how the real bitches do it."

Will's chest puffed up behind Norman's back and Mel, noticing, lifted a finger in warning to him.

Norman strutted to the stage, unbuttoned his coat, ran his hands back flat against his slicked-back hair to applause and whoops through the room. The opening riff of "You Shook Me All Night Long." Gus and Mel's eyes met.

Gus stepped off through the thin crowd to grab the binder, explaining to Mel it was their civic duty to sign up, save the room from a Norman concert. Mel tilted her head, beer in her cheeks.

Norman shrieked monotone, *She was a fast machine. She kept her motor clean.* Gus turned back to Mel, widened his eyes. She shook her head and smirked. Eyes lowered, Will cut through the film of muck on the bar floor with the toe of his shoe when Norman exaggerated the *told me to come* part as if anyone didn't already notice it. The audience, petering out after the first few lines, joined Norman again for the chorus. *YOU—shook me all ni-ight long.*

Returning with the binder, Gus flipped it open on the edge of the bar for him and Mel to look through. Will waved off the offer to join them.

"By artist or by song name?" Mel asked.

"Whichever," Gus said.

Too old to have really been a punk, Gus turned thirty in 1978, but loved Public Image so much that he began every karaoke session of his life with the same disappointment, looking up "Public Image" by Public Image Limited. No karaoke place ever had it. Though its two note riff with no surprises was perfection itself to Gus, it would, he had to admit, be a very tough song to sing karaoke. The "melody" was all in the sneering attitude. Except for the repetition of the words "public image," few lyrics were comprehensible after the opening line, "You never listen to a word I'm saying."

"No Public Image," Mel announced, flipping back to her place in the book from the P's.

"Figures," Gus said. He reached for the slips of paper, stacked a stretch away on the bar top. Norman humped the air aggressively while singing.

"You know," Gus said, leaning back close to Mel. "It really does make sense that if Norman did in fact attempt to mount someone, it really might create a shaking like an earthquake and those after-shocks might conceivably take all night to pass."

Mel rolled her eyes. To free both her hands to flip through the big book, she kept her cigarette in her mouth and had to tilt her head funny to keep the smoke out of her eyes.

Will couldn't help but study Norman, his panting between phrases. The lights spun a tempo independent of the tempo of the song, a longer song, it seemed, than Will had ever realized. Norman, having never peeked up at the monitor, invested in every syllable, simultaneously proud and ironic in a way in which neither pride nor irony negated the depth of his experience of the other. Proud and ironic, he delighted in the public display of his ability to laugh at himself.

The room cracked in applause. Norman lifted a fist.

"I'll be back," he said dropping the microphone with an amplified thud. Like a robed boxer after a victory, he kept his eyes to the ground, marching back to Mel, Gus and Will at the bar. He planted his feet, undid his ponytail and shook his hair dry like a dog shakes itself dry, drips of sweat landing on each of their faces, on Will's bottom lip.

Gus looked at Norman stunned. Mel couldn't even look. Gripping his pint glass more tightly, Will straightened his back. Mel turned to Norman, glaring, but seeing the look of rage on Will's face, caught herself and—deep breath—put her hand to Will's wrist.

Pulling his hair back into the rubber band at the back of his head, realizing his faux pas, Norman cleared his throat. Gus handed Mel a bar napkin and wiped down his face with another one. He offered one to Will, but Will wiped his face on his sleeve.

"Sorry," Norman said. Mel shook her head in disbelief, wiping her face.

"I'll go sign us up then," Gus said, folding a couple pieces of paper in half and stepping away. Norman looked Mel in the eye, nodded with his lip curled. She patted him on the shoulder.

"You killed it, Norman," she said and he smiled real big.

"May I?" Norman gestured to the binder.

"But of course," Mel slid it to him.

The bartender leaned across the bar, tapped Norman on the shoulder, "Hey, buddy."

Norman looked up confused.

"Who's next?"

"Huh?" Norman didn't understand what was being asked of him.

"Who's singing next?"

Norman shrugged. "I don't know."

The bartender shook his head. "Look, Jammin' Josh isn't working here anymore."

Norman sat up excited. "My god, yes. I'll do it."

Mel closed her eyes, shook her head.

"I'd be happy to host," Norman said, confident that his grace and charm had been so immediately apparent and the bartender, no fool, recognized charisma when he saw it.

"No, no, no," the bartender said. "It's cooperative or self-service or whatever."

Norman looked confused.

"When each person is done they have to call out whose name is next on the list and plug in their song number."

Norman nodded, considering the setup a moment. He stood and shook his head.

"That's a bad system."

"What?" the bartender said.

"Too confusing. I don't mind. I'll do it."

Mel put a hand on each of his shoulders and pressed him gently down toward a stool.

"No really, I don't mind," he said. "I volunteer."

"That'll just confuse things, buddy," the bartender said. "That's nice of you, but we have a system."

Having waited long enough, a young woman near the stage stepped up to the microphone and called out into the microphone, "You're Norman?"

Norman looked up.

"You?" she pointed from the stage. He started to stand again. "No, no, it's fine," she said. "If he's Norman, next up we have Jeremy and Todd."

Two men hopped toward the stage. The bartender returned to serving drinks. Norman shook his head. "That's really a stupid and confusing system," Norman said.

"Well," Mel shrugged. "That's their way of doing it around here."

Norman nodded. "Let's get some shots."

THE RUSSIAN INVASION THE NIGHT BEFORE THE FUNERAL

Donna Summer's "Last Dance" fading, The Russians settled at a table they'd pushed into a corner. The lights on all at once amplified their snickers. The quieter Russian held the shared date they'd arrived with—and exhausted by dancing across the room—between them by the bicep. Her eyes followed the few people stumbling toward the door. With a booming thump, Norman dropped a big binder of song listings on their table. Leaning across the shared date, forcing her to twist back with effort to balance her drink, the more gregarious Russian whispered to his friend. Their expressions increased in severity and both men looked to Mel wiping down the bar, who had been pretending not to hear their laughter, the only sound in the now silent room. Mel knelt under the bar to count the beer list.

Love lift us up where we belong, the shared date shouted. In a cloud of smoke, Oh, no, no. *9 to 5, 9 to 5*.

The more gregarious Russian waved Norman forward and leaning in toward his whisper, Norman looked to Mel. Standing straight, Norman shook his head No, shrugged, shook his head again. He leaned back down, The Russian's breath on his ear.

The Russian pointed. Norman pointed and nodded. The

Russian nodded. Seeing Norman approach, the bookish cocktail waitress with no chin pressing wadded bills against a table, scooped the bills into her large wallet. She walked off mid-sentence, leaving the young girl who'd come in a little earlier that night for an interview, Sarah Ann, alone, flattening the red wig cut short on the table.

4

A tight ring of stinging bites ran under the fold of Sarah Ann's knee. Her stomach throbbed, suppressing spinning, spitting. The simplest gestures, a scratch or a lean up on one elbow, remained unreachable, distant, the burning, a pulse behind her knee. On her back in the west end zone, looking up across the foreshortened distance of the practice field, she couldn't siphon experience from expectation, the breeze licking against her ribs. The moon, a suspended field goal centered between the far posts, never dropped. Negotiating the itchy to cool cost-benefit ratio of the grass, maybe two AM? Maybe five?

Homecoming, another supposed gate to pass through. She resented recognizing it as such. Imposed sentimentality always fell flat for her, opened her into a cycle of loathing and self-loathing. Faking smiles at everyone who couldn't recognize the phoniness of the situation, she'd assume them all idiots for getting anything they themselves might mistake as true feeling from the ceremonial imposition of emotional response, and then she'd feel guilty for being so judgmental, but justify it to herself as her inevitable right to feel free to look down on the idiots but then feel even more guilty for ruining everyone's good time with her sulk. She was not cut out for fun.

This realization confronted itself in the tighter and tighter curves of a quickening cycle until finally, that night, she crashed in on herself. She told herself hysterical paralysis could not possibly be real, not real as the breeze and the burn of the bites below her knee, the moon in its silent hang.

Rob, stupid singing and dancing debate champion Rob with all his arrogant friendliness, thumbs-ups and winks, climbed on her. Some tripping pair laughed at the fifty-yard line. Faraway, moaning dogs called back to sirens. She fended off one dumbass's pothead philosophizing with a moat of silence as her sole defense. Yes, it is weird how the whole world is upside down and backwards, but if it always remains so, then it is in fact right side up and just appearing to be upside down and backwards, so what? Adapt and coast.

Rob's curdled breath and cold nose against her cheekbone and neck, his tongue a sponge in her ear all at once, his hands scuttling—up, down, back, here, forth, there. He failed to recognize her indifference as an obstacle, contented himself with her as his means of doing so. No wonder she'd avoided the boys from school. She wanted to want them. Wouldn't that be nice? But going through with it hardly seemed worth the discomfort. She'd rather live with the gossip: lesbo, prude. Rob pinched her in counterpoint to his whisper and tickle, but provoked no awakening in her.

He mumbled, "I love you," and to squash her will to kick him, she mustered a Herculean charity. Instead, a sigh leaked. She hoped he didn't mistake it for delight or encouragement. His eyes lifted into her sightline, his nose on her chin.

Submission took hold. Rob was the conquering imperialist and the indigenous had the right, she firmly believed, the responsibility even, to defend themselves from invading powers. But submission took hold. Burmese immigration officials are complicit in human trafficking, water wars, CIA Black sites and she's going to bother fighting Rob?

She pulled him close to avoid the look into each other's eyes and figured letting him go ahead was her quickest way through it. Her vision fell above and behind her, her chin lifted and crown planted in the soil to wave her white flag to him. The aluminum bleachers upside down, huh. The people all fallen off, floated away? Did candy come tumbling when the concession stand flipped? Candy wrapped in paper, the morsels in a nacho cheese and cola broth in the big bowl of the concession stand's tin ceiling? Okay, Cortez, Apollo, plant your flag. Claim your mineral rights to the moon, Halliburton. Go ahead and mine.

Her breath fell in with the rhythm of a low, glowing green, smeared wool cloud passing slow. Maybe the cloud wasn't passing at all. Through its coral fingers in the endless miles of night behind its float, Rob's dull beat returned shallow and returned. In back-float she could see the cloud contained everything she herself might ever project up onto it and into it all at once, always. Clouds never took on a shape. A cloud never looked like anything. The clouds existed only for each of us, when in need of them, to pull from by projecting upon. The cloud, the cloud climbed on her, and any cloud was all clouds, so what choice had anyone then?

THE LEGENDARY SHHH... THE NIGHT BEFORE THE FUNERAL

Norman insisted Sarah Ann wear the red wig cut short, as he stood over her. She had fallen in for the night after catching Norman just as he was walking out earlier, then sat watching, waiting around to see what would happen. The bookish cocktail waitress with no chin slipped her a couple whiskey-cokes. One of the girls, the thick, milky-skinned one, took Sarah Ann in back, had her try on a couple different wigs. She liked the red one with severe bangs on Sarah Ann so much, insisted she wear it back out into the club for the night, get a feel for it, the room in a wig.

A little tipsy, Sarah Ann had scared the girl away. The thick, milky-skinned girl smiled and nodded politely as Sarah Ann explained that the hyper-sexualizing of the Black man was a power issue, a manifestation of the oppressor's fear of the uprising. But when Sarah Ann kept pontificating— the classic rock station is obviously a conspiracy as passive nostalgia creates a sense of timelessness, ironically a sense of ahistoricism, and this comfort in retro culture means only passivity in social and political progress until the people, subordinated by this constant deluge of a prescribed experience of romance, are eventually, and inevitably, politically awakened—the thick, milky-skinned girl didn't want to hear about it, took it personal.

Seeing Sarah Ann in the wig, the more gregarious Russian

feigned breathlessness with an animated flail and the quieter one applauded. Sarah Ann took the wig off quick. The men all shouted, "No, no."

The last drunks seemed loud continuing to speak at the same volume, lights on and music cut. "Goodnight," the doorman yelled, "We're closed."

Sarah Ann stood, tilting, moved toward the door and Norman, with a light hand on her back, marched her to The Russians' table. The quieter Russian, leaning heavy on an elbow, burned a cork with his lighter, smudging his fingertips black as he spun it to scorch each side. The other spoke in a soft, steady voice to Sarah Ann, "What kind of song you like sing for us?"

Sarah Ann shook her head, uncertain how to answer. These men, she thought, the smell, must be some kind of fishermen. But working in the industry, they must know about the depleting sea life, the devastation to the entire food chain. They must know and continue the job anyway.

The doorman smiled while grinding his jaw, his gentle hand to lower backs, herding the staggering toward the door. A couple of the girls had gotten a head start changing. Anxious to head out, the thick, milky-skinned girl insisted they go to the after-hours bar to show off her new boots. The bookish cocktail waitress with no chin, preferring the diner if not bed, finally gave in, anything to get away from having to chat with the bar staff.

Mel wiped the bar down, scooted the coffee maker and condiments to wipe beneath them, Z'd out the register, scooted the coffee maker and condiments back, silent, her ankle throbbing, tired. She eyed Norman in the corner with The Russians. Their shared date, having lowered her head on the table, stirred with a moan. Sarah Ann squirmed.

The doorman grabbed the beer list. "Keys," he said.

Mel turned from wiping the bar, tossed the keys from the register. Muttering curses, the doorman moved to count bottles in the beer closet. The bar-back stacked glasses. "Those doofuses with the matching Panama hats, goddamn," he said, shaking his head.

With a concise smirk, Mel dug into a damp rag hard against the bar top. Pushing each glass against thick fur coils suctioned to the bottom of the steel sink, the barback washed glasses with a punching four-step rhythm. Mel dipped her dirty bar rag into the water and pressed hard against the sticky coating on the bar top, paused to massage the flesh across the top of her arm, wrist to elbow.

The kitchen having closed an hour earlier, Gus sat with his notebook open, waiting for Mel, consciously ignoring the laughing and belching group in the corner. The quieter Russian broke out in a half-measure of "Lady" by Kenny Rogers, and Norman turned it into a joyous sing-along. Gus stepped behind the bar, pulled the Guinness open with timidity, sprayed and spilled. Mel circled back to re-wipe the taps. He apologized.

Gus, who danced through his kitchen, knowing which pan needed tossing precisely when, sorted piles of fries or tater tots with casual consistency. Visit twice and count the exact number of tater tots plated months apart, in varying degrees of busyness and distraction juggling, variable sizes of courses the fries or tots are set beside, and still the same exact number both times. Rich, the bar lore went, could tell you exactly how much a stack of twenties was—the difference between $2120 and $2140. This attribute in itself, or whatever character trait it's symptomatic of, could've solidified Rich and Gus's connection to each other. Yet somehow, somehow Gus never could master the chimp-work of pouring himself a beer.

With a hand on Sarah Ann's knee, his eyes locked hard into hers, the gregarious Russian explained flatly, "We like the rock and rule. We like the disco dancing queen club music for to make a party. We like the sentimental love songs for you to show your heart and feeling to us."

"I want to rock and rule all night for party every day," the other Russian called out, hands thrown in the air. He stood up quick, his chair banging out from under him. With his burnt cork he had drawn two thick black lines across his cheeks like a linebacker.

"Whatever you like to sing," the seated, gregarious Russian

said to Sarah Ann.

"I don't know," Sarah Ann said.

Attempting to squeeze through the narrow opening to the sound booth, Norman got tangled in microphone cables. He swatted the air and spat, turned back toward the stage.

"Gus," he called out. "Gus, I need a hand."

Gus looked to Mel. She rolled her eyes. He remained seated, notebook open in his lap, untangling its spiral binding coiled up in his sweater. Ballpoint pen to his bottom lip, he closed his eyes, concentrated. Between each quick dip into actually writing, the actual action of pen-tip to notebook, Gus hung suspended. Each word suffered over on its own, he never knew what word would come next.

"Look at all these choices," the seated, more gregarious Russian said, flipping through the songbook for Sarah Ann. His friend, the quieter one, sat back down, his nostrils flared.

"I'm not sure," Sarah Ann said. She asked for a cigarette. She saw the woman with her head down on the table between The Russians, the shared date, peek at her.

Sarah Ann spent as much time pretending to be asleep as anyone alive ever had. There might be someone older than her who had spent more cumulative hours, but no one had ever spent as high of a percentage of their time pretending to sleep. She never meant to pretend to sleep. She was surprised every time to find herself having occasion to, stuck at a party suffering a vast sobriety barrier, dragged along blindly to a double date, getting home from work, mom felt chatty. It's simple, much simpler than not pretending to sleep. Breathe deep, slow. Keep your eyes closed and keep a straight face no matter what anyone around you talks about. But, the shared date, she was a lousy faker.

"Yes, yes, a cigarette." The diplomatic, more gregarious Russian pulled a cigarette from his chest pocket. She took it in her lips and he cupped his hand around the flame to light it for her. Sarah Ann inhaled.

He glanced up from the lighter to her eyes. She was looking over his shoulder, beyond him. And in the pinball game backboard, which he could see over her shoulder, he saw Mel's reflection. At the bar, behind him, Mel signaled to Sarah Ann, turning a steering wheel, pointing to herself and then Sarah Ann.

Sarah Ann nodded, bouncing her cigarette from The Russian's flame. Glancing up to see if he had noticed her nod, he was looking her dead in the eye. She gasped and he didn't flinch.

The doorman struggled to balance a few loose bottles pinched under his arm, elbow to rib, while attempting to lift a few cases of beer up to the bar.

"Yeah, fuck those guys. You know? Those," the barback stammered, "douchebag motherfuckers."

Mel said, "I don't know what you're talking about."

"Hey, come here and give me a hand," Norman called out to no one in particular, one leg thrown up on the stage, unable to hop over the turn of the plane.

"The Panama hats," the barback clarified.

The doorman balanced the bottles and smiled. "Oh, who cares?"

"No, fuck them for real," the barback said, shaking his head.

Looking to the corner table, Mel reiterated, "Who cares?" They returned to work in silence.

Sarah Ann looked for her backpack, there, under a table across the room. In westerns, that trope, a guy breaks a bottle on the corner of the bar, holds the whole room in check. She thought through how to do that, but too many gaps in the choreography.

Gus let out an "A-ha!" and wrote for one second. Coolers hummed.

"My employees!" Norman shouted.

No one responded. Gus closed his notebook and returned to the kitchen with a sigh. "Maybe I can fix my bike with a butter knife," he said.

Mel nodded.

"Sabina," the gregarious Russian with his hand on Sarah Ann's knee called out, "or whatever your name is, you liar."

With a heavy, drunken clomp Norman stepped, head

down, to the center of the room. He turned, surveyed its occupants. He snorted through his nose, threw both fists up over his head and let out a sustained party shriek. "Whoo!"

The room silent, Sarah Ann watched her smoke curl, ashed on the table. The Russians' shared date shifted her weight in her seat, but remained pretend-asleep. Sarah Ann figured the shared date might be fifty years old. Shouldn't she have somewhere to be in the morning?

The doorman locked the beer closet. Dropping her head, Mel focused on stacking bottles in the cooler. Feet planted, hands on hips, Norman threw his head back and cleared his throat with purpose. With conscientious diction he projected, "My employees, friends, I bid thou all good evening."

Only the doorman smirked, "You have a good night, boss?"

The term "boss" obviously still retained its charm to the doorman, the only employee, not counting a couple dancers of course, younger than Norman. Nights running around, if not together, at least near each other, still fresh in his memory.

Such a fundamental lack of meaning in anything, Sarah Ann thought, except sustaining the systems we live within, continuing, continuing in and of itself the only value and its value only for the sake of the system, never the individual.

With slow steps, everyone watching, Norman moved around the side of the bar, stood silent until Mel looked up, pressed his smile against her face. She blinked, dropped her head again, the ding of the bottles stacking. Norman took his time squeezing past Mel, forcing her to abandon her task, stand up straight.

"Why yes, thanks for asking. I had a fantastic evening and I'm pleased to see someone here still has some manners," Norman said.

Norman looked around the room, everyone motionless and attentive except Mel stacking bottles. With a large stage gesture, he stood up straight to address the room with purpose. "First, a friend and I, a beautiful young lady, went and we had lamb steaks with mint sauce."

"You're going to get gout," Mel said without looking up,

bottles clinking into place.

Norman lit his cigar, took a dramatic puff in response. "As I was saying, me and my lovely friend enjoyed exquisite lamb steaks with mint sauce so succulent each bite melted in your mouth, garnished with seared sweet onions and crisp fried onions, so delicious we could hardly speak."

Mel coughed. She turned her back to Norman, leaned back on the cooler, an aching pull in her ankle. The doorman smiled. "Oh yeah, and then what?"

Norman looked to The Russians. "Well, and now the party will continue. We are hosting guests."

The more gregarious Russian raised his glass to Norman and Norman realizing he had no drink, waved. "And now we'll sing," Norman shouted.

"Heavy metal party rock!" the other Russian yelled. The shared date mumbled and threw her arm over her head to block out the light.

"Sabina," the first Russian turned in his seat and called out, "or whatever your name is, you refuse a song to sing for us?"

"Yeah," she said. "Sorry."

"And even one nice song, you won't allow my friend and I sing for you?"

She sighed. "Well, it's just I got a long day tomorrow, funeral in the morning."

"Oh no," he said.

"We need to toast," the quieter Russian blurted.

Norman scooted aside Cheez-Its, chips, nuts, and chocolate bars to retrieve his personal bottle. Tilting it to the light, he called out, "Someone been pulling from this?"

"No, no," Mel said. Arms straight to stretch her wrists, she leaned on the bar. "It's fine. No toast necessary, thanks. I just have to get home."

"Too bad," the more gregarious Russian said.

"And I'm driving her," Mel said, pointing to Sarah Ann.

The men all looked to Sarah Ann. She turned her gaze downwards.

"It's true?" the more gregarious Russian asked. Sarah Ann

nodded slowly, deeply, took a long drag from her cigarette.

Mel opened the ledger, wrote down the ring. Arranging the smear of his face into stern inspection, Norman surveyed them all. "Who's been touching my bottle?"

"Jesus Christ, Norman, everyone knows," Mel said. "No one would dare touch your bottle."

Norman nodded and, taking a neat glass into his paw, poured himself a large shot. Mel lifted the bills from the drawer into the moneybag. Dropping his glass to the bar, Norman grunted.

"What?" Mel asked.

Swallowing the bourbon swishing in his cheeks, Norman said, "Hold on," took the money from her.

"What?"

"I'll deal with it. I just need... I'll deal with it."

"Norman," the more gregarious Russian called out, remaining seated, gaze locked on Sarah Ann, hand on her knee.

"Yes," Norman responded. Starting to count, distracted, he stuffed a wad of cash in his pocket. Set the rest down in a pile next to the register.

"Your new girl," The more gregarious Russian said softly.

"We want to hear her singing," The quieter Russian yelled.

Mel checked her closing duties off the ledger, scratched out the ring she'd already written down. Norman poured five vodkas neat. Bending slowly to open the refrigerator, he sighed. "No lemons?"

No one responded. He stood up straight and repeated, "Mel, no cut lemons?"

Without looking up to him, eyes on the wad of cash, she responded, "Just ran out."

"You didn't cut more?"

"Literally ran out as the lights were coming on." She glanced up at him. "That's the afternoon shift's job, cutting fruit."

"But what if someone needed a wedge of lemon?"

"I told you, ran out as the lights were coming on."

"Norman," the more gregarious Russian called out.

"Norman," his friend repeated.

"I'm sorry, just one second," Norman responded. "How about in the kitchen?" he asked Mel. "Any lemons cut back there?"

Mel shrugged. Norman hadn't counted that money before stuffing some in his pocket. Wouldn't know how much, how much was there, how much should be left, he wouldn't know.

"Cut me a lemon," Norman demanded.

Mel nodded. She grabbed the money Norman had left in a clumsy stack, dropped it in the moneybag and set the bag aside.

Norman stood up a little taller, "Come on. What the fuck, we got people waiting."

"Mel," the barback said. "You spaced on paying me."

"Me too," the doorman said.

Sighing, she reached for the moneybag, unzipped it.

"Mel," Norman said, "I have guests waiting to sing."

She grabbed the wad of money from the bag, dropped it on the bar.

The ring of stinging bites behind her knee, Sarah Ann preferred her own bed to this version of noir she'd unwittingly turned up in.

Stupid, arrogant, friendly, singing and dancing, debate champion Rob wiped his hand off on the grass, zipped his pants. Rolling over on his back next to Sarah Ann, he saw only a low, faint green cloud drift. Passive and vague, he flattered himself.

Sarah Ann lit a cigarette. The next afternoon, maybe less than twelve hours from then, she would comply with the administration's request and walk across the stage at the pep rally, with the only other senior to have received straight A's up to that point, though that girl would never condescend to even look at Sarah Ann. She—student council president and first chair cello and founder of the school's chapter of Habitat for Humanity and winner of the drama club's female performer of the year three years in a row—also placed all-state in gymnastics and planned to punctuate her award acceptance with a series of flips down the center aisle from the stage back to her seat. And Sarah Ann did all the admin work for Habitat for Humanity. That jerk just stood in front smiling big, took the credit. Sarah Ann dreaded even the dignified walk back to her seat in the wake of that jerk's flips.

She couldn't worry about what other people thought of her. It is insanity to report catastrophe with an upbeat, chipper tone and yet, arguably, the entirety of contemporary American culture is based on that practice. She's going to worry about what the participants of such a system thought of her? Anyone that didn't reject it participated.

Maybe the next day her nerves would boil up to a point, nothing else would be appropriate but to kneel down at the bottom of the stage's steps and do a long series of slow somersaults, pause to tuck her shirt in, straighten herself out when she bumps into the feet of a row of seats, her course askew. The bleachers and the sky would tumble over one another and resolve, the polite smiles of strangers and rolling eyes of judgmental acquaintances would each flash for a second as she passed them. Maybe she'd sputter like a damp Roman candle when she ended at her seat, flat on her back, arms out, exactly as she lay in the end zone now, imagining this.

She wanted only to bundle up in a blanket under the bleachers, watch the sun come up over the practice fields. Was this an inherited memory prescribed by the geometry of suburban architecture? Nostalgia before an event even happens.

But the sunrise, the sunrise would require a silence too deep for Rob, even if he was quiet for once, present in body alone. The only appropriate punctuation for the night was to get up and walk home alone in the chilling dew of dawn. Say goodbye to no one.

She imagined she'd sleep all day the next day. The kind of sleep that feels like you're lying awake, until later you wake up and realize maybe you had been asleep all along. Without shame she'd invest the entire day to that in-between state, plenty to process. Maybe she'd work through some stuff without having to pause or focus on any specific detail if she simply remained still.

Maybe she'd surprise herself Sunday morning, witness herself simply a passenger swept along by momentum, seeing through decisions she would not remember ever having been consulted about. Somewhere in the daze of half-sleep maybe some committee deep within her would have come to some conclusions, and the armed wing of this committee would tie the wrists and ankles and gag the sensible captain of herself to see its own agenda through.

Maybe she wouldn't dress for work. After five years of nights and weekends, even feeling like a member of her manager Jimbo's family, babysitting and visiting on holiday afternoons, maybe that morning she wouldn't put on her khaki pants and Craft Shack uniform shirt. Instead, maybe that morning, Sunday, she'd crumple the top into her backpack, head out in jeans and a t-shirt. Maybe a moment, getting on her bike or pulling into the lot, she'd be aware, that it was indeed unusual behavior. But at no point would it occur to her that she had any choice in the matter.

She'd show up fifteen minutes early, as expected of her. A few women would already be milling about outside, moaning toddlers twirling in circles, waiting for the store to open. She'd smile at the widow who found some excuse to come to the store every day for at least as long as Sarah Ann had worked there. But this day Sarah Ann would not stop to chat.

Jimbo would call out to her from far away as she let herself in.

"Kat called in sick, and it's the last day of the patterned fabric sale. So I'll need you at your register, but you're gonna be alone on the floor until noon too. 'Kay kiddo?"

She'd float over to him. Maybe only a quarter inch, only an eighth of an inch above the shine of the floor, but she would float. Jimbo would look at her as if she were maybe unknowingly drenched in blood. This mustached man with his thick-framed glasses, nothing but kind to her since she first walked up to him with a work permit at thirteen years old. Even when clumsy with his communication, maybe especially when he got tripped up in his talk, forced to negotiate his way out, he was kind. She knew him as nothing else but kind, even if he had been the exploiter of her labor for years, hawking sweatshop goods. It would satisfy her, however kind he was, the hard jolt, his shock of frustration.

"Ann and I got a little late birthday gift for you."

She'd nod. "You guys didn't need to do that."

"Where's your uniform? Why aren't you dressed?"

She'd pull the crumpled shirt from her bag, hand it to him.

"Sarah Ann, I don't know what, but there are ways to do things, and I know you're going through an intense... a transitional time. But this is not how things are done."

"I'm sorry."

He'd drop his head and she'd feel bad, because she knew she'd be smiling at least a little bit. She'd want to follow her body blow, which would wind him, with a quick upper cut while his head remains lowered. But before her verbal combination came together, he'd be back up, looking at her teary-eyed, looking away quick, a deep sigh, fists to his waist.

"You gotta give me two weeks."

She'd shake her head. "Sorry, Jimbo."

"Katerina called in. I got the patterned fabric sale."

"Sorry."

Maybe he'd let his anger soar.

"I never imagined, it never seemed possible, how could we end up in a way that I could not give you a good recommendation?"

"I don't care."

"Well, I guess not. You're not leaving me a choice."

She'd pivot and start off. She'd wonder how she had never before recognized the deep hypnotic effect that zigzag floor had held over her. It would all make so such sense. Her palms would press flat against the cold metal of the door handles. She'd take one last conscious breath of Craft Shack oxygen.

Jimbo would call out, "Please, Sarah Ann. You don't have to. Don't do this. We'll forget this happened."

She'd smile. He really had been kind in a way she could never doubt, even if at that moment being kind would be his most self-serving strategy.

She would push and with a deep click and punch the doors would fling open and she'd dive head down out into the warm fall morning. Get on her bike.

Rob dropped an arm over her chest. Straight As and continuous employment notwithstanding, no one ever expected her to make it, stay in town all the way until graduation. The sunrise moon reflected peach. Leave town without explanation. Say goodbye to no one. The ring of bites under her knee, scalding. If there is no hope for the future, what is at stake if the present were not to continue?

Mel took a lemon from the fridge, Tupperware, the knife and cutting board, washed the lemon and cut it into neat sixths, sliced each wedge across its center and handed the first wedges to Norman, standing over her.

Balancing five drinks in his hands, Norman asked the diplomatic, more gregarious Russian, "What can I do for you?"

"Your new girl," he said. "She no wants to singing for us and says she is to go."

Careful: stop first and balance—Norman set the drinks down on the table, sighed deep as he settled into his chair. He nodded toward the shared date. Head down on the table, she snored.

"I don't understand," Norman said, looking to Sarah Ann. "Where do you gotta go?" He split the shared date's shot, pouring it between the other four glasses.

"Gus and I are driving her home," Mel said. Thrown off counting out the doorman and the barback's pay, she gave them each a look, started over.

"Oh," Norman shrugged, "well, don't worry about it. I'll drive her home later." He wiped ash from the table with his hand, knocked a small glass vial of cocaine out on the table.

The seated, more gregarious Russian clapped, "Okay then,

let's sing." Giddy, the quieter Russian stood up quick to hop in place with the songbook in hand.

Cutting the cocaine into lines with a credit card, "I like that song 'Venus,'" Norman said. "She should sing that first."

"'Like a Virgin,'" the excited Russian said. "I'll sing it."

Norman sat up straight, squinted at him. "I got new talent here," he said extending a hand toward Sarah Ann. "You think we want to hear you sing now?"

The quiet Russian looked disappointed.

"You think I want to sing?" Norman asked. "You know I always want to sing. But, no, it's all about the young lady here tonight."

Sarah Ann cleared her throat, her backpack under that table across the room. The multiverse, she thought, infinite dimensions. She shifted her weight, conscious of breathing deep, bounced a little in her seat.

"No really," Mel said. "We're just about to leave and she's coming with me." She handed the doorman and the barback each their pay.

"Get the door behind me," the doorman said.

"Oh, I never finished telling you all," Norman said. "First, the appetizers—fried cream cheese, like Crab Rangoon but with artichokes—but the dessert, my god."

The doorman waved and smirked and the barback stepped out without saying goodbye. Mel locked the door behind them, walked back to the bar.

"No really," Mel said louder. That kid was real young-looking, jeans and a large t-shirt on, hoodie crumpled in her lap, gym shoes with no socks. Smeared make-up across her face, the smudge of a wide wiping left in a dark swoosh, her hair pinned down and the red wig cut short on the table. Mel couldn't even look closely before in the low light, afraid to strain and see, but yeah, too young. Way too young.

"Really," Mel repeated. "I have to go now and I'm her ride. So," she dropped the cutting board in the sink, "sorry about that."

The seated, more gregarious Russian looked to Norman. Knocking his credit card against the table a couple times, the lines cut before him, Norman sat back in his chair and looked to Mel. He smiled, took a deep breath. "What the fuck is your problem?" he said.

"No problem," Mel responded, straightening herself up tall, her ankle throbbing.

"I was supposed to interview this young lady tomorrow afternoon. Now that we're all here, we'll do it now," Norman said with a smile to Sarah Ann and a slap to her knee. "And we want to see her sing."

"Sing!" The quiet Russian, pacing, called out. "I want the singing!"

His friend turned, sliced the air with a down-turned palm to quiet him.

"Norman," the more gregarious Russian said, leaning closely across the table, hushed. "We get you very many things for great deals and now," he pointed behind him at Mel, tilted his head and raised his voice, "now you no can help us because a wild bitch you have here?"

"Let's go," Mel said, dropping her towel on the bar. She walked in long steps to the kitchen, called out, "Gus, come on, Gus. We're going."

She grabbed her coat from the coat rack, walked over to the table where Sarah Ann sat between Norman and the more gregarious Russian. Stepping up behind her, tight against her back, the quieter Russian pinned Mel in position. The seated, more gregarious Russian pressed Sarah Ann's hand flat to the table. Sarah Ann thought to take a deep breath.

"Norman," the seated Russian said calmly, "what happens?"

Norman smiled to Mel standing above him. He shook his head. "The problem," he began, then paused to smile and shook his head with a sigh. He downed his drink in one gulp with a satisfied grimace, "Ahhh." Knocking his glass back down against the table, the shared date stirred.

"You see," Norman began again, turning his head to smile big to both Russians. "Mel and I... she... you see, I'm fat and I disgust her and because I'm such a fucking fat loser she can't even stand to look at me she feels so bad for me."

"What's happening?" Gus called, popping his head out from the kitchen, bike grease across his cheek. "I could use another couple minutes."

"Nope," Mel called out, standing straight. "We're going now."

Seeing her surrounded, Gus jogged over from the kitchen. "Hey, whoa here," he said. "What's going on?"

No one responded. "Norman?" Gus said.

"Really," Norman started to say, but Mel cut him off.

"I'm flattered, Norman, that you've ever even wondered for a second if I like you," she said.

"I'm disgusting and I like to have fun and you hate that," he replied.

Mel shifted her weight. "But that's not what's happening now, Norman."

"I know. You think I'm pathetic."

"Norman, I've known you so long."

"So what? Doesn't mean you like me."

"It means I don't ever think about if I like you."

"You don't have to. You know."

"Jesus."

"Really. I get it. You think I'm wild and insensitive, you should see me naked."

Mel grabbed Sarah Ann by the wrist, above where The Russian had her hands pinned, pulled her up. "Sorry," she scrunched her nose to The Russian. "Wish we could stay and make a night of it."

"No really. I'm disgusting, you'd puke," Norman said.

The Russian looked to Norman. Norman shrugged, shook his head. The Russian let go of Sarah Ann. Sarah Ann stood up, the knock against the table forcing the shared date to re-position her pretend-sleep position. Grabbing her by the wrist, Mel pulled Sarah Ann to the door, grabbing Gus by the arm too.

"You're locking up then," Mel called out to Norman as they walked out the door, her swollen goddamn ankle aching. Sarah Ann pulled away, raced across the room to grab her backpack out from under a table, caught back up with them at the door.

In all the infinite dimensions, all the infinite possibilities within each, Sarah Ann thought, crunching across the gravel parking lot, sobered quick by the chill of night air on her skin, this place, these two. She thought, This guy.

"Um, Mel?" Gus asked, pulling his arm from Mel and lengthening his strides, his arms swinging, to maintain pace without walking so fast. "What the fuck?"

"Karaoke," Mel said. Waiting to be let in the car, Gus had a chill in his short sleeves.

"Where are we taking you?" Mel asked Sarah Ann. Sarah Ann was silent, staring at Gus as they all climbed in the car.

"I forgot my jacket, my keys," Gus said, sitting down shotgun. Spinning, an arm over the back of her seat, Mel backed out of the space fast.

"Fuck it. Get them tomorrow," she said.

"Ah fuck, really?" Gus said.

"Not going back in there," she said. "Where do you live?" she asked, turning to Sarah Ann. Sarah Ann shrugged.

"You okay?" Gus asked. Sarah Ann nodded yes.

"Where should we take you?" Mel asked pulling out of the lot.

Gus asked again, "You're okay? You're sure?"

Sarah Ann shook her head, looking at him. He wanted to protect her, she thought.

"Hey," he waved for her attention. "They didn't touch you or..."

"No, no. I'm okay. I'm fine," Sarah Ann said.

"Where are we taking you then?" Mel asked again.

"Uh, I don't know," Sarah Ann said. "I just got here."

"Just got here?" Mel asked.

"To town," Sarah Ann said. "I just got to town."

Mel nodded, looked to Gus. Shit, hardly legal, if legal, this kid looked young. Gus turned, looked out the window. A cop cut the ropes from a man in his underwear, laughing and crying tied to a tree.

"We need to stop at the grocery store," Mel said. She was cuter than this kid when she was that age, hotter. "You can stay with us tonight."

5

Grocery shopping, most of all, more than anything, had always made Mel lonely. Not sure why. She never had been in the habit of grocery shopping with anyone else. A few times it happened, a bottle of wine and some ice cream, a frozen pizza late at night through empty aisles. When, on a few different occasions, a third or fourth date with someone ended up grocery shopping, it invaded the solitary ritual, too much of a leap forward in intimacy all at once. What they each pick up, would eat without thinking, what they consider and put back, the calories and the budget. But no real reason why it would make her lonely.

She had always shopped alone late at night. Clinical lighting heightened by contrast the blue outside, the space cavernous, so sparse with shoppers. Labels repeated and changed. Boxes stacked with boxes, jars with jars, better in a half-awake dream state. Helped resolve the wound-up exhaustion after work. And she preferred to drive during those few hours before dawn when the college radio station played the Classical show.

After Gus moved in, after he'd ended up not leaving when he said he would and not leaving still, his dirty dishes piling from the sink and spilling out across the counter, an empty glass left on its side on the floor next to the couch for weeks, he started buying the groceries, an unspoken approximation of rent. And she could use the help ever since Norman and the money.

ABOUT NINE MONTHS BEFORE THE FUNERAL

Mel folded her nice coat, the one Rich had bought her and she always thought was too nice to wear, across the high back of a stool, picking it up and re-folding it. She bounced in place, imagining some burdens eased some. She'd worked for a caterer, been a freelance illustrator, too tough to hustle up work, waitress, grocery store checkout lady. Never expected to settle at The Shhh..., a summer job that had sprawled out across fifteen years. She shook her pill case, the soft pull of her belly straining her lower back, maybe psychological. She dropped the pill case back in her purse.

Norman popped through the door coolly calling out, "Row-row!" He started past her without breaking stride to pour himself some coffee, but Mel stopped him and grabbed his hands. Norman sighed and nodded. Mel shivered and pulled him close and held him a moment, unable to believe her impulse to do so, figured must be hormones making her sensitive. Norman's sweet hairsprayed shell crinkled and tickled her nose. His sour girth swallowed her. She gave an extra little squeeze to signal a friendly let-me-go, but Norman held on another moment longer to defend himself against her assumption of his implied rejection. His good manners, as he understood his sustained hug, celebrated her, his friend, and after years of friendly conflict they were now friends, soon to be family, sort of, in a way.

She knew Norman didn't like her for some years, and she was fine with that. Eventually, when it had become clear that neither of them were going anywhere, he tried to make her laugh, and if she sometimes laughed—he was pretty funny sometimes—then they'd be okay for a while.

The two of them stepped apart and Norman took her hands in his. Mel lowered her gaze while Norman looked her up and down. Mel nodded her head and looked up to him and he, sensing her about to tear up, pulled away quick in a fluster of self-consciousness over their spontaneous sentimentality.

He forced a chuckle and poured himself a coffee, bent to grab a bottle to make it Irish. "Well, go on up there," he said.

Mel turned for a heavy and deliberate step up the first stair but floated by the time she leveled out at the top of the flight. Whenever a new girl began working there, the impression of the first trips down that goddamn hall must have made for chilling remorse and self-reflection. Maybe it was the stark contrast of the blinding white light reflecting without compromise but bound to its limited little halo within all that blackness. The light fell where it did and stayed where it fell and did not dispense in any functional way and who could help but think, seeing this lighting strategy in action for the first time, What kind of place have I agreed to surrender all of my younger self's hopes for my future self to? What room might lie at the end of such a hallway?

Maybe Rich liked this distinct contrast. Building up the suspense of the journey to his office only made the office appear more welcoming by comparison. Lowered the standard of how kind he actually had to be to seem kind. Mel, as all the girls had to at some point, had learned to accept the hallway, but still couldn't help kicking her languid default settings up to a brisk strut.

After years of practice the effect was not the same at all, approaching the office. It had changed. Approaching was nothing. Headache lighting through a chalkboard itch-scape tunneling toward a quick drop and flip into one's self, suddenly before Rich's door. No biggie. But the walk away, Rich must have known what that did to the girls, mocking them, making them confront themselves and their situations so the first moments immediately following any interaction with him they had to justify back to themselves exactly how not-so-bad they each had it.

The constant black tunnel demanding reflectivity spread out in every direction. By high noon in the hallway's independent time zone the gravity of the moment hit her as the clip construction lamp blinded her. Her shadow shot straight up above her for a moment, folded down into its most compact, dense potential, a dot on the ceiling, a flat hole in the matte mirror of the light glaring back at itself. She glanced up to the red dot of the security camera.

So little had ever happened as she hoped it would, but it had all happened somehow. This was certainly not how she ever expected to become a mother, that slob, and Rich stepping in. But the means of dream realization couldn't be judged by anyone living within the dream's course. The whirlpool of opportunities, however small, grasped just after they each seemed to pass, which she recognized in hindsight like uncoiling string behind one's self through a forest hike as her life, appeared to her as a two-fold blessing—first, to have had the awareness at the time to grab quickly and take what's a moment short of too late. But then beyond that, knowing it all had happened as it should've and the only way it could've. What little she ever did get, she had fought for. No bedtime story, no goal to aim for, no family around but Nana to celebrate with—when would she tell her? No emotional infrastructure she herself had not designed and built. But there she was, passing under her own shadow, a UFO in the sky of a hallway of a Stone Claw Grove strip club and into the last patch of her own shadow before Rich's door. She was old enough that her years at the club were in such a proportion to her lifetime as a whole that she felt at home there, even if self-consciously so.

She appreciated catching Rich in his silent stares. He radiated furnace warmth to his girls and perhaps, she thought, never so effectively as when in one of his dazes. Quiet men led her to the club. Her father, Dell, with his bouncing knee and spitty thumb, both of her brothers' appropriation of his silence, Mel trusted she must've loved them all, even if in some inverse proportion to the day-to-day of her feelings toward any one of them. Now, after running from them as she had to, she remained predisposed to mistaking the quiet of quiet men for strength and security specifically, and love at all in its grossest expansion.

Rich. She'd been there at The Legendary Shhh... fifteen years and he, in the most passive and simplest manners had become her family. At his desk, Rich was silent. The cloud of smoke hung at its familiar height. Only when she recognized Rich was dead at his desk did it hit her—he'd never really specifically promised her the $2500 lying flat under his palm, but had only implied it in his playful way.

Gus went broke self-publishing the follow-up to his poetry collection, *Safe Art: Poems to Be Read Out Loud*, too soon. Should've waited to sell all those before publishing *Fundamental Illness*. Had big boxes of those two books and not much else to carry when he moved in with Mel.

Mel liked Gus's cooking. He deferred to her purchases, combining those same staples she'd always eaten in ways she'd never imagined. Through the grocery store, he kept pace with her silent strut, the blank execution of her memorized route. Charlie Chaplin steps, a head of dangling, dark lettuce as a wig, he entertained himself with spontaneous goofy poems, "Iceberg Wilt" and "Saltine Popsicle," or his tribute to their grocery shopping ritual together, "Cold Tooth Headache."

One night he segued into a poem from his notebook inspired by their shopping. She said nothing, but he knew it lightened her step some, even with its clumsy attempt at corn syrup and corn stalks as ostentatious symbols for dying alone and lonely. She liked it. She liked Gus.

Mel had historically been a relationship flamethrower. She had never not gotten a man she wanted, never been dumped once in her life, had no experience with the sick ache of rejection as anything but a concept. After her surgery—the first one fifteen years earlier didn't give her pause at all, her ex such a deadbeat, didn't even bother telling him—but this time, the surgery had zapped all desire from her to return to that same script with each new lover, never any down time in between them.

Gus had been staying with her and stuck around when she found out, figured she might need help. Then after the surgery he just didn't leave. He appreciated watching her, happy just to watch, root for her, her flat tone that of one who rarely externalized her experience of the world.

Side by side after work, 4 AM, she done up in all black, leather pants and a halter top, he smelling of grease in stained baggy jeans, he would read her his poems as they strolled the empty grocery store. It was good to have an audience.

But that night they were quiet, moved quick. Mel wanted to skip it, just head home, too tired. But Gus insisted, no, with the funeral the next day, they'd have no time. He would've fixed his bike, ridden home an hour earlier instead of waiting around. Had to be that night. Sarah Ann said she'd wait in the car, but was gone when they returned ten minutes later.

After only four hours sleep, Gus's hoodie choked him a little as he rolled over, half-woke him more than he admitted to himself, clinging to sleep. He arched his back and balanced on butt and shoulders, untwisting himself, pinching his eyes shut tight. Untangling his legs from the braided blanket, golden brown, darker brown, gold, rust, and orange in simple zigzags between wider white zigzags, he reorganized his boxer shorts' bunching.

Each of the cartoon plastic patio chairs in a block pattern across the purple background of his boxer shorts read "Girlfriend." When choosing that pair to wear, Gus never failed to appreciate what fun the underwear designers must have together in the afternoons, one busting into another's office with a thrilled bounce. "I got it!" Arms stretched out before him as if spelling it out across the clouds. "'Girlfriend,' over and over, 'Girlfriend' on patio chairs."

The couch—wide, long, and low—lent itself fine to bed function, but faded daily from the wear. Shades of dirty sunshine fanned out into simple bold floral patterns. Bone shade became dirty bone shade in wide, irregular spirals. Unraveling yarn set small snares, but no one ever sat on that couch with pants on. Gus slept in nothing that could potentially catch. One flower's bulb, perfectly centered in the flat field of the single cushion, fell precisely on one of the pins pinching fabric to foam, functional mechanics placed aesthetically. Too perfect, Gus always thought, took it as a wink set in the seat. A wink sent out toward the future from whatever man made the couch to whatever man would end up in constant proximity enough to someday notice such subtle detail through all that orange.

He willed his eyes to open. Soon enough his eyes did open. The first conscious deep breaths of a day always pleased Gus. He was biased toward assuming that whatever state he woke to find himself in would persist unshakably through the course of his day. Though the wave pattern of his mood variations remained consistently narrow, Gus felt his spectrum's ends deeply. What might be called "chipper" at the crests cast a shadow on the comparative dark valleys of "bemused." And that day, sitting up with a stretch, he anticipated as "just fine," not only despite the funeral, but because of it. Anxious as Mel was, he knew the day would be just fine. Dropping a toe to the carpet, he lowered his head and ran his fingers through his thinning hair, gripping and pulling at it a little.

Strange night the night before, the Russian creeps, the new girl hanging out not saying much, coming with them then disappearing while they were in the store.

WHEN SARAH ANN ARRIVED TO STONE CLAW GROVE

The streetlights downtown looked like shattered pudding cups glowing orange in the light, cold rain. Sarah Ann had never seen anything like it.

In the front window of an empty grocery store, twisted butcher paper taped on one side hung like a crinkled curtain, a kite frozen mid-swoop. Cardboard leaned up to different heights in the window from the floor inside.

Through all the melting hours, minutes flipping around to bite their own backs, constantly spinning over in her seat, unable to fold herself up comfortably with her sweatshirt crumpled up as a pillow in the hot-piss dank, she hadn't thought about what to do when the bus pulled into town at 10 PM.

All those pawn shops, the military base and the casino, the Indian Reservation, all those pawn shops made sense. The ultimate American myth, just like every penis is average, everyone is middle class whether one makes $20,000 a year or $300,000. How does the American class myth hold up against all those pawn shops?

A gas station down the block was lit like a stadium. A mural across the street, a painting framed from about an elbow deep beneath soil reaching up to blooming shoots, honored community roots and public safety in flat greens and browns. It appeared freshly painted.

Across the street, a windowless box of a two-story square building was painted shades of purple, the first floor deep artificial grape, the second pale lavender like the lifted cusp of a fading grape-jelly milkshake. On one of its walls, a faded fashion ad was torn open, sloping and splintered.

The other two dozen people who disembarked scattered at once, while Sarah Ann spun in place. Half had idling rides waiting for them when the bus arrived. Train tracks cut a tilted paved valley through the empty downtown. A few people, hunched and bundled in the chill, scurried toward the footbridges and tunnels twisting through these angles.

Some people crossed the street to the local bus stop. They lined up with their backs turned to the copy machine repair shop's window. Behind them, form-cut and stacked, the near-identical machines looked like robots interrupted while mingling on a coffee break, plotting to sneak up on the unsuspecting humans.

One other person getting off the bus—a heavily scarred little man, stocky and short with a severe flattop—stood around the station, restless a moment, struggling to hold too many plastic bags, each stuffed to maximum capacity. Sarah Ann couldn't look at him without feeling like she was staring. It hurt to look at him. When he caught her staring as he bit open a marshmallow bar, he offered her a bite before walking off. Saying no thanks felt like rejecting him.

A flimsy new aluminum door hung strangely against the old brick and frosted windows on the one-room bus station.

Inside, chipped paint flaked like skin run once quick through a cheese shredder. Two dirty gym shoes sat on a bench as if on display. A scrunched menthol cigarette pack floated in a shallow puddle in the middle of the room. The room was silent except for an unseen fan, which clicked twice quickly then took a longer breath before clicking twice quickly again.

A flyer announced the Freemasons and the Shriners each had a timeshare at the dental co-op. Sarah Ann took a couple steps to the window but looked out only for a moment, realizing turning her back on the room scared her. She swallowed a pill dry.

Across the street was a 24-Hour Laundromat behind a spiked green iron fence. The stare of a woman leaning under its awning in the patter, by comparison, seemed inviting.

Waking each morning, Gus always found his nightly reading, *The Oxford English Dictionary*, open on the coffee table. Spinning around, touching his knees to the coffee table's edge, he remembered his discovery the night before with a shiver. He scooped up a handful of mixed nuts, and after a quick jiggle to settle them within his grip, tossed them into his mouth to break up the thickened saliva of a night's sleep. His cheer required he speak it out loud to himself. He cleared his throat. "Pneumonoultramicroscopicsilicovolcanoconiosis." And what day wouldn't be just fine if that's the first word you say out loud?

Gus had met Kent a couple times, when he'd come home for his quick and infrequent visits, and he really liked him, looked forward to seeing him. Ronnie and Joe, in passing, were easy enough, almost funny if not so sad, always scratching themselves. Will, however, he had no idea what to expect after the last time he saw him. He'd have to tell him about the situation with Mel, the money. Maybe Will could help like Shane from the old Western riding into town. Absent, Will had become more like Dell, the legend overtaking the man himself.

Walking from the bus station, the cold drizzle stinging her face, such a shit hole, red mud and concrete, Sarah Ann felt aware of herself as a dramatic cliché, the teenage runaway. Finding The Shhh... from the bus station would be simple. The bus had passed it pulling into town. No reason to put it off, no other reason to be in Stone Claw Grove. May as well head over there that night. And being in a strange city, the textures of its decay severe under blasts of streetlights, she thought about noir.

She realized noir had of course appeared around World War II as a stylized representation of life. Its stylization defined it. And no more or less than any other aesthetic movement did it ever entertain the pretense of being anything more than a lens through which to view the experience of life itself. But with postmodernism emerging only about a generation later, in a postmodern culture in which life itself had been relegated to secondary importance after its representation, she considered that at least tonally and thematically, noir could be an appropriate term to describe the experience of life itself.

Sure, in terms of plot, everyone she'd ever met, with very few exceptions, lacked the energy—even if motivated by appetites sexual or otherwise—to realize any plans. And contemporary conspiracies, business hidden within politics within religion, the conspiracies were all too fragmented to tie any plot up neatly. But tonally and thematically it made sense. Life itself had become noir. She wasn't about to wear a stupid hat. That's not what this was about.

But the formal qualities of noir: dream-like, strange, erotic, ambivalent, and cruel. Defined by off-balanced compositions.

All of the defining elements were present in the day-to-day experience of life itself. Post-industrial consumer Capitalism practically prescribed a dream-like state as every citizen's default setting. Of course this dream-like experience of the world was strange and of course it was erotic—as information itself became the currency and grounding of experience, the strangeness of physicality would of course be fetishized.

Ambivalence was not a passive state. People often misused the word. It required summoning reserves of strength to sustain ambivalence. And assuming one keeps up with bleak world news, however zapped of strength most people seemed to be, even the least engagement in the world would necessarily be ambivalent as any motivation to continue living at all required one to impose a positive spin to some degree on such a cruel world. Cruelty was of course a given.

Noir as a genre existed in the specific historical moment it did because it was a premonition, as every art form springs from the fringes of a culture, betraying its potential. Noir anticipated the obsessions and motivations of a culture, which sucked the life from those living within it, while still hanging on as it had to, to the comfortable belief that a narrative was possible, even if its twists were not totally believable. It required stylizing and in this way it appeared quaint and comforting to the contemporary viewer. But our world, however alien, was already recognizable then. Even if the protagonist was required to navigate an urban maze, at least the protagonist had a maze to be grounded in.

The greatest comfort Sarah Ann longed for, if she would never be able to name the mystery, was to at least be able to recognize the mystery that required her solving when she saw it—meaning. She always kept an eye out for its clues, meaning of any kind to at least draw out the shape of the maze.

Since its cultural moment, noir could exist only self-consciously as a tribute or a parody. Unless, Sarah Ann considered, it became the experience of the world itself. And she, she by intuition and impulse had become one of its tropes, a teenage runaway.

In the morning, when the overnight attendant at the Laundromat left, Sarah Ann headed out on foot into the city of brick. She had walked back the night before from the grocery store to the bus station, looking over her shoulder the entire time, ducked inside the Laundromat to wait. When the attendant approached her, she pretended to be asleep, hunched forward on her bag in her lap.

"Just this one time, okay? Okay?" He shook her knee.

She opened her eyes and nodded. "Thank you."

She had never really fallen asleep, but knew to leave, as to not get the attendant bending the rules for her in trouble with the man taking over the next shift.

The city scared her even more in the daylight than it had the night before. The buildings were like shallow step pyramids. An abandoned factory in the middle of town loomed above all the other abandoned factories, a pale blue square painted flat on its front, its windows all wood. The edges of its pale gray frame reflected bright in the rising light.

She considered going back, spending the whole day at the bus station, waiting for the next bus heading west, staying on it all the way. She liked the idea of L.A. being somehow beautiful. All the sprawling paved openness, no one to hear you scream, whole neighborhoods, mazes of caves of highway underpass, parking lots, and lots and lots of strip mall.

An entire block was lined with ankle high windows along the sidewalk. She hurried past, uneasy, imagining people on their tiptoes below in a basement. The man from the bus station the night before, the deformed man with the flattop, sat on a parking block with a lot of plastic bags, smoking in a suit, waiting for the funeral home to open.

She really should head back to that bus station and make her way to L.A. Consciously deciding L.A. must be beautiful was a necessary gesture of redemption.

The totality of the development of consumer Capitalism generally consumed her thoughts. Yes, she did love Hugo Chavez and Mao conceptually and loved her concepts deeply, fed on them even. But acceptance as a virtue was distinct from her conceptual sustenance. She believed acceptance had to be the life force she would feed her concepts to. Acceptance was the hinge all must swing from. Because all did swing, whether one preferred it so or not, and facing this was in itself acceptance.

Down by the tracks she picked up her pace. Would it be quicker to turn around? Quicker to where? No one was around. The Hell's Angels Club was painted red with flames taller than she was. A loading dock ran along its entire front behind a wide gate chained shut.

She visited L.A. once for ten days as a kid, part of a cheerleading championship. She hated every second of it.

Turning, unsure exactly which way was back to the bus station, she swam in a wall of glass bricks' reflection of mechanical waves.

Glancing up at his reflection, warped in the convex of Mel's television set, thin hair matted greasy to fleshy scalp, Gus shuddered, recalling a line from one of his own poems, "The TVs Really Are Eyes." Hidden cameras projecting back to some master brain, keeping tabs of everyone's blank stares and masturbation habits and pizza boxes didn't scare him. The required mirror culture, which would have to survive unseen and mimic our own in order to sift through all the data its surveillance would acquire, seemed too ambitious a bureaucracy to pull off.

His fear, and the ironic flip that buttressed his poem, was a more subtle style of eye: the television's broadcast, which kept watch not by taking in images, but by outputting its addictive drone of illusory options. The projections as fences kept people within the parameters they passively established collectively.

Gus spoke of this rarely and then only hushed in the most conciliatory tones, as people take their televisions personally and take any questioning of television as a simple and self-righteous attack they'd all already considered and seen through. Gus was sensitive to peoples' feelings like that, even if completely baffled that what seemed so obvious to him was somehow taken as a radical stance. And, as always, didn't want to be seen as an old crank, not a generational thing. Stupid Norman, in his attempt to redesign The Shhh... to please everyone all the time, had even hung a couple TVs in the club, as if a room with naked women dancing in it needed a distraction, any more spectacle to look at.

Gus hated waking up to that funhouse mirror, Mel's television, every morning, his own fish-eyed reflection. Through the wall, the neighbor's television sang and banged away continuously, always, every second, every day, without pause ever, under any circumstances, ever. Gus felt bad for that guy. Lived alone, must've been lonely.

Part 2

Jesse's stories went on and on and on and on and sometimes it was a long time before one part of a story came back and at those times he was always happy when it did, happy to see those same story-people again. Wallace walked through and said "Hi Jesse," and fed him. Jesse was scratchy and sore. But he never saw story-people scratchy or sore. He and Wallace were different. But all the story-people had different problems than being scratchy or sore, and he saw the problems of them repeat and get fixed and happen again and the problems pile on top of each other to make more big problems. It was one story over and over all the time. It always changed, but it was always the same story, one big story really.

Little fun problems happened when the nice men and the nice women liked each other but were all scared, and sometimes when they looked good, even though they all looked good, some of them especially were not scared to go up to the other people, and sometimes one of them would like the other more than the other liked them, and then they always said and did the most embarrassing things because they wanted to be liked. But it was always funny and fun, not like the real life problems, being scratchy and sore, the dragon on its throne with eyes of fire.

And in the stories bad guys and good guys, who was who could change. So Jesse watched close, easy come, easy go. He wanted to understand their feelings and a lot of the time when he laughed at their mistakes, he knew they would feel better soon and it was okay to laugh because he heard other people laugh and the story-people did not really feel bad.

And they did not itch. That was why the stories happened, so the story-people did not have to itch like Jesse itched. The story-people had problems, but the problems the story-people had were more good than Jesse and his no problems stuck inside. The story-people all had "The Freedom,"

Wallace explained, which was how Jesse knew they were the story-people.

The story-people showed Jesse so many kinds of happy it made him happy to see them. The story-people got sad too. But they knew so many kinds of happy that sad was just another kind of happy to them. It was okay. People clap for the story-people's secret other stories.

Mom and Dad used to make Jesse say prayers and when he and Wallace got together he prayed by himself a lot for the first time. It had been a long time since he prayed. So long that he forgot what praying was like. Wallace talked about God all the time, but not so much in a praying kind of way. And now that he was friends with so many story-people, it was like, why would he need to pray? They showed him their life, so that was his life now too.

Wallace said the story-people's lives were fake lives for people like Jesse to watch so it was okay to not go outside while they all waited out Babylon's collapse. But Jesse knew the story-people lives were very real and better than his and better than his itching. Jesse would see the story-people in his mind when he closed his eyes. They would chase away the dragon on its throne with eyes of fire from his mind. And so now, would he pray to God to be like the story-people or would he pray to the story-people? So, he did not pray.

The story-people said the same things they had said before a lot. These times were funny because you never knew what crazy situations would happen. Kissing your sister on accident, or you had a boyfriend and his mom came to visit or the neighbor was a bad guy spy or the new boyfriend was an older man and was very nice, but had to say he could not be together anymore for some reason no one could explain but everyone understood. Jesse could never imagine a whole sports team lying to cover the crime of one player.

It did not matter. It always kept its shape, his itching and the days. It all kept the same shape always and he knew because there were always so many ways to end up saying the same thing, "What are you talking about?" and "Here comes the big one."

It did not matter. The stories went on and on and were always different, but the story-people always said the same things, many short songs with spinning colors, people jump over tall buildings, that same sing-song sound of laughter. So it really was one big story.

The story-people never really got happy, but they never really got unhappy. It made Jesse happy over and over to watch close as the story-people tried hard to be more happy. They were so much more happy than him or Wallace with all their itching could ever be and they never feared the beasts of land and sea. But the story-people did not even know how happy they were.

Jesse was happy when they were happy, but he was not as happy as them when they were happy. And he was sad when they were sad, but he was not as sad as them when they were sad. And they might have always looked to each other or just to the side of Jesse and never at him. But it was okay, even if they never spoke to him. They knew he was watching. They never forgot it was for him that they felt happy and sad. They felt happy and sad so that he could feel happy and sad. So they were never not speaking to him.

Sometimes he wanted to be exactly like the story-people, no itching, no dragon on its throne with eyes of fire. He wanted to drink coffee and drink it all day and go in the colorful maze living room where other friends came to visit and explained their stories, this or that, and then go to the coffee café and see more friends, chase fast cars with a robot in a tuxedo. He wanted to explain himself every day and every day have new things to explain to his friends.

But, he knew, like Wallace said, that that was not how life was. It was okay. He did have the story-people's lives. Their life was his life. Wallace had made it so the television set, the channel could not be turned and it could not be turned off. Jesse was scratchy and his sore body moved slow.

This nice cake Wallace brought Jesse home from the grocery store bakery, the frosting must have been an inch thick.

Never seen such a cake, beautiful under its thick plastic top, painted pink and blue.

He brought it home with him in the morning after work. On his couch, in his pajamas as always, Jesse was concentrating on *Judge Judy*. That boy watched his stories so closely, Wallace never knew, coming in, if he was awake or asleep. So he always waited for Jesse to say hello first so he wouldn't wake him. But then if Jesse didn't say hello, it still didn't necessarily mean he was asleep. Wallace remembered being moody at his age.

It was a crisp morning. Bright blue and really made you feel alive. Wallace felt great bringing home that cake, sticking it in the refrigerator without Jesse noticing. He didn't know if Jesse knew it was his birthday or not, but Jesse never said anything about it. Wallace never knew what that kid knows.

It was a shame maybe the way that boy lived. It was a shame a boy would have to live like that, all bent up and never moving from his couch. But it was just not safe otherwise, for either of them, really. Shit, Wallace never planned on having a teenage boy around to take care of. Happy falling asleep in the sunshine, he looked forward to that afternoon, surprising Jesse.

Wallace and Jesse both always left the top off the toothpaste. It made the tube harden in the time between it being squeezed and being squeezed again and Jesse did not know about Wallace, but there was something about the hard part at the end that he liked. It made him feel like he was eating candy, and eating candy two times a day was better than brushing your teeth two times a day. It tasted like candy anyway, but when it hardened a little bit then it was really like eating candy. So he did not mind that, eating candy two times a day. He really did not usually know how long a day was, so it was good that he liked it.

And Jesse did not know if that was what Wallace liked about it too or if he liked anything about it or if he just let it happen because he knew Jesse liked it or if he never thought about it. But it happened.

Slowly there was a little toothpaste on the top of the toilet tank where they would always set the tube down. It was no big deal, just the little bit left from the lip of the tube when you would put it down. But slowly, that muck grew some. And Jesse did not know if either of them noticed it happening, but it became so the toothpaste tube had a little hardened toothpaste valley they would always put it down into. Before that, he did not think either of them ever thought about where to put the toothpaste down. They just set it down on the back of the toilet. But as it began to leave a little bit of itself behind each time they would pick it up, they began to think that was the toothpaste's spot. So then they always put it down there. But the repetition made the sticky clump it left behind grow. So eventually it was like a wad of gum. It was like a wad of gum that would not ever really harden. That was the thing about toothpaste. Even if it hardened at the tip when there was a little bit exposed, when you got a lot of it together on top of itself, it stayed the same. It really kept its consistency. And it was thick. Jesse first noticed it when it was the size of a wad of gum. It was like a greenish-blue wad of gum on the back of the toilet.

Scraps of tissue began to stick to it then. It was on top of the tank at the back of the toilet, so it was not like either of them were putting toilet paper or tissue there on purpose for any reason. But toilet paper and tissue both have a dusty quality to them. You pulled out a tissue and you saw the trail of dust it left behind in the air.

Enough time for just the little lip of the toothpaste tube to grow into a wad of gum, that was a long time. The end times really did go on and on in a way. So even if that dust from toilet paper or tissue was even that littlest bit that came off each time, well, it had to land somewhere. And over time, it built up enough to give it a different kind of texture. Jesse watched parades on TV and it was like one of those floats in a parade with bits of paper all put together to make some strange shape. Except it was not any shape anyone could recognize. It was just its own shape.

And then there was Wallace's whiskers and body hair. He was pretty bald. So sometimes there were longer hairs and those longer hairs could have been Jesse's. But longer hair did not catch in the same way. Long hairs had too much left dangling disconnected from the wad. So longer hairs could get pulled off or float away. But Wallace's short whiskers and curly private hairs both stuck to the wad. Jesse did not know how the curly private hairs got up there. They must have just floated around the bathroom some. Jesse knew he did not have so much curly private hairs like that, a little, but it must have been Wallace. And Wallace had no reason to be pulling out his hairs and sticking them on the back of the toilet, so they must have just floated around some. And his whiskers: obviously Wallace shaved in the sink looking into the mirror and that was to the side of the toilet by a foot or two and a little bit above it. But for some reason he must have missed the sink a lot because the wad of toothpaste eventually had a sparse beard.

And then it began to harden. Not just the toothpaste stiffened, but all these things that stuck to it made it thicken. The things it picked up gave it shape. And so it grew to be of pretty significant size. It was impossible for Jesse and Wallace to deny it anymore, but they did. By that time, it was too late to clean it very simply. But neither of them wanted to clean it. Jesse had never cleaned anything in his life since living with his parents years ago, and he would not be strong enough to scrub that. So they both continued setting the toothpaste down in this glob because not setting it down in the glob was admitting that the glob existed.

Then the glob started to grow around the toothpaste tube. At first it would just grip it a little bit and it would take a little effort, like pulling weak magnets apart, to get the toothpaste away from its glob. Jesse did not know how this happened or what happened to make it happen, but then it got tricky to pick the tube up at all because the whole thing was lying in this sticky mess.

They were both able to deal with it. They ran out of

toothpaste and got a new tube. It was not like all this happened from one tube. But they got a new tube and put it back down in that same spot and it just became part of the same mess. It took no time at all for it to get buried in the mess. It was like the glob had grown to have its own personality. It started making decisions or at least getting aggressive, like it was hungry. It would swallow the new tube so that you put it down one day, after carefully picking it up, and then the next time you returned to it the whole thing was covered. And it got harder every time.

And then it began to curl up around each new tube. By then they had gone through so many tubes that it had a lot of different layers and the layers were all different colors. It was mostly sea green and blue and white. It looked like the ocean. It looked like nature. So maybe that was what made Wallace and Jesse think they should just leave it alone. But of course, there were all different colors. And there was at least one tube in there some time that was red and white striped and that was weird. Even if different brands stuck mostly to the same colors, they all looked different from each other. They aged differently too. The muck curled up around each new tube and the bottom was of course a different color than the top. It had been changing colors slowly. A little at a time, each new layer faded into the one that had just been on top, so they never really noticed the change. But when it began to curl over and show its bottom, it was like they could see the history of all the different toothpastes they had ever had.

Then, not too long ago, Jesse walked into the bathroom and the top of the glob was scraped flat. It was smeared up and to the left and left like that. It looked like a frozen wave. A piece of toilet paper was stuck to the top. So he figured Wallace thought to try to scrape it off but then gave up. Even if the toothpaste had no hungry personality, just giving it the time to pile up on itself made it strong. It was at least strong enough to fight back against Wallace trying to clean it. Maybe he was trying to wipe it off, but that was not going to work. He should have known that.

Or maybe he just stuck the piece of toilet paper to the top

so the wad would stop grabbing things. If the toilet paper was spread out wide enough then the whole surface of the toothpaste would just be grabbing that, the toilet paper. And the toilet paper would not grab anything. It would work like a shield. But Wallace put the toothpaste back down on top of the toilet paper. That meant that every time you picked up the toothpaste you got toilet paper stuck to your hand, because the toilet paper would stick to the toothpaste and the toothpaste would stick to your hand. And then you would have to roll all the little bits of paper up into little balls to get them off your hand.

It was after the toilet paper got stuck in the glob Wallace stopped brushing his teeth. He could not stand to even try to pick the toothpaste up anymore. Jesse did not know how long Wallace had gone without brushing his teeth, but he found out about it that day Wallace pulled him close for the first time in a long time. Wallace's breath smelled like manure, that day Wallace caught Jesse trying his clothes on.

When Wallace was Jesse's age, when he was a boy, he'd run around. Well, he didn't really run around that much maybe. He was never athletic but he sure loved it whenever he did get an opportunity to run around.

Really, he walked around a lot, sauntered. It was quiet back in Louisville. Especially back when he was a boy it was quiet. You might hear the factories on the river late at night and you'd hear the quiet rush of the water. He'd walk around the woods. Not actually in the woods. He was usually pretty afraid to do that.

But he sure walked those roads through the woods and he'd listen in, mystery scuttling ankle-high, the thick brush of a tree against another high overhead, whistling. He'd get halfway through and start hurrying. It was the same every night. He'd trick himself into walking those roads at all, those country roads, no one around. Start slow. Tell himself that maybe he wouldn't actually go all the way through. He'd sort of peek in and take a step, a few steps, each next step in answer to a dare to himself.

Quiet neighborhood, everyone knew everyone else. The quiet made it fun. In the afternoons, he, his best friend Strawberry Meat, and all the kids moved around both as a big group and each on their own, like spies behind enemy lines.

There was the Schroeders, old and uninterested in everything. The Simmonses, Mr. Simmons would decide to buy all the kids lunch some days when he'd spot them, not asking anyone what they wanted but instead showing up with a big bag of a few of everything off the menu from somewhere, burgers and sandwiches and mountains of fries. He'd show up and tear open a bag between all of them, and Wallace would imagine him placing that order. "Yeah, and give me two of those, and what's that? I'll take four of those."

All the Jews in Louisville were right there in those few blocks, and they were all friendly enough despite whatever Pa always had to say about them. They drove Pa crazy. Looking back at it, Wallace guessed it was because Pa felt his family had always just been there and then slowly they were surrounded. They lived in their old house they'd always been in, full of mice and drips, while the Jew houses all got built up around them. Wallace couldn't understand Pa's racism like that since Pa obviously knew the Jews were part of all of it, with the Revelations and the end times. That was Pa, though, and maybe Pa didn't know that yet back then.

That neighborhood stayed cool all day, all year round under all those thick trees. The kids, they had constant construction sites to climb around, shit. It was their Cold War espionage jungle gym to sneak around in. Strawberry Meat always cut himself up on some old jagged piece of metal and Pa, on the porch, always called all the kids "furtive" whenever they'd slip past.

And then there was what they all called "the path." Between two houses, right straight ahead of where the road turned back on itself in a cul-de-sac, if you were walking down the middle of the street and went on straight ahead, you'd go straight on into and through the path. It was only a few steps, a sidewalk. It was really just a sidewalk, twenty feet long between two houses, through a few tall bushes. That was it.

But beyond it, at the end of the next street, past those last few houses, there, there it opened up into the woods. And you could get lost in there, boy. "Yea, though I walk through the valley of the shadow of death," alright.

After supper Wallace would walk off alone and take only a few steps at first. He would have to remind himself every time that he had done that walk plenty of times before. He'd survived it over and over. But still he would have to leave himself that little escape route in his mind. He'd tell himself "Okay, no big deal Wallace, you're just gonna take a few steps in and see what's going on in there tonight, and then turn around and head right back out." And the entire time, no matter how immersed he got in the croaking of the toads or the deer tracks in the mud alongside the road, he still never lost this pounding fear in his head. His steps would fall into the rhythm of his heartbeat in his head, and this pounding would be the combined sound of his steps and his heartbeat. The fear would get thicker and thicker, fifteen minutes, twenty minutes. He wouldn't stop walking. He never slowed down.

All at once it would hit him—he was in the middle, the air cool and musty, the shapes abstract around him, as alive as not, all of it together, never still. It would take him as long to get to the far end as it would to turn back. He would swoon. His mind would fall through his stomach or his stomach would lift up through his head. He didn't know. But there was a floating that would come over him. This depth of the woods he had ended up in would hit him, and then at that depth there'd be no option but to float. He'd see the forest from above and himself within it, floating along, breathing in the rhythm of his steps.

He could never really see the first half of the walk up until that flip through all his fear, and then once that flip had happened, he could never really see that second half of the walk through his blind float until he'd appear at the end. All at once the forest would be behind him.

He might loop back around along the tracks. There was always something going on down there. Everyone knew how friendly all those old bulb-nosed drunks living out there were, no matter how desperate they might've seemed to all the grumps and religious hypocrite types. They'd offer you their beans from a can or whatever fish they had to split between them. You couldn't get away without taking a pull from a jug of their sweet wine, and there was no bigger insult known to them than wiping the mouth of the bottle on your shirt first. They were all sunburned and glazed in dirt. Mostly they just wanted to tell you their same stories, this one's best friend crippled diving off a pier into shallow water. This one preached universal harmony with a far off gaze and this one once lived in a diamond ice castle in Alaska or whatever. They enjoyed an audience and some nights it was nice to sit and listen. Each time they'd think they were meeting you for the first time.

But mostly he'd circle back the other way along Old Tower Road. There wasn't much there, just the road itself through some fields, and he'd prefer the quiet after the woods. It used to get farmed out there and everyone knew it was the Heinzinger's land until one day those lands just weren't farmed anymore.

The kids used to steal strawberries. One year Heinzinger had a raspberry patch in the back and the kids used to come home all purple and sour with their mouths stinging and if you ever did see old Heinzinger he might used to play like he was mad, but it really wasn't any fuss to him, and he let them all know it. He'd call them names, commies and hippies, and yell some and threaten to have a talk with their folks after church if they didn't immediately stop trespassing and pilfering from his property. But he'd do it all with a smile and his big hand across your shoulder. His wife would bring you out a soda or a milkshake and they'd make you sit and tell them all about what classes you were taking at school and which ones you liked and how the different kids were doing, and they knew all about which teachers everyone dreaded ending up with. Then when you headed home, he'd smile again while wagging a finger at you warning you not to come back around, while his wife would be on the porch shaking her head and rolling her eyes at him.

But then they just weren't around anymore. Wallace would guess probably by '76, '78 those fields were flattened and a sign was put up saying 'future location of such and such properties incorporated' or whatever. Their house was still far off in a corner of all that land, but no one ever saw them anymore.

Wallace would walk home along that long slow bend, like a big half moon, back to his house, and it'd be flat for who knows how far before there was a little lift in the distance and the clinic sat alone atop that small hill. Very few cars would pass. You'd see their lights coming from a long way off, a mile away. And even though you might be the tallest thing around there in all those fields, even then as a boy, those cars wouldn't see you at all. The whole road was one long bend so the lights would scan the horizon without ever seeing straight ahead. They would have no idea Wallace even existed until he flashed through their beams. He'd feel invisible really.

After making it through the woods and the rush every time, unable to believe he'd lived through the croaking toads and the deer tracks in the mud, walking home then feeling invincible—invisible, safely invisible—it was a great reward. He loved the riddle of exactly how far away this lightning in the distance was. How could you know sky distance?

By the time he was twelve, thirteen years old he wasn't walking so much anymore. So then when he did walk, it was always that much better. One night, it was as dark as it ever was. Clouds must've covered the stars. The light of the clinic up on the hill, the orange smoke of the factory over by the river and then that lightning in only that one spot far away. The air had a charge like it might storm and Wallace had a chill in his bones—and not a cold chill, but like the chill from the charge of being hyperalive, like he felt overwhelmed with himself in the world and it was a miracle to be there and to be himself at all, like the whole 3-D of the world might shatter at any second.

And so he walked straight off that long open road into what were once fields, and then were just dead fields in the night's thick cloak of darkness. And he knew he was the tallest thing standing in these fields for miles around, but he also knew the night was covering him and it wasn't very late. But sometimes out there it was just so lonely it could feel like the middle of the night just after supper time. So he walked out there into the middle of those fields and into and across that dry dirt there where there used to be strawberries and then further off where there used to be wheat. Now it was just him in the night and the night making him invisible and he was just so overwhelmed by it all that he didn't know, he couldn't remember thinking about it or making any decision, but the whole charge of being himself in the world overtook him and if the world wasn't gonna shatter itself then he'd just go on and shatter it and he didn't even think to do it but it was happening before he even knew it and he just had to do it, he didn't know he just did it, he played with himself.

He just did it. He did it and did it. He didn't feel any shame and he didn't think of anything except the night and himself standing out there, invisible, the tallest thing in miles hidden by the darkness and he didn't know what it was but he just did it and it felt good and it felt real in a way that he didn't really know if he'd ever really felt before then—him and the land and the night. He must've carried the glow of that night around with him for he didn't know how long. He really did feel holy for a while.

And Jesse was right about that age now himself.

Wallace gave Jesse two minutes' notice every time he ever came home. He had to click open lock after lock. A little song happened by the order in which he opened the locks. The overall rhythm of lock after lock was constant, but then also each lock was a little bit different than the others. It was like a small marching band announced him right before he arrived home and right after he left. He was like an army hero, a powerful general from one of the war stories with his own theme song.

When he sometimes forgot something and had to turn around to come home again right after leaving, Jesse always felt bad for him. He always had to do that. If he was only stopping home for a minute, he should have been able to cut down the song in some way. But there was no doing that. It had to play through completely each time. But the fact that he could not shorten it if he was popping in for only a minute, that, sometimes, made it seem dumb.

Wallace woke around one PM and, sniffing at his hands, walked blinking, half-asleep, in on Jesse. He scratched at his pajama pants, and his hairy blond belly hung out a little bit at the bottom of his tiny t-shirt. He yawned with arched back to announce his entrance.

"Morning."

Deep in his dent on the couch, in flannel plaid pajamas under piled blankets, Jesse did not respond. He watched *The Three Stooges* with a furrowed brow and pursed lips.

"You sleep?"

Jesse still did not respond. Wallace strut-stumbled slowly to the couch and gave Jesse's dirty-tube-socked foot a shake. "Hey!"

Jesse snapped up. "What?"

"Good morning."

With an askance look upwards, Jesse responded, "Good morning."

"What's up?"

"Dunno. Nothing. What?"

Wallace strained a smile. "Nothing. Good morning. You sleep?"

Jesse shrugged and tilted to watch his story around Wallace. Wallace sauntered the few steps over to the kitchen with a sing-song moan. His bare feet stuck to and peeled from the tile. "Hungry?"

Jesse did not respond. Wallace took a box of Cocoa Puffs from the shelf, shook it and listened. He tilted the box steeply out into two bowls, the second one topped with sugary dust from the bottom of the box. He poured milk in each bowl. The dust of the second bowl melted, thickening the surface of the milk. He walked this bowl over to Jesse and gave him a flick on the arm, "Sit up."

Jesse scooted up to a shallow angle, took the bowl, and balanced it on his lap to eat. Wallace walked back to the counter. He stood chomping at his cereal with demonstrative satisfaction, the whistling wheeze of his quick inhales punctuating his long smacking exhales. He said nothing for a while watching Jesse watch *The Three Stooges*.

"Happy Birthday."

Jesse glanced away from the television a second, grimaced and returned his gaze to the screen.

"It's your birthday."

"Yeah?"

"Yep," Wallace nodded, popping the spoon in his mouth and smirking.

"Hmm," Jesse set his bowl of shallow brown milk down on the floor next to him and returned to the Stooges.

"Thirteen."

Jesse nodded. He would have sworn he was already thirteen, but who knows? If it was already his birthday again, which he would in fact have no way of knowing, he would have guessed he would be turning fourteen, maybe fifteen.

"How's it feel? Huh? Thirteen, you're a teenager now."

Jesse responded with a blank look sideways, skittering past a response to Wallace's question without even a grunt. Wallace drank down his milk and sighed, resituating his weight, leaning forward on one arm on the counter. He sniffed at his armpit. "You alright?"

Jesse snuck a glance and Wallace, catching his eyes, reiterated his question with a shrug. "You alright?"

"Yeah, of course. I am fine," Jesse said. "Why?"

"I don't know. I just thought," Wallace tilted his head to throw a long dangling hair from his eye. He lit a cigarette. "Maybe it seemed, like I don't know, maybe something was bothering you."

"No, Wallace. I am fine."

"Well, then," Wallace said, playing it cool to heighten the drama of his surprise. "I thought for your birthday I'd go out and get us some ribs."

Smiling, eyes widened, Jesse pushed himself up with effort.

Wallace clapped. "That's right, boy! We're gonna throw you a birthday party, you and me! That's right, rib dinner, your favorite. We'll get the wet naps and get all sloppy and I even got us a cake!"

Jesse spun over and nudged himself up taller on one elbow. The Three Stooges spanked and whooped. Jesse and Wallace bobbed their heads together, smiling with excitement. Everything would be okay from now on. Ribs! Frosted bibs with barbecue, and soon *Green Acres* would start.

Jesse's pale blue fibrous blanket spilled across the corner of the wooden coffee table, tangled colorful dead lighters, scrunched packs of cigarettes, and a dirty mug up in it. Jesse scratched at his crotch. Wallace sensed some sadness shade Jesse's celebration, a distraction. "What is it? What?"

Jesse poked with a toe at one of four crusty socks crumpled at the foot of the couch. Wallace prodded, "What?"

"Well, where you gonna get the ribs?"

Wallace said, "Well, you know, your favorite place, Barry's, of course." Wallace shook his head, "What? I don't get it. Why?"

"Dunno."

"You don't like that? It's your favorite place right?"

"Yeah, it is," Jesse said.

"Then so what? It's your birthday and we're gonna get your favorite ribs."

Jesse lay back again and looked to the television. Wallace stepped around the counter shaking his head, "What?"

Nudging Jesse's feet back into the deep fold of the couch,

Wallace sat down on its edge and leaned forward to block Jesse's view of the screen. "What?"

Jesse sighed. "Well, Barry's is a restaurant, right?"

"Well, yeah."

"So, what I mean is, well, people eat there right?"

Wallace's feet pulled back onto their heels. His hands wrapped up into one another.

"I mean, right?" Jesse sat up in response to Wallace's weight shift.

"I don't know."

"Well, I mean, that is what a restaurant is... does?"

Wallace stepped up and knocked Jesse's bowl of milk. It didn't tip. He bent and picked it up quickly, squelching the urge to hurl it toward the wall with a deep breath.

"Well, I don't know. I mean, yeah, I guess maybe, yeah, people could eat there."

Jesse sat forward. "Yeah?"

Nostrils flared, Wallace stared down at him. "But that's not how it is, you know. A restaurant," Wallace stepped forward and dropped the bowl on the table. "A restaurant, it's like, you know, a place that makes the food for the people."

"I see it on my stories, Wallace. People eat at those places."

Wallace gasped. "Listen to you. Thirteen years old today, and you're gonna talk about believing what you see on your stories?"

"I am just saying Wallace, today is my birthday and if now I am thirteen, I am just saying maybe just this one time we could go to the restaurant to eat."

Wallace picked up the bowl from the table and returned to the kitchen. He dropped both bowls in the sink. Running water over the last of the milk, sudden-born clouds twirled themselves out from the center into nothing.

Surprising himself, Jesse decided to continue pushing. "This one time, just this once."

"What are you talking about? Eat at a restaurant?" Wallace spun and loomed. The Three Stooges were stuck out in a storm under thunderclouds like gray cotton.

Wallace continued, "Go to eat at the restaurant? I'll go out there. I go out there, every day I go out there so you don't have to. Every day." He brought his hands to his hips and jutted out his chest. "I'll go get the food and bring it back here for us, end of discussion."

"But I just mean if it is my birthday—"

"And ribs aren't good enough for you now? Then forget it."

"No, Wallace, ribs are great. They are my favorite. You know that."

"Then what's your problem? You don't appreciate—"

"Yes, Wallace. Of course I am happy to have them. I just meant—"

"You wanna go out to the restaurant?"

"Yeah."

"As if that's safe—"

"Wallace—"

"As if everyone can just go wherever they want as if life were just like one of your stories."

"Wallace, I know—"

"No, you don't act like you do. You act like you think life is just like one of your stories and everyone can just go out to restaurants."

"Wallace, of course I know—"

"What about the other stories I show you? You don't believe those?"

"Yeah, Wallace, I do. I know."

"You see how people kill each other and how people torture each other? You see how people cut each other up into little bits? People keep each other alive just to make each other suffer. The earth opens up and swallows people, shakes their homes down on them and crushes them."

"I am sorry Wallace," Jesse said, so tired by the apocalypse.

"You think everyone's happy about it, thugs attacking old people and mamas throwing their babies away in dumpsters? You think other people don't all wish this wasn't how things are?"

"I know, Wallace. I am sorry."

"But this is how it is. This is just the way shit is. So we just have to deal, okay?"

Lip quivering, Jesse turned back to the television. The shapes of the Three Stooges, flowing compositions without pattern, drawn out in shades of black and gray on white, floated abstract behind the glow of the screen.

"Not everyone has someone like me to take care of them, you know?"

Jesse inhaled deep, lost his voice in his throat. "I know." He cleared his throat, "I know that."

Wallace ripped the plastic bag from the empty cereal box and crinkled it up loudly. Collapsing the box, he wrestled with its stiff corners. "You act like you don't even appreciate me."

Jesse turned back and sat up on the couch again. He would not cry, he told himself. He would not cry. He lit a cigarette.

"Of course I do, Wallace. I just thought—"

"I know what you thought."

"If I am a teenager now and you go out there every day."

"So you don't have to."

"I know that," Jesse said, so tired of living in the end times.

"Eat at the restaurant," Wallace said, shaking his head.

"I am sorry."

Wallace walked back toward his room with his head down. "I gotta get dressed."

"Wallace, I am sorry."

"Yeah, it's fine."

"No, really I am."

"It's fine, really."

Wallace leaned his head up against the door to his room. Shit, shouldn't have gotten all flustered. What did that kid know? That stupid kid didn't know anything, didn't mean no one any harm. But shit, he wants to go out to the restaurant. Shit.

Wallace sighed, spoke quietly without looking at Jesse. "You want ribs? For your birthday, for real?"

Jesse pinched his lips to one side and blinked hard. He took a deep breath and looked up at the ceiling. "Of course, you know that is my favorite."

Wallace smiled and shifted his weight against the

doorframe. He smirked at Jesse and held the quiet until Jesse looked over to him. Wallace nodded, "Alright, then. Good."

He walked over to the couch and pulled Jesse's head against his chest in a one-armed hug. Wallace's breath smelled sour as the whole apartment, same smell as the whole apartment, but concentrated. Wallace held Jesse that way a moment, running the fingers of his other hand through Jesse's hair before kissing him on the forehead softly.

"Darling?" Wallace said, his voice lilting.

Jesse smirked and rolled his eyes, sighed before responding, "*Darling, I love you but give me Park Avenue.*"

Wallace patted Jesse on the knee. "Weren't you just acting just like a little Zsa Zsa there?"

Jesse shook his head embarrassed, swatted at Wallace lightly.

"Alright then," Wallace said. "Well, I gotta get dressed. I got some other stuff to do too." He released Jesse, and Jesse nodded. "So I'm gonna be a little while, alright?"

"Yep." Jesse responded.

"So maybe you wanna get some sleep sometime."

"Yep."

"And then I'll be back with ribs in time that we'll throw you a party before I have to get to work. Okay?"

"Great."

"Okay, then. Get some sleep."

Jesse said, "Yep." Wallace walked into his room to get dressed.

Jesse did not know why he did not tell Wallace about this thing. He just felt wrong and was afraid to tell him, thought maybe it would make things like they used to be a long time ago again.

For a long time he got this feeling sometimes, sometimes more than once a day and sometimes it felt like it would never end. He would get so bothered and frustrated, like all he wanted was to bite down on something and it never mattered how hard he bit down on a blanket or his sleeve. It could never be enough.

His peanuts would stand up stiff and it would burn and he would think he needed to pee. It felt like he needed to pee so bad, but he never could. He would be angry and just need to push his peanuts against something. He would push the blankets up into his lap. He would bunch them all up and press and a few seconds later with a shiver he would pee and make a mess in his pants. The burning feeling and the anger would be gone. He would be sleepy. And he would be so embarrassed he would not know what to do. He was too old to pee himself like that, and it would be sticky pee.

He would stuff the shorts he had messed under the cushion on the couch. But then later he would need to do it again and he would make a mess of his other shorts and stick those under the couch too. After a while he stopped wearing shorts under his pajama pants. But then he messed up all his pajama pants too. He had to pull out shorts he had already messed and put those back on because even if they were crunchy with pee at least they were not wet still.

Once he figured out this feeling was just going to keep happening and it would not go away, he felt so bad all the time. He did not know why. He knew he was mean to Wallace then because he was so afraid Wallace would find out he kept making a mess of himself and he was too old for that. He did not want to, but he could not stop pressing the blankets up into his lap and squeezing.

He thought a lot about when he first met Wallace, the first days in the motels when Wallace would hug him hard and it would burn. He had forgotten all about that for a long time. He did not know if he was remembering or dreaming those burning hugs.

Most of the time he could not control when it happened. But sometimes he would be watching his stories and then he could not help it. Every time he watched the dancing party stories, the pale redhead with the thick curly hair, and every time he watched the people on the beach stories, the blond women running barefoot in their slick swimsuits, it happened. All the time he was angry or sleepy. Sometimes he would get angry and then rub against the blankets and get sleepy and then he would want to start rubbing again even before he began to feel angry again.

It would not stop. He started to go to the bathroom to do it. He would imagine the dancing people or the beach people and go to the bathroom. That was when he realized it was different than pee. He would wash his shorts or pajamas in the sink, but it would still be a messy, cloudy smear, thick pee in bursts, not streams.

The way he felt bad all the time changed him. He was embarrassed and ashamed all the time. He missed his family like he had not missed them in a long time, their collaborative hurry early every morning. New memories of them emerged because he knew he had become a different person than the person that lived with them. That person never felt embarrassed or ashamed. That person never would have made this kind of mess every day. He never would have spent most of every day, thinking about making this mess. He was hardly able to watch his stories anymore. He watched them just waiting for the parts that would make him want to make the mess.

Things were not so bad for him, he would tell himself. Wallace took good care of him and mostly was nice. Wallace told him all about end times, so Jesse knew how lucky he was to have someone that took care of him. It was hard to believe, with the end times, that there was once a time and a world when kids like him could go to school, walk to school by themselves even. He watched the Bible stories and knew they said he was lucky to have Wallace who was brave enough to go out and get things they needed, brave enough to face the beasts of land and sea and the ten-horned dragon on its throne with eyes of fire and the wars. A lot of people were not so lucky and they were locked in just like Jesse, but without a Wallace. Jesse knew he was lucky.

He used to wish he could be in that perfect place where the stories came from, before Babylon. But he was young then. He did not understand. He was still imagining a world like before, when people could go to school, go out, and have friends. Back then, before the world changed and before he understood the change, the stories were all that the people had left. The stories were the most important and more real world than the world. When he closed his eyes and saw the dragon on its throne with eyes of fire, the story people chased it away, until the burning.

Only when the burning started and the thick pee started, did Jesse ever start to become unhappy with the stories. For a long time, many years, he forgot that he was watching the stories. He just thought the story-people's stories were all there was to his story. But when the thick pee started it was a separate thing that happened to him. It did not happen in the stories. It was like the itching and scratching had always been, but so much worse. He never thought about the itching too much before then, but then he felt like maybe being itchy had been everything to him all along. Once the thick pee started, the stories and him were made totally separate by it. And that was his new sad idea that changed everything. The stories removed, he could see that the itching was all that had ever been there beneath everything else, always.

When he felt bad about making the mess, he would cut himself. When he felt like he just wanted to be in the stories again, to believe in the story-people again, he would cut himself because he was so angry at himself for separating from them. With the spoon he had sharpened against the bottom of the tub, kept tucked it in the couch, he would slice little stripes above his elbow on the inside of his arm so Wallace would not see them, lick the salty blood from his fingertip. He knew the lamb with a sword on horseback would not like that. Might even leave him behind in Babylon if he knew. And the lamb knew everything, but Jesse could not stop himself.

And Wallace, Jesse thought, started to know that something had changed about him. It made Jesse worried. Before Jesse could tell for sure if Wallace was treating him different, he could imagine that he was just imagining things were different. But Wallace was definitely treating him different, so things really were different. It was not Jesse's imagination.

Jesse figured it was just end times getting to him, fear of the pirate armies taking him to the camps, or the microchip. But really it was all just the thick pee.

Jesse used to have a mom and a dad and a bigger brother and a little sister. He was always small and he kind of could not keep up with a lot of stuff. But Mom and Dad loved all of the three of them the same. They treated them all the same. But Jesse always felt like the favorite. He was agreeable. Wallace still always told that to him, "Jesse, you are agreeable."

Now Wallace loved him like Mom and Dad used to. He made him toasted cheeses or mac and cheese. Every time Wallace came home he stood at the counter and made Jesse some food up quick. He always came home bothered, like Dad used to. But then once he started making food he became more calm, like Mom.

But Wallace did not care or notice when Jesse woke up or went to sleep. So it was like when Jesse's big brother would baby-sit him, except Wallace never held him down by his wrists, dangling a string of spit over his face, or grabbed his wrists and made him hit himself. Jesse and Wallace had figured out how to get by good, just them two. Wallace took care of him.

Even when he tried really hard to remember Mom and Dad and his sister and brother and his old life, he could not remember them really. All of them seemed like a dream. He could not make their faces appear.

He could hear their voices sometimes. His sister talked out her nose. His brother sounded like his voice stayed stuck in his throat. Mom smelled like laundry. Dad smelled like sweat and oil and smoke. But he could only picture Dad from far away, mowing the lawn, and his back was always sunburned.

Sometimes in a dream one of their faces appeared to him

clearly. Mom's sharp chin and dimples, his brother's vacant gaze, that might be the entire dream, his brother grinning or Mom holding his face in her hands. Sometimes they would all be together and those were his favorite dreams, when it was no big deal and nothing even happened. They were just all together. Their faces all came back to him real clearly then. He could see all of them perfectly. They were in the old yard or they were not even anywhere. Mom's dresses were so light. He had never felt any kind of thing like that again, fabric so soft and thin.

But he could not make those dreams happen whenever he wanted. When he woke from one of those dreams he would try to hold onto it. He would not open his eyes. He would stay completely still, trying to linger in the dream for another minute. But that never worked.

Things were not bad with Wallace. It was like when Dad used to take the cushions off the couch and make forts. That was what his room was like, living on a couch in a small room of blankets and cardboard always lit by the TV.

Jesse knew it was impossible. But he sometimes thought some day they could all be together again, his family and him. It had been so long. Everyone would look a little bit different. He knew it was impossible. He understood it was impossible. But if they could ever just all be together again somehow, nothing would need to happen. But he still always imagined that day, even an hour, a minute.

It should have been simple, knowing it was impossible. But the fact it was impossible was what sometimes made it so hard. Afterwards, it would be no big deal to come right back there to Wallace and live with him exactly as they had learned to live together. That one minute with all of them, just to make sure they did not dream each other, they all remembered, the past was real. Then continuing there with Wallace would be simple, if he could have only said goodbye.

Even when he was little Jesse was always sick. He was always a bother to Mom and Dad like that. He had been with Wallace longer than he was ever with Mom and Dad. He knew life with Wallace was his real life. It was as real as his old life was before he ever knew a life could change.

Mom got real strong whenever he got sick. The sicker he got the stronger she got. Dad always tried to act tough, but mostly he was always tired. He never sat still. He worked and worked and always found something else to work on.

Sometimes, Jesse would pretend to sleep, so Dad would play with his hair. When Jesse was sick, Dad would only approach him when he was asleep or at least playing along and pretending to sleep, all along knowing Dad knew he was faking.

Part 3

1

One of those nights, bloodied, Will first spent a night at The Carroll Motel. Sometimes the bartender, seeing Will approach, would call his brother at the police department. If Will found the door directly from the parking lot to the bar locked, then the upright civilians in the lobby behind the tall desk, in their suits or skirt suits, polite but stern, following orders, had to ask Will to not enter. He never argued, respected citizens. But worth stopping by, try the door to the bar.

That night's tangle at The Cave was a loss decisive enough for Will to not bother cleaning himself. But he walked off head up, got in his own car. Drove himself away, waved to the crowd in the parking lot, smiled for a photo. The guy who'd been pounding Will's head to the pavement, he fell back against a wall gasping, near tears.

A couple exited The Carroll Motel bar, crossed the parking lot arm in arm toward Will. His every heavy step an effort, Will advanced. The man, tall and graying in a dark suit leaned on the woman, younger, blond with roots. The man timed his story through the short gaps in his laughter and passing Will, the woman glimpsed him blood-caked, a look away, brief eye contact, her painted face dropped, pleasing Will. The man's story reached its comedic apex, and confused, never noticing Will, he laughed alone, his pride stung. Will almost chuckled, but cramped, he couldn't.

His reflection in the door came more clearly into focus with each step, a man with no business standing, Jesus, zombie apocalypse battlefield. And through the blur of his own reflection, the tiny bartender with his big Yosemite Sam moustache stood behind the tinted glass, his hand set to lock the door, frozen. Gus stood by his side. With a scorching deep breath, Will paused, creaked against the ache of his own weight. Hardening his grimace, the bartender shook his lowered head, straightened himself up tall. Gus put a hand on his shoulder, insisted.

With a deep sigh, his shoulders lifting then settling, the bartender opened the door slowly. Will's cloudy reflection spun aside, revealed the bartender still shaking his head, unable to look, and Gus staring at him. Neither said a word. Blood burned Will's twitching eye. Lighting a cigarette, the bartender stepped back into the bar. Will passed Gus close with deliberate thumping steps, careful not to bump him, careful not to smear blood on the doorframe.

A hot dog ski stunt montage flashed across two televisions mounted high in opposite corners. In the other corners, two televisions cut between suited men in different studios, a ticker running continuous numbers across the bottom of the screen. Crowded beer logos drawn out in curved neon moderated the glow of the televisions. Except for this fuzzy light from the walls, the bar was otherwise dark. Will had to scan the many empty chairs of the room closely to determine it was in fact empty except for the bartender, sitting back in a chair in the middle of the room, staring at the ground a few feet in front of him, the goddamn Aerosmith at full volume.

Abandoning his attempt to grab Will by the wrist, Gus walked ahead of him toward a low, cushioned chair at a small table in a corner.

"Wait. Don't sit," the bartender called out.

Jumping up, the bartender walked heavy to the bar and cut open two garbage bags, tricky with dull scissors, then, bags crinkling in his grip under blasts of air conditioning, he returned to Gus and Will. Like picnic blankets he spread the garbage bags open across the chair, nodded. With Gus's assistance, Will settled into the soft rumble of the bags across the cushions, suffered to balance his weight in the least painful manner.

Standing over him, lip curled, the bartender studied Will more closely a moment before hopping off to lock the door. Crossing the room in a few brisk steps, the bartender unlocked a closet, ducked in and emerged with an armload of white towels. He dropped the pile in a sink, opened the faucet over them only long enough to spin and cut the stereo. The room silent, the bartender unfolded each towel from the others one at a time, wrung each out over the others left in the sink.

"It's okay," Will said after a moment. The bartender glanced up, but returned to his task without responding.

"It's okay. You want to play that, the music," Will said.

Cradling the towels, each now folded separately, up into his arms, the bartender shrugged, returning across the room.

"Well, it's not for my sake, you know, the loud music. It's so people can feel free to talk without other people hearing them."

Will nodded. The bartender dropped the towels to the side of the chair where Gus, kneeling in front of Will, nodded thanks.

"Sit up," Gus said.

With a groan, Will scooted his weight toward the back of the chair.

"And," the bartender extended a palm toward the room, "here we are, alone." He returned to the bar, head down, sat leaning on his elbows, his back turned to them.

Setting his arms symmetrical on the armrests, Will propped himself up. Gus pulled Will's knees apart from each other gently and leaned in. Looking up into Will's eyes for a second, seeking his gaze but unable to get a glimpse through the swelling, Gus began to wipe Will down in silence, across torn clothes and torn flesh in continuous, even strokes. The warm towels dampened Will, their paths waking each inch from dull ache into startled stinging. Crusted brown blood flakes became red liquid again, upon contact with the towels, and as each towel got quickly saturated in blood, Gus threw it aside onto a pile. One towel almost enough for both hands, another for one wrist to elbow. One towel soaked up the back of his neck, but his face saturated two alone.

Not a word was spoken between them. Will had never said anything about it, but Gus knew. Everyone knew, ever since Will had beaten that gangly olive-skinned blond kid who tried to stick him up at work with a pointed finger in his pocket. Tears in the kid's eyes, the crack in his voice betraying the gruff tone of his commands before Will even touched him. Will hadn't fought any less since then, but he'd been insisting on getting beaten up. If anything, Will seemed to be fighting even more, taking great pleasure in suffering public beatings, fighting back only enough to draw out and deepen his punishments.

THE LAST OF MEL'S KARAOKE BIRTHDAYS

Leaning against a wall alone, Will knew that bassline. The claps and snapping pattern sounded cool, never noticed that before, but he hated that stupid song, "Ice Ice Baby." The two men who had gotten up didn't rap, though. One began by scatting, and these two guys were old enough to know the joke of a stupid song gets old long before the song ends. Guitar came in. This was different. Right, he forgot about where that bassline had actually come from, it had been so effectively recontextualized.

From across the bar Will watched Norman push shots toward Mel and Gus, who each reluctantly accepted one. Norman scanned the bar with another shot in his hand, and Will ducked a step back into a shadow. Toasting, Norman drank two shots in rapid succession.

That song, Will couldn't believe the strange scatting moments. Like ribbons within the stoic chants of *people on the streets*, as if the scatting was itself an attempt to break free from the oppressive lockstep chants of these people on the streets. The scatting voice did find language, only for a moment, to cry, *Let me out*. Maybe Will had never really heard the words to "Under Pressure" before. The whole world, the terror of knowing what the whole world is about. Well, yeah, that would be terrifying.

Van Halen had always been Will's favorite band, and it had never occurred to him that they might at some point not be. But in the last few years, listening to those same songs he'd lived with his whole life, his focus had shifted. He'd come to really like only the bass playing. The singing and the guitar playing and the drumming all always had to be so kick-ass. He was over it. Seemed like insecurity to him, pathetic battling pleas for attention. Every song, everyone fighting to be the most kick-ass while the modest pulse of the bass was actually the entire song.

But this song, "Under Pressure," was different. He wasn't offended by the singing or guitar playing or drumming, fanciful as any of them might have been. Everything was in service to the song, toward a greater end.

When the song seems it's gone as high as it could within its own harmonic framework, then it climbs even higher, *Why can't we give love one more chance?* Really, *why can't we give ourselves one more chance?* The drums pick up to double time and it's building and building until finally, as the drums drop to half-time and it's no longer a question but a statement, a statement of purpose and resolve, acceptance, *This is ourselves.* Back in a shadow, next to the knock and spin of the pinball machine, Will's head swam. He'd promised Mel. He'd doubled up on his chill pills. Under Pressure.

For a while, some months even, when his brawling compulsion first began, all the bars—Sluggo's, The Cave—took Will's side without question. Sniffling blood bubbles, beat red cheeks, his chest heaving, he'd push his way through a startled crowd, eyes open wide, vision stunned clear. Always him they held back. And he hung back agreeably once pulled off, the other guy always taken away while Will poured any beer in reach over his own head howling, "It's raining beer!"

Didn't matter who got the worst of it, torn open flesh, bone cutting from within, who puked, spit out a tooth. Whether they jumped on each other like magnetized cats in the middle of a room, or stepped outside with the stately graces of a pistol duel, those first few months, the bars' staff always took Will's side.

Took his side every time, until he got in the habit of running over to The Shhh... for closing time every night. Outside in the parking lot, covered in blood, he would dance just outside the front door. Some nights wild ghost dances, other nights Tai Chi-inspired interpretative dance, but always soaked in blood, always beaming smiles.

He began to get warnings, pulled aside as he arrived anywhere, talked to sympathetically, Come on man, what is it? Hard times, etc. The warnings intensified quickly, and there weren't many stern warnings before he was being mocked, given taunting messages, threats and challenges from Norman, who he would never actually see. Soon he was brawling every bouncer in town. Got to be so he'd show up, do nothing but approach and plant his feet before the entire security staff at a bar where he'd so recently been a face everyone was happy to see, and they would stand around making small talk with each other while kicking him in the ribs. One time they beat him until they could prop his teeth up on a curb, left him like that a long while in suspense. The crowd hushed, queasy. Finally Will rolled over and smiled, stood up and brushed himself off, "Send Norman my regards."

They would toss him between them, spinning him, one knocking the wind from his gut with a hard elbow, another biting open his nose. But he could stay on his feet. People screamed, unfamiliar voices pleaded, "Just stay down!" But he could stay on his feet. He couldn't stop himself. They'd stand him up, back pressed against a wall, throw his head back against the bricks. They would finish, strange voices sobbed, "Please just stay down! Stay down!" But he always got up, stayed up on his feet. That was his magic trick, wide wounds—ta-da! Stay up on his feet was what he could do.

That first man that sang Harry Nilsson as they arrived to the karaoke bar returned to the stage already, this time to sing "Everybody's Talkin'." With exaggerated yawns and stretching, Norman made a display of his boredom, embarrassing Gus a little bit with his bad manners. The high trills again, Harry Nilsson's fake horn mouth sounds nailed, Mel and Gus impressed. Norman leaned in. "That guy's a hack. I know his type."

"Sounds great," Mel protested.

Norman shook his head, a look of distaste. "No, no. Look, he can't *sing* sing. He can only impersonate Nilsson."

Mel shrugged. She looked to Gus. He looked her in the eye and they shrugged together. "Sounds really good though, Norman, doesn't it?" she said.

Norman, sweaty, rolled his eyes, shrugged. "Yeah, sure, whatever, because it's Nilsson. Anything else, the dude would be lost."

Mel nodded. She looked to Gus. He looked her in the eye and they nodded together.

Finishing, the man forgot about his responsibility to announce the next singer. Norman, seeing his window, got to the stage in four long steps, took matters in his own hands.

"Gus!" he called out. "Our very own Gus, ladies and germs."

Stepping to the stage, Gus attempted to wrangle the mic from Norman, but Norman continued.

"You know, Gus here has been working for me for a long, long time now."

The song starting, Norman released the microphone to Gus.

Will felt dull, separate from the room, aware of his skin as a distinct boundary between self and world. Gus was a dumpy little phony, Will thought, always working so hard at appearing kind, but his intention to appear so, was always obvious. Really, he was so condescending, always judging everyone with his coy smirk, a poet, constantly squirming.

Feet apart and shoulders back, one hand in his pocket, Gus twisted at the hips a little through the opening bars of Jim Croce's "Operator." Not a particularly dark song, more wistful, it tells its story in few bumping words. Really only when the song descends in the chorus did Gus's little twist appear a twinge forlorn. He knew the song perfectly, but the ball bouncing along the lyrics threw him off. Its bounce off time during the chorus, delayed a smidge, made him doubt that he actually knew the song.

Gus had always liked the basic premise of the song. The operator anonymous, it didn't matter to the singer who would listen, the meaning of the act was in the expression itself. The song itself had a cool shuffle and did not sound urgent, but it was about the urgency of expression. And calling just to tell her he's fine, the act would negate its own true meaning and everyone would know it but him, the singer. So which experience was more real, his, the singer, or everyone else's? Gus liked all that about the song, the irresolvable tension in such a seemingly simple ditty.

Jesus, Mel thought. What blow had Gus overcome? Who'd he need to call just to tell them he's fine? What exactly had he learned to take well? Barrel-shaped in baggy jeans, Gus confronted loss with the same cool as the accompanying drums' soft shuffle.

Wasn't it just the most common mistake in the world, Mel thought, the quintessential experience of modern life, thinking this love would save him? And *they* may say that's the way it goes, but who cares what *they* say? Mel always remembered that part in Catch-22, she read it twenty years ago and always remembered the part where the main character said that these people were trying to kill him. His commanding officer said, You're crazy, we're at war. They're trying to kill everyone. And he replied, Well, just because they're trying to kill everyone else too doesn't mean that they aren't trying to kill me.

So this vague *they* in "Operator" told the singer love would hurt. But being told that meant nothing to him compared to the experience of his pain. He may *wish his words could convince himself that it just wasn't real, and that's not the way it feels*. But the true experience, hurt feels more real than logic.

Closing his eyes, a deep breath at the end of the song, Gus

was received with tepid applause. Mel though, bouncing on her toes, clapped enthusiastically, shouted, "Bravo!"

The applause grounded him back in the room, returned from the song.

"Who's next?" a stranger yelled at him.

"What?"

"Read the next name."

"Oh yeah, right."

"Sam? Sam?" he called out, looking around the room to no response.

"He split." Someone yelled. "Got too drunk too early."

Gus squinted to plug in the number for the next song. Norman threw his arm up in the air. "I'll do it!" he shouted. "I'm up next anyway, just do them both."

Stepping offstage, a big smile, Gus considered his seniority on its own might've generated more applause back home in Stone Claw Grove. Bar kids did respect someone so old like Gus, who could still muster the energy to make it out to bars and hang out late.

With a panther's stride—Oh no, "Eye of the Tiger"—Gus passed Norman on his way back up to the stage.

"Good job, Gus."

"Thanks."

"Yeah, weird though."

"What?"

"I don't know. Just figured you'd sing "YMCA" or "We Are the Champions" or something gay like that."

Seeing Norman return to the stage, Will decided he could use a little fresh air.

In The Carroll Motel bar a vent belched on, kicked off, on again, the slow breathing pattern of the bar. Will grunted occasionally. Gus sighed once or twice covering the surface of Will with a bar rag then repeating the process, covered the surface of Will again.

When Gus stepped to the bar to speak to the bartender, the

bartender turned the stereo back on.

Gus returned, grabbed Will by the wrist.

"Come on." He pulled and Will moaned.

"Let's go." He pulled again and Will leaned forward best he could. Gus cupped him under the armpits, chest to chest to help him stand, gripped him by the shoulders to steady him.

"Come on," Gus repeated, grabbing Will by the wrist again.

"Hold on," the bartender called out, pouring them each a shot. Gus leaned Will against the bar. Will had trouble lifting his glass to the silent toast, dribbled the bourbon down his chin. The bartender slid a couple pills across the bar. Will insisted no blood-thinners, makes bruising worse.

On the short march to the lobby through a long hall of doors, his stride limited to a shuffle as if his ankles had been cuffed, Will felt aware of feeling captured.

WILL GETTING SILLY

Goddamn! Tear the fabric back! Head in flames!

One guy, a little older, his ankle was sideways, flipped inward perpendicular. Fucking flesh pressed flesh, a tooth cut in Will's knuckle. A cartoon of silly tornado limbs, the pile of them locked weighting themselves against the doorframe. The doorman pushed the pile out the door.

A guy lifted his friend from behind, grabbing him under the arms.

"Hey, whoa, my boot's come off!" But it wasn't his boot.

In Will's dreams stretching flesh pressed flesh, bone and flesh pushed out flesh and hair, stretched and blemished, a continuity of mind in warping shape, but not when inside it.

Will slammed a head into the doorframe. Leveraged an arm against the doorframe, pressed all his weight on the bicep and wrist, wait for the snap.

Goddamn! Head in flames! Love was just such imprecise logic.

AT THE FACTORY-CHURCH WILL GOT SERIOUS

Administratively, the scene was structured kind of like the anonymous blowjobs in men's rooms triggered by a coded foot tap. A couple men meet up at a predetermined place, an isolated place, used to be a barn just outside of town. Then it moved to behind the factory-church.

A flat powder blue square, two stories tall and equally as wide, painted on the front of the abandoned factory on the west side of town—a church had salvaged exactly that much of the building. Ornate bulbs popped from the double-belted centers of the two new pillars at the big front doors. The rest of the building, the majority of its front, remained untouched. Granite shades of grit and gray, the depths of its seams in shadows and dirt behind the powder blue box, the rest of the building, a frame frozen in continuous expansion, fading into the background of the dull sky, day or night.

In the open yard behind the factory-church, late at night, early morning, men met anonymously, the meetings coordinated through scribbled code in men's room stalls, near payphones. The keys whispered in passing in the fury of battles in bar parking lots. Will was offered the key many times before recognizing it as such, slow to realize a code to break even existed.

In the parking lots, only once a night had exploded into scattered chatter and threats, tears and heat, did Will ever feel peace, hunger satiated, his mind still. Shouting men with chests puffed out pointing, many sides retelling a single event all at once. Commands and appeals cancelled each other out, became a single roar. And in these moments, Will would hear the whisper close up in his ear. A small man he never caught sight of, bumping up against him, moved on as soon as his message slipped. "The factory-church, 3 AM Tuesday and Thursday."

Repeated, the message took on the power of a dream's

command.

Giving in to his curiosity one night, Will pulled around the back of the factory-church, waited in his car, nothing to see, but this must be the place. Pulled up as far as he could drive, up to the fence, sat in the warm purr and rattle for a while. The windows began to fog. He leaned chest to steering wheel to wipe the windshield with his sleeve. Static on the radio, the reception so weak the scan function skipped over all his presets. Skipped through the whole dial again. Cracked the window and smoked, heard silence.

Finally got out. Stood next to his car under the big moon. Walked through the open gates, dragging his feet loudly through the gravel. The yard empty, a darting rodent, he sauntered, hands in pockets.

"Hello?"

Maybe he had imagined the whole thing. The feeling of being watched was very similar to the feeling of suspecting you were being watched. The entire dark flatness of the factory's backside, the empty stands of a stadium. Breath quickened. He hopped a few steps up to the tracks to better survey the yard, still empty.

Suspense doubled back on itself became boredom. Scraping metal to gravel, he peeked in the drawer of a file cabinet on its side, nothing, turned to return to his car. From above, the plunk of metal came down on his skull, a deep grunt of muscles collapsed him. Flattened in a blur, he raised his hand over his head to stop the next blow. But no more crashes followed the first. Opening his eyes, nothing, no one anywhere. Lay on his side in the gravel under the big moon, pulled his knees up fetal. Far off, a rodent scampered eye level.

He stood, dusted himself off, dust stuck to blood clumps. Stood up straight and called out, cleared his throat and called out, "Well, come on then! You come out now!"

Whir of silence from every direction, he spun, no one. He shuffled back to his car, kicking up dust, scanned the gravel for a long pipe, a heavy car part, anything he might be able to swing. Looked back over his shoulder every few steps. Wheezing, he opened the door to his car. Turned back to the yard, threw his head back and howled to the factory's backside, black against the night sky, howled.

Grabbing the car door, he bent at the waist, slammed the door shut on his head and bolted upright as the door bounced back. Turning, he expected applause from the dark flatness of the factory's backside, the empty stands of a stadium, but nothing. Howled again, his nose filled with blood. Eyes burned and the scream of wind rushing in his ears forced him to concentrate on his balance. He opened the car door again, held it open, bent, held the pose, stood and looked around smiling. He sat down in his car, sat a long while stunned before heading home.

The high of the mysterious single blow lingered for days. Will had become quite a local celebrity in the parking lots of the various bars, people applauding when he arrived. Challengers traveled from nearby towns to find him. He thought of himself as living out the montage scene near the beginning of *Conan*, equally pleased to identify himself as a barbarian of pre-history and, while actually in battle, to truly experience time pass as in a montage sequence.

People recorded every fight. Posted them online and argued his technique, his intuitive strategy and passion tailored to the specific challenger he faced, on street fight message boards: "Astonishing grace," "Awesome power," "Relentless." He tried not to look, but sometimes didn't know what else to do with the computer time he'd signed up for at the library.

But the vanity of the parking lots meant nothing compared to satiating the needs of his ever deepening dependence. His tolerance increased, like anything, the body's learned resistance, he needed greater and greater amounts of pain to yield the same rush. A drinker, after a while, might come to need three or four times the drink to feel the same drunk. Will's tolerance, though not measurable in such terms, came to be more analogous to that of an opiate abuser, eventually requiring twenty-five or as much as a hundred times the original amount.

And this single blow at the factory-church, the shock, dropping from the sky and then nothing, maybe it was a trap. He tried to shake the thrill, distracted for days, but couldn't. He had to return to the factory-church, try to figure out what had happened.

Sunday morning, children scampering off during the post-Mass mingle, climbed a short stack of railroad-ties, found a tooth among the gravel.

On Gus's arm in the lobby of The Carroll Motel, Will stood like an enemy combatant. The bartender leaned forward on his toes, pulling himself up over the desk on his elbows. He whispered something to the young man behind the counter, who could have easily helped him out by leaning forward but chose not to. Will looked to the fireplace, imagined its gray ash sticking to his dampness. An empty plastic bag of orange juice concentrate sat deflated on a counter next to its spigot.

The clerk was dressed up to appear older than Will thought he must have really been, giving the impression of having a moustache penciled above his lip. He responded to the bartender in tight nods with pursed lips and terse shrugs. Listening, he eyed Will sideways, never turning his head toward him, heightening the judgmental quality of his expression. Dinosaur ferns held up with plastic ties to short stands were plastic. Washington crossed the Delaware next to a flag on a wall in the breakfast nook.

The bartender spun, winked at Gus. He twirled a room key on his extended index finger, approaching Will and Gus slow and self-satisfied as if they were his own freshly waxed Corvette. Planting his feet before them, he pointed with his head toward the hallway.

"Well, go ahead if you insist," he said.

Taking the key from him, Gus held his hand a moment. "Thank you," he said, and the bartender shrugged.

"I got to close up," the bartender said and started back

toward the bar. "Come visit me for a night cap still?"

"I will," Gus said, taking Will by the arm.

Through the hallway, the worn carpet dimpled in cigarette burns, Gus spoke without turning to Will. "We had a room tonight anyway," he said. "Kind of a special occasion, but not really. And he gets a good deal, so no big deal."

Grateful, Will nodded with exaggerated thoughtfulness, swollen dull, unable to parse out the complexity of the arrangement. A hand-written sign read, "Please do not bring infants into the Jacuzzi." Burn and ache threatened to tumble Will, the rhythm of his steps acutely relevant to his remaining upright, and the pulse of his tightening skull, the grand dusty ballroom, the abandoned theme park, beat in this same rhythm.

The end of the hallway constricted to a distant pinpoint somewhere endlessly ahead. Gus's cool pace past room after room falling away and fading behind their steps, over and over Will thought, Is this it? This is it. Is this the room? This is it. Over and over the doors fell away until the sudden flat blankness of a wall before them engorged and overwhelmed Will, swallowed him.

"Whoa, you okay buddy?" Gus propped Will up, bumping into him for a pause before the turn of a corner toward the next long hall. Gus tilted him upright, by the shoulders. He lit a cigarette, put it between Will's lips and grinned before spinning off.

"Come on. Right here."

Deep breath, Will followed in silence, struggled to hit that same rhythm in his steps he had going to keep him balanced, that same pulse in his skull.

Passing only a few rooms Gus stopped and clicked open a door, a sharp waft of detergent and wet dog, stale smoke stench seeping from the cracking of the seam. Gus stepped in and turned on the light. He held the door open, for Will to stumble inside. Another few steps in, Gus inspected the room with quick glances.

"Got you a late checkout."

Will nodded.

"So take your time."

Will nodded and Gus studied him more closely. "You alright?"

Will nodded. Gus grabbed him by the shoulders again, turned him carefully so his back was to the bed and lowered him. Seated on the bed Will looked up to him, but Gus broke the gaze quick and shook his head.

"Yeah, well, you owe me."

"Thank you, Gus."

"You owe me."

"I mean it. I know, you know," Will said, sighing.

"What?"

"You know," Will shook his head. "I mean, I know you don't like me."

Gus swatted the statement down and stepped off, turned on the bathroom light and left the door open. The ash from Will's cigarette fell on the bed and Gus took the cigarette from him, dropped it in the toilet.

"I'll leave this light on for you."

Will nodded. At the door Gus turned back and smiled. "Well, I mean, no one likes you, Will."

Will grimaced, shrugged.

"That's your thing, right?" Gus widened his smile, softened his tone. "I mean, you like that, right? No one liking you?"

Will shrugged. Stepping out the door, his expression serious, Gus popped his head back in, his feet still planted in the hall. "Will?" he said.

Will focused his gaze and nodded.

"How—" Gus stopped and reconsidered his question.

"I mean, when—"

Will wanted to understand.

Gus smiled.

"No, I guess, really, I mean, why?"

Will nodded then kept nodding. Gus cocked his head, pulled his baggy jeans up at the waist. "Yeah, why, that's my question," Gus said. "Why?"

One time Nana told Kent upon his arrival that maybe Mel's ex-husband had reappeared, and she said Mel said he said maybe they could work things out.

The strange piece of furniture something like an exercise bike made of leather and wood, seemingly constructed only for the indulgence of crumpled clothes, Kent moved that thing from the corner of the guest room to near the door. He picked up the pair of seashell owls, glued on googly eyes, from the dresser top, swapped which one stood left and which right.

Upon Mel's arrival one time Nana told her that Kent's son, sitting in the dugout, caught a foul line drive in the face and she said she thinks Kent said he needed about sixty stitches.

Mel moved the hamper to the other side of the dresser, the potpourri to the other end of the dresser top.

Victory! Kent declared, returning more than six months later. The seashell owls remained on the dresser-top as he last set them.

Nana's jewelry case was always on top of the dresser in front of the mirror after Mel had visited.

And Dell was in just one photo, blurry in the background, chest high in the water, leaning along the side of a blue pool, smoking. In a splash in the foreground Kent heaved Mel over his shoulder.

Either Kent or Mel always took that photo down, put it in the top drawer. The other one always hung it back up. Whether Will found it in the drawer or on the wall, he always flipped it face down on the top of the dresser, left it like that.

If he could determine the pattern of occupancy to distinguish which one of them emptied the closet of Nana's dresses to hang their own clothes, versus which one of them emptied the dresser of linens without returning them, Will thought maybe he could figure out who put the photo in the drawer and who hung it up again. But really all he knew was just to move things.

Returning to the factory-church early another evening, Will slipped into the basement through a broken window on the backside, moved a desk through tickling cobwebs to the window, careful not to knock too loud around the crowded machine room, surveyed the yard. Nothing moved.

Trying to not sneeze passed the time, hours in his hiding spot. No one approached. The yard darkened, the jagged details of its littered landscape faded. A bird pecked at a sweater, took it in its beak and struggled to pull it from a puddle. The glow of streetlights far off beyond the field emerged from being blended within dusk, held vision in particulars. Only by remembering the lighting of the scene before, holding its hues and shades firmly in mind in comparison to the present, could Will sense time pass. Watched close, nothing moved.

Will imagined a family of raccoons might have made themselves a fighting circuit there at the factory-church. This raccoon family probably set up a boxing ring and one wore a referee's striped shirt and maybe it was a wrestling ring and one leapt with an elbow from the top rope before pinning the other, the raccoon referee dropping to his side to count, raising the other's paw over his head in victory, a raccoon in a hooded robe, silly.

Some hours of darkness later, through the burn of lower back and thigh cramps, thirsty enough to suck sores from the inside of his cheeks, Will's bowels gurgled. Took his eyes from the yard for the first time. The door to the hall blocked from the other side, the broken window to the yard was the only way in or out of the room. Shit on the floor? Squat among clutter and bent metal, rats, in the dark with no toilet paper, he decided otherwise. Climb back out the window. He looked, nothing.

Someone else, anyone, if he could have just seen the moment from the outside, if he could see an attack, maybe he could understand his own compulsion to return, return to be attacked. All the sport of battle removed, all strategy removed, the brutality falling in an instant, an otherwise unrecognizable, singular flashing second with neither suspense nor follow-up. Such perfect barbarity, the temporal aspect negated, and with it, all improvisation, the impulse to strike back suspended indefinitely. One strike, the totality of satisfaction. Will needed to see it from the outside, the set-up. He couldn't be the only one who showed up for this, needed it.

But nothing. Surveyed the yard, all the training as a child, playing spy in the tree-house or sharp shooter, any sign of movement, anyone else planting themselves in a base, or anyone else approaching for a rendezvous, but nothing. His stomach imposed its priority. The sun cracked over the distance, surprising him. The night had passed. The whole night, the yard entirely still, he could see it all from his hiding spot.

Careful to grip between shards in the frame, he hoisted himself up into the window, pulled himself up to his waist, arms extended, kicked a leg up onto the sill. Planting a foot to stand, the blow dropped, the back of his head, a crashing elbow maybe. Pointy bone on the back of his skull, hunted while hunting, the audience had become the game. He toppled from the ground, back through the window, his wrist under his tailbone against the steel desktop, and his ankle too against cold concrete.

The rush of the parking lots: everyone fought differently. The combined trampling weight of a throbbing mass, directed like a Ouija board, in snow falling without wind, a thrill, but more so, the individual participants.

Some followed codes of honor closely. Others basked in bad taste, unquenchable rage. Some were sneaky about transgressions into poor sportsmanship. One never knew who carried a battery in his pocket to add pounds to his punch, kept fish hooks hidden.

A few rivals, the most worthy opponents, among the people Will had ever felt closest to, provoked re-matches monthly. But the strangers were the real thrill. Will could look around, not looking for anything. He never started anything himself. Looking around, he couldn't help but wonder about certain men.

If that guy were to start something and if Will couldn't walk away, how would the guy do it? If Will had no choice, how would the guy come at him? Would he be patient, conscious of dynamics, respond uniquely to Will? Or would he have an overall attack plan scripted and rehearsed, zero spontaneity? Would the guy maybe strip to the waist as some of these cocky dorks thought to do? Would he lose himself, overwhelmed, overcome by urgency and unable to pace his throws, exhausting himself prematurely? Would the guy wrap Will up tightly against him for close jabs or keep Will dancing a step away, forcing them both to full extension?

Will could measure a good guess at someone's technique immediately, the length of his nails, did he keep them clean? Teeth, but you could never really know. Shoes could tell a lot, though often nothing. And he enjoyed any considered fighting style. Sloppy and reckless could be executed with equal mastery as rigid and methodical. Will enjoyed all of it. He was silly that way.

But the factory-church was different. Inspector Clouseau instructed his house servant Cato to attack him when he least expected it, all suspense and self-defense reflexes kept sharp. Maybe some light housekeeping and a certain amount of flattery required, but surprise, surprise within the agreed-upon-context, the real expectation.

Will had never seen *Fight Club*, but it sounded a little plot heavy, dull and abstract, according to anyone he knew who had seen it. The twist—the two main characters the same guy, one the other's projection—seemed unnecessary to Will.

Drawn to this community—if that would be the word for himself and a rival he could never see, in the community between these two poles of Cato and Brad Pitt—Will found a certain peace. Lacking in practice both the Panther's slapstick and the psychic-meta-qualities of *Fight Club* as buffers, one big blow, a stun, the sole intent. No sustained fight or punches thrown in defense. Blows were not to be seen coming. One never knew what landed, impossible weights dropped, only that one toppled after one waited to topple. A crooked two-by-four to the back of the head, an impossibly hard kick to the balls, asymmetrical attacks, the rush and point.

Will continued to frequent the bar parking lots, but after becoming involved at the factory-church circuit his focus dwindled, his drive had dried up. Worked out fine for him, as all he had come to desire was being beaten and he could hardly be troubled to return a blow. But soon, not only the security, but the audience, those tilting around at closing time, had turned against him, booed, spat. And he had come to bask in it, his drawn out passion play on slick pavement, no pretense of redemption but through compulsive repetition of the ritual. Resurrection never even occurred to him.

Sitting on the bed at The Carroll Motel, Will looked back up to Gus and shrugged. Gus traced a finger over the framed emergency exit route hung at the door, then stepped out of the room.

"Yeah, well, you got a late checkout."

The door closed behind him.

Sitting on the side of the bed, Will looked around the room for the bar, unaware of the distinction between hotels and motels, his only idea of hotel rooms being Cary Grant as a bon vivant on some far-flung foreign holiday, or young Paul Newman clinking cubes into a glass. He felt for a second just like he imagined young Paul Newman felt, the moment before helping himself from a spread of carafes. The possibility of ending up somehow okay, the defeated champ everyone roots for and never doubts will end up back on top somehow, back on top. Paul Newman suffered because he himself felt defeated, and the tragedy was that no one else ever thought he was defeated. But how will his beautiful accomplice, the aging actress, or even Paul Newman's warm-hearted and humble mentor, the old coach or sympathetic deputy, ever convince him otherwise? Those clouds will part, in his mind those clouds will part, and then he'll recognize what everyone else already knows. He'll hit his stride. His capacity to hold the aging actress's cheek softly in his palm will return.

Plastic flowers, leather Bible, murky plastic shower curtain, phone book, plastic cups wrapped in plastic, coat hangers. The comforter had a coat of some manufactured idea of softness, a fragrant grimy shell encasing it, crisp. But it was not in fact soft. Faraway sirens surrounded the silence.

A knock at the door, Will struggled to stand. Gus popped the door open.

"Don't bother getting up," he said. He tossed a vest and some big pants over to the bed.

"Sorry, only change of clothes I could find around here," Gus said. "And I forgot to leave you your key." He tossed the room key to the bed.

Will nodded, "Thank you."

"You got a bartender's vest, no shirt, and a janitor's big overalls," Gus smirked. "Bartender says please shower before you put them on."

Will nodded, "Yep."

"And I'll leave you alone, won't intrude again."

Gus closed the door behind him.

Will laid still a long while. Passing lights revealed the smeared fingerprints along the sides of the window, greasy smudges on the wallpaper.

Unplugging it, Will quickly moved the lamp from the desk to the nightstand. Tracing its course, he unraveled the phone's cord from behind and between the legs of the empty dresser, and moved the phone from the nightstand to the dresser.

Dropping the lamp on the bed, he pulled the nightstand from the wall, spun it around, and put it back, pressing its drawer and shelf against the wall, careful to fit its feet backwards into their dents in the carpet. He replaced the lamp on the nightstand.

The bruising didn't hurt as much as the sting of the air conditioning on the torn dangling bits of flesh. Pierced unevenly, some gaping holes big as if scooped out with a spoon, shallow pools of blood returned to the surface. He squeezed his hand behind the television. Lift with your legs not your back, a few slow steps to heave the television up crooked into the sink.

The small table next to the window fit standing upright under the sink. Tilted, the chair fit next to the table. A passing car's lights cut across the bottom of the window, climbed the window's side.

Another night, parking blocks away, sticking close to the fence, low to the ground, Will arrived behind the factory-church after midnight. He had tried to resist the temptation, scoped out Sluggo's and The Cave, but neither would let him in, both chased him away. The yard always silent and empty when he arrived, careful each time to not be seen approaching, he had been frequenting the factory-church for blows. This time, another man. For the first time Will walked up on someone. A man he'd never seen before turned circles in the yard, didn't see Will.

Some afternoons, not the appointed fighting hours, Will had walked the yard seeking evidence of struggle, a rusted pipe, heavy shattered porcelain. He knew there had to be others, bunkers dug into the trash to hide in. A pastor or an administrator, a choir leader might pull past him slow while he inspected the yard, not shy about stopping and staring from their big old cars. But in the back, at the appointed hours, never saw anyone before that night. He stooped in a crevice between leaning tin-shed pieces, careful to remain in shadows.

The man sat cross-legged in the open. No sense of time, he remained still in the ring thrown from a reflecting streetlight, head down. The breeze and creaks, hours, perfectly still. Will too, so still a squirrel sniffed his cuff.

Standing finally, unbuttoning his coat, the man called out in a high lisp, articulating every syllable particularly, "Oh, well, good evening. Well, I'm here."

The man undressed in the yard. Will watched. The man took off his over-coat to reveal a suit, loosened his tie, unbuttoned the top couple buttons of his shirt and pulled it over his head. Folding his pants, he set them down in the dust. In his boxer shorts and a v-neck tee, he paced the yard, placing toe, heel, toe with conscious effort.

"Oh, how I do look forward to this and then at the time, when it's happening, I get so troubled, my mind, such doubts." His circle widened.

"I do so need these times, as I am certain you know." A fake British accent? Quiet and nothing, his steps crunched gravel.

"Oh, I get so nervous. I just talk, you know? Helps I guess, the talking. I talk as I figure things out, you know? In times like these, I mean. I mean, at times like these I don't talk because I know what I want to say, I talk to figure out what I want to say."

He fell straight down, legs crossed again, bowed his head between his knees. Picking gravel, shards of glass from the undersides of his thighs, his shoulders bounced, tears? Like a landed octopus, he crawled in place, squirming, but never peeked up.

The wind rumbled the tin Will leaned under, the sound of thunder. Unable to watch the man squirm and suffer any longer, Will took a step, knocked the lean-to and ducked back into the shadow. The man looked up, a wild smile through tears, "Oh, thank you."

As Will approached him slowly, the man with a shivering whisper repeated over and over again, "Oh, thank you, thank you. I knew you'd come. I knew you'd be here. Thank you."

Having been seen, Will thought it only fair to linger over the man's head for a long, long while, his arms jittering from exhaustion, balancing the large sheet of glass he had found, before he finally dropped the single, impossibly hard blow.

Someone paid the cops off to ignore the complaints of the factory-church owners. And none of those involved in the community would ever go to the police. That simplified things for Will. And after some time, as much as he had come to peace with his hamminess, how much he loved the public aspect, the standing around parking lots smiling, covered in blood while people had their photos taken with him, the jolt of the single blow drew him in.

Videos of these meetings—they weren't battles—began to appear on the internet as well, always the same crack across the lens, the same voice that first lured him there from the parking lots always narrating, always framed so tightly on the waiting man that the blow could never be seen except for in its effects on the victim.

Satisfied with his room at The Carroll Motel's rearrangement, Will carefully sat back down on the bed. Peeling his shirt from the sweat and blood-crust underneath it felt like a slow series of small bites. It was a tight sixty-fourth of an inch between the sculpted inner core of his work shoe and the crushed black nail of his big toe. A mouth-hot athletic sock blanketed and tucked in the shedding dead talon. Leveraging his shoe against the top of his foot to remove his heel, it couldn't be done subtly, he pulled fast and hard and his entire inner circuitry crashed in the sudden throb, the fizzle of water dumped over a robot brain. He lay down on his side at the foot of the bed for a minute, deep breaths before untying the other shoe, turning his socks inside out from their tops to remove them.

Barefoot and shirtless, he tilted his weight on his outer foot to hobble to the bath. Leaning hurt. At the bath he gripped, he needed to grip, steadying himself against the pull of the handle, he pulled and nothing until the faucet tore open and his balance thrown off from his outer sole and water, see-through water, crashed on hard rubber and thin plastic.

Needed to lean again, lean even lower to plug the drain.

To catch his breath, stay up right, he leaned, palms flat, against the mirror and thought, Paul Newman. Paul fucking Newman—what am I supposed to do, donate the profits from my Alfredo sauce to charity?

His reflection, injury—a triggered awareness of the integrity of form that he had taken for granted. Only troubled does anything point back at itself. And the looking back at itself can be the trouble. Doesn't matter what comes first, the trouble or the reflection. They collapsed into one injury.

The water roared upward toward the tub's lip. The pitch of its rumble lowered. Leaning into the mirror, Will's forehead, an open gash, stuck to its reflection. His thoughts as stilted as his movements, he couldn't distinguish between the steam gathering on the mirror and his own vision dimming. Lifting his lip to flash teeth at himself, one new, one cracked, each outlined in salty red. He ran his tongue along them—tongue taste speak, salt. Speaking of taste—lick tongue back of teeth tooth teeth bite brush bite—

Adam's apple, what other part of me is so artfully birdlike? What else threatens to pop so simple and definitively, a single gesture, puncture or slice? A bird-skeleton-fragile birdcage expanding and resonates, croaks and ribbiting unnoticed until its pipes whistle breath.

Will reeked of beer ceremoniously poured over the other guy's head before the fight, over his own head after the fight, the sour stickiness of having been wiped down with bar rags.

My smile is a man in drag's Adam's apple. My smile is the scarves a man in drag wears to cover his Adam's apple. Adam's apple and evil long ago became one in young people-core, Madame's apple core.

It rained beer, wasn't that silly?

His weight back on his heel to keep it off his crushed toe, in one motion Will dropped into the tub, water rushing into every cut, heat releasing tension, healing heat.

His calves offered to the slaughter, the slaughter, laughter. On the one hand, he had his arm, his fist, the armed militia of his psyche, the little bit of Michigan in him. But on the other hand, an open palm, a map of Michigan. His paws grab, can't wait. Water rushed in.

His plunk in the tub smile, his smile was like, like a melting hand castle in the rain, washed away in waves. And pause, the hordes fed him, paid him. A parking lot did cheer blood, and words, a cramped crowd hidden in the barn in the storming forest, his skull. Through the electrical storm of hair, say. Couldn't stick around for it. He couldn't respond, jaw swollen shut. *Jaws*, the first movie Ronnie rented, over and over. The kids didn't know there were other movies to rent. Renting a movie meant renting *Jaws*.

Wage earned wagering, bet, better, best in the parking lots. Chest puffed, his ribcage the central security apparatus, sustained crib rage. A caged panther's stare and stride guards his heartbeat, the beatings relentless phallus defense. Don't fail us in inches thrust, sin for the sake of seeing how to seek redemption, protect the nest and the eggs hidden in it. And we fallen, spined like tree trunks, spies up in a tree house, a sharp shooter on one knee needs keen vision. I lash out.

My mind, the Venus flytrap, the fear area within earshot I witnessed at the hearing. Elbow below, a blow bends or breaks. And fingers, what's the point? Fists first, wrists—risk trying, tried, trial, and triumph.

It was clear. The sentence was silence. Will couldn't explain himself, but knew, one can't explain one's self. Only in a new place, somewhere no one would say hello. His crushed toe could not grip the plug to drain the bath. Took a deep breath to sit up and reach for the drain, hurt. He sat back, let the night air dry him, closed his eyes, wanted quiet, blindness evermore, numbness in every way, deeply, numbness without end.

Will once thought himself solved, briefly. Tammy. Didn't she solve him, couldn't she? She'd easily, without effort it seemed, explained him to himself. Cornered him, daring vulnerability. But the ultimate lack, the self-absorption pulling inward toward, the hollow like a drain, not possibly language enough to fill it, promises made smiling, grotesque. No codes, no destinies, empty, Will left with his silly fists.

It was a good name for him. He always liked it, free will. If he had to turn his head, if there must be a sound he couldn't help but turn his head toward, will, it was good, free will. Funny, the only sound he had no choice but to respond to, a muscle decision. Will was a funny word.

It embarrassed him about Tammy, about how he thought he felt. Must've been some misunderstanding, a case of mistaken identity, projection, imagined ease, a simulation. He understood "will," but how he had thought he felt, too abstract, stupid. He preferred hunger, the uprising to the revolution.

He had learned to allow her to touch him, but then the stakeouts, ringing a strange doorbell at four in the morning, the shame. He had only one photo of Tammy, a photo booth. On his lap, she was too far foregrounded to remain in focus, and his big, dumb smile.

In seeking to repeat their perfect harmonious ambiguity he'd mistaken dull satisfaction, manic desire, flattery, total pussy, perfect technique, the acceptance of others, drama, spit, content habit, specific conditions, awkward cohabitation, and even pity. But it was a state, passing, a passage. No possible outcome but feeling made a fool of, not good enough for his own hunches.

He could no longer accept the intuitive hunt. He needed new intuitions. Self-consciousness of the hunt insured the hunt's failure. Commit to quiet, commit to quiet or accept the shame that vulnerability inevitably opens up into.

So he got quiet, five years above The Saigon Restaurant in southeast Ohio, worth it just to say it every morning, "Saigon, shit. I'm still only in Saigon." Especially funny those first days enduring the strange withdrawal symptoms of compulsive fighting, hardly able to crawl out of bed, but never able to stretch enough. Worked nights at the in-patient home until the temptation to fight back against the patients got to be too distracting. Found work as a hood cleaner, balancing on a stepladder above hot grills, spraying water up into the hood, it dripped down onto the grill and sizzled, the constant balancing act.

Got to town, home for one long day, walked directly from the bus station to The Shhh... to find Mel, got lost. Norman sent him away. Thought about The Carroll Motel but couldn't face it. Walked and walked and got turned around and walked past Tammy's. Morning rush hour by then, slept sitting up back at the bus station.

Tammy hated his hands, those disgusting hands of his, bangers nicotine yellow and dry as salt flats, crisscrossed in cuts and slashes. Shallow canyons across his palms. His hands, granite symmetrical turkeys, symmetrical turkey spider-soldiers he commanded intuitively.

After he quit the hood cleaning job, the temptation to flop down spread eagle on a hot grill too distracting—figured he could work at a convenience store. But the shame from back home, the olive-skinned blond kid, the association followed him. In the bright store, he grabbed a bag of "traditional fruit snacks," too ashamed to ask for an application. A Native American family getting a hot dog each for dinner was so disappointed to learn there was no mayo on hand.

Tammy lived in an apartment by the highway that always smelled like a deep fryer. He would call her from a pay phone at the self-storage. Tell her to come down. The thick mustard colored skin around his nails, the blood-beat under each tip's husk, two small smiles and a soft frown under each finger, his hands made her sick. Their smell made her sick.

It's a long walk in the cold. Rush hour's line of lights, they each had a place to be? Pinch me awake or just point, lost in an endless parking-garage maze, lost in the corn outside of town, just point. It's a long walk out here in the cold.

What loving evolutionary impulse sprouted opposable thumbs if not the need to pinch one's self awake? As many dreams as there could ever be, there must be exactly that many ways to wake up.

His fingers never asked anything of him but to be kept out of dark places, down drains, between rocks. They needed only to see where they were going. In return, they should point or pinch, not only clench.

Tammy ate pickles with her frozen pizzas. Will would help her do the dishes in the bathtub. She had a proper way to crack an egg, a recipe for ice cubes.

He was five, six years old. Nana's backdoor slowly faded closed. He was just steps behind Mel running, running, hopped the couple stairs from the garage, turned the hall and through the kitchen. But the door clicked shut as he hit it. He shot his little claw through the pane, each digit, up past his wrist, hit with thousands of blistering hot pins.

Yeah, put through a glass door, manual sex, broke a glass—Will would no longer take this history of his American signature for granted.

A group of children screamed "Monster" when they saw Will return to the funeral home, sweaty from a quick jog. He felt bad ditching the funeral for a bit and did consider skipping his daily run, might be uncomfortable in his suit, but just cut it a little short instead.

Grunting, he chased the children around, hid in the bushes out front and leapt out at them. Wrestling in the vestibule, they climbed his back. All fun until one kid started crying and Will couldn't quiet him.

Paintings hung chest-high lined the funeral home's walls, in the lobby, in the tight locker-room-looking area outside the restrooms, the wide halls. The paintings were all of rivers, rivers through a twisting copse of dead old trees, rivers through low fog, rivers through small Dutch towns, rivers through prairies with broken fences, a mountain with mist up to its waist in the distance, near clock towers. Never a boat moving along a river, but one painting with a boat docked along a quiet shore under an industrial bridge. Creeks and the waterways of Venice in thick impressionistic oils and translucent water colors.

In the snack room, a pale green backstage for the family,

the cushioned patio chairs were scattered. The plastic bags and crumbled papers of fast food wrappers were piled on the few round glass tables among half-eaten sandwiches and cold fries, the squeaky bottoms of melted ice and soda in paper cups. Among the functional décor, a steel coffee pot and a microwave, hung pastel paintings, not of rivers, but of birds in flight, birds launching from branches, never a bird still, but always floating gracefully and free. The window looked out over the parking lot and beyond that, the parking lot across the street.

Her ankle killing her, Mel sat quiet, her arm around her mother as Ronnie shook out her pill bottle, sorting pills in her cupped hand. Joe had fallen asleep on a couch, so Ronnie was free to visit. Mel remembered dancing on Ronnie's toes in the kitchen, Ronnie singing that she loved a rainy night, Mel was so beautiful to her. Maybe she should've just had the goddamn kid, Mel thought, would've been due this week.

"It's actually not that strange, honey," Ronnie said. "People didn't keep the kinds of records they do now, so plenty of people Nana's age never knew exactly how old they really were."

Mel nodded, but didn't think much of it. "Interesting," she said.

She stretched her arm over Ronnie, picked her bag up and dropped it in her lap to dig for her cigarettes. She had always been afraid, as a young girl, of growing up to look like Ronnie. Maybe sorting through Nana's house would inspire her mother. About time, twenty years later, to think about maybe peeking inside her own place she'd locked up, walked away from, left sitting for twenty years.

"What about your boss, Rich? Has he come by yet, or any of the girls you work with?" Ronnie asked, tilting her head back to swallow a pill dry.

Mel was surprised. "Oh, you don't know?"

"Hmm?" Ronnie asked.

Mel lit her cigarette. She'd turned out alright, she thought. She never felt pretty as a kid, and there'd always be fresh-faced new girls coming through the club. But if she was going to end up shaped like Ronnie, she would've already. "Rich passed away just about nine months ago," she said.

"My god, I had no idea. That's horrible," Ronnie said, scratching at her arm.

"Yeah, Norman has taken over the place."

Ronnie nodded.

"He said he's going to come by," Mel said. "We'll see."

Ronnie nodded, sighed. "You making any paintings, designing any flyers these days?" she asked. With a sigh Mel took a drag from her cigarette, scanned the room.

2

Sarah Ann showed up to The Shhh... at four o'clock, an hour later than she'd agreed to the evening before, before Norman came back and The Russians, before she left with Mel and Gus.

Norman was alone, measuring a wall out according to the lengths of his steps. A strange, familiar song was loud in the room. She couldn't place it exactly, but knew she knew it. She had to approach him, get up close, before he even noticed her. Startled, he had to start over counting his steps, returned to the far wall. He asked her to take a seat at the bar, he'd only be a minute.

Her backpack bunched in her lap, the bar chilly, empty in the afternoon, she sat at the bar alone, put her hood up. A couple cigarettes left, both bent but not broken in a crinkled soft pack, but damp matches. The music surprised her when she recognized it, my god. Without that horrible shrieking, it had never occurred to her before, but perhaps without that horrible shrieking, AC/DC had created one of the most diverse and affecting bodies of work within the entire discipline of twentieth-century Minimalism.

Joining her at the bar, Norman explained, "I gotta make it quick. Late for a funeral."

"Oh." She sat up.

He waved off her concern. "No, nothing tragic. One of the girls, been here a long time, her grandmother."

She nodded. But for AC/DC to be considered in that context, Minimalism, of course, all the singing would have to be the same. If it were expressive to any degree beyond stagnant repetition it would intrude upon the true expressive quality of the group as a whole, Minimalism.

"I may have already missed it," he said.

"Is this... are you listening to instrumental AC/DC?" she asked.

Norman thought a second, tilted an ear toward the ceiling, and shrugged. Noticing her bent cigarette in hand and the damp matchbook on the bar, he leaned in and flipped open his Zippo for her.

"Last night," he said.

Shit, her eyes widened.

"Left the machine set up from last night," he said.

Right, she nodded, karaoke.

"I like it on in the background, good background music," he said.

They looked at each other a moment. Last night. AC/DC ended. Maybe she had been stupid to come back. Shit. She took a drag from her smoke, looked around at the disrepair of the club, a large mirror waiting to be hung, tools left out. Silence, she didn't want to get into last night, would he insist on an explanation? Maybe Gus wasn't even around. He might be at that funeral. Shit, she was stupid to come back.

The first notes of "Under Pressure," those bass notes broke the silence. Norman smiled.

"I want to show you something," he said, stepping away. "Be right back. I want to see what you think."

She nodded. He crossed the room with a lumbering gait, stepped out a door, leaving her alone with "Under Pressure." He wanted to show her something, something he needed to grab from the back room, okay. Strange to be in a bar, all the lights on, alone, and though she appreciated hearing the song without that scatting, the absence of the words like a father or a phantom itch, singing in her head, she didn't know she knew them, she considered the words to "Under Pressure" for maybe the first time.

The terror of knowing what the world is about, yeah, the world all at once, Gaia, Borges's "Aleph," and Jesus, of course these people on the streets scream to be let out, like a Hieronymus Bosch, let me out from the fruit of knowledge, the burden of five senses, time. Shit.

Maybe she should split. What would he want to show her? No one knows where she is. She should get out of there. This was her chance.

And "Under Pressure," seems it's gone as high as it could within its own harmonic framework, but climbs even higher, why can't we give love one more chance? Really, why can't we give ourselves one more chance? She'd come all this way, got on the piss-stink bus straight from the Homecoming field, stupid singing- and dancing-debate champion Rob's cum still on her hoodie. She could wait this out. Norman had something to show her.

The "Under Pressure" drums pick up to double time, Norman's been gone a while, and the song builds and builds, higher and higher until finally the drums drop to half-time and it's no longer a question but a statement, a statement of purpose and resolve, acceptance, *This is ourselves.*

This is ourselves. So perfectly simple and what could be left to say? The promise of rock 'n' roll, what religion might've once done, transcendence and redemption fulfilled through form. And instrumental, the words only in her head, karaoke production values slightly off in a way she could never explain specifically, maybe executed perfectly and only the circumstances of the recording proven singular, Borges's Pierre Menard, tones familiar but different. In the act of this conclusive achievement of the promise of the rock form, "Under Pressure," the promise of karaoke is also fulfilled.

How could anyone, these very *people on the streets* the song addressed, ourselves, ever find true expression, contrary as it might seem, but through a script, the limited available script of one's historical circumstances?

"Under Pressure," in perfectly achieving the form, begged the question of the workings of the form. What could it mean, symptomatically, this form? What could it mean for this culture it blossomed from, that the pop-form, the sonic analogy of the culture itself, could only be expressed in three-minute blasts?

From the trance-inducing inclusive drum circles of primitive cultures through the oppressive complex soaring twists of choirs under stained glass in sixteenth-century cathedrals, it hit Sarah Ann, alone in a club in Stone Claw Grove, orange neon beer signs dim under the afternoon houselights, *people on the streets,* those people in the drum circles and cathedrals, those people with their five senses on their mud streets, standing on their two feet and chewing their food to the greatest potential of their dentistry, they accessed and interacted with their own cultures exactly as she did each day without noticing. Commercial jingles often stuck in her head.

"Boo," Norman said, standing close behind her. She gasped and he smiled, stepped around the bar.

"I fucked up, missed the funeral already," he said. He dropped a sheet of pink paper on the bar.

"Sorry it took me so long," he said. "I had to print this out."

She picked up the piece of paper.

"Only paper I could find." He shrugged. "So, you seem like a smart kid. What do you think?"

He kept talking as she began to look it over. He wasn't above that shit. Fuck it. It wasn't an act of desperation. He wasn't desperate. It's not like he needed to do it, but fuck it, he had a free hour, which was rare, and the girls at the club, they just resented him because he was the boss. He didn't owe a single one of those bitches anything. Fuck it. He'd take what he could get thank you very much.

CHARACTERISTICS

GENDER: <u>Male</u>
CURRENT STATUS: <u>Single</u>
LOOKING FOR: <u>Casual Dating, Romance, Long-term</u>
<u>Relationship, Friends with Benefits, Some Action</u>
BODY TYPE: <u>More to Love, Athletic</u>   HEIGHT: <u>5' 09"</u>
EYES: <u>Brown</u>   HAIR TYPE: <u>Long, black</u>   AGE: <u>28</u>
SEEKS: <u>Woman for Dating, Woman for Friendship</u>

PROFILE

EDUCATION: <u>Some college</u>
ETHNICITY: <u>Hawaiian</u>
RELIGION: <u>Spiritual, not religious</u>
POLITICAL LEANINGS: <u>Liberal, Conservative</u>
NEIGHBORHOOD: <u>Campus</u>
CITY: <u>Stone Claw Grove</u>   SMOKING: <u>Cigars regularly</u>
OCCUPATION: <u>Club owner</u>   DRINKING: <u>Regularly</u>
HAVE CHILDREN: <u>No</u>   DRUGS: <u>I'll try (almost)</u>
WANT CHILDREN: <u>No</u>   <u>anything twice</u>

HABITS

PERSONALITY

I GET AROUND TOWN VIA: <u>My jet-black 2008 Viper</u>
MY DIETARY PREFERENCES ARE: <u>Conscious omnivore</u>
I SPEND MY FREE TIME: <u>Working out, Watching movies,</u>
<u>Hanging out, Dining out, Watching TV, Live music</u>
          CHECK ME OUT!

FILL IN THE BLANK

MY THEME SONG IS: <u>Don't Stop Believing!</u>

<u>Working up a sweat dancing (or however else)</u>
IS MY FAVORITE WAY TO END AN EVENING

IF YOU HAVE A PET, IT BETTER NOT BE A
<u>woman! People are uptight about that.</u>

IF I WERE A SUPERHERO, I WOULD BE
<u>psyched about my X-ray vision.</u>

THE QUICKEST WAY TO MY HEART IS <u>long legs</u>,
THE QUICKEST WAY TO MY BED IS <u>just say the word</u>,
AND IN THE MORNING I LIKE MY EGGS <u>scrambled</u>.

THE KARAOKE SINGER'S GUIDE TO SELF-DEFENSE

THE PERSON I'D MOST LIKE TO TELL OFF IS too many to list.

Hard work _____ MAKES ME SWEAT

THE MOVIE VERSION OF MY LIFE SHOULD BE TITLED
"work hard, play hard."

SOMETHING I SAID I'D NEVER DO, BUT DID Anyway WAS
own a business.

TWO THINGS I CAN'T LIVE WITHOUT ARE
my music and fine dining

IT'S SUNDAY MORNING AT 10 AM IF I'M NOT SLEEPING I'M
still up.

I CONSIDER MYSELF AN OPEN-MINDED PERSON, BUT MY DEAL
BREAKERS ARE loudmouths and bimbos.

MY IDEAL MATE HAS THE BRAINS OF Steven Seagal ,
AND THE BODY OF Kelly LeBrock .

ONE THING I LOVE THAT EVERYONE ELSE HATES IS:
MTV. Everyone acts like they're too good for it now, and
complain about how it's changed, and sure it's different
than it used to be, but it's still good.

Hello, my name is Norman. I live in my own apartment
with a nice view of the sunset. I own the Legendary Shhh...
Club, but don't let that intimidate you. I love traveling to
Las Vegas, Miami, Los Angeles, Orlando, and San Diego.
Some activities I have done on vacation are hot air balloon,
parasailing, climb into caves, paraglide, snorkel, hang glide,
walk thru hanging bridges, boat tour near an active volcano,
wave runners, and all-terrain vehicles. I love to listen to
music. I work hard, so when I get to blow off some steam I
don't like to hold back. Some people can't take it, but that's
not my problem. You only get one go around in this life so
I'm not gonna waste it trying to please everyone else. I'm
going to have fun! Join me?

Sarah Ann read it over, trying to not squirm. What was the big deal? Life will inevitably exist soon enough as pure information anyway. It's one's right to cultivate his or her own future cloud-body identity, whatever a dumb-ass he or she may be. No right to judge Norman.

Time accelerated and collapsed, the subjective experience of time, in so many countless, small ways that the process was rendered functionally invisible. Sarah Ann resented her smart phone, left it back at home. She could no longer tell when a game of Scrabble began or ended, and always kind of playing Scrabble meant never really playing Scrabble. Time collapsed. Its borders slipped, the game no longer had a beginning or end.

She understood the people living within the model of a culture, blind to the experience of the culture as fish are to water, could never foresee the looming leap in consciousness to the next stage of cultural evolution. Hunter-gatherers could not anticipate agriculture, the shift in thinking a food surplus would bring. Hundreds of generations of farmers with their cyclical experience of time could never have imagined the industrialist's sense of infinite progress.

And as the accelerating upward arc of the subjective experience of time approached a vertical ascent, leaving everyone with neither grounding in the past nor the ability to foresee a future, why wouldn't people be distracted, grounded even, by immediate comfort, gratification, the emotional porn of reality-TV and the straight-up porn of cooking shows? Environmental devastation, mass-species die-off, what could possibly be left but pure information? Norman wants to be known as that guy, beginning-and-end-of-Norman all according to that form. Great, good for him.

Evolution evolved into self-consciousness. The biosphere sprang from the minerals of the geosphere and consciousness sprang from the biosphere. As unchecked Capitalism kills off the biosphere through resource depletion, choking the earth with garbage, evolution accelerates through self-consciously crafted identities, digital ego-projections that will soon no longer depend on us in our mineral forms to guide them. These new life forms will be neither representations of us nor independent from us, but we will have become them.

Still, it had been a while since it first occurred to Sarah Ann that her MySpace profile no longer reflected the her she thought herself to be. Social networking was obviously little more than the sunny cultural inversion of terror cells, the final clinging to some sense of community or belonging that the last stages of consumer Capitalism would allow. And the habit had been knocked to the back of her mind, so only occasionally did she cringe, recalling the state of her identity as she'd left it projected to the world. But, she did cringe. May as well get it right.

HEADLINE:
"Life shrinks or expands in proportion to one's courage." —Anais Nin.
She'd been waiting for that one. She knew when she first read it, that'd be going up there.

ABOUT ME:
She can't believe she had that dorky rant about doing her best in school and getting into college up there still. About me? About me...
"I am now more myself than I have ever been before and this happened by letting go. Like the wind I am unable to help but touch everything I pass through."

I'D LIKE TO MEET:
Simple. Take down the dumb band-dudes—how could she have not been so grossed out by the vanity? And no more Janis Joplin. Sure, she still loved her, but that's not who was on her mind. Post new photos, no more Audrey Hepburn in *Breakfast at Tiffany's* and young Goldie Hawn. Susan Faludi, Howard Zinn.

GENERAL:
"Traveling alone, getting lost, writing letters, the dust of the road on my jeans, rice pudding, the playground at night, dumpster diving donuts."

MUSIC:
"Okkervil River, Bright Eyes, TV on the Radio, Rahsaan "Roland" Kirk, Joni Mitchell, Erik Satie, Iron and Wine, Mahjongg, too much to list..."

FILMS:
"John Cassavetes, Jean-Luc Godard, Orson Welles, *Chinatown, Last Picture Show, Midnight Cowboy, A Clockwork Orange, Breakfast at Tiffany's.*"
These didn't need to change.

TELEVISION:
"*Frontline, Charlie Rose.*"

BOOKS:
"Anais Nin, Henry Miller, Richard Brautigan, Rainer Maria Rilke, Virginia Woolf, Jean Rhys, Kurt Vonnegut, Camus, Flannery O'Connor, Miranda July, Kundera, Gabriel Garcia Marquez."

HEROES:
Freud or Marx, Freud or Marx, hmmm...

Norman dropped his big pepper-spray keychain on the bar. The interview would be casual.

"Yeah, I always knew the place would be all mine someday," he started, "and let me tell you, it took a hell of a lot of work to get this place up and operating like it should."

Sarah Ann, still wearing the same jeans and hoodie she'd traveled in, was afraid that maybe she smelled a little sour. She lit her last cigarette, arranged her backpack on her lap.

"My dad, I'll give it to him, he made the place out of nothing." Norman continued. "What do people want? Girls. Give it to them, bang, simple. And he made money. He did alright."

Norman looked to Sarah Ann and she nodded. Should she tell him it's not really him, not really a job that she'd come looking for? That song "Shiny Happy People" came on. She'd always hated it, so cloying.

"But times've changed. People aren't turned on by a little flash of tit anymore. Come on, you gotta give the people more than that. But my old man..." Sarah Ann thought Norman sounded especially affected when he referred to his dad as his "old man."

"I guess it's because he was successful with the place on his own and so he didn't wanna change anything, wouldn't listen to anyone. It's like he didn't know times change. People change. What brought people in, what turned people on fifteen, twenty years ago, it just ain't gonna work now. It can't. Of course people have had their fill of what's been around. Don't get me wrong, The Shhh... is a fucking institution, okay?"

Sarah Ann nodded. Maybe "Shiny Happy People" is actually lyrically critical of shiny happy people? Maybe its popular reception had always been in the completely wrong terms, celebrated exactly for what it mocks.

"It's a staple of the local community and economy," Norman continued with increased volume. "Doesn't matter the factory closes, doesn't matter guys can't put food on their table for their whining little brats, The Shhh... does alright. We're the last place that's gonna go and everyone from the mayor to the garbage man knows that."

Norman had always been impressed with the minor local political power that came with owning the bar all the city boys hung out in. They could've called the liquor or public performance licenses into question anytime, always simple to find a signature out of place.

But with a constant smile, Rich held that power over him in check by always having enough to get any of those city boys in the papers or divorce court. The shallow waverings of a mutual blackmail checkmate maintained the trust. Rich knew to let his influence accrue, call it in in small ways, always refracted, overlooking a little coke in Norman's glove compartment, a bargain to get Will out of town before standing trial for beating some street urchin, that olive-skinned blond kid. Even if innocent that time, plenty else he'd gotten away with.

Norman continued, "But you can always do better, and somewhere along the way the old man got soft."

There it was, Sarah Ann thought, "old man" again.

"The old man started getting charitable to all the whores and forgetting that's exactly what they are—they're whores. And when the whores aren't whoring, what are they? Well, they're bitches, okay."

He smirked to Sarah Ann. She pursed her lips, nodded. "Shiny Happy People" was still a lousy, annoying song even if it was supposed to be clever.

"Whores?" she asked.

He shrugged, "Well, bitches."

She nodded. It occurred to her she was never really not shocked. He took a swig from his drink. "Sorry."

Sarah Ann shrugged. Of course the same culture that accepted environmental devastation would find satisfaction in porn. She wanted a pornography that was like life in the world. She'd always liked nature films well enough, lions chasing zebras on the plains, gorillas grooming each other with tenderness. She never sought nature films out, but couldn't look away when she came across them. And that's the pornography she wanted to see. Though this place would be more like a zoo than a nature film. And she wasn't even there for a job.

"Well, what's that make the old man and I?" Norman continued. "I don't know. And I don't know when he ever got it in his head that a club owner is supposed to be some kind of humanitarian. That's real nice, you wanna be a humanitarian go ahead, fine. Fine and nice and the world needs you and God bless you and I hope you reap all your rewards in heaven, fine and good. Even if the old man wanted to be a humanitarian on the side, okay, whatever. But business is business and our business is bitches. The old man is lucky that I haven't lost sight of this like he did. The money was there to be made all along if he'd stepped aside. But he was too proud. It was his baby, this club, made in his image. You'd think he'd have felt lucky to have a son that kept up with the trends, that knows what people want. I'm interested in fashion and music. You know, those things aren't what people are here to see, but those things don't hurt."

Sarah Ann nodded.

"The audience," he continued, "what they want is their bitches to get dirty. They want to see bodies bend and open and they want their goddamn minds blown. That's the simple part. A young girl, pretty enough with okay tits, fine. But she can't get up there and just wiggle her hips and expect that to be enough. The bitches gotta blow minds. They gotta be fearless with their bodies. They gotta be above shame, fuck humility. My dad had this idea people were here to appreciate little wiggling hips, fuck that. He thought a shot and a beer and some timid little hip wiggling was gonna get all of us off forever?"

Nature films would be cool, Sarah Ann thought, but always all that exploitation. Couldn't pornography just be straight nature films? None of those hang-ups and insecurities, the need to desecrate the beloved's face with seed, the aggression. None of that was a turn-on. She didn't even really like it when her mom told her she loved her, so it wasn't about feeling, about love. Love was embarrassing, and this nature-film pornography couldn't be embarrassing and still turn people on. She understood that. "I say fuck no," Norman went on. "Why'd the old man..." He said it again, "old man."

"Why'd the old man think the room was half-empty five nights a week? And even on the weekends there was still always a seat. Fuck that. That's not how it should be. If he would've done things my way, seven nights a week, anytime, you show up to The Shhh... you gotta wait for a seat. I'd have asses in seats seven nights a week guaranteed."

Love wasn't even an emotion, she thought. People always assumed love was an emotion. But emotions drift through the mind like clouds, subjecting one to their shading. Love would be more like the sun. Love wasn't the clouds. People were so stupid. Love was a conscious decision and effort to build a sunroof, a skylight. People thought love was an emotion, subject to desperation, like the clouds, but that wasn't it.

"It's simple," Norman said. "People don't want a shot and a beer. They want pomegranate martinis and blueberry martinis and fresh ginger syrup and egg-white rums. Take down these black painted walls and make the place look classy. You know, some varnished wood or those metal walls with the swirls on them. The people should feel sophisticated, flattered. That's what people want. The real appetites are simple. They want their whores humiliated and their sense of taste flattered for wanting that. A shot and a beer isn't good enough for humiliation. That's fine for wiggling hips, but I'm talking about widening the entire experience of The Shhh... in every direction."

Sarah Ann nodded. Marx and Freud, she thought, Marx and Freud. Wouldn't the nature-film pornography be interesting?

In a suit, his jeans and a big t-shirt crumpled in his arms, without a word, Gus walked quick across the far wall of the bar and straight into the kitchen.

Norman grew up in that room, The Shhh.... A shy little nine-year-old from Hawaii, dropped in the Midwest with his mom gone and all those girls just about his mom's age, parading past in her place. But his mom, she was a delicate flower and what did his dad replace her with but a dozen bimbos, who wouldn't have half that woman's beauty and charm and elegance if you melted them all down and extracted the best parts from each of them. That's what Norman had always thought.

He was nine years old. Putting a nine-year-old on a plane and dumping him in the middle of some barren concrete wasteland with a bunch of pale, young, hip-wiggling bimbos and expecting the kid to figure it out was not, he thought, the best way to explain to a nine-year-old that his mommy had died.

He spent the first year looking at the tropical fish tank. It was three feet wide or more and two feet deep and the only thing that felt like home, a little box of home in the corner of that dank dump—colorful, beautiful, bright fish and colorful coral and the little diver always one step away from the treasure, never reaching it and never giving up. Alone down there, the deep sea diver with only a little tube to breathe through and that was how Norman felt. Like he might suffocate at any moment, cut off from everything again, and left to choke.

One girl, Mary, Maribel, tried to get him out of his shell. A lot of the girls were playful with him. They'd come over to him while he was at the fish tank staring, and maybe they'd even run their fingers through his hair to break the fish tank's spell.

He'd show up after school and walk in on the old man auditioning some bimbo. Rich would let him in and tell him to buzz off. He'd give Norman a stack of quarters for the pinball machine, but he didn't know how to play pinball so of course that would take all of ten minutes. He'd get some pretzels or potato chips or nuts and endless sodas and watch the fish while Dad worked away at the books or on the phone.

Delivery guys would come in and out all day. Norman got to be pretty friendly with some of those guys. But however friendly he got didn't really matter because one day they got a new job or a new route or whatever and he'd never see them again. He noticed that the first Tuesday he would expect to see a particular guy, that would be the day the guy would be gone. The new guy would explain, "New route" or "He moved, his mom got sick" or whatever, but then Norman would never really get too friendly with the new guy for whatever reason, no reason really except that he wasn't the old guy. So he learned to never expect anyone, or anything from anyone.

Some of those delivery guys, Mike the pinball guy and Eddie that carried a lot of the kegs, some of those guys were the same guys who had been coming around twelve years, fifteen years, but Norman was still only cordial with them. This one's a lifelong Cubs fan and this one's old man was stationed in Hawaii in World War II and it was the same friendly script each week. And it was an okay script. Everyone was very friendly with each other. But still, no one was particularly invested in knowing anything more. Just getting through the day as they each had to and there was a moment here and a moment there one might enjoy. Rich always talked about highlights.

Norman always thought highlights was a funny word because it meant like, slam dunk was a sports highlight or that Ping-Pong ball shot out of her cooch was a highlight of her dance, but whenever Rich used to say it, Norman always thought first about hair. He'd always heard the girls all talk about highlights. He knew it was the blond streak across a brunette's head. So when the old man talked about how living had its occasional highlights and living only for the highlights, Norman always pictured bright sunshine through total blackness, coming out through a crack, real intense-like, blinding.

Rich always said life was 99% banal or sad, but it had its highlights that people lived for. Norman always remembered that. It was the old man's unofficial slogan, 99% of life is banal or sad. Norman never really knew what banal meant, but he knew he didn't like the sound of it. And God forbid some highlight might happen when he was with one of the delivery-guy acquaintances—what had been a highlight, a bum tripped on the curb or someone had some banana bread to offer—it would just become the new banal script for each week. "Remember that bum tripped?" every week, or, "Yeah, no banana bread this week, but sure was scrumptious, huh?"

But Mary, Maribel, knowing her was a highlight. He'd get there after school and play his quick games of pinball, rip through a bag of chips and stare at the fish tank. Rich, when he thought about it, would tell Norman to get his homework done and then he'd do it. But mostly it didn't occur to Rich to ask. Eventually dinner would show up and they'd sit at the bar and eat it, watching TV. Rich ordered from the same few places a lot. Made it easier for him. He never had to ask Norman what he wanted, fried fish and deep fried balls, ribs, whatever. This was before Gus was around.

By the time the club would start to fill up and the girls would start dancing, the old man would bring Norman up to his office and he'd fall asleep on the couch, watching TV. The club was technically open all day if anyone wanted to come in at any time, but it wasn't worth it to any of the girls to show up until later.

Mary, Maribel, started showing up on her days off to take Norman for walks. At first he was suspicious and didn't want to go anywhere until she appealed to the old man, and then he made Norman go. At first they'd go on walks around the neighborhood. They had to walk a little ways from The Shhh..., through boarded-up pawn shops, weeds growing from the cracks in the concrete, to get anywhere that had a sidewalk. She'd hold his hand and they'd walk on the slim gravel shoulder along the side of the road. They'd arrive at some houses, a small neighborhood, go to the playground and sit together.

She always asked about his day and he never had anything to say, but she'd keep pressing. Every day she'd ask, "How was your day? Tell me about school." And what was there to tell?

He didn't know when it happened or how, but eventually she couldn't shut him up. Days she couldn't come by the club to get him for some reason, he could hardly cope. He'd stare at that fish tank but no longer saw whatever it was he used to see in it. He saw only his own reflection without Mary next to him. It got to be so that he depended on her showing up and all he'd have to do was see her and then he'd run up to her and just start gabbing and gabbing and he'd make her laugh and tell her stories and it got to be so that it was like she knew all the other kids, just through him telling her about them. She would say, "Oh, I really wish I could meet so-and-so, why don't you invite him out with us some afternoon?"

But Norman could never invite any kid over to the club. He

understood that even then. And what kid could he expect to understand how he and Mary hung out? What kid wanted to go sit on a bench and talk to some adult he didn't know? But she knew all the kids through his stories and remembered them all and remembered everything he told her. "Oh, I can't believe the bus driver let that Will get away with that," or "Cheryl got sick chewing her pencil again?"

When she wouldn't show up, some days he'd have quiet tantrums. Then when he did see her, he'd play it all cool. She'd show up and he'd be playing pinball or sitting with his chips at the bar and she'd approach him, "Norman," and he'd pretend like he hardly knew her. He got so defensive. And she'd apologize, and it didn't take long before all his defenses were down and he'd babble.

It was after one of those first times she didn't come by, for some reason, that she took him to her home for supper to make it up to him. She lived in a real small apartment. There wasn't much in there. She made Sloppy Joe and he'd never had it before, but it became his favorite food ever. So after that, half the time they'd go sit on the bench and talk, and half the time they'd eat supper at her place. But they were always back in time for her to start getting ready, and he'd still go up to the office and fall asleep on the couch, watching TV.

Then Rich told him that he couldn't be seeing Mary so much, that she was busy, had her own life and things to do and he would only see her a couple times a week. Norman didn't know if she told Rich that or Rich told her they were spending too much time together, but however it happened, everything was different between them after that, forced and phony, polite. By that time he had learned to no longer get mad when he wouldn't see her for a couple days, instead just be happy to see her when he could. But then she pulled away even more, made her distance official. He knew he was still the same. She was the bitch that changed.

He just didn't know then that that's how bitches were. He knew things changed, moms die, Hawaii gets left for Stone Claw Grove, whatever. But he thought that change was one big thud. He didn't know then that change happened in glances, change happened in the way a bitch tensed her back up when she greeted you, change happened when you're no longer lonely watching TV, but lonelier when you stopped watching TV and started talking to someone else.

By that time he was eleven or twelve and tits started looking pretty good to him. Maybe they didn't yet hold the power over him that they eventually would, but at first there was some deep mystery he was drawn to. He started coming downstairs some nights.

Back then, Rich was still behind the bar a lot of nights, so he'd be scanning the room but he was busy. Norman could slip out the door and check out the show for a minute. He'd peek his head out. Around that time he got pretty comfortable if the girls saw him in the hall upstairs. He no longer felt like he was locked in the office. He'd wander in and chat with the girls as they dressed and sometimes they'd play prudish and motherly a little bit, but he could tell some of the girls kind of liked having a little kid around. He figured they liked knowing they were the first impressions he'd ever have of naked ladies, even though he never really saw them naked, only in various degrees of lingerie. But some of them would flash him to get a rise out of him. He never saw any snatch and he didn't understand why asses were supposedly a turn on. He didn't understand curves yet. But tits he just went crazy for.

He was still seeing Mary once or twice a week, so he knew her nights. Things had cooled down between them, and she'd cancel plans half the time he'd expect to see her. But he knew her nights, so those were his TV nights. He didn't really think about it. He didn't know it was what he was doing, but Mary was still like a mom or a big sister to him, so he didn't stick his nose out of the office on her nights. He didn't mingle in the dressing room, and he certainly didn't take a peek out into the club those nights.

But it turned out the more he mingled, the more some of the girls would ask him how come he never watched them dance? Bitches wanted attention. They didn't care if it was a limp-dicked eighty-year-old or a peewee eleven-year-old. Especially the girls that ended up there, they just needed the approval of any male. So they started asking him, "What did you think of my dance?" "Did you notice my new corset brings out my eyes?" "That five pounds has gone straight to my hips." So he started spending more time on the floor.

Of course he knew girls switched shifts all the time, but then what did he know? He just wasn't thinking. Eleven years old, Mary's night was Mary's night. How could he have expected to barge in on her dancing on some not-Mary's night?

3

The Funeral Home hallways were a series of small lobbies, each opening up into the next small lobby. Shiny wood tables and desks, cabinets everywhere, all empty, were placed among the many couches along every wall. Some couches were lush and others covered in crinkling plastic but all were muted pastels. Strange to sit down in a hallway.

The room itself, the room of the event of the casket, opened into various sizes and shapes according to how the molded curtain partitions were drawn on dollies across the ceiling. The room should always appear at capacity, comfortable and at capacity. Along the walls flowers flowers flowers flowers flowers exploded from plaster pedestals and thin wire stands. In the center of the room, plain and straight wooden chairs were lined in a few neat rows. The front row before the casket was a couch, flanked by two plush La-Z-Boys, their fabrics stitched like digital interference up their tall backs.

The walls were all shades of peach, the fleshtone of make-up, darkening and lightening at each of the room's many shallow angles. Lamps on low tables, as many lamps as Kleenex boxes, the lamps had little hands up their long, slim brass trunks, clamps to grab envelopes of condolences with cash or checks. The hands molded to appear as leaves. Lamplight alternated in the curves of smiles and frowns, up or down from the same height along the walls. As the peach shades changed, the wall's textured Persian-looking pattern remained the same, swirling seashells, visible only according to how the light fell at a particular spot.

Three circular space-age air vents were on the low ceiling; white, vacuums looking to the sky, industrial. Between the vents hung two chandeliers with teardrop-shaped bulbs in concentric rows like shark teeth.

Behind the purplish-gold casket, a wide doily curtain covered a window with a view of a close brick wall. Two women, Nana's neighbors, stood before the casket, their backs to the room, and hidden under one of them was a child. His arm emerged and moved playfully along the casket's edge, unaware it was not to be touched. The illusion, brief, but very real, frazzled Joe half-dozing in his seat—the reclined corpse had given up the possum gag with a restless stretch. Joe ate a pill. And in the casket, the chickenbone hands crossed over chest, cloaked still in their own loose skin.

Ronnie could not blame Kent even though, of course she wished things were different. She had to respect his decisions. She would not be strong enough to forgive herself if she were him. She wished he was strong enough, but she couldn't blame him.

He'd tolerate her, speak to her if there was absolutely no escape. Nowhere to glance away to and pretend he hadn't seen her. When that happened, it was always only for someone else's sake.

She ran into him alone for a moment outside the funeral in the hall, just the two of them. She smiled, opened her arms. "Hello Kenny." But he turned up his nose, snorted and huffed off. In bigger groups he had the good manners to just pretend he didn't see her, like when he had walked in late that morning and everyone said hello at once. His sister got a kiss and he had a hug for Will, but not even a hello for his mother. He just ignored her. But alone, he'd mock her, mock her teeth when she attempted to speak to him and then of course at the funeral they were both cooped up in that small area.

A half hour after Ronnie ran into him by the water fountain and he had sneered at her, Mel's friend Gus who she had brought with her, said, "Oh Kent, I was just talking to your mother." Ronnie sat on the far side of Gus and Kent, not seeing her, walked over to say hello to Gus, this friend of his sister's he'd met maybe twice before in the last ten years. He approached Gus with a big friendly handshake and a pat on the shoulder, as big and hearty a hello as Kenny could muster.

"I've thought about what you mentioned, your idea," Kent said. "I think if Mel really needs the help, we should ask my brother. I think it's okay to ask him."

And Gus replied with a big smile, "Well, look at that, Kent, here's your mother."

Kent looked the same but grown. To Ronnie it seemed he was still a kid, playing at speaking with his voice low in his chest.

Gus said, "Oh, I was just catching up with your mother," and of course Kent didn't have a second for Ronnie, but he'd hate to embarrass Gus. So he nodded, "Ronnie," obviously trying to keep things quick between them. She knew the hurry he imposed. When she did get a minute with him, every five, seven years somehow, a cousin's wedding or a graduation party, he hurried the whole time, like she was leaning on him and his precious minute, keeping him from something important.

She said, "Oh, Kenny," because she didn't want to embarrass Gus, but more so she wanted Kent to know it was okay. She understood he didn't want to talk to her. Looking at her sickened him. Just looking at her sickened him, okay. But, excited for her goddamn minute with him, she'd take it. Gus studied them, aware he had somehow unwittingly created a situation.

ABOUT NINE MONTHS BEFORE THE FUNERAL

Leaning over a large cutting board on an island in the center of The Shhh... kitchen, Gus chopped onions. The quick rhythm of his even chop pattern extended at regular intervals with a scrape of each small chopped onion pile, the back of his knife across the board into a large metal bowl. He dropped the next onion in place to signal the pattern's reset.

His apron cinched his baggy jeans tight just below his

waist, twisted his stain-layered baggy white t-shirt across his belly. His process, mechanically precise in its choreography, banged through the otherwise silent room.

Norman stepped into the doorway, didn't say a thing, and Gus didn't notice him. Finally chuckling with self-conscious over-friendliness, Norman entered, lifted Gus's bicycle from the counter it leaned against and wheeled it to the back door.

"Oh, geez," Gus looked up, startled. "I'm sorry."

"No problem," Norman said, setting the bike against the back door.

"I was going to bring it out. I don't know. I was anxious to start on this."

"It's fine," Norman said.

Gus shrugged. Norman lit a cigar. Dangling it from his mouth, hands on hips, looked over the kitchen. "How do you do it?" he said.

Gus wiped his watering eyes with the back of his wrists. "What?"

Norman circled Gus with long, patient steps, looking him up and down while smiling. "This quiet. You don't want the radio on?"

"Oh, I guess not. I don't know," Gus responded.

"It's right there, the radio," Norman said.

Gus set his knife down, shook his head. He leaned back against the counter, throwing his head back. "I don't think about it, I guess. I mean, I don't notice."

Norman nodded, stopped pacing. "I wouldn't be able to stand it. This must be the concentration it takes. I'm lucky to witness such a thing, a master deep into his craft."

His eyes red still from the lingering onion, Gus shrugged and bowed playfully. Norman smiled and approached him, putting his hand on his shoulder as a gesture of faux-comfort.

"There, there, you'll be okay, Gus. Don't cry."

Gus smirked with some effort, stepped away from Norman's hand on his shoulder. He opened the refrigerator and stuck his entire head in. Picking up a slice of cheese from a pile on the counter and folding it into his mouth, Norman began to speak, paused to chew a second, spoke. "You must've gotten here early today."

With his head still in the fridge, Gus responded, "Hmmm, nope. No, this is just about my regular time, been here about an hour now."

Norman nodded, cleaned his teeth with his tongue before speaking again. "So, what happened last night?"

Gus peeked from around the fridge door for a quick second, but replaced his head fully back inside, began rattling stuff around.

"What do you mean?"

"I mean, what happened?"

"Well, what do you mean, 'what happened?'"

Norman raised his voice. "I'm asking you."

Gus stepped back from the refrigerator and dropped a couple Tupperware containers, each the size of a boxed sweater, on the island with a heavy thud. With flared nostrils, he looked Norman in the eyes and took a deep breath. He shook a cigarette from its soft pack on the counter. "I'm not certain what you're talking about."

"You wouldn't serve the Big Daddy Famous Burger."

Gus shook his head and smiled. "No. I couldn't. We ran out."

"We didn't run out of patties, did we?"

"A burger is more than the patty, isn't it?" Gus stepped around Norman to the counter and stood behind him a moment. "Excuse me, please."

Norman smiled large and pivoted, crowding Gus a moment before chuckling and stepping back to give Gus room to work. Gus spoke with a measured cadence, "The Famous Burger has always been stuffed with pork, and I need wasabi sauce."

"I told you before. We can no longer afford that," Norman said.

"Well then," Gus said, "I guess I can no longer make the Famous Burger."

Pointing a finger, Norman said, "No. That's not what I said."

Gus dropped his head and sighed.

"What did I tell you before?" Norman asked.

"I know what you told me before," Gus said quietly.

"You do?"

"Yes."

"You remember our conversation about the Famous Burger?" Norman asked.

"Yes. I remember the conversation," Gus said.

"Because it doesn't seem like—"

"Yes. I do," Gus cut him off. "I remember our conversation about the Famous Burger."

Norman threw his hands up in the air in exaggerated exasperation. "If you remember our conversation—"

Gus spun around and looked at him directly. "This is not how your father... Rich did not run things this way."

Norman widened his eyes large and cartoonish.

"I'm serious, Norman. This is not the way things were with your father."

With a grin, Norman blinked a quick flutter. "I know that," he said. "That's the point."

Norman woke on his office couch, considering a curved ax may have been wedged in his skull in the night. Almost noon, the first kegs would arrive in a minute. Still hadn't gotten used to it, that his dad wouldn't come knocking down that long black hall from his own office to wake him. Norman never had gotten around to repainting that hall. His storage-room-turned-office was further away from both the stage and the dressing room than Rich's office was, meaning he couldn't keep the kind of eye on the girls that Rich could. But he made up for this in other ways beyond The Shhh..., fake names on social networking sites, the gossip of the doormen at other clubs.

His suit crumpled, long hair pressed greasy to his face. Standing and stretching, a moan, he ran his palms flat down the front of his coat, untangled his shirt collar from under his coat collar. A flat cola left overnight on his desk, a swig, his mouth gluey-dry. He sniffed under his arm.

The record player skipped a tedious thud at the center of a record. This pulse had infiltrated his dim sleep. Dropping heavy into the chair at his desk, he pulled a folded v-neck from the bottom drawer. Pressed his fists to his temples, hoped prompting the blur, squeezing it, might hurry the process, like steeping tea, the fermented agents clouding his thoughts. I am Norman. Ache. Norman.

Setting the t-shirt on the desktop as a pillow, he scooted the chair back, dropped his head. The weight of his head against the desk held his eyes open, his feet through waves of pain. Fun, fuck it, fun. Remembered, had to get through work quick that day, make an appearance at the funeral and get back to interview that kid, if she still came around after The Russians, that mess.

To pull a boot off, leverage the toe of one foot against the heel of the other foot. Leverage, nope, failure. Not about to bend. A moment of nothing passed. He stood, struggled to breathe. He shifted his weight. Kick that boot back on. Deliberate steps, lop-sided with one tall heel. Approach the record player. Lift the needle, Journey's *Greatest Hits*. Right, last night, even before coming back to The Russians at The Shhh...

After a toast shouted in dizzy lights, Norman bumped back to the dance floor, fists pumping. Good lighting, the projectors placed at strategic angles, could make half a dozen people seem a swarm. Sour breath on a pretty and thin-lipped girl's cheek, "You really gotta come by and try it. It's excellent. I make the ginger syrup myself, not easy."

She needed a breather and he followed her back to the bar. "Norman, you're so sweet. I mean you're such a good friend. You're like a brother."

Tugging at his lapels, Norman nodded coolly to the beat. She had pushed back meeting him an hour, dinner hurried before the restaurant closed.

"And things aren't as bad as you say," she said.

Norman shrugged, looking past her to scan the dance floor. Lamb steaks with mint sauce, dry and expensive, and she sat sullen, text messaging.

"Really, you are such a good person," the pretty and thin-lipped girl said with a tug on Norman's coat. For dramatic effect she repeated, "Such a good guy."

He buttoned his coat, displayed his disinterest with pride.

"Things aren't so bad," she said. He had had enough.

"Well, Jesus Christ, I mean, shit," he said. "What the fuck, really, how would you know? What do you know? I'm telling you about me, about my inner state."

Demonstratively taken aback, her coo softened. "You got a million friends, Norman, who care about you."

He shook his head, sighed loud.

"You do. Everyone thinks you're a lot of fun."

He couldn't take it anymore, shouted, "Oh my fucking god, will you please, goddamn it, please, just shut the fuck up."

She stood up straight and chilly, collected against Norman's acrimony.

"Please, really just please," Norman pressed both hands to the bar, "Please, just shut the fuck up. I'm disgusting."

"Well," she said, throwing her head back. "Well, if that's how you really feel, maybe you should work out. Go to the gym at the college. They got a gym there."

"Ah, Jesus."

"Really, anyone can join."

Norman shook his head, his lips pinched, almost a smile.

"Or maybe if you just watched what you eat a little."

"Oh my god, fuck you," he sang out.

The pretty and thin-lipped girl, shocked again, self-righteous, "What? I'm just trying to help."

Norman turned to step back to the dance floor. "Oh my god. Shut up. Fuck you, fuck you."

The ashtray piled high, Norman's nausea brewed, the short glass of straight bourbon on his desk. A gag, gravel in his throat. This next morning, finding the un-drank left from the night before. This might be reason enough to drop a single cube into a drink: it'll melt overnight, appear less menacing in daylight, diluted as the hours dilute the ache. The ache of joy, night!

The Russians took off before even singing, sat only long enough to berate him. Slumped low in his seat, Norman wouldn't flinch, wouldn't even look at them as the quieter Russian, cheekbones striped with burned cork, shouted, waved his arms in a tirade, knocked over a chair, leaned in close to snarl. The other appealed to him coolly, things will be different between them if Norman can't control his own club, the girls. "Are you a man or a mouse?"

Picking up the shared date by the arm, she was struggling to stay awake, he repeated it hushed and intense before walking out. "Are you a man or are you a mouse?"

Alone, Norman sipped from his drink, stared off at the blurred middle ground in silence for a lingering moment. Next thing he knew, the sun coming up. Standing on stage, his throat dry, he set down the mic and flipped off the machine. After hours, singing alone redeemed his shit night. No audience to pander to, no waiting your turn.

There was a shift somewhere between Norman's eighth and thirteenth drink, always. The conversation, monologue, turned, as it often did, from extraverted output, the irrepressible expression of the energy a crowd fed him, to a lament, the gaping hole at the center, a drain sucking inward, hollow.

His date having left, he shouted over the music to the DJ, a bearded acquaintance, flipping through his crates. "I'm disgusting. Look at me."

Glancing sideways at Norman, the DJ continued to look at his records without responding.

"Really I am, man. Look at me."

The DJ pulled out an album and looked over the song titles

on the back. "Oh, come on, man. Things aren't that bad."

"You don't know."

The DJ shrugged, took the record from its jacket and looked close at the label. Norman leaned in closer to shout. "Really, you don't know anything. How would you know?"

The DJ set the record down. Pinching the needle between his fingertips, he bent to catch the lights in the record's grooves.

"I got a small dick," Norman shouted.

Snorting, the DJ looked up at him, dropped the needle. "Oh come on, Jesus, man."

Tipping his glass without noticing, Norman spilled the top of his drink. Irritated, the DJ bent down, ran his fingertips along the top of his crate, checking for conspicuous wetness.

"No, really I do. I got this little dick," Norman continued.

"I don't know, man," the DJ said, neck bent to his shoulder to press one ear to a headphone.

"No, I'm telling you. Really, it's true."

The DJ stood up straight and looked at him a moment, shook his head. "Well, okay, well, maybe your dick is small, or maybe your dick is normal-sized but it just looks small compared to your body."

Norman tipped his drink again, waving big. The DJ grabbed him by the shoulders to steady him. "Ah, Christ. I got this tiny, small pencil-shrimp dick and I'm fat."

The DJ shook his head, faded the bass on one channel and slid the fader, turned back to Norman.

"You think it's just a coincidence," Norman asked, "just bad luck that I always only find ladies with giant vaginas?"

The DJ shook his head. "Man, you know what it is? Your problem: you're just always watching so many pornos."

Norman grimaced, lifted his hand against a spinning light blinding him in flashes. "What, so... what does that got to do with anything?"

The DJ rolled his eyes. "Those guys are professionals, man. They don't get that job because of how average they are."

"Shut up," Norman said.

"No man, for real. You don't see like basketball games on

TV of like, whoever, your mailman Joe-Schmo and the guys playing at the Y or whatever."

"Just shut up, okay?" Norman cut him off.

"What?" The DJ bent down again, flipped through his crate. "Makes sense to me," he said.

Norman buttoned his coat. Steadying his lean against a tall speaker set on the floor, it tilted under his weight. Couldn't help but take a headcount of the dance floor. He didn't feel like dancing anymore. Fuck it. And what the fuck was Will lurking around the parking lot for, that goblin retard?

The DJ stood. He took a record from one turntable, put it in its sleeve and placed the sleeve at the back of a stack. He put a new record down. Norman leaned in close, looked him in the eye, hushed. "You mean you got a little dick, too?"

"Fuck you, man." Shocked and pissed, the DJ shouted, "No."

Nostrils flared, Norman shook his head, finished his drink in a single gulp. "You don't know what it's like, see?" he said.

"No, I certainly do not," the DJ said.

"See? You were just trying to be nice," Norman said, turning to step away. "Okay, I get it. You're a good person. You should go feel good about yourself."

The DJ grabbed him by the arm.

"No really. I'm sorry," Norman said.

"What?"

"I'm sorry. You don't wanna hear this shit. I'm sorry you gotta hear this shit. I'll shut up. I'm sorry."

"No man, for real. It's cool. Just have a good time," the DJ said.

"Yeah, I'm sorry," Norman said, "It's unfair. No one wants to hear this shit."

The DJ shook his head and touched a fingertip to his crate. He gave Norman a wide-eyed look, meant to be encouraging.

"I'll shut up," Norman said.

The DJ shrugged, "Whatever, man."

He flipped through the first few records quickly. Norman turned to walk off. Spinning back after a single step, he leaned low, close to where the DJ kneeled. "But you don't know. I mean, I just wanna fucking kill myself, man, you know?"

The DJ bolted upright. "Well, alright, man, Jesus, man, I mean—"

"No really, look at me, pathetic," Norman said. The room spinning, his tumble almost toppled a nearby booth.

Yesterday's coffee cold in the pot, Norman poured what was left into a dirty mug, black. Balancing, conscious of the bathroom door, the few steps necessary to reach it. A few bites of a sandwich left on his desk, thirteen dollar sandwich. That was at least three dollars in mayo gone sour. Wadded it up into its paper. Dropped it in the garbage. The Russians would come back at him somehow.

No one expects to come to need cocaine all day, just the hangovers get so tough, and the hangovers, well, the loneliness. One goes out. When The Russians came back at him, maybe Will would stick around, be agreeable. He should've asked Will the night before, Stick around, help me out.

Norman stepped, stepped again, alright. Splashed cold water on his face. Couldn't make his face out in the mirror. Strange, one can't really know what one looks like without one's glasses on because when one doesn't have one's glasses on, one looks in the mirror and sees only a smeared shape, a smear. Back to the coffee table, his glasses, thick and sporty purple plastic, returned to the mirror. He removed his ruler from the medicine cabinet, unzipped his fly, and leaning an elbow to the wall, tugged at his penis. If he could get hard, he would hold the ruler as far back to his testicles as he could press it.

THE LAST OF MEL'S KARAOKE BIRTHDAYS

From the parking lot Will could hear glassware clinking over the rumble of shouted conversations and bass. He shook a pill from its bottle. Breezy September night, felt good.

Tammy's family had money. Will's desire—compulsion even, he'd pant, get an erection even hearing her name—was all because she'd told him for years that he embarrassed her. The attraction on his part was all about class. She may have had everything handed to her, worked for nothing, appreciated nothing, but when he fucked her like no one else ever had or ever could fuck her, all was leveled. Class was obliterated. He fucked her to redeem all the class shame he'd ever felt.

And she—they really were a perfect vacuum yin-yang of unhealthy need—she never felt anyone else had ever really even liked her, let alone loved her or desired her, in her whole life. So she shamed him, calling him stupid all the time, impersonating his walk to make her friends laugh. She humiliated him because she could, having never been appreciated in any kind of way. She had to humiliate him to prove she had some power over him, a power over anyone.

The mutual humiliation kept the cycle spinning. He thrust as if the continuation of the world depended on it, and eventually she could not bear the depth of such responsibility. Not just he himself and not just the two of them—not just culture, its biases, mores, comforts and hidden violence— but the natural world depended on the blank aggression of his thrusts. He was never naked without a chill until her and it was this feeling he attempted to recapture when first attacking Beau. Fighting, if not resembling love in any other way, at least staved off the suspense of collapse. The moment of violence grounded him in the immediate in the same way, blankness, shut out the constant waiting. Then this violence kept the cycle spinning.

Will returned to the room to witness the opening bars of "Crosstown Traffic" and Norman, air-guitaring. Nothing more exhausting to Will than fun continuing. Without the terse wailing bleats of AC/DC to approximate melody, maybe Norman was impersonating Jimi Hendrix's throaty warble, but Norman simply moaned.

What an idiot, Will thought. Jimi couldn't sing. That was

the idea. That's why his singing was good. His guitar playing was so phenomenal that he didn't have to sing. His singing was a version of karaoke itself, boldly flawed or at least confidently average. Norman was dumb not to realize this, thought any song he liked was a good song to sing.

"His singing is croaky," Mel said. Gus smirked.

Gus could understand the *tire tracks all across your back* part being the sort of sexual innuendo Norman was drawn to. But in what way exactly was he trying to *get through* to this *you*? That seemed to contradict the sexual innuendo of the *tire tracks all across your back* part. But actually— *crosstown traffic*—what the hell was he even talking about?

What was the "audience" in Norman's mind was actually composed of performers-in-waiting. The binders passed around, drinks ordered, toasts. Everyone in the room collaborated as DJ, the background, the audience, all active participants. The songs, some hardly audible anymore, overwhelmed by layers of associative cultural baggage, the songs were all left incomplete. Everyone, performers-in-waiting, a drink or two to loosen up, took turns tackling the task of completing them.

The more gross the nerves under layers of masking, like scabs—gold jewelry, pre-stressed denim, logos of sport and industry—the more the embarrassment, the deeper the insecurity, the greater the testament to sensitivity. Unsustainable otherwise, but singing, all these people, each wanting to be needed to be heard, revealing some warped true self they couldn't otherwise reveal, and then, when their turn was up couldn't conceal, however much they may try. Friday night, what if the world never does actually end, but the experience of subjectivity continually dims, its half-life endless?

And "Crosstown Traffic," Norman hit it at the top with a proud moan, but, realizing the room hardly noticed him, just a familiar song in the background anyone might be singing, he got bashful. Sang with an ironic detachment, a shield, eventually a monotone moan.

The room more dense with people now, Norman stepped

off the stage to polite applause. A song had been played. Gus and Mel attempted to convince Will to sign up. He shrugged them off, downed a shot Norman handed him.

"You ever think about it? This is such a goldmine, just sitting there, waiting for us," Norman shouted over Mötley Crüe. "It's like, if we don't grab it, just ours to take, it's like we're pissing away our money?"

Will nodded, took a slug from his beer. The man singing onstage stood with his elbows spread wide, pointing the microphone straight up at the bottom of his chin from a foot below it. His neck veins bulged and though his mannerisms were full volume, his voice was inaudible.

"You ever think about that?" Norman asked, leaning in even closer to Will.

Will shrugged. "I don't know. I mean, Mel's birthday and we're celebrating."

Norman shook his head, "No, no, no."

"Besides," Will continued, "you're rich. You're out every night."

"That's not what I mean," Norman said. He took a long slurp from his bourbon, scanned the room. Tough to hear each other over the music, Norman practically stood on Will's toes.

"What I mean," he continued, "is these backing tracks."

Will lifted his beer to his mouth. Norman, waving his hand over his head to vaguely imply the whole room, poked Will in the eye.

"Jesus fuck, Norman," Will reached for his eye.

"Sorry," Norman said. "But someone is making a killing re-recording these songs." Will nodded, his eye tearing, took a deep breath. Held his beer to his rib with his elbow to grab a cigarette from his coat pocket.

"Really," Norman went on. "How hard could it be, for a musician I mean, to record all these songs and just leave the singing off? Make it sound exactly like the original, simple."

Lighting his cigarette, eye pinched closed, Will shrugged.

"A fucking goldmine for the producer, the agent or salesman or whatever." Norman had a faraway look, scheming. Will considered the bottom of his beer, hardly a drip left to pour over Norman's head.

"Brilliant, really," Norman said. "And I bet it's fun in a recording studio. Don't you think?"

He turned to Will, Will squinting.

"Excuse me," Will said, stepping away, head down with a deep sigh.

A guy that really, really looked a lot like Steve Perry, the singer of Journey, sang "Don't Stop Believin'." Puffy, unbuttoned white shirt tucked into jeans, the guy really, really sounded a lot like Steve Perry too.

Soon as the song hit its first chorus, it never occurred to him not to, Norman charged that second microphone. Moaned again, moaned more than sang, Quasimodo-style. The thrill, just overwhelming impulse and cheer, joy, thrust him up to the microphone. This song cannot possibly proceed without me singing it! The guy that really, really looked a lot and sounded a lot like Steve Perry, though at first shaken by Norman's crashing of the stage, threw an arm around Norman, just like Steve Perry himself probably would, and they finished the song with their arms over each other's shoulders, *Don't stop believin'. Hold on to that feelin'*, yeah. But *streetlight people, living just to find emotion*, whoa.

Norman felt good. He liked this guy, high five. They held hands above their heads and bowed. Next song, that was Norman too. No need to go anywhere, STP or something, maybe Creed.

The room, the audience of performers in waiting, Heart may be an epiphany, thought a woman flipping through the binder, *Barracuda*. One guy poked a finger knuckle deep in the payphone's coin return slot. The disco lights doubled in their reflection on the pinball machine glass, and in doubling, top and bottom panes each reflecting, they came apart from each other, a smear or echo of light in time. Must've been duct tape on this one wall for some reason, hmmm. Oh, goddamn it, it's on my coat. Hasn't that big Steven Seagal-looking guy sung a couple times in a row? There's always that one dork that thinks everyone else secretly likes country music. Tell her you like her shirt, it's a strange enough shirt that one might innocently comment on it.

Norman swung for the fence, the top, back corners of the room. Emptied his breath from deeper than he thought breath could reach, below his navel. A mad animal for this final soaring chorus, These bitches and children and queers will hear my voice, see me, and that guy over there looks maybe Polish, the cut of his brow, fuck the Polacks too. In the nourishment of smoke and depressants and laser lights, life-force itself warped.

No one noticed Norman walk off the stage. An ice puddle melted a coaster, bound one bill left on the bar to another.

ABOUT NINE MONTHS BEFORE THE FUNERAL

"Your father never interfered in the kitchen," Gus said, tugging at the waist of his baggy jeans, attempting an authoritative tone.

Norman held an exaggerated shrug, hands high up in the air, did a little bounce on his tippy-toes. "Well, Gus," he said, "my father is dead now, isn't he? It's not up to him anymore? Has nothing to do with him, far as I can tell."

"Your father built this place."

"And he left it to me."

At odds with his own mannerisms, squirming in an attempt to hold his words back, Gus shook his head.

"And we're... I... I am making a lot of improvements around here," Norman said. "I'm just trying to save a little money where I can."

"Yeah, sure. But at what cost?"

Norman shook a finger at him and smirked to acknowledge Gus's quick play on words. Gus continued, "Your father built something. People appreciate it and expect a certain standard of quality."

Norman nodded in agreement.

"Don't you see? Everyone's watching you now. Everyone wants to see how you're gonna do, following in the old man's footsteps, and so far this... this cutting corners—"

"Things are different now," Norman cut him off. "My father ran the place like a goddamned fool."

Gus threw his arms up in the air and spun around, his back turned to Norman, the lugubrious manic asshole with his ostentatious improvements, thinks purple always equals drama, drama always equals depth, too stupid to recognize where the value lies within his own inheritance. Breathe deep, okay. Gus tapped on the countertop. Regaining his composure he sighed, shook his head slowly. "Just change the name." He spoke softly. "Don't call it the Big Daddy Famous Burger."

"But that's what everyone orders."

Exasperated, Gus raised his voice again. "This place is what it is because of your father's love."

Norman nodded in agreement. "Very true. It is and I appreciate it greatly." He stepped to one side and leaned back. "But you know how long I've been waiting for this?"

Gus let a simple grunt of disgust slip.

"I've had my whole life to plan. Waiting, just hoping the old fool wouldn't drive the place into the ground with his stupid big-hearted..." Norman paused, searching for the word. Gus tilted his head and looked at him over his shoulder.

Frustrated, Norman blurted, "Whatever it is he thought he was doing."

Turning around slow and standing up straight, Gus looked Norman up and down. Norman puffed out his chest a bit and tilted his nose up. Gus took a deep breath and held it a good while just below his chest before letting it slip slowly out his nose. Back and forth, Norman leaned his weight one foot to the other. Gus squinted in concentration, could've counted to twenty, took so much time to raise his extended index finger to his forehead before waving it at Norman a few times. Hands on his hips, Norman shook his head.

"You," Gus said. He took another deep breath and cocked his head hard to one side and back.

"You," he continued, "gotta give Mel that money." His shoulders—his entire balance—dropped, slack with relief. Norman stood up tall, buttoned his coat with a guttural, "Harrumph."

Gus pressed on, "Give her what's hers. It's not right."

"What do you know about it?" Norman unbuttoned his coat, tugged at his collar.

"I know."

"You don't know anything."

"It's not right, Norman."

"Why are you talking about things you have no business in?"

Shaking his head, Gus stood with his hands on his hips, put his cigarette out on the cutting board. "It's not right, Norman. It's just not right," the cadence of his repetitive talk boosted his confidence. "It's just not right, Norman. It's not what your father wanted."

"Oh, and you know exactly what Rich wanted."

Gus nodded with the same vigor he had been shaking his head.

"Yes I do. I do. Yes I do."

"You have no idea know what you're talking about. You're so full of shit."

"No sir. I knew that man. I knew your father well, knew him a long time."

"Oh yeah?"

"I know what he wanted for Mel."

Norman shouted, "You don't know shit!" He began to pace. Shocked into sudden submission by the violence of Norman's volume, Gus hopped backwards, half-sitting up on the counter, recoiling from Norman.

Pacing, Norman stared at his feet, repeated himself in a hush. "Okay? You don't know shit."

"This place," he continued, raising his voice. "This place is my place now." He threw a fist up in the air to punctuate his point dramatically. "My place. It's no longer my dad's place and it's certainly not your place. You know whose place it is?" He stopped moving and looked at Gus. Gus looked away. "Mine. My place."

He chuckled and returned to his pacing. Staring at his feet, he shook his head, searching for the right words. "Mel, I mean, my dad wanted to reward some bimbo tramp for being so fucking brilliant as to go and get herself knocked up." He looked at Gus. Gus scowled.

Norman continued, "She couldn't afford to get knocked up, but she did and he wanted to help her out, that's his deal. But me, I don't see fit to do so."

He paused and looked at Gus again.

"I just don't see how it's my place to reward someone for their lack of foresight. Maybe it's just me. But I couldn't live with myself if I did that. That's just not the kind of man I am. That's not within my code."

"Was his baby," Gus said, the words a quiet whistle from his throat. He cleared his throat. Norman smiled at him.

"Said her."

Gus repeated himself. "It was your dad's, Rich's, baby."

Norman shook his head. "I don't believe it, woman like that? You know how the bitches around here are."

Gus considered he could grab a handful of flesh under Norman's chin, rip out an entire handful. Neither Mel nor Rich ever told Gus anything about it, but he knew the situation. Knew there was no possibility that Rich had actually been a part of the conception, but that in no way gave Rich even a moment's pause in thinking of the baby as his own, would be thrilled to openly claim it as his own. And the money, it was supposed to be just enough to give her a few months off to be pregnant. Enough so she could have the baby then come back to work.

Norman continued, "You do have a code, right?"

Gus shook his head.

"No? Every man has a code."

Gus let himself slip forward off the countertop, planted his feet on the kitchen floor, not allowing Norman's eyes to slip from his stare. He spoke slowly, enunciating. "You are disgusting."

Norman laughed and turned away.

"You are. Who are you?"

Norman shrugged.

"She can't work like this."

"Not my problem," Norman replied with a flat tone.

"Especially in those ridiculous new, rinky-dink little thongs you want the girls to start wearing."

Norman smiled a playfully ashamed smile.

"She's not a dancer anymore. And she... she's not even a cocktail waitress."

Norman shrugged, let his mouth hang open a little to mock the idea that he would respond.

"Jesus, Norman, really," Gus continued. "She's been here since she turned twenty-one years old. This is all she knows and you know she can't work like this. It's not good for her. It's not safe. It's not good for the baby."

Norman hopped toward Gus, looked him square in the face. "None of that is my problem."

Gus shook his head. Norman knew Gus would've agreed to raise the baby as his own, tell everyone it was his if that was what Mel wanted.

Norman continued, "It's not. How is any of this my problem? She's so stupid."

"Now you quit saying that."

"What?"

"You quit calling Mel stupid, you bully."

"Oh I'm sorry. That girl whose livelihood depended entirely on her ass was a fucking genius to get knocked up."

Gus shook his head and looked down, raising his hand slowly to Norman's chest. "You just better watch your mouth, Norman."

"Oh, I'm sorry. I forgot it's her superior intellect got her in this situation. She's a fucking brilliant fucking floozie."

Gus took a deep breath and both of them remained still, Gus with his hand raised lightly to Norman's chest. Stepping back, Norman laughed and swatted Gus's hand away. "And get your fucking hands off of me."

Gus took a deep breath and cocked his head up at Norman. "Your father told her he had that money set aside for her."

"Oh man," Norman feigned shock. "But where could it be?"

"Norman, that money is hers and you know she needs it. She has nothing else."

"Man, who would've ever thought he'd just fall over dead like that?"

"You know he was crazy about Mel and thrilled about the baby and he told her that money was set aside."

Norman scratched his chin with sarcastic thoughtfulness. "What if he would've just fallen over dead, just like he did, but before he even told her about the money?"

Gus looked confused. Norman continued. "I mean, he did just fall over dead. He wasn't sick. I mean, not really. It could've happened at any time, right?"

Gus shrugged, "So?"

"So nothing. I'm just saying, a shock like that, you don't see it coming at all, do you? He could've fallen over dead before he ever even had the chance to make any promises."

"Bullshit." Gus began to pace. "That's not the point."

Norman smiled and straightened himself tall, unbuttoned his coat. He remained silent until Gus glanced over, and finding him still and silent, Gus stopped pacing. He shrugged. "What?"

Norman only smiled in return, widened his eyes, but remained silent.

"What?" Gus asked again.

Shaking his head, Norman continued to smile in silence.

"It's just," Norman began, pulling a cigar from his pocket. "It's just that you're such a fag."

Diminished, Gus shook his head, lowered his eyes. Almost sixty, the kitchen walls sticky with thick grease, almost sixty and plenty of goddamn practice shaking off name-calling and isn't it so simple, someone wants to kick him in the gut, always the last resort, so predictable. So predictable and dull, and still, almost sixty and still. He sighed, looked up at Norman, the fat fuck, as if to ask him why, or even just "Really?" but Norman's gloating smile, fuck it.

"It's weird," Norman said, puckering on his cigar. "Sometimes I don't even think about it for a little bit at a time and then it just hits me, like, Oh right, isn't that weird Gus is such a fag. He, like, craves dick. That's so weird, right? How sometimes I don't even think about it until I do."

Gus mustered his composure, inhaled deep and stood tall, but had to look at his feet to do so.

"She put you up to this." Norman said.

Slow to respond, Gus shook his head. "Nope."

"Come on. Yeah, she did. She was afraid to come to me herself."

"No, no. She's never even brought it up."

"Really?"

Gus nodded. "She'd be mortified. She'd kill me if she knew I talked to you about it."

Norman nodded, "Hmmm." He stepped up next to Gus and fingered a pile of tomato slices, popped one in his mouth. Both men were still.

Gus spoke softly. "A petty tyrant."

Norman nodded to acknowledge that he had heard the statement and continued nodding to imply that he was considering it. He popped another tomato slice in his mouth and waited for it to melt against his tongue. He took a puff from his cigar.

"Maybe, Gus, things aren't working out here between us."

Gus took a deep breath before looking over to him. Norman shrugged and Gus nodded. With careful movements Gus removed his apron, crumpled it in a few folds and put it down on the counter. He turned slow, but paused before stepping off. He looked to Norman. Norman did not flinch. Gus took a step away, paused, took another two steps quick before spinning back to Norman.

"Look, I'm sorry, Norman. I don't know what got into me."

Norman cocked his head and squinted, holding Gus in the crosshairs of his stare.

"I mean, you're right." Gus felt sick. "This is your place now. You're the boss. Who am I to tell you how to run things?"

Norman held him in his gaze another moment. "Yeah?"

"Oh yeah. I was being crazy. I don't know. I'm sorry."

Norman nodded in agreement. Gus chuckled and continued, "I was. Jesus. I'm sorry, I don't know what I was thinking."

Norman smiled at him, put his big hand on Gus's back.

"Alright, alright. Get back to work."

Gus unfolded his apron.

"The Big Daddy Famous Burger," Norman said.

4

Joe slept sitting up in his chair next to Ronnie. She slapped his arm. "Well, what do you say, Joe? Isn't it ol' Kenny?"

Joe had been drinking all morning. She told him to please don't. But he complained how seeing her family, of any day, was the most wrong day to ask. Said he hated funerals, as if everyone didn't. "We're all, the rest of us," Ronnie laughed, "just pleased as peaches to be there."

She asked, "What do you think, Joe? I'm thrilled for the treat of my mother's funeral?"

He answered in his stammer, like he answered everything, "Just because you don't... because don't like it too, doesn't mean I like it more, just because... because you don't like it too."

Ronnie wasn't so naive as to think there was anything she could say to keep that man from his drink. They weren't even going to come. She figured Oh well, hell, no one there wanted to see her and if that was the way it was, she sure as heck wouldn't go alone. And she was okay with it. Made her peace with the decision. She didn't know how, but somehow ended up they went.

Joe and Kenny, they had no qualms about making faces, letting their faces show, both of them not bothering to hide for one second the feelings they had for one another. As if they'd ever even sat down and talked, man to man. Joe rolled over in his seat with a grunt and a scowl. Kenny, Ronnie was afraid, looked like he was setting his shoulders square to spit on him. So she stepped in between, pushing past Gus to give Kenny a hug, knowing he was too vain to let anyone see how he really treated his own mother. She'd take it however she could.

And she didn't blame him. She didn't. She was young, seventeen, when she had Kenny. Last half of her senior year, she walked around ready to drop him. He was heavy all at once. She had no idea he was even there until he was heavy all at once. Then at the end, she knew it, was trying to hold on to him. Didn't want to let him go. She never did get along with Cancers. She kept hoping he'd be born early. Geminis got along with each other well enough. How easy things would've been. When he didn't come early, and it did seem like any day, then she spent every second trying to will that baby to not be born. She just knew. She had always known she just didn't get along with Cancers. She knew it and he proved it and proved it over and over.

Dell was a good bit older than her. Dell, he really was an ugly son of a bitch. But he was so cool. Lean and mean and silent and cool, above all else that son of a bitch was cool. A dream with those careful sideburns and those mirrored glasses. He always kept his clothes so perfectly neat. He was so particular about his appearance. And was a lot older than her. He knew about plenty she didn't know. And he was sadistic. She couldn't blame Kenny one second, she didn't.

Those last years before Dell left, that man just had such a chill around him. He blamed her it seemed. Like he had some other real life waiting for him somewhere, some life he deserved and Ronnie and his babies were not it. They kept him from that life. That man, he did remain calm through his cruelty, looking curious at his own experiments. At least if he'd delighted in the torture, delighted in shaming Ronnie, humiliating her and Kenny, humiliating them together. If he didn't, wouldn't, and never would feel bad, at least he should've been delighted. That could've explained, or at least motivated, his behavior. They at least deserved that, if not conflicted, at least he should've been delighted. But not Dell, no. He remained perfectly cool. He never raised his voice. He kept those eyes with heavy lids still, behind those square glasses of his. He was tall, denim shirt tucked into denim, cowboy boots tucked under his jeans' cuffs. Long neck and his hair kept in a neat fade, that man was so particular about his appearance. His hair always longer on the top, falling back perfectly, and he'd speak slowly in that quiet voice of his, never with any tone whatsoever.

He'd calmly announce, "Ron, tie Kent down for me."

"Excuse me?" she'd scream. She'd howl, "You don't touch that boy, you monster."

But he loved it. That was his true love, his true calling, cruelty. The wilder she protested, the deeper his calm got. He'd untwist a coat hanger, stand silent with it over the humming stovetop.

Kenny had made his own life. She let him have it to himself, never went barging in on him. He wanted nothing to do with her. She knew it. She left him alone. He didn't need to worry about her. Some women, they got to be her age and they're always bugging everyone, requiring everyone take care of them, telling everyone how to raise their own kids, but not her. She'd love to meet Kenny's kids. She wondered about them every day, every day. A boy and a girl, half East Indian, she worried about them. That's a hard life, not that she was racist, but other people, not fitting in with either the white kids or the other Indians. But she bet they must be beautiful and she wondered about them every day.

He should have been thankful, Kent. He knew she knew she screwed up. He knew she knew she screwed up so bad that she couldn't ask for anything, couldn't ask to even know him. She left him alone. She had her own life. She didn't need him or anyone else who didn't want her. He didn't want her and she couldn't blame him, so that was that.

Her life, she thought about what she'd imagined at sixteen, seventeen years old. She wasn't thinking nothing, but she could not believe this handsome, cool stranger, ugly as a muskrat really, this cool, cool, cool older man had any kind of interest in her. She could not believe it. She was just always wondering what he was thinking about, with that blank face. That's all Dell ever really let anyone think whenever anyone was around him. There wasn't any thinking anything else with Dell around, he'd be so quiet and, in this way, always seemed to be judging everyone. Not that he'd ever say anything. And his face never did give anything away, of course. All she knew was she was just a chubby little girl with a little brother to take care of, a little blob who thought he was all that, but he wasn't. You think he'd even come back for the funeral? Wherever he was.

Ronnie had Patti and Lucy and Joanne and they were just all such nerds. With their pinups—Johnny Mathis—and their crushes and their dolls they'd dress up and next thing Ronnie knew, this silent cowboy on his motorcycle, she always thought Dell thought he was Peter Fonda, and he wanted to take her in his strong arms. Okay, what was going on there? Next thing she knew, there was little Kenny, little Kenny sitting there inside her through all her classes, heavy that senior spring. Little Kenny sitting there through home economics, algebra, philosophy, science, and then Kent, named after Dell's own dad he never knew, Dell and Kenny and her.

She didn't ever have time to picture her own life. She never did imagine how things might be when she grew up. She never imagined how she wanted things to be because she never had a minute to do that. Before she knew it, there she was, a part of Dell's world, grown up. Dell was like a Merlin, still in the middle of the storms he set spinning. It's how that man was happiest.

She couldn't say, "Kenny, you know I'm sorry." She has. She didn't talk to him for some years and then she was on the phone with Mel and Mel put Kenny on the phone, "I got a surprise."

For Mel's sake he spoke to Ronnie a minute, was polite, told her about his kids, a promotion at the factory. Didn't ask her any questions and she was pleased not to volunteer. She had nothing to say. She and Joe had each other, had a room. What would she have had to tell him? But after a minute, he was always impatient and she couldn't blame him. He was getting off the phone, handing it back to Mel, and she called out after they already said Bye and Good to talk to you. He's handing Mel the phone and Ronnie called out, "Kenny! Kenny!"

He got back on the line, "Yes, Ronnie."

And she didn't know she would say it. She didn't know she'd ever say it or that she even wanted to really actually say it. She needed to keep him on the line a second longer. This man was, of course, a grown man, his life all his own, and her little Kenny was no more, didn't exist anywhere, in any way. Not anywhere, that little Kenny was gone for good, as gone as wherever it was old Dell ever disappeared to, only kind thing she'd ever known that man to do for anyone but himself. That little Kenny that was gone, that Kenny was nothing but her mistakes, every day she had to think about what she should've done. And they didn't exhaust, the memories. One might think they'd burn themselves out, leave nothing but ash, but no. They deepened each day, like a groove a little harder each time to step out of.

So Mel got Kent on the phone and he was with his sister and she'd set up this getting Ronnie on the phone and what was Ronnie about to say? Kent had already been as nice to her as he had been in years, just telling her about the kids, and then she called out to hold on and she didn't know, it just came out. She didn't want to push things. He had already been so nice. But she said it.

She said, "Kenny." He didn't respond.

She said, "Kent." She spoke slowly.

She said, "Kent, you know, I am so sorry."

And then quickly she repeated herself, "I'm just so sorry."

He didn't say anything. The line was quiet for a moment. Ronnie figured that's Kenny's playful way, silent, making a promise. Things would be different. Mel got on the line and they finished their conversation.

That was the last they spoke to each other before the funeral. She saw him come in. Saw his brother take his coat and put an arm around his waist and Kent pulled back. Ronnie waved when she thought he saw her. But she couldn't blame him—he didn't come over to her. There were other people there, lots of people. But at the water fountain, that stung. It stung and it hurt like a kick in the gut, making a fool of her there with her open arms and big smile. She thought, I don't know. Things could change. Then he acknowledged her, squirming as she kissed his cheek, just for the sake of this Gus standing there.

But time came to head out to the cemetery and everyone

milled about sorting rides and excusing themselves to pull their coats from the back of someone's seat. Gus excused himself, Mel was gonna run him home quick on the way to the cemetery for something. He climbed clumsily past Ronnie's knees, she leaning back in her seat to make room. And with a spin, without having really said anything, Kent slipped away.

He found Will downstairs, down a long hall, playing hide and seek with some kids in the coffin showroom. Was supposed to give him a ride to the cemetery. Everyone was leaving. Kent felt hurried for everything, all the time. Had to wait for Will to gather all his plastic bags, too many to carry easily. Taking a slug from his bottle of Crown, Kent walked a few steps ahead, didn't offer to help.

At the toothpaste factory, breaking momentum was worse than the redundant task itself. Kent's musculature had long been addicted to the repetitive choreography. Quick lift, turn left, return. A decade and a half passed taking a tube off a belt, flipping it over and putting it on another belt running parallel to the first one.

Almost two years since he'd taken the management position, no small feat, Kent felt, for a lefty, and he still hadn't truly fallen into the cadence of the new twist. Twelve flattened boxes came through at once, insides turned upwards. Machine straws spit glue in the seams and a machine claw folded all the boxes closed in one motion. Kent stacked the boxes on a pallet, as bad on his back as the old job was and worse for his wrists. The set-up, of course, biased for the right-handed.

Management meant every eight minutes he looked at the clock and wrote the time on the crate, in a wide fluid gesture with a thick red marker. Such accountability translated to a ten percent higher hourly wage than his co-worker Juan, who otherwise did the exact same job alongside him. Ten percent raise meant affording the Florida trips more easily.

With the frequency of looking at the clock, however—has it been eight minutes yet, can't miss it—the shift felt twice as long, ten times as long.

And with the change in position came a change of awareness he was also reticent to welcome, a sudden ability to read the codes. Kent had never before had reason to be aware of the codes at all. Now, he personally contributed an element to each code assembling into its own form.

In the end, wherever any tube ended up, a box store in a valley, ninety minutes from the nearest of the surrounding small mountain towns, or some high-rise on the Upper East Side with a doorman, whoever ended up looking in the mirror behind a sink with a frothy mouth with any one of these tubes that passed through Kent's hands, identical as the endless stacks of tubes may have appeared on the line, day after day, hour after hour, tube after tube, the sequences of overlapping codes in four-point type on the spine of every tube could trace it back to the moment it passed through the factory's doors.

There were three shifts. The factory ran twenty-four hours a day. Kent knew one sleepy grouch he relieved and another caffeinated slob who relieved him with a grunt. "Morning." Kent had no illusions of any more than one-third of the output of the factory having ever passed through his hands. And it was not that he had any pride or connection to the specific tubes of toothpaste birthed from his shifts.

It simply occurred to him. And he would've rather it didn't. Each tube, despite appearing to be identical, was a unique individual with specific tribal loyalties, accountable to that shift's manager. A single cracked seam would leak goo enough to mess up the entire belt, throw off an entire day. That cracked seam—Kent's accountable. The turning of the cranks, the continuing operations of the factory, could not help but produce each tube with its unique code.

Kent did not entirely appreciate the responsibility, being squeezed between a sense of power and the brunt of the accountability for circumstances largely beyond his ability to wrangle. He wanted to shake it all, the process and the ends, from his thoughts and return to the simpler times of work at the factory.

Before, before he had to remember to look up to the clock and scrawl the code, shifts passed in a yogic zone. The factory fell away from his movements. The tubes and the belts fell away. Only Kent's body in its constant pattern remained, and his body was the pattern and the pattern itself was his body and the pattern continued in blankness, endless white above and below, and no form within either reach or keenest vision on any side. But once thought, Kent could not help but suffer the knowledge. He returned to the clock and returned again to the clock and in doing so stilted his movement among the machinery.

The belt began to jitter in the familiar foreshadowing of a halt. He'd have to climb under and around, palms and knees to cold concrete, careful between what belts and bolts his fingers poked. A superficial pass would suffice to determine his own culpability. Most often the break happened far down at the tight turns and kinks, nothing to do but sit and wait. But his quota—

Kent and Juan exchanged a glance and a nod. Shit, there's no not admitting it if he recognized the belt's skitter too. Kent popped a Nicorette in his mouth, layered on the ChapStick.

Kent had agreeably covered for Juan a couple times, calling the line-tender over and improvising a scattered story about why Juan should be relieved, just to give him some minutes to sneak off, wander around the old factory. Juan could not return the favor due to Kent's obligation to initial each crate. Kent knew Juan did not think this responsibility was worth a ten percent wage difference, and he never felt comfortable enough with Juan to attempt to convince him of what a drag it truly was.

The horn bellowed like a loud cow awakening. Kent scooted a plastic milk crate over with his foot and offered it to Juan. Juan wiped his brow and sat, dropping his head between his knees. The collective moan of all the workers in the huge room echoed the horn.

In the two years since Kent had been set apart as

management, stories had circulated. He had been unable to confirm them with personal experience, but the workers exhausted the line-tender, taking turns seeking adventures through the closed wings of the giant old building.

A series of dusty crimson curtains covered the far wall, the size of a football field. There was a gate someone had pried open with a screwdriver, without management ever noticing, in the wire fence behind the folds where two curtains overlapped. Through this gate and down a long unlit dusty hallway, those closed wings of the building opened up into a maze of identical metal doors lining identical gray walls. The lengths of the hallways differed. The distance between doors differed slightly. The workers had drawn and circulated a map to a door that remained unlocked, seemingly forgotten.

In this room under a greasy sheet was a pale vanilla 1928 Duesenberg, long and low, its license plate "LUMNOUS." Upping the ante on the superlatives the men adopted to praise the flow of its curves, the precise ornamentation of its grill, the radiance with which its shine cut the floating dust of the room, had become the furtive cafeteria talk. Competing camps contested which old-money town benefactor's name was on a little plate displayed in its window, compromising claims of who had actually seen it.

With the break imposed, Kent anticipated Juan's request. He was unsure, however, how to explain that he would have to insist Juan sit and wait out the belt's repair alongside him in an effort to help keep the secret of the car, knowing the rush of workers lost in the halls all at the same time would only draw attention to it, blow their cover. He'd promise Juan they'd corroborate their stories for the line-tender, after the belt was up and running again, so he could go on his adventure.

Kent would resent Juan for having gotten most of his shift off, his expensive sneakers, not packing a lunch. But he'd prefer to press the grumpy line-tender to meet the quota. Better that than prohibiting Juan from sneaking off to ogle at the glowing-golden, hidden car.

Will stepped in goose shit, and each step he took smeared it more into the cuff of his suit pants, unrolling out over his heel. The duck-footed minister led the parade to the grave, head down. The duck-footed minister was very sincere.

Back at the funeral home, the twenty people sang a murmur, a little less loudly than the flipping pages of the lyric sheets handed out. The duck-footed minister, hunched at his keyboard, murmured most loudly of all, snuck a couple bites from a hoagie, when Nana's neighbor stood for her public whisper.

In the cemetery geese wobbled and meandered in big groups, nothing to do that afternoon. There was a creek and shallow hills, gold and auburn leaves blew, and goose shit everywhere, puddles.

Kent held up the procession a moment, insisting the pallbearers all balance the casket and swap positions real quick, on account of his being left-handed. He took a quick pull from his bottle of Crown. The smell of mud hung in the moist air.

The grave was squared perfectly, deeper than it was wide or long. Two Latino men in sweatshirts and dirty jeans, gardening gloves and baseball caps, lowered the casket slowly, with a system of pulleys and long straps. The teeth of whatever machine dug the hole had stripped its sides in evenly spaced vertical lines.

Kent announced that he'd decided to spend the night after all, head home early tomorrow. Hearing that, Ronnie announced she and Joe had decided to head back to their place, wherever that was, straight from the cemetery. They'd be back to help Mel sort everything later in the week. Will dangled a cigarette from his teeth, wiping mud and goose shit from his plastic bags with napkins he'd pulled from one of them.

Geese barked. Joe, tie loosened in the back row talked over the duck-footed minister to no one in particular. "My daddy, my dad died, years ago, my daddy died, his funeral, my daddy, what a turnout."

It wasn't about Ronnie's teeth. Joe didn't want to go for his own reasons, but Ronnie was convinced he was embarrassed. He just didn't want to go. It was simple. He could probably use getting out of the room, beyond the short string of parking lots connecting motel to bar to diner to card game to bar to motel. But a funeral, with her family, that was not the excuse he wanted.

He didn't care about her teeth. He loved Ronnie. But he knew her kids would be shocked and offended, pick on her. Or worse, pretend to not notice, which everyone always did the same way, smiling with his or her own mouth closed, lots of smirking. And the kids, especially Kent and Mel, always asking him about work. They knew about his knee, his disability. Why did people insist on shaming the sick and injured, exasperating the conditions they already suffered?

When he and Ronnie met, Joe had been a security guard at the mall. Sixteen stacked screens, four across, four tall. Each screen cycled through five camera angles. Each camera angle held for five seconds before it flipped. From screen to screen, the edits were staggered within splintered seconds so the stack as a whole flickered. With the tap of a button Joe could stop the constant motion, hold on any one screen when his scan deemed it necessary. Oily fingerprints remained on the screens from close inspections.

Sometimes, certain paths one might have taken if, for instance, one parked in the North lot and walked to the Gage's Superstore in the Southwest corner—Joe could trace the entire path from the far left second screen to the top, next across with a bump up to the top row, then back down across the second to bottom screen for the last two horizontal rows. This depended on the edits falling in sync to an unlikely degree, but that happened with greater frequency than one might have expected.

Joe pleaded to Ranger. Todd Rancher held tight to the nickname he had given himself, Ranger—everyone's right, Joe figured, to reimagine themselves through the eyes of how they wished other people saw them. Joe appealed to Ranger, restack the screens so North was on top and West to the left, etcetera, and Ranger, indifferent to the idea, said he didn't mind if Joe wanted to do it himself.

It stumped Joe, how to find the right time to unplug everything, rearrange it. If something were to happen in that moment, Joe caught not surveying the scene, "sailing," he and Ranger called it, mall management would not be pleased, no matter the reason. And it didn't mean enough to him to stay late. The far left screen did in fact point North as it should have. But from there the system scattered, partly lined up to the orientation of the room within the mall, but even that was no more than Joe recognizing blips of order in the statistical inevitabilities of a random system.

One time some little rat face, Joe saw him right there on the screen, daring him, he lifted a baseball hat from a kiosk while his friend distracted the kid working there, put it right down the front of his pants, turned, and strutted off and Joe saw the whole thing, the monster balls of that little rat. Joe leapt up and off he went and he tucked in his shirt as he stood and he was off to go and he was walking off, thinking he knew right where the little rat was heading, tracing his path beyond the frame of the screen and walking right along the paths of those screens, and goddamn it if Joe hadn't looked at those screens so long that he'd forgotten which way the goddamn mall itself was oriented. He marched right over to Panda House near the angled bricks, thinking he knew that little shit's escape route exactly and he was going to cut him off at the pass but he didn't realize it until he was already over to The Donut House and this kid had vanished, he'd walked off straight the wrong way.

That's when Joe learned the good-goddamn sense of borrowing a minute's time from one's self from time to time. When security there at the Oak Towers Brook Plains mall stepped away from those screens, it was an exception. The higher-ups assumed, if Joe hadn't noted a quick minute, "in pursuit of a culprit," and if he hadn't noted "gone to the john for a minute or fifteen," the assumption was he was there and he was sitting and he was watching those screens careful-fucking-ly. He was accountable, his ass on the line.

And the little blue pills kept him focused. Not only helped so he could drink more and not feel it, but just made him stare—Bing!—at those screens all day without anything slipping past.

Sure, Ranger dealt with the home office. Ranger signed the report when mall management called home office, complained stock disappearing or vandalism. But Ranger passed any blame, said it looked bad for the whole operation if the leadership were questioned, and nowhere but Joe to pass any blame to.

Ranger was the boss, no mistaking it. In the original plan, when Joe needed the favor and Ranger took him on, Joe should've remembered how Ranger always had been, but the plan was they'd split the shifts, maybe switch it up every hour, one out on foot making his presence known among the shoppers to give the workers a sense of security. That's what they were, what they personified. Security.

Out there, anywhere outside the office, Ranger wasn't Ranger and Joe wasn't Joe. They were both their uniforms. People needed to see them, know they were out there, on foot on the frontlines. Thing was, though, Joe was really pretty sure when he got the job that Ranger said they'd split the shifts, take turns in the office while the other's out on foot.

Couldn't really call it an office, even. It was a room, definitely a room. Joe stepped through the heavy door each morning at seven-thirty, took two steps and sat in front of the monitors. Leaning in his seat, he could touch either wall with his fingertips. The walls were thickly painted light yellow, lemon but more muted—muted lemon.

Sometimes the light above blinked on and off. Would do it for a whole day or two every time, right before it went out, and Joe tried asking maintenance but they wouldn't change the thing until it went out all together. After a couple days of its flicker, he would continue to see the flicker even when maintenance changed it and the new light was steady. Seven-thirty in the morning until ten at night, Thursday through Tuesday.

Ranger failed to understand the basic concept of what they did there. Joe watched him browse the newsstand daily, lean forward heavily on his elbows, tipping his hat back to flirt with some fine young thing at the yogurt stand. He would return and tell Joe he'd been in meetings or following a lead. And Joe—"Black Monday" and the trickle-down of the Dow drop as a pretext—Joe the one who got let go.

When Joe returned to the parking lot the next day, to knock out the windows of Ranger's car with a shovel he'd shoplifted from the hardware store, he failed to consider that the shovel would be too heavy for him to swing over his head. His wild swing toppled him. He banged his knee hard against the pavement.

When Ranger watched the surveillance footage and saw Joe so ashamed and angry with himself that, limping, he turned the shovel on the headlights of his own car, Ranger was so moved he got Joe on disability real quick and never did stop signing off on it, every month since, twenty years. That was the bond fighting together to defend this nation in some far off land established between men, loyalty. And Ronnie's goddamn kids would question him about work? Mock him for that? He'd rather just skip the funeral and all of it altogether. Had nothing at all to do with Ronnie's teeth. It was love at first sight for them and within a year she had moved to be with him.

1988

Unable to settle her coffee's hazelnut-to-rum ratio, Ronnie poured a third finger but still didn't like the taste. In her ratty robe she sat, sighed, Wait for it to cool then drink it down quick.

Time came she should have headed out for the hospital, but she didn't budge.

She'd listened to Dawn and Judy since that one semester of college what, Jesus, a little over twenty years ago. Two girls her own age had commandeered their own radio show. Ronnie always suspected one of them must've been *somebody's* daughter. Driving across town those mornings, fall turning into mild winter, roads and lawns all the continuous pale gray and yellow of dirty teeth. Everything dead, but the snow never showed up to bury anything.

Before that one semester, she would've already dropped Kenny off at Nana's and been at work by the time Dawn and Judy came on. But in school, able to leave a little later, just after rush hour, she sat in the car with their laughter every morning. Never could determine whose laugh was whose, the two laughs a unified, melodious refrain. Usually couldn't tell what they laughed about, didn't matter. One hardly gasped a word or two between sobs of laughter to get the other one going again.

That morning at her table, with her coffee, in her robe, Dell ten years gone at least, Kenny off a couple years already, and even Mel hadn't been around for some months, Dawn and Judy cackled.

Ronnie observed herself with curiosity but without emotional investment, like a scientist, Hmmm, isn't this interesting, this day she has decided to not move. The her-that-watched-herself-sit began rooting for the sitting-her, Go on—get up girl! Get on with it, the day awaits! But nothing. She didn't know why this day—could have been any day.

She ran water over the top plate's crusted egg yolk smears, but wasn't about to deal with all that crash and clatter of unburying dishes out from under each other. Clear plastic pressed coffee grounds speckled ground beef blood to blue Styrofoam at the top of the trash. She knew picking up the bag meant balancing that. She had no balance to spare. There'd been this dead mouse smell in the kitchen the last few mornings, but after sitting with it a few minutes one didn't notice it anymore. Ronnie had little interest in searching it out or scooping it up.

My thinning goddamn hair, do I really think I'm fooling anyone pulling it out and teasing it like this?

Rust and gray, silver and copper, her pale reflection in the window drawn out across the back lawn, striped by angled blinds. Dead mouse smell, coffee grounds in blood, that laughter.

AT NANA'S AFTER THE FUNERAL

The neighbor's security light flashed on in response to every creak and knock of the wind, blinding them each a second. Its reflection off the bone-colored lawn lit them each from below in long slow strobes. Shallow angling and intersecting concrete planes made up the few steps of the patio. The yard was continuous pale gray and yellow, the coloring of an olive-skinned blond. Faded wooden fences in various degrees of tumble behind bent wire boxed in Nana's small square of thin grass, dead year-round.

Kent adopted the airs of an admiral allowing himself the indulgence of setting his own best judgment aside. Mel kicked one high heel off into the lawn, felt the second kick in her ankle and dropped that shoe in front of her. Unable to contain her sprawl even with all her effort to appear so casual, she cracked open a can of cold beer with a heightened sense of ceremony.

Among his plastic bags, Will crouched his muscled bulk down to a catcher's stance on the astroturf stoop. The last times he had seen Nana, years ago, something about her had scared him. He stood up with a fist on his hip a silent moment. Only at the funeral could he finally begin to understand what it was that scared him about her. Having spent her entire life in Stone Claw Grove, always content, he didn't get it. He dropped his arms against his sides. She must've found some meaning somehow that he couldn't recognize. He leaned against the aluminum siding, its molded ripples icy on his back. But how, where did she find meaning in that stupid life of hers? What did she know that he didn't?

Will resigned himself to decoding and negotiating each swoop of Kent's hand as he knocked his weight from one hip to the other, and each stretch of Mel's back for a throaty drawn out syllable. He regretted not having gone straight to the bus station.

In need of a harmless enemy in common, they laughed about the funeral home director. Every finger ringed, two pierced ears, two bracelets each the size of another man's necklace. His cloying regrets, he appeared inflated under his neat suit. A man without a straight line anywhere, a dense arrangement of twisted tubes with a raccoon-hat pouf of hair far on the back of his head, permed and gelled. All his whispering and cooing, the forward ease with which he'd lay the wide heat of his open palm across one's shoulder or lower back, all compromised by that hair.

Kent laughed. "He may as well have tied a teddy bear to his head, like he goes to work each morning as Baby New Year in a diaper and ribbon with a teddy bear tied to his head."

Approaching the cracked door of his office, looking for a funeral flag for traffic, Will and Kent overheard only a single unguarded phrase. The funeral home director asked the teenage parking attendant standing before him, "She got a new boyfriend yet or she still seeing that thug?" This question, their only glimpse behind his public front.

They agreed that his hair, the deliberate gesture of his hair, was so extreme that if it were tempered and integrated in an evenly distributed percentage throughout his entire person he'd still be doused in a thick floral fragrance, passing his afternoons at the counter of a homey café eating a donut with a fork and knife wearing a bowtie and a linen suit cut for a woman.

Will, with his lifelong tight flattop, thought the outburst, the tantrum of the funeral director's hair, pointed to the repression the man must have otherwise imposed on himself. How to explain a peacock Tourette's in such a pigeon?

"Don't you just want to kick a guy like that's ass?" Kent

laughed, downing the last drops from his bottle of Crown.

Mel became taut. Will shifted his weight.

"What?" Kent went on smiling. "Really, don't you?"

"Kent," Mel shot him a look.

"What?' he responded. "Will always liked a good pounding."

Will shifted his weight. "Well, you know, I haven't fought in years, you know?"

Kent waved him off. "Yeah, well."

"Five years," Will said.

Kent shook his head. "Yeah, well, you still could fight if you had to, right?'

"I mean," Will wanted to be clear. "It wasn't really fighting I was into."

1. He admitted he was powerless over fighting—that his life had become unmanageable.

Mel threw her hands in the air. "Don't try explaining it again."

Kent shook his head, leaned his elbows to his knees. "No, what do you mean?"

Will shrugged. "Never mind."

"It's fucked up." Mel shook her head. "You were crazy. You know that, right?"

2. Came to believe that a Power greater than him could restore him to sanity.

"I thought that was your thing, look at your face." Kent said. "That was your thing, fighting."

"Just never mind," Will said, biting open a marshmallow bar.

"Good," Mel said. "It's weird."

3. Made a decision to turn his will and his life over, his Will, his life, to the care, turn over his Will, turn over his life, to the care of this higher power, this higher power as he understood It.

Out there on the interstate, Ronnie stopped for a drink at the Indian casino. All those bells, the electronic bells of slot machines like electronic church bells, they cast spells quickly. "Wait for that payout, just one pull away, you've fed me this long, may as well wait for my payout."

The casino was the furthest out of town you could get and still be in town in any way. So she stopped. She thought, Ronnie you better just think about this a minute, girl. Will is only thirteen. Sure, Nana will take him in, but not if I ask her to. She was driving and it hit her so she stopped and went in.

But she made it quick. She passed real quick through all those electronic bells and flashing lights and she sat down at the bar and she got a double Jack and Coke, and in as long as it took the young man, eager and smiling, and in just as long as it took him to turn around and pour that drink she knew she had to keep moving. Because if she stopped because it hit her, if she stayed stopped, it'd fall right on over her and pin her down and she'd never keep moving, so she took that drink down in one long pull, laid a fiver out by the time he'd come back with that drink and she took it down in one gulp and was up and a few steps away already, by the time she shuddered, and he called after her if she wanted her change and she waved him off over her shoulder, back into the flashing lights and electronic bells.

She knew then, This is hitting me, but this ain't really hit me yet. I could still turn around.

And that's when the decision really happened, once it was already done and she decided not to correct it. That's when she knew she didn't want to turn around. That's when she knew she couldn't think about it and she couldn't stop driving, because if she stopped she'd think about it, and if she thought about it then next thing she knew she'd be on her way back home to break a window, or she'd go straight to the hospital and look for an extra apron and hairnet to borrow and then tomorrow, no.

It's like credit. She knew all about living on credit, and she made the decision on credit. She knew it'd really hit her later—days, weeks, months, years, hours, minutes. She'd pay a little interest each day but she'd learn to live with the debt, outstanding balance. She had nothing if not outstanding balance. If nothing else had ever really been her own, even if she put this down on credit, with who could know how steep an interest, shit, this would be all hers. She wasn't gonna stumble along anymore, Uh-uh, she'd wipe out, all on her own. Yep, a wipeout. Wipe out her life.

Mel had been gone a couple months, never said goodbye. Her room at Nana's would be open. Will could stay there. Can't make a plan with Nana, though. Anyone Ronnie said goodbye to would try to talk her out of leaving.

Pulling out around the far side of the parking lot, scaffolding ran all up and down the casino's side. A man moved through it and whatever mission he may have been on, Ronnie thought it hard to believe he wasn't simply playing through the repetitive piping all locked into each other, itself.

Mel complained about Norman, his constant clueless chatter, and the laughs continued to come quick but each breath came up closer to the surface. Will's blank stare mapped the cracks through the porch in the static chill of the Stone Claw Grove night air. Night there had always had a high pitch to it, a harmony of the drone of the interstate, far away with the buzz of the electric lines at the back of the yard, the wide bleep of the moon against endless purple.

Mel insisted Will share her seat, a gesture of generosity. He declined and she unfurled across the creaky swing, her right, she figured, as neither of them had bothered to come around, watch Nana shrink, and her ankle felt better raised. Kent spun. Silhouetted by the neighbor's security light, his ponytail, like a small thumb, jut out from just above the nape of his neck. Will had grown tired of laughing. The couple quick marshmallow bars eaten in a panic expanded in his belly. He felt oppressed, obtuse.

"Done any interesting graphic design work lately?" Will asked Mel. She shrugged, took a long pull from her beer. Baby would've been due this week. They all sat quiet.

Kent and Mel both always expected a small performance,

a cynical and cold shotgun critique bordering on brutality, any time either of them saw Will. Will, perpetually the baby, playing the curmudgeon still held some amusing disconnect for them. But it had been years by now, and Will disliked the idea of doing the cantankerous rant routine for both of them at once. Like maybe they each assumed he reserved this indulgence of bad taste exclusively for each of them. Letting either of them see his performance in front of the other might betray the trust the playful tantrums nurtured and suggest a true and deeper mean-spiritedness. They were the only two people who had ever thought Will was funny, but it was never in the way he longed for—silliness. And now, a monster. Well, appearing a monster was enough to improve anyone's manners.

3. Made a decision to turn his will and his life over to the care of this higher power as he understood It.
4. Made a searching and fearless moral inventory of himself.

Nana's death cast a heavy woolen quality over their talk, more out of respect than immediate dread or shock, but really had little to do with Will's reticence to participate. He dreaded the fighting talk, the self-righteous lectures about his fighting, the intervention every time and how to prove to them it was all long behind him, as if either of them knew anything about him, his day-to-day. Taking a seat on an upturned plastic bucket, he was careful not to lean into the shallow puddles of rainwater that fell just short of the molded peaks of its ringed bottom.

Kent was caught up in a boisterous review of the roller coasters of their youth. They had all internalized the rhythms of each, exactly when the quick spin would fall into a drop on the sheen metal screamer. They could each still whistle the melodies of the creaks of the old wooden classic. Its thrill depended on layers, the course of the ride itself and the threat of the strain of the cars against their rails, finally reaching their crunching climax, twisting off into the parking lot.

But Will found Kent's appreciation rehearsed. He

suspected maybe it had gone over well at some Iowa City bar some night when roller coasters came up and Kent thought it only appropriate to resurrect the act for a hometown performance.

Mel limped inside to change, bumped her head on the chandelier hanging in the middle of the room, popped a pill, studied the dents in the carpet in the guest room. No way to know how long ago the bed had been scooted.

Kent's appreciation morphed into a lament. In Florida, taking his kids to an amusement park last summer, he found being raised ten stories only to drop straight down sensationalistic. He thought it pornographic that a sleek speeding train continued to spin on its axis while going through a loop. The epic emotional journey of the amusement park, the blank thrill of autopilot reptile brain, reflecting a mirror maze between all the expectant faces, waiting waiting waiting waiting waiting hours in a line in the sun for a ninety-second jolt, Kent could squash anything.

At the kitchen table, still in her robe, her night-sweats, Ronnie reached for her purse, grabbed her keys. The Ronnie-watching-Ronnie didn't know what the sitting-Ronnie grabbing for her keys was doing. She looked calm. The Ronnie-watching-Ronnie was calm watching her. She felt no anxiety to find out what she was doing. She simply watched with curiosity, what's she doing?

Sitting-Ronnie looked to the coffee grounds in ground beef blood under plastic on Styrofoam. She jiggled her keys lightly in one hand close to her chest. She dropped the keys to the table, worked her neck with both hands. She closed her eyes, inhaled deeply. The dead mouse smell was gone. It's not gone. I'm too in the middle of it, can't smell it. Dawn and Judy's laughter stabbed away.

First she removed the house keys from the chain, took off the front door key, the back door, the garage. Slid them off one by one around the ring, through the pinch of the ring and off. She laid them neatly down next to each other. She took off the key to her locker at the hospital. She laid that down next to the others. She read them left to right—front door, back door, garage, locker.

Was this Joe, living on disability in a weekly rate motel, worth this? Didn't feel like a choice.

She had a key to a file cabinet in the laundry room that she hadn't opened in years. She unwound that from the ring and laid it down at the end of the line. She had two keys to Nana's. She laid those down next.

There were two keys she'd been carrying around who knows how long, she had no idea what locks they opened. What doors did she have access to that she no longer had occasion to pass through? Something of Nana's? Didn't look like a car key with its wide oblong swoop. The other one, small, looks like she might've once been able to open a desk drawer or a briefcase.

Ronnie put them down on the table. She looked at the keys lined up in front of her and straightened them out so all their tops were lined up straight across and they all reached down to different lengths. She flipped them all over so their teeth all pointed left—bronze, silver, silver, round and small, bronze and smaller, silver, silver, lopsided and small.

Blustery and gray out, she pulled the front door locked behind her, only the two keys for her car left on the ring.

"But come on, you must miss it, right?" Kent said, leaning forward with his elbows on his knees, layering on the ChapStick. Will shrugged. The neighbor's security light flashed on and Will considered for a moment how identical his own shadow still was to what it always had been, no disfigurement in his shadow.

"I don't know," Will said. "No."

"No, you must. I miss drugs. Every day I miss cocaine. I miss cigarettes, oh my god, I miss cigarettes."

"Sure, it was a struggle at first," Will said.

"I miss all that fucking," Kent said. His polyamorous phase before he moved away, organizing orgies at unsuspecting house parties, dancing turning into a striptease turning into stripping other people as they danced, that always embarrassed Will. He didn't respond.

"All I mean is, if you were really addicted to fighting, to violence and brutality or whatever, then you must miss it now," Kent said, conscious of speaking in a patient and reasonable tone.

"Wouldn't it feel great," he continued, "just once, if you had a really good reason—this one time—someone really deserved to be pounded?"

Will lit a cigarette, hated how the charred taste lingered in his mouth when marshmallow coated it. He spat, it dangled a second, thick.

"Look," Will said, sitting up. "Getting my ass kicked was a high, right?"

Kent nodded, kind of loved it when he could get the classic imbecile to pontificate.

"And like any high, when you eventually have to give it up because it's taken over your life, you replace it."

"I think I'd actually have a great advantage fighting," Kent said. "Being left handed."

Will rolled his eyes.

"Really, I would. People aren't used to that. They don't know what a difference it really makes."

Will shrugged.

"And so?" Kent asked, tilting his bottle of Crown to his mouth before realizing it was empty.

"And so what?" Will responded.

"You replaced the high?"

4. Made a searching and fearless moral inventory of himself.

"Yeah, simple things. Running, my marshmallow bars are a treat, my vice."

5. Admitted to himself, to God and to himself and to another human being the exact nature of his wrongs and

6.   Six, he was entirely ready to have God remove all these defects of character.

"My days," Will continued, "are all very much the same, you know?"

Kent shrugged, "Well, everyone—"

"No," Will cut him off. "That's the thing about getting straight, about staying straight."

Kent leaned back, sighed. "Five years," he said. "I mean, I don't know, I figured maybe you were in jail or dead or living in a broken-down station wagon with a dog somewhere. I don't know. I just wasn't supposed to ask."

"It takes a lot of work to make every day the same," Will said. "That becomes the central priority every day."

Mel returned to the porch in oversized flannel plaid pants and a puffy teddy bear sweatshirt, mistaking creepy for cute, as Will had always found her inclined to do. "What's up?" she said.

Her brothers shrugged, said nothing. Kent popped a Nicorette into his mouth. Will blamed himself, should've gone straight home. He opened himself up to this, could be watching his old television commercial tapes at that moment. Instead, among gangly dead branches in the blond light on the olive-skinned concrete of Nana's back porch, Kent attempted to justify a relapse.

Seeing Mel dressed like a toddler reminded Will of his favorite game as a child, a continuum of games most often played out at Nana's, the opposite of grown-Mel dressed as a kid.

Kent had nicknamed Will "The Professor" by the time he was three, four years old. Everyone loved it, loved how much he hated it. His deep discomfort with the nickname confirmed how astutely it mocked various dimensions of his constitution, beyond his control and braided together. Will's serious tone and stately demeanor as a toddler might have been funny enough to his family even if tempered with some modesty.

But by the time he was four, five years old he intuited the only effective defensive response would be to reappropriate the nickname and embrace it. He could fall into character at any moment when cued to do so. Often he would fall into character without knowing he had. Then when someone responded to him, with rolling eyes, "Okay, professor," he'd have no choice but to smile and play along by exaggerating what had only a second before come to him so naturally. He never had much interest in learning, only the appearance of being smart. The authority interested him.

Hours each day, he formally adopted the persona and refused to break it. This was how he played. He submitted to whatever was expected of him in that time, but did so in character. If he were expected to be watching television, he watched the Three Stooges down the slope of his nose as he imagined a British gentleman might, or thoughtfully considered the plight of the Munsters. If he were expected to be playing with the neighbor children, he would sit sullen on ratty carpets until the opportunity presented itself to correct their approach to stacking blocks. Accompanying Nana grocery shopping meant an occasion for his dignified silent parade.

The ease with which he, as a toddler, could slip into a Sherlock Holmes costume, two baseball hats worn as a double-billed cap, one forward and one back, overcoat thrown over his shoulders as a cape, could not be missed, even by Ronnie. It was his first Halloween costume, Sherlock Holmes in cowboy boots. It was months before anyone could get him to take it off.

Not that he had much choice, being limited to either Kent's oversized hand-me-downs or the mothball scented thrift store outfits Ronnie brought home, but the humble workman-like nature common to the entire spread of his childhood wardrobe pleased him. Navy blue matched brown, and gray matched everything, thickness and durability the only relevant virtues. The cuts of his jackets had remained the same since he was five, six years old. The tint of his jeans faded and saturated a few times over the years, but the fit remained without variation. Simplicity, he recognized, even at eight, ten years old, gave him an authority to play-act as an adult.

He would shiver at the opinions of his peers in colorful striped sweaters. What privileges he assumed, making up statistics of baseball players he'd never heard of or specifications of remote control cars he'd never seen, all justified by his muted exterior. He would declare the exact value of comic books he could neither confirm nor deny even existed. And everyone laughed, thought him too stupid to bother hiding doing so.

As an adult, Will was sometimes still overwhelmed with the feeling of catching himself somehow playing dress-up, pretending to be an adult and a citizen, shocked everyone bought the disguise. Until, a little at a time, a beating at a time, one lump, one rip, one gash or cracked tooth at a time, he became the disguise he could never take off. He considered how he would explain all this—about the disguises—to Mel if Kent weren't around, though it was Kent he most wanted to explain this to. Mel understood.

FOR YEARS

Lit from below, Mel kept her eyes closed mostly. If she looked up, the light reflecting off the mirrored ceiling lit her face. Long time, but still she never recognized herself in the dull masks of pleasure, Sabina's fake abandon bubbling underneath all she allowed to surface, total indifference.

The bill of a baseball cap pulled down low, sitting deep in the chair. Her indifference most of all always turned them on. And she couldn't help the indifference, so, in a way, they were real, the dances.

But if she looked up, back arched for friction against his fly, any glimpse of Sabina was goofy, still couldn't not laugh if she saw herself in the mirrored ceiling. It was all a little goofy. Made her drop the front. So she couldn't look up.

If they knew she had a face, once the men determined her face okay enough to not notice, if they saw her eyes closed, they all chose to understand it as enraptured, in the throes. They read everything as heat.

Behind the mirrored ceiling panels, the cameras. She did feel safe, knowing they were there. Sometimes when it was busy and it was loud in the main room, the music thumping, you couldn't hear a thing. Always the same kind of creep brought his hands in with him. The same kind of creep always took the flattery at face value, forgot he purchased it.

Widening her eyes to the mirror the only alarm necessary, and the bouncers would enter in seconds, grab the creep by one arm each, tell him with regret, It's time to go, and, Sorry no refunds, the time had come. And the creep, always in his daze of self-satisfaction, always taken by surprise, would plead, unable to understand the fundamental fiction enabling the transaction, never able to recognize he'd done anything wrong.

So yeah, in a way the mirrored ceiling made her feel safe. She knew she was always being watched, those guys, the bouncers, whatever asshole-morons they were, they were always there, to protect her or whatever.

But in another way, more often, it kind of shook her up.

Nothing ever really happened. Maybe twice a year, maybe four times one year and then not even once the next, and of course it was nice then that those guys, the security, were there. Maybe it was only once a year and felt like more. But more often, mostly the mirrored ceiling, the camera behind the mirror, was a reminder. Looking up, she saw herself looking down on herself, Sabina hanging upside down, and it was a reminder. She didn't know of what exactly. But if she were really safe they wouldn't have even needed the mirrors, the cameras—the layer of security masqueraded as an extra layer of turn on.

And what kind of turn on needed security? She'd kept steady, unflinching, through enough twisted arms, car bumpers pressed to shins in garage-light, showing her hands and no sudden moves, one bat behind the bar and another tucked near the door, both always barely beyond her reach, safewords. She didn't want one more potential need for security. She was tapped.

The curtained rooms were each hardly bigger than a booth. The cleaning ladies had to turn the spotlights on to clean.

Some girls had gotten in trouble, resented the cameras behind the mirrors—without them they might have made a little extra money. Not an issue for Mel. For her the mirrored ceiling was another stage, the whoever in the chair, granted an audience to himself.

Those mirrors, the cameras behind the mirrors, kept her self-conscious, while it was exactly her job to appear above self-consciousness. She got a chill if she glanced up, and it was not the vents. She was used to that. It was seeing her skin made her cold. Couldn't direct herself seeing herself from the outside.

Like a bloody steak looked in a mirror and saw a dull cow in the pasture chewing cud as its reflection.

AND YEARS

You ever lay awake wanting to fuck the sleeping person next to you so bad you feel like you can't move, your whole body a pulsing halo of a toothache, and every soft turn between blankets clangs like dropping an ashtray in a marble hallway, and her breathing is so soft, constant it just wrecks your mind to realize it's always there and only at that moment has the rest of the world quieted down enough to let it emerge and so you dig your nails into your palm in the hum of the apartment, consider your dick has gone so numb from sustained suspense you can't imagine the potential for future sensation, and so you count the refractions of the streetlight between the windowpanes, wonder what might have happened if certain characters from different television shows had been placed in the same fictional universe, anything, anything except stroking her side lightly or pressing up to her back turned to you, think of anything but fucking the sleeping person next to you. And then, well, take that feeling and multiply it by itself, every night, long as you can remember and into the future without end. That was Iowa City life.

So, you go and you sit on the couch and look out over the snow and decide you'll sleep on the couch to prove some kind of point which you can just as easily excuse as no, nothing wrong, just fell asleep, and you're so sure this is your plan, but then eventually, you just want to be found, because eventually you have to admit that it just sucks to sleep on the couch, so you crawl back to bed and she's been asleep the whole time anyway and never knew and never would know anything about how you felt, what you've been through. That was how Iowa City felt for Kent.

Will excused himself from the porch to use the restroom, didn't want to hurry back. A couple steps down the hall to peek into Nana's guest room. Once his teenage bedroom, a fort built up around his helpless self-conscious reflection, Nana's remodeled guest room had the soft focus of a toilet paper commercial, the potential shine of swirling wooden furniture surfaces diffused in cotton. Will had inherited the room from Mel. She had split leaving its walls plastered in tacked up, low-contrast black-and-white photos of her friends posing in cemeteries, her vast series of thick purple color-study paintings.

The photos now on the wall proved Kent's features had grown prematurely in proportion to his head. And his head did look abnormally small in that shoulder-padded blazer, sleeves rolled up to the elbows, at a cousin's wedding. Will could trust the drift of his memories. Leaning heavy on the handlebars of her ten-speed with shelved bangs shot stiff, Mel's eyes pursed ablaze.

Will sauntered back to the porch. He had to leave home and return to really see it. Had to see it to feel it, that his family, all the people he'd ever known and everyone he'd ever met had each chosen an archetype, cliché, or stereotype to approximate. This was more than just the necessary playing of particular social roles or even the awareness of that necessity, being polite or whatever. The archetype, cliché, or stereotype was the sum of the necessary roles each person had to play and how the roles found balance between themselves within the individual. Will had to see this in his family and everyone else to recognize it in himself.

The archetype, cliché, or stereotype each person unconsciously chose set a standard of success or failure to judge one's self against, how dutifully he or she could fulfill the expectations of this archetype, cliché, or stereotype.

Mel, if Will had ever loved anyone, well, he truly always thought Mel the coolest. Mel was trapped with Gus the dreamer and Norman the small town club owner, who could never be skinny and could never really be a tough guy. Kent, the vain working stiff so proud and lost, conservative by way of fear, and toothless, scratching Ronnie and her gambling loser boyfriend Joe, living in a motel off the interstate. Dell and Nana, the haunting specters most of all, identities fixed in the memories of others, no longer able to negotiate their own subtleties of character. Will the brawler felt as exempted from all of their judgments as they each did from his. Only from the outside did experience flatten into archetype, cliché, or stereotype. Returning home, Nana's porch with his siblings, flattened Will.

He couldn't place or articulate the vacancy he experienced even within experience itself, this lack he assumed everyone else felt too. Standards, the absence of any true, fixed standard, made the archetypes, clichés, and stereotypes necessary. In a world in which God was optional, God was not an option. Socially, the bosses, the elites benefited from the imposed role-playing. A limited assortment of archetypes, clichés, and stereotypes could be kept clamped down on more easily. But Will was neither religious nor political.

He could accept the archetypes, clichés, and stereotypes as means to freedom, freedom from confusion. So many people, billions, each individuals, all cramped on small earth, all subject in various degrees to the same global culture, how subtle were the distinctions one should require of an experience or an individual to consider it or him or her unique? And why should being unique have become a meaningful prerequisite for respect? The truly irreducible was the shared experience, the suffering in common. The truly unique was the experience of the collective at an historical moment.

And if escape from the limitations of one's insufferable archetype, cliché, and stereotype was not an option, then it only made sense that most of all, more than anything, all anyone longed for was to suspend disbelief, disbelief being the default setting. Belief, as flickering of an experience as it might be, was more than anything else, a means of coping with disbelief. Everyone wanted to be absorbed, coddled even, in a fiction greater than the fiction he or she could recognize as one's self.

Will resented feeling he lived in a romance novel or a soap opera, gestures toward escape as impossible to ignore as they were to achieve, some kind of entertainment for the elite, the sensationalism of the trials of the underprivileged. But accepted the sentence he, as they each, had to serve. Getting through the archetypes, clichés, and stereotypes built character. They all had only their sentences to serve and he accepted it like Socrates or Christ accepted their sentences. Will had transformed himself, one rage at a time, scar upon scar, into a monster, a new archetype, cliché, or stereotype, sure. But he had, however, transformed himself.

He considered for a moment, how he would explain all this to Mel if Kent weren't around, though it was Kent he most wanted to explain this to.

"I really did like fighting," he said, embarrassed as soon as the words left his mouth.

Mel understood. She would tell Will everything if Kent weren't around. How she hid the pregnancy at first so she could keep dancing. How she could've had the baby if she could have kept dancing but couldn't keep dancing if she had the baby—Goddamn it, maybe she probably should've had the kid. How Norman had been squeezing her and couldn't

Will maybe do something, even just scare him, just this once?

But Kent was talking about his remortgaged subprime tax break insurance kid's sports team past glory with a snappy comeback Florida getaway I prefer a bargain or something. It was getting late. Will lit a cigarette.

WHEN MEL ATTEMPTED TO RETURN TO DANCING

Mel cut off awkward ramblings the same way she broke awkward silences. You just break them. Mel's nap that afternoon, an awkward silence, she snapped to, a surprise to find this material, her body, home; she had shared it, sublet nutrients. Ronnie had three kids, the oldest about to graduate high school when she was Mel's age. This life? Bed at dawn and up by happy hour every day, Gus's boxes of books cluttering the living room, his bike leaning in the narrow hall, its handlebars catching any dangling strap. Shouldn't have fallen asleep, sitting up on the couch with her coat on, feet planted, Gus's dirty blankets bunched under her. Always tired, shit, late for everything, all day hurried, shit. Should've known she didn't feel right, not the day to try to dance again after some months.

"Hey, sorry," she said, walking in.

Norman babbled at a couple of the girls, made-up and nodding—the girl with the pin-up style who had gone too far getting her tits done, could hardly dance anymore, and the fair-skinned serious girl who couldn't make eye contact and had a boy at home. Mel appreciated when girls got their tits done, like putting on a badge to announce their investment in the job. And Mel knew that she herself really only got along with the girls who, like her, were always just about to quit. Been a while since one of them had passed through.

Norman was telling them, he really thought he was gonna bag this babe, had a new Dark and Stormy recipe, spent the afternoon grinding down his wrists on a homemade ginger syrup for her, went out dancing, worked up a sweat, invited her back to the club and she was all over him.

The girls sneered at Mel as she entered, no response from Norman. In front of their mirrors, each with feet pointed toward the door, drafts from the vents piling down on them. Goose-bumped, Norman pinned them down with his long-winded account, shirt open to the waist, stretch marks under his arms and sweat stain in his armpits, a few long strings of hair dangling, not pulled back into his ponytail, "She was going for it and, I don't know, what the fuck..." Mel popped in, "Hey, sorry."

Norman groaned. "I don't know," looked to Mel. "Yeah, shit, what time is it?"

"You need my station?" The girl with the pin-up style offered. "I gotta make a phone call."

She and the fair-skinned serious girl who couldn't make eye contact and had a boy at home both popped up. With a glance down her nose to Mel, stepping out the door, the girl with the pin-up style said, "Gotta call my modeling agency."

"Oh forget it, shit. I'll tell you about it later," Norman said. "I don't know what the fuck, ugly bimbos."

"I don't know what happened," Mel explained. "Fell asleep after grocery shopping, dropped the bags on the table and don't remember even sitting down, was just gonna put everything away then take off, had to stop by the doctor for, you know, the follow-up exam, but fell asleep. Got there in time to bang on the door, and no one answered. I left the car double-parked out front with the hazards on to run the groceries in. Drained the battery, but my weird neighbor Terrence walked out with us, gave me a jump."

Norman nodded, not too interested. Looked to the clock, "Shit, what the fuck? You're late. You're late for Classic Shhh... night."

Mel shrugged. "That guy is so creepy," she went on. "But whatever, glad he walked by when he did."

Norman got up. "Hurry up, okay?"

"He kept saying 'Give you a jump' with this eye contact, and I was just like, 'Yes, Terrence, I need a jump.' 'I can give you a jump.' 'Okay, Terrence, I get it, my car needs a jump, my battery died.' Such a creep."

Checking himself out closely in the mirror, inspecting a zit, Norman nodded, half-listening. He swallowed a pill with a sip of water.

"He gets his rickety little car that sounds like gravel knocks around in it and he keeps staring at me silently, not even looking while he connects the jumper cables, just staring at me. Finally, I can take off and he's asking me something, saying, 'Too bad neighbors can't see more of each other.' Then every fucking light is red and then this goddamn yellow light the guy in front of me won't go through and then I'm stuck behind a school bus, what the fuck is a fucking school bus driving around this late for anyway, but lots of stops to make and then a fucking... one of those slow crawling trains comes and god, shit."

She sighed. Norman chewed on his cigar, looking at her. She shook her head. Earlier, she had truly for a moment considered—before catching herself—she did actually consider flicking her lit cigarette into a passing baby carriage on the street.

Part 4

One night, right around the beginning, Jesse did run from Wallace. When Jesse was little, he and his brother would sometimes camp in the backyard, and one night their tent collapsed in the rain and they did not know what to do so they tried to stay asleep, pretend to sleep until they believed it themselves, make it until morning lying still under the collapsed tent. That was what he felt like that night he tried to run for it. Just staying awake at all felt like fighting the weight of a collapsed tent.

His arm thrown over Jesse, pinning him, Wallace snored like a pig hiding from a storm in a clogged drainpipe. Jesse was confused. It was as long as he had been able to stay awake in a long time, probably weeks, but maybe months. He did not know how long.

Wallace's arm crushing his side, he wiggled out from under it a little bit. Wallace continued snoring, his pattern uninterrupted. A centimeter at a time Jesse crept out from under him, a millimeter at a time. He held his breath, counting six or ten snores before he would move again at all, first flexing a muscle before scooting to gradate his movements more finely still, absorb the shock. Wallace's hot breath on the back of his neck. A gargle in Wallace's throat, a complex counter-rhythm against the rise and fall of his chest.

With a deep breath, Wallace shifted his weight. Jesse snuck a few inches away in one motion. Wallace fell right back into his snore, but Jesse stayed still a good long while. Seemed like the whole night should have passed, how many times to reconsider and convince himself again before Jesse finally tilted, only his ribs then under Wallace's fingertips.

Slowly, he slid off the side of the bed slowly, balancing sideways along the bed's edge to keep his weight steady under Wallace's fingertips. On his knees next to the bed, he slowly lowered Wallace's hand slowly to the mattress, softly set it down. Wallace's fingers clenched and released, but his snoring bumped and clanged along without a clip.

Jesse lowered his palms to the carpet, felt a pull in his back. He felt weak yet alert, red-alert aware, awake inside a dream. A distinct line of light from the bottom of the door, he crawled toward it, first one knee forward. He would pause after each soft thud, one hand forward, wait.

At the door he lifted himself up on his knees, the line of light, the finish line he had aimed for finally at his knees, palms pressed flat against the door, found the knob. It creaked. Turning the knob faster, it kept creaking and pulling at it, it clicked loudly. He turned around, Wallace a dark pile on the bed. Across the room in the mirror, his own reflection was a shadow outlined by the little light coming in from under the door. Perfectly still, Wallace. His snore, a rodeo horse let loose at the demolition derby, continued.

Reaching up, Jesse clicked the lock open quickly then pulled at the door quickly, and it was his own dumb fault the door slammed shut against him and he didn't know why, because he didn't think about the chain lock so he pulled at it again three or four times, each time harder and more frustrated, and then he figured out it was the chain lock. So he jumped up quickly and slammed the door shut quickly and so he could reach the chain lock, he got on his tippy-toes and he looked over his shoulder and Wallace turning over in bed moaned a little bit, and the lock stuck so he wiggled it and he pinched his hand in the lock like a quick bite snapping, but then finally the chain slid open and he threw the door open and ran out and after just a few steps running he heard the door slam behind him and hardly able to breathe, he stopped, unsure where to run.

He was in a parking lot. There were only a few cars parked there. Most were parked by the doors of the building. The lot was surrounded by woods. Everything was lit in purple at the edges. The sun would be up soon. The trees and the cement, all the same gray. He spun out into the middle of the lot. A couple cars zipped past quickly behind the trees. He heard himself moan and whimper. He ran to the car parked furthest from the building, ducked behind it. A sign lit up said "Office," the lights off in its window. Low to the ground, his hands ankle high, he moved to the next car a few spaces away. He looked to the dark office. He looked to the woods, orange filling in the greens of purple vision.

From behind, beyond, out of nowhere, before he could move, Wallace swallowed him up into his arms. Jesse couldn't distinguish between the blurred boundaries of Wallace's growl, biting down hard on his ear, and his own crackling screams as he kicked wildly and punched wildly against Wallace's grip around his waist which, tightening in a single thrust, knocked his breath from him. Wallace carried him—gasping—easily back across the parking lot, threw him in the room through the open door.

On the ground, sitting up on one hip, a palm flat to sticky carpet, he saw Wallace's silhouette in the doorway, shutting out the sun coming up orange and purple behind him. Wallace pulled him up to his feet. He collapsed again. Wallace pulled him up and slapped him across the face with an open hand. He collapsed again, stinging. Wallace picked him up and tossed him across the room easily. He hit the far wall. By the time he hit the floor Wallace was already on top of him, his knees on Jesse's chest. Wallace punched with his fist, once on Jesse's eye at the top of his cheek, a knuckly bonk. Grabbing Jesse's hair with both hands, Wallace tried to pull him up, but his own weight on top of Jesse negated the effort. Wallace punched the wall hard and jumped up, rubbing his tiny fist in his hand.

Wallace howled. His voice cracked. Jesse didn't know who this guy was. Jesse was six years old. This guy was familiar. He had seen him in flashes over the last few days or maybe weeks. He didn't know how long he'd been with this guy, but he'd never really seen him before. The guy was familiar like he'd stepped out of a dream Jesse kept having. But in between the repeating dreams of this guy, instead of returning to his normal life, Jesse slept. He had not been awake like he was at that moment in a long time. It felt like maybe he had never been awake like that before. This familiar stranger was breaking down, turning green and purple, shouting and sobbing with snot hanging long from his nose and Jesse had no idea where he was. He did not know this room. He did not know this guy. A dark maze of pavement and woods sprawled jagged outside the door.

This man was shaking at the foot of the bed. Jesse squeezed around the corner of a desk, next to a sink. He did not breathe.

With deliberate deep breaths, slowly, Wallace finally quieted down. He lifted his shoulders and let them drop. He let out one last deep breath, sitting on the bed, his elbows on his knees, his thin hair in his hands. He approached Jesse. Swiping at his side and pulling hard at his shirt, almost tearing it off of him, Wallace pulled him out from the corner he was wedged in. Wallace scooped him up into his arms. Jesse tried to make himself heavy, plant his feet. He set his weight against Wallace, but didn't dare really fight back.

Wallace buried Jesse's face into his chest, squeezed him tightly. Wallace smelled like rank cheese covered with copious sharp cologne. They took a few slow steps together. Wallace sat down on the bed and pulled Jesse up against him. He kissed Jesse's forehead softly, hugged him tightly. Jesse didn't know what to do. He ran his fingers through Wallace's hair.

The sun up, they tilted over on the bed. Wallace fell back asleep, big in Jesse's arms.

Early in the afternoon Wallace and Jesse got into Wallace's big car and drove off. They had a mission. Jesse stayed awake all day that day. Wallace let him sit up front and told him funny stories. He told him the real reasons why the Road Runner and Wile E. Coyote chased each other and fought so much. Jesse could not repeat it, but it made sense when Wallace explained it.

Jesse laughed a lot. They stopped for burgers and ate them in their laps. Jesse liked the heat of the sunshine on him through the glass and the whistle of the wind hard against him through the bent seam at the top of the window. Hours at a time he saw nothing but trees. He never asked where they were going. Wallace never told him where they were going. Jesse played along cool, Of course we have a mission together. Of course we need to just drive all day.

They stopped at a room that night as the sun was going down. It looked like the last room they had stayed in, but with the furniture moved around to different spots. Jesse did not recognize his own clothes.

Even though it had gotten a little bit chilly outside and the pool had green slime on its top, they decided to go swimming in their underwear. They wrestled in the water. Wallace would pick him up and fall backwards to drop Jesse into the water over his head. Jesse climbed up on Wallace's shoulders from the front, his feet on Wallace's thighs, and then Wallace would throw him backwards. Wallace got out and ran around the side of the pool, bare feet slapping the slick tiles and jumped in, pulling his knees up into his arms to make a big splash on Jesse. When he got out to do it again, he slipped and fell in the pool sideways after a couple steps and they both laughed, but Wallace kept holding his elbow.

When a big woman walked up, Wallace quickly announced they were tired and it was time to head back to the room. Three kids about Jesse's age followed her, swinging towels at each other. Wallace spun Jesse away from them and pulled Jesse's shirt over his head before drying him off, pulled him by the wrist the long way around the fence while Jesse still struggled to get his shirt on.

Jesse liked restaurant food. They never had it much back at home, and he liked eating in Wallace's car. And he always liked the drives during the days. They would have fun talks. And it was also good to look out the window in silence. The car made a bumping sound and the wind and the road hissed and whistled.

At night, when Jesse could keep Wallace calm, they would fall asleep watching television, and Wallace never rubbed up against him or made him do any of the strange things that hurt, that he remembered from those days when most of the time he never knew when he was dreaming or awake. When it did happen, he would burn and ache so much the whole next day. It was almost a relief when it was actually happening. When Wallace was in the middle of pulling up against him, as much as he hated the feeling, that was the time that it hurt the least.

Jesse learned how to live his new life. He was still himself and Wallace was his friend.

Things between Jesse and Wallace were always changing. Wallace liked to imagine he was like Merlin because he was like an adoptive parent and like any parent, he imagined Jesse destined for some greatness. Jesse was The Chosen One. Like Merlin did for Arthur, Wallace needed to secret Jesse away. And though maybe Jesse did spend all day scratching and picking at himself, lost in his stories, someday they would get the big cue, from the cosmos, know it when they saw it, and Jesse would emerge into his destiny, walk right out into the glorious light of the New Jerusalem.

They'd know when the time was right. When that happened, then everyone would realize Wallace was a hero. He had the courage to see what needed doing and did it. He had the eye to recognize The One, fulfill the prophecy. He raised Jesse to be modest and with virtue. And though Jesse had not yet had occasion to test it, he would be revealed at the time of his unveiling to possess vast reserves of courage. Those years would then be redeemed. He'd been saving up his energy. Imagine, years redeemed.

Wouldn't be any need to run. Not even any need for justification at that point because everyone would be so happy. They'd all wonder how it was that Wallace saw the big picture all along. They'd hardly believe him when he explained, "Well I was just doing what I thought was right. Didn't even think about it much, really." Then it'd be clear, he was just a mechanism to serve the prophecy.

Of course he would never expect anyone to be able to

recognize this yet. But when they got that sign, whatever form it might take, and they knew, well at that point, the whole mission, the courage and patience would be clear.

Wallace would tell funny stories about what a pain in the ass Jesse could sometimes be and no one would even believe it. How Jesse's moods would flip and one second he'd be bouncing up and down giddy, then his face would drop into a straight dead expression. He'd refuse to answer direct questions with even so little as a shrug. He'd just plain flat-out pretend that he didn't even hear Wallace, the little son of a bitch.

Or how Wallace would hand him his macaroni and cheese exactly the same as it had always been, and he'd take one bite and sneer. Wallace would ask What's wrong and he'd complain he must've made it wrong, or maybe something spoiled. And Wallace would be eating the same goddamn thing in the same goddamn way it had always been, but no, this time Jesse guaranteed something had changed. Somehow it was Wallace's mistake. Jesse would complain how hungry he was, as if he couldn't put a piece of cheese on toast himself or pour himself a bowl of cereal. And finally, just to shut him up, Wallace would make him something quick and Jesse would leave it, not even touch it.

Boy, that shit got to Wallace and Jesse knew and he would just sit there scratching himself, the little shit. He knew exactly when Wallace was in a mood and he knew just how to turn it around and around, so that he could make it seem like he was trying to cheer Wallace up and then he'd spin that cheer up around at the last minute, the little prince he was, charming little bastard, yep. Always starving and needing to eat immediately or on a hunger strike and Wallace never knew which one was coming when.

Everyone would laugh then, the reporters and the authorities and general well-wishers, about how Jesse had even learned how to unplug the TV sometimes, just to make Wallace worry. Wallace would hear that silence and it'd take him just a minute before he could figure out why what was weird was weird and he'd peek in there just to see

Jesse sitting there in silence. He'd ask What's wrong. And Jesse would say "Oh nothing, just thinking." The little slob couldn't walk anything to the sink, his little piles next to the couch, well, fine.

But he couldn't shake Wallace, no. He may not have realized it, and Wallace sure couldn't see what exactly it was yet, and such a fate may be hard to believe about that sloppy bedsore-covered sloppy, little guy. He may have hardly been able to move, true. He'd been sitting still so long he struggled every step, could hardly hold himself upright. But that was just going to make his comeback—the prophecy, the emergence—that much more spectacular. The longer they remained like that, the greater Jesse would appear to be.

Wallace made an oath to himself, a solemn oath. He never had much of anything he had to think about before to do his best at. But he became a better employee at the store. He was invested in his work. He was polite to the customers. He was never too nosy with the regulars, but was always certain they knew that he knew them. He showed them dignity. He kept the store spic and span, all the merchandise on the shelves at neat, ninety-degree angles. He thought this professionalism showed and people appreciated it.

And all that he had thanks to Jesse and the discipline rearing a kid required of him. For Jesse's sake he learned discipline. He worked at plenty of those kinds of places before and he always did as little as he had to. Now he had someone depending on him, someone the world would know someday as a great one, a great one made great by his rare upbringing. Well, Wallace did have to be in tip-top shape for that, now didn't he? He was just waiting for that sign. They were both going to know the sign soon as they saw it.

Nine years he and Jesse had been together. Wallace thought Jesse was probably fifteen. Third time Jesse thought he was turning thirteen. Might have seemed like they were in a rut, but Wallace thought that just happens to any two people been together so long.

McRaskin the cop and some of Wallace's co-workers, they joked with him. Of course they all thought he, Terrence, lived alone. They didn't know he had his secret, his secret that made it all meaningful. They tried to get him to go out with them, drink and party, probably thought he was a prude or a teetotaler. Not saying sometimes he didn't think about it, might be nice to make another friend somewhere, somehow. But he knew that was just not a possibility and it didn't bother him, knowing like he did that a man's life was private, his meaning was at home and no one else needed to know what any of that was about.

And sure, he could see how maybe some aspects of his life at home might have been construed as leaning toward the dishonest side. But he never lied to Jesse about the world. Maybe he'd exaggerated some, but he hadn't told him anything that wasn't exactly true as the world was, brutal, cruel beyond belief. His views were not extreme except in that he was honest and it was the world that was extreme, Babylon was extreme. The chaos was extreme, extreme enough that he saw no problem understanding one man's medicine was another man's preventative medicine, vitamins.

Other kids that had to go out there, live in the overcrowded anarchy, they needed their ADHD drugs. Why wouldn't Jesse need his benzos? Wallace may have been Terrence at the store and Wallace at home, but those two faces weren't any more deceiving than what any other man showed himself to be at work compared to how his family knew him. Seemed to him he was more honest than anyone, keeping his identities clearly defined like that.

A dishonest man, a less virtuous man wouldn't have been able to keep Terrence straight as Wallace had. A less virtuous man would've given in to Terrence, given in to the fear, and panicked to save himself, do whatever was necessary to hold on to some imaginary unified version of himself. Terrence would've harmed Jesse bad, hidden the evidence. But Wallace took responsibility for his actions and adopted Jesse as his own. Wallace never said he was perfect. But he tried to be. And wasn't that the absolute best any man could do?

Circumstances, events Wallace couldn't understand at the time they were happening, determined that he would dedicate his life to the welfare of another. He was a nurse. Even as a boy, while the other boys were snatching up frogs to have contests—who could throw a frog against a tree with enough force to make it explode—Wallace was nursing sick birds, squirrels. And by the very same charges some would call what he'd done abuse, he would defend himself only by saying he took care of weak things, sick things.

He may have been Terrence at work overnight, but he was fucking Merlin at home. Who could say? The story had always been told from Arthur's perspective, but maybe when Merlin disappeared from Arthur for long periods of time, maybe he was just at his day job. And no reason, like Wallace, Merlin couldn't have maybe worked third shift.

Not that Wallace expected the Archangel Michael to appear to him. He didn't expect to walk up on a burning bush one day. But he never expected that when he finally got the sign, recognized the sign as the sign and its message unmistakably apparent, he never expected its obvious and decisive message to tell him there is no message. Nothing else it possibly could've meant, so many days all exactly the same. The sign could only mean no sign, no emergence, no message.

After they had spent a few days in a cabin, Jesse finally asked Wallace about his family. They no longer drove every day. Every afternoon they would walk around in thick woods, far in every direction, without seeing anything any different than anything else. Trees and trees fallen over on each other or trees cracked open with green growing all over them or sometimes, fuzzy white. After every long walk Jesse would be surprised to end up back at that same cabin.

After a few days in that same dirty place—sleeping on scratchy blankets on the wood floor, Jesse beginning for the first time to be itchy all the time, they carried heavy buckets of stinky egg water a long way and had to work hard not to spill it and the electricity came from a small box and only lasted a little bit of time—Jesse asked about his family.

Wallace told him he had bad news. His family had all been hurt. But that was a long time ago and Jesse was very lucky because now he had Wallace to take care of him, his family had loved him very much and asked Wallace to take care of him because they wanted the best for him. Wallace said the accident was so bad Jesse couldn't even remember it.

Jesse looked at his blond hair in the mirror. Wallace said from then on he would call him Jesse and if anyone ever asked, that was his name.

Wallace couldn't say what it was, you know, what happened, what went wrong with him. He did always feel out of place in the world, even while somehow knowing and believing deeply that he alone had it all figured out. No one else really got it. He had some girlfriends as a kid. He hung around with a lot of people, had friends, Strawberry Meat. None of them really understood Wallace, but he didn't know if any of them ever realized that. He understood all of them just fine. He understood everything. And he got a joy from all of it, the espionage of being a teenager.

He provoked very little. But he could always keep up with the foolishness, the stunts, and usually he was seeing three, four steps ahead of what the other kids were up to, even when they themselves didn't really know what they were up to. Most fun to keep quiet about it, he figured that out early on. No one wanted him to ruin their good times decoding their heartbreaks, their pacts of allegiance or vengeance.

It was all pretty simple for him, really. Just as happy to be around his friends or not, he was fine. He could drink a lot more than most of the other boys. He could smoke some weed, eat some mushrooms before school and get through the day just fine without no one noticing a thing.

His body did always hang strangely. He was just a boy still, very young, when he first started thinking about his breath consciously, thinking about how he'd be taking in the whole outside world all the time, filtering it through himself before blowing it back out and how everyone, each individual was just a filter of sorts, all feeding each other. And there wasn't any way he could ever figure that no one was any better or worse than anyone else. Everyone had a value and everyone had something to contribute to the world. It was all just politics, what banded people together against any other people. Politics was just a sport, and he never did much go for competition. Just wasn't in his nature. He kept quiet, watched whatever he watched get set in motion go into motion. That was his conscious contribution, not interfering, not spoiling things for everyone else around him, everyone in awe of the spin of their own machines, which they never realized they themselves set spinning.

He tried out quite a few things really, at the Louisville library downtown, Pushkin, Kafka, *The Upanishads*. He went through some time, a summer, as a ping pong champion, having never picked up a paddle until the day he did and then he didn't put that paddle down until the end of that summer, having taken up residency in a neighbor's garage and beaten every taker in town. When school started he never did pick up a paddle again. It was just a way of breathing for him, a zone he could enter.

He knew it was the nature of the harmonica that everyone who picked one up and blew into it for the first time thought, Shit, I'm a harmonica-genius and I never knew it. That's why he put down the harmonica and started playing a three-note wooden flute he found. He'd sit in the front stairwell of this office building downtown that left its door unlocked. Of course that first day, all the office workers—dental technicians, and even the collection agency brutes who spent their entire days hiding behind fake names and barking at poor, suffering strangers over the phone, that first time he walked in there and sat down on the third or fourth step and started blowing, playing along to himself with the reverb quality and resonance off the glass and the hard steps—they all took turns coming out to the top of the stairs and listening. But no one ever said "Stop" or "Go on from here. Scram." So he would sit there and blow for them all day.

Nights around that time, he'd concentrate on spending half an hour to turn a doorknob, a meditation technique he'd heard made you aware of every muscle and how when one muscle clenched, another had to stretch in response. It was all breathing to him. It'd drive Pa just nuts to walk up on him, concentrating on moving as slowly as he could. Pa would be just getting off work, a long day of tarring some rich Jew's driveway, Pa probably thought blacktop was an international Jewish conspiracy invented only to taunt him. And he'd be beat and hungry and he just didn't have the time to find Wallace, standing in the doorway of his bedroom, concentrating on moving as slowly as he could, "letting his gaze drift," as the books called it. And Pa would start hollering and Wallace would just be still and not fight his yelling, but just let it drift through and accept it. He'd try to give him quick headshakes or whisper, "Go on, Pa, I'll catch up with you later." But Pa would keep screaming, "What the fuck, you've lost your mind?" Pa always thought Wallace was sad when he was quiet, and sadness disappointed Pa. He got angry when Wallace would walk home early from a party.

But of course, all this, the flutes and ping pong, slow-motion door opening technique and running around with the boys, keeping quiet, all those different ways of breathing, all that was all just copying. He was just doing his best to figure out how to be, play dumb and play along, studying everyone he ever met, this is when the head tilts, this is how to speak with one's hands.

That was just who he was. He didn't know how to dress except what he thought was funny because it might upset someone, contradicting accepted style in subtle ways. Only trouble he ever got in at school was for lying down in the doorway during classes changing, making people step over him. Nothing he thought was funnier than bothering people, even the people he liked, but even his modes of rebellion were basically passive. He could understand it was all copying, all everyone did, and he could understand that was how a boy needed to be, to an extent, copying.

But Jesse, besides his TV, he had only Wallace to copy. Wallace figured the TV, the classic reruns channel, that was a lot of possible characters to copy, to learn from how to be.

Jesse was walking to school when Wallace approached. It was sunny and he was walking alone. His brother and sister were not around. He did not remember why. Maybe he was late or maybe they were both sick. He only remembered he was alone.

Wallace pulled up to him and said there had been an accident and your mother has sent me to get you. This was in northern California, near Oregon, where they both lived then. School was not far from his house, but there was not much around.

Jesse was walking along the side of the road. It curved around through a short bit of woods. They were a block from the gas station where he always saw Wallace sitting in the mornings when he walked to school. They had never talked but the man seemed friendly, or at least he seemed familiar.

Jesse did not know that Wallace even knew his parents, but he was so worried and shocked about what Wallace said, about some kind of accident, so he got in the back seat and Wallace drove really fast and kept talking really fast and he drove really fast for a long time and Jesse was really worried and confused but Wallace just kept making him more confused, talking about this accident and Jesse did not know where they were or what this guy was talking about. And the further they got, the guy kept saying, "Almost there," and then they stopped to eat hamburgers they unwrapped from paper and that was the last thing Jesse remembered, unwrapping the hamburger, and then he must have fallen asleep for a long time.

He woke up sometimes, always in different rooms he never recognized. A long time, he was confused. He did not know how long it was. He never knew where he was or what was going on. He would wake up sometimes and be so groggy.

Sometimes he thought he was back in his bed or at the school nurse. Sometimes the road would zip by. He would sleep across the backseat. Wallace's car was as big as a boat and it shook like a big boat and was as loud as a boat in a storm.

Wallace cut Jesse's hair at a picnic table. He washed Jesse's hair in a bathtub with burning shampoo. Jesse's hair turned orange. They did it again and Jesse's hair turned yellow like Wallace's. They never woke up in the same room twice. The rooms were always almost the same but never exactly, always a small room. The bed and the bathroom and the sink and the television set would always be moved around. They would walk out the front door, a couple steps to the car.

At night Wallace would breathe heavy and hold Jesse tightly against him and Jesse would feel like he was choking and his stomach was being torn open like he was going to be sick, and he would pretend to sleep but he was scratchy all over, and it burned everywhere Wallace touched him, and the burning would wrap around him and he would imagine screaming but then, more importantly, so Wallace would think he was asleep, he would imagine swallowing the scream and the scream would go deeper and deeper down into his belly. And the more Wallace scratched against him, the more it burned everywhere, like flames were coming up all around him and the higher the flames got it did not matter, because he could bury the scream that much deeper.

A lot of the time he would fight to stay awake. But those times, those times when Wallace would wake him up and try to keep him awake, he would fight the feeling he might never sleep again.

And Wallace had regrets about some stuff, things he should've stood up about when it was time and he didn't, because he was just a copycat. He always did feel awful for Strawberry Meat. Wallace was standing right there freshman year in the locker room shower when he saw Strawberry Meat get that regretful boner. He saw it there right before his eyes and he thought, Thank God it ain't me, and he hoped he wouldn't ever have a boner he'd have to regret like he knew Strawberry Meat must be regretting that one. The body's just got a mind of its own. And he tried helping Strawberry Meat out when the other boys surrounded him and began to start at him all mean. Wallace tried saying, "Come on," and to some of those boys who were his friends even, he tried saying, "Now, let's all just cool it, here."

But that wasn't going to happen, and Strawberry Meat looked at Wallace and he knew the beating he had coming, just as inevitable as that swollen little prick of his standing right up of its own accord. Wallace stepped back and let it happen, blood on the tiles, washed down the drain.

Strawberry Meat transferred schools after slogging through that whole rest of the year, spat on, failing classes when he could no longer muster the spirit to pick his books up one more time after so many people tumbled them from his arms. And they just didn't see each other after that, Wallace and Strawberry Meat. But Wallace never did bite into a strawberry again without some regretful feelings.

He did always like to smoke some weed and he'd gobble up some mushrooms and it got to a point where he didn't know how, he was watching some public access television shows about the rapture and the Holy Land and Nostradamus and yeah, Wallace was a seventeen-year-old holy man.

All he really wanted to do was, he meant to explain—how, yes, he did nab Jesse and they did each end up with a whole new life together, Jesse and him—but there wasn't nothing in his life as he ever knew it, or that anyone who ever knew him, or even someone he didn't know, some outsider who looked at his life could ever point to, to mean they saw that coming. He just wasn't ready to be tired yet, but he got tired.

He had what some of those people, once more prone to loving him, called "a restless spirit." And he was "a creative type," not in any kind of way in which he did the same thing and got better at it, but just as a way of approaching everything, whatever he approached. But what it took to pay the bills, when making money wasn't what interested you and work was something you'd resigned to doing just enough of to get the bills paid, well, it did take over your life. Work made you over in its own image. You get tired. And he just got tired was all and tired wasn't a way he knew how to be.

So yes, he did intend to explain grabbing Jesse and all he meant to say about it was, well, he did what he thought he had to do, and then after he did it, he just kept doing the next thing he felt necessary to keep up with what he'd already done. He needed some variation of a lightning bolt to strike him, some burning bush. And he loved making plans. Always did surprise him, the plans he made, like dares to himself, You really gonna? You got the nerve? When it came time to execute those plans, he was still just trying to surprise himself even when seeing a plan through.

But this trouble, this Jesse situation he suddenly had, was a whole nother kind of trouble than he'd ever seen before. The Book of Chronicles says "God allows trouble, but is always in control." But this, this wasn't sneaking off and leaving his date sitting at a restaurant when he got bored, or walking out of work and pushing the dumpster over to block the door and trap all the customers inside. This wasn't peeing his pants on a dare or shimmying up the window well to the roof of the grammar school, jumping off and grabbing the flag's line mid-flight to carry him to the ground gracefully, rope burn leaving him unable to grip for weeks, or deciding, Shit, maybe he was a gay after all and that's why he hadn't never felt at home nowhere, the dare of the first sweaty penis he ever tasted. He bet it all on Jesse. And he did mean to explain.

But before he could do that, he just needed to get through some things he needed to get through. It's okay, he'd figured out finally, to stay angry. Not that he thought of those things so much any more, those things that made him angry and that he wanted to forget and got more angry about because they wouldn't let him forget, but he remembered sometimes the things themselves and he did get angry. But that was okay. And he was gonna go on and show the world, shit, he didn't know. He had nothing but fronts, from every angle fronts. And from fronts, what?

He never knew what it was, or anything that he would do with Jesse, no plan. He didn't know. It felt right at the time. But then it ended up, he's taking care of Jesse.

He had gotten to some point back in Northern California, he trusted it would pass, but it was lingering, this point where he didn't know exactly. It was simple and he could deal with it simply, but he didn't know really how to take care of himself. That happens. He never felt hurried or too concerned. He'd moved and then moved again. Sometimes a couple teenagers might crash with him for a while. But it had gotten to maybe be a couple years since he'd really had any kind of contact, anything meaningful, with anyone. And he'd always spent a lot of time on his own, so that in itself, it wasn't enough that it occurred to him to worry. No one knew his name. It was okay.

All he meant was Jesse had a good time with him while they were traveling, and sure Jesse was mourning his family and all, but Wallace thought for a boy the age Jesse was then, if they kept up enough of an adventure, Jesse would be able to not think about it too much. So they kept on the move. He gave Jesse some of the medications he was on and it kept Jesse cool just like it kept him cool, benzos, bennys. They were on a road trip any boy would love, and Wallace thought Jesse felt Wallace was just like some camp counselor he used to have, and sure, Wallace thought Jesse did find his body gross, as he himself had also come to find it. But that was okay with him. He told Jesse they'd both call him Wallace.

Jesse slept best to a game of Mario Brothers on pause, the looping song better than sleeping to a TV story, no dynamics, no risk of sudden bangs, the melody repeating enough so that he lost all sense of where it began or ended. He would drift in and out of sleep while his stories were on, roll over for a minute to turn on the game, pause it, and fall back asleep.

Quiet made him nervous. Unplugging the TV revealed

all the sounds outside, the beasts of land and sea and the dragon sitting on its throne with eyes of fire. Always there, tiny grinding and moans he could not hear with the TV on. Figured that out one time when his room had gone dark all at once. The TV and everything else, the ankle high nightlight and the microwave clock went off. Rain beat against the shaking windows.

Wallace came home that night soaking wet, his keys clicking and knocking, stood dripping in the doorway a minute before whispering, worried, "Jesse? Jesse, you okay?"

He always sounded worried about something, poor Wallace. But that night walking in really scared him, walking in, no glow from the screen, no sound. The nightlight had come back on and the microwave clock blinked 12:00, over and over, 12:00, like all time had stopped and the TV's broadcast had not returned. Jesse had not fussed with it. He did not try to turn it back on because he did not know that it could turn off. No idea what to do with his blank vision, the silence, he sat in constant anticipation of the first blow of the seven trumpets.

Wallace peeled his wet boots from his wet socks, left a damp path to the bathroom to dry his hair. A towel hung around his neck. He turned the TV on. Jesse saw how he did it. With Wallace's modifications to the switch so that it could not be turned off, he had to unplug the TV and plug it back in. Jesse saw this and remembered it.

Leaving for work the next afternoon, the door closing and keys rattling, the locks clicking out their little theme song, Wallace woke Jesse. Jesse suspected he had maybe dreamed that quiet, the experience of quiet, did not remember the TV ever having really been off. But the potential for quiet distracted him for a couple days.

First Jesse just pulled the plug. Shut the TV off for a minute. After a few experiments with this, when Wallace left for work late in the afternoon, he would turn the TV off, be sure to have it back on by morning, when Wallace came home. Jesse still could not sleep in quiet. And by the time Wallace would get home, Jesse would be so wound up from the quiet, always thinking he heard the lamb with a sword on horseback about to come cracking through the clouds any second, he would have to pretend to sleep to avoid having to explain his mood to Wallace.

During the day, when Wallace slept, the sounds outside were louder. Wallace snoring, Jesse would unplug the TV for a second to listen. That was when he realized that there was not anything strange going on at night. It was always going on, but the TV covered the sound. And during the day it was not really louder sounds, just more of them.

He could never sleep with all that racket outside. It scared him real bad, warfare and earthquakes toeing up to the window. He did not know what was making all that noise. Warbling, constant moaning like a whistle with a scrape to it, and the whistle and scrape would rise and fall over and over, hissing.

The quiet got him so wound up Jesse did not sleep for a couple days. But that was not such a big deal, really. It happened anyway, sometimes. He would sleep for a couple days straight and then he would not sleep for a long time. No big deal.

This feeling Jesse got sometimes, he did not know what it was or how to describe it, but when it hit him he always knew it as that same feeling. It made him unhappy and it also felt good. It was familiar and that was what it mostly felt like. That was what made it strange and how he recognized it. He felt happy to be unhappy. All of the days that ever felt like that felt like a different life. A day feeling like that just started up where the last day that felt like that left off, like none of the days in between had ever happened.

Oddly, he felt a little bit stronger on those days than he usually did, needed to kick back at something. But he did not know what to do with that strength. He felt it coming up in him and it made him uncomfortable. Days like that he would unplug the television when Wallace left, listen to the soft groan of the outside. See how long he could stand it.

Eventually he got bored by the quiet, the charge it pulsed through him. Not bored, but the suspense became less interesting than the stories. And it was too tiring to always feel that charge. So he would forget for long periods of time that he even knew how to unplug the TV.

Wallace always told him how bad things were out there in Babylon, how dangerous it was. They had special secret food set aside, if Wallace ever did not come home from work. Wallace always worried about that. He told Jesse things were so bad that of course it was dangerous to go to work, and if anything ever happened and Wallace did not come home from work then Jesse should go into where the secret food was, do not let anyone into the apartment.

That might have been the first time, unplugging the TV, the first thing Jesse ever learned to just not tell Wallace about.

Wallace walked out in a fluster. That was the word he always used that Jesse came to recognize as that way Wallace always was. Usually he came home in a fluster. He always came in from work smiling, "Hello, Jesse." But it would be only a couple minutes before he would be slamming cans down or smearing a burrito all over the counter and cursing the microwave. "It's still fucking frozen in the middle!" He would usually quiet down quickly and explain, "Oh, I'm just in a fluster."

But that day he left in a fluster. He said something about it was his birthday or something. He would be back before work with ribs. In a hurry for something, he forgot to lock his room behind him. Jesse did not move. That bright crack of Wallace's open door was in the corner of his eye, behind the TV.

The Three Stooges ending, *Green Acres* starting meant it was about the time Wallace would usually leave for work if he said he had to go somewhere first. But that meant he was not in a hurry. He might stop back in at any moment if he realized he forgot to lock the door to his room.

Flustered as Wallace may have seemed, they were polite with each other, a tenuous peace. Wallace paused at the door before stepping out, gave Jesse a look. Jesse sighed before melodiously saying, "*Darling, I love you but give me Park Avenue.*"

Wallace nodded and smiled before stepping out. The first couple locks clicked, and then a pause. The same locks clicked and Wallace popped his head back in, "Until I get back, there's macaroni in the refrigerator."

Jesse could not hear him over the TV. Wallace walked out. Bothered and needing to think, Jesse considered unplugging the TV, maybe he felt restless in that way, wanted to summon that feeling, creepy quiet. But it was not worth the ache of bending and pulling. He heard Wallace say something again, could not understand. Jesse called out, "What?"

He heard Wallace talking, but the locks did not click. Annoyed, he did not want to get up. What was Wallace doing? He called out again, "Wallace, what?"

Jesse struggled to stand and walked over to the door to hear what Wallace was trying to tell him. It was strange for the clicks to not happen exactly the same as they always did. He heard Wallace through the door. Wallace said, "Oh, no, no one, talking to myself. Living alone too long, I guess. Can't stand the quiet."

A woman said, "Come on, let's go. Nice to see you, we're late."

The locks did not click. Jesse, weak up on his tiptoes, looked out the peephole and could see only Wallace's forehead. Wallace stood, head turned, his chest flat up against the door.

A man said, "Okay. Glad to hear everything's okay, but I'd swear, Terrence, sure sounded like a real heated argument. You sure you don't have any lady troubles?"

Wallace laughed. "Oh, me? I wish I had a lady to have troubles with, but, you know, no time."

Losing his balance, Jesse stumbled a little bit, knocked

and rattled lightly against the door. Wallace turned, looked directly at him, convex through the peephole. A pause in the hallway conversation, Wallace knocked clumsily against the door, mimicking the sound of Jesse's light tumble. The first lock clicked locked, a long pause before the second one.

The woman said louder, "We have to get to the cemetery. Everyone's waiting. You got my keys. Let's go."

"Okay, yeah, I'm coming," the man said. "But, Terrence, sorry we got to run. I forgot my work keys at work, just grabbing hers."

Wallace nodded, clicked the third lock into place.

"Why don't you come on by the club sometime," the man continued. "It's not my thing, but I guess a lot of lonely young men like yourself seem to like it."

One at a time, Wallace clicked the locks locked. Leaning against the door, Jesse counted the locking pattern out, but lost track of its usual melody, Wallace doing it so much slower than normal. Another one, or maybe he was unlocking the first ones to come back in. Maybe he realized he had left his room unlocked.

"Find you a nice young woman to argue with," the man in the hallway said.

"Oh, well," Wallace said with a forced chuckle, "I don't have much money to spend on partying. I don't really party."

"Spend it all on electric bills, I bet," the man said. "Keeping that TV on all day and night."

Wallace laughed. He stepped away from the door and Jesse could see the other man through the peephole. This man did not look scary, talked about a fun visit to a place. He did not appear worried about going outside, the ten-horned beast or war, no itchiness. It was like he had The Freedom.

The man said, "Come on, I'll walk out with you."

The last lock clicked. Wallace's keys scraped against the door. He said okay.

"I'll make you a mean steak. Plenty of people say they come for the food as much as the girls."

Jesse pressed his face to the door. Did the man mean a restaurant?

"Oh, I don't really have the money to eat supper out," Wallace said.

"Got yourself some tight security there," the man responded.

Wallace turned, stepped back to the door. That wasn't the last lock. One more clicked.

Jesse waited a good long time. He tried to watch his story, but that crack of light out of the side of his vision, Wallace's open door, oh man. He had never been in Wallace's room before without Wallace around. Wallace never told him not to. He had stood in the doorway and talked to Wallace while Wallace was in there. He did not think it was a big deal for him to see it or not. But he had just never really looked around in Wallace's room before. It was always locked, always.

Jesse got up, got some nacho chips and returned to the couch. Sitting up straight, he cracked away at them in a pattern like a drummer. That cracking got louder and louder, and soon he realized he was hardly even watching his story. He had not paid attention to a word anyone said. He watched the *Green Acres* people move around and then it was *Family Ties* and sometimes he could hear the laughing while he cracked away at those chips. But honestly he did not know what anyone laughed about. He watched the story-people all walk around. He always liked the *Family Ties* story because it was a little bit like how his family used to be—mom, dad, brothers and sisters. But that would have made him the little girl and that did not make any sense.

But that day Jesse watched the *Family Ties* story-people walk around their own couple rooms and he did not hear a word any one of them said to another. All he heard was that cracking of those nacho chips in his own head, staring at Wallace's door.

Finally he made a handful of the shake at the bottom of the bag and filled his mouth with that spicy mush and the cracking stopped, all at once like that, but he did not even care to sit and watch what happened on the story. They had all been moving along to his chewing and once that snapping stopped, he could hear them, but he did not get it. He had missed too much for any of it to really make any sense. He sat up straight and smoked a cigarette.

He was thirsty, but instead of going to the sink he thought maybe he would have to pee soon enough anyway, so he would just go to the bathroom and then he could get a drink in there and he would not need to get up again in a little bit. He walked right past Wallace's cracked door. He walked straight into the bathroom without even turning to peek. He cupped his hand under the faucet and drank some water before trying to pee, so that his hands would be clean enough to drink from. He liked the taste of the water from that sink more than the water from the kitchen sink anyway. He could not really pee, but he stood there and thought maybe if he stood long enough, he could. Finally he felt okay, knowing that he would not have to pee for a little while still, so he would be able to relax again once he sat back down.

Walking back to the couch, he peeked into Wallace's room. He could not help it. He walked right past it. He listened for the front door. He could not really see anything in there. Both of their rooms had the same continuous carpet. Wallace said it was "beige," and Jesse always remembered that word because he never knew if that meant how thick it was or how soft it was or just the way that it would stain easily. Even though Wallace insisted on him drinking his Kool-Aid medicine twice a day, every time he would say, "Be careful, sit still when you drink it," and he had to be careful because the carpet was "beige."

The carpet looked much brighter in Wallace's room. Jesse had to crack the door open a little bit wider to make sure it was really the same carpet. He did not move his feet. But he stuck his head in the door. It was like all the light in that room came up from the carpet. He could see dust floating around in the light from the window.

The kitchen was always piled up with empty boxes of cereal or mac and cheese and frozen pizza cardboard, bottles and cans. Their living room, his room, was crowded with piles of video games on the table and blankets. He always had to shake the video game controller out from blankets. But Wallace's room did not have much of anything in it. His room looked like it was mostly just light.

Wallace had left almost two whole stories ago, but he still might come home at any moment. Jesse took one step in. He would still hear the door. Around the corner, clothes were piled on the floor. There was a bronze lamp and a plastic clock radio on the small table next to his bed. Wallace's bed had a pile of old blankets on it that had all faded into the same color. They were all fallen apart and shredded up together into a thick web. A short tower of videotapes all had numbers written on the labels.

Lots of magazines stacked on one side of his room, some were old and wrinkled and turning yellow. Jesse crossed the room. *Extreme Prejudice, Reason, Militia Monthly.* There were new ones too. It was so quiet in there.

Sunshine poured in through the window. The yellow curtain was mostly pulled closed but the sunshine was bright, a lot brighter than it ever got in his room, the living room. The window in Jesse's room was bigger, but Wallace had taped it up with cardboard when they first moved in there years ago. The curtain hanging over each of their windows matched.

Jesse ran back to his couch and covered himself up quick. Maybe it was a bang on the TV.

He could not really see the window in his room. The TV was below it, in front of it. When he looked up past the TV set to the window, the rectangle glow of the TV followed his eyes. Even on blank walls he could only see a glowing rectangle a lot of the time.

Wallace's room was so still. The few things in there, everything seemed sharp in that light. Jesse's room, the living room, lit only by the TV, was the same half-light all day and all night, every day. Even with the same curtains pulled mostly closed, Wallace's room was a different world, a shining afternoon.

Still on his couch, he decided to destroy Wallace's room. He would kick the magazines over, rip the tapes from their shells, smash holes in the wall with the lamp. *I Love Lucy* started. She never meant Desi any of the trouble she caused him.

The front door, all its locks locked. The door to Wallace's room, Jesse had left it cracked open wider than Wallace had left it. Wallace would not know the difference if he never meant to leave it open in the first place. But if Jesse closed it, maybe he could play dumb to ever noticing it was left open.

This time it was easy. He walked right in there. It was so quiet. And sure, he sometimes got nervous in quiet. But he figured it was only the quiet itself that made him nervous, all the moaning and groaning of the beasts of land and the beasts of sea, that ruckus was always there with or without the quiet, always, like his itchiness hidden under the stories, so the quiet lost its power to make him nervous.

He considered where to begin the destruction, tear down the curtains, knock over the stacks of videotapes, rip up the magazines, swing the lamp and smash a hole in the wall. In the middle of the room, in sunlight, he spun.

But really, ugh, Jesse was just so achy, all that walking around the apartment since Wallace had left. The adventure was exhausting him before it really even had a chance to begin. So tired and he was really not even angry with Wallace. He knew he was lucky to have Wallace. The way Wallace always came home in a fluster, he knew the end times and Babylon really must be as bad as Wallace always said. Jesse knew he was lucky. And tearing things apart, magazines, videotapes, throwing things, so much work.

He picked up some pants that were thick and green and heavy. At one point, he did have jeans and stuff like the story-people wore. But it had been a long time since he had had any clothes but pajamas and a few big t-shirts.

After that string of hotels when they first got together, Wallace took Jesse, stayed at a cabin he knew his old friend

Matty's brother kept but never went to. Matty's brother had blown his hand off a little below the elbow. Got himself a colostomy bag, hammering closed the end of a pipe he'd stuffed hundreds of match-heads into. Between keeping that bag clean and the work around the cabin with only one hand, Matty's brother never did go up to his cabin anymore. But broke his heart too much to think about selling it or giving it up.

So Wallace knew that old place was always sitting empty. And out there on the road, driving circles on the state highways, never being sure exactly what made sense, certain he was being looked at in the grocery store of an old logging town in Oregon, always raining and even if it wasn't, Wallace remembered it like it was, always muddy. He kept them on the move until Jesse one day told him about a trip with his camp counselor and he remembered Matty's brother's cabin.

It was a good time they had there, like camping. And it gave Wallace time to figure out what they were doing, make a plan. Spent a month cooking in that old wood stove, sleeping on the floor wrapped up in thick old Indian blankets. In town, Wallace loaded up on canned beans and hot dogs, canned chicken, butter crackers. They got cold water from the creek in buckets. He killed some squirrels, but they were no good without any seasoning, even if they were a warm meal.

Raccoon meat, Matty's brother always gushed about raccoon meat, but Wallace didn't know. He shot one. Those buggers were dirty, scary even when dead, like they're about to pop up awake and hiss at you. Jesse helped him carry it back. Jesse grabbed it by the back legs and Wallace had the front, its little snout dangling just under his balls and Wallace kept thinking this little vampire raccoon was gonna come to and slash and mangle his manhood and he deserved it. Its dead top lips fell and its ugly little fangs were twinkling up at him. Jesse had to drop it every few steps and grab it again. Made Wallace itch just to carry the dead little beast, same size as Jesse. It was cold out and neither of them had gloves. They got it to the side of the cabin on the small cement patio with a drain and dropped it. But it was so cold Wallace could hardly hold on to the dull knife.

He found one ripped-up gardening glove in the toolshed. He wondered if Matty's brother really got rid of the other glove, now that he only had one hand. Seemed like more effort than it'd been worth and he couldn't even imagine how to put one glove on if you don't have a second hand to pull it on. And he could swear it was the left hand Matty's brother lost. Made sense, right-handed meant: swing a hammer with his right hand meant: the left hand was holding down that pipe when it went off. But there was only the left glove there.

So maybe he wasn't wanting to have to get into slicing up that raccoon. It was the same size as Jesse. From the shed he peeked out over to that small patio with the drain where Jesse was standing, and the raccoon was lying there on its side, its goddamn eyes still open while Jesse leaned his nose up closely to the raccoon's face to look at it closely. But he could tell by the way Jesse was leaning in, keeping all his weight turned back from the raccoon, that he was ready to leap away at any moment. He stood there in that shed flopping that one left-handed glove. Guess Matty's brother may have taken the one hand he needed and left this one behind.

He told Jesse, "Now go inside," and "I'm gonna take care of this."

Jesse had helped him with the squirrels. They were no bigger than birds and Wallace was sure the boy had seen his mom prepare a chicken before. But this raccoon, Jesse's size, laid out there, he didn't want Jesse to see this.

But Jesse kept insisting, "What are you gonna do, Wallace? How come I can't stay around and watch and see what you do and how you do it?"

And Wallace kept explaining, "It's just like the squirrels, what I gotta do—it's nothing much to see."

And so Jesse said, "Well then, that's no reason."

And Wallace said "Well, that's plenty reason. You got a lot of other things you can be curious about. You don't need the repetition of something what you already know."

But Jesse insisted, and that little dead raccoon's legs were just pulling in toward each other, contracting stiff quickly, so

Wallace said, "Fine."

They spread it out. Wallace stepped on its two legs, its left side, and pinned them down under his feet. Jesse had to spread his arms wide and really use all his strength to keep those two right legs pinned. Jesse's head was down, his hair dangling just over the raccoon's belly. With its legs pinned, the raccoon's belly popped up like a balloon and looked like it was just about to pop if Wallace had a needle to poke it with. But that dull knife was so dull he couldn't get it to puncture. So he couldn't slice it open.

Jesse began panting, resetting his weight to hold it down. Even dead, that raccoon's leg muscles were strong enough to make Jesse work. But its wiry hair was enough to keep that dull knife from cutting. So Wallace was pulling a long line across its bottom and nothing. So he pressed down harder and retraced the pull of that long line and nothing. He reset his feet so he was standing over it in a way that could get all his weight down on it, and as he lifted his foot its little foot would pop up and he had to nudge it back down with the side of his foot, then stomp on it hard so he could push his whole body weight down on it.

But that sort of approach and posture meant he lost some of the subtlety of his cut. So even with all his strength, all he could do was carve away at it in short strokes. But he knew that was not the way to cut through the meat, get all that blood running all over and getting into the meat. But even those short careful strokes that he could really lean into weren't doing anything.

So, finally frustrated, he put both his hands around that knife and pulled his hands up high over his head all the way back as far as he could reach, like Abraham over Isaac, and he saw that raccoon's belly all inflated there and he brought his hands down with all the force he could, right into the peak of its belly, and just like popping a ball, a basketball more than a beachball, because he could feel the thickness it had to pierce. But his hands followed through with the stroke and pushed on way down deep into its belly, and his hands were so cold he could hardly grip anything, and he only had the one glove on anyway and that dull knife made a little piercing, but really it was his hands that pushed on through into the raccoon's guts and so his hands were suddenly no longer stiff from the cold against the metal, but were warm and wet and slick with blood as its intestines bubbled out and Jesse let go and jumped up away from the gushing-up innards. And him getting up let the weight of the whole raccoon slip, and made Wallace's hands go on up into its sides and he felt its ribs from the inside, from behind and, even relieved to finally be warm, he had to pull his hands out of that raccoon, but then they were stuck and he knew this was no proper way to cut meat, he was infecting everything with the blood, and pulling his hands back in a panic he pulled the bloody raccoon back up toward him, but it was so heavy, even with all that strength of the panic charging through him, that he pulled himself down into it too. And Jesse wanted to help so he grabbed Wallace's arms and began tugging and shaking so they got the whole raccoon shaking, looking just like it came back to life just like they were afraid it would, with its open eyes and sharp teeth.

They wasted all the water they'd carried back that morning, just cleaning the blood off of themselves. Had none left to run that raccoon's blood down the drain. Wallace had to keep his cool, not let Jesse see he was shook. But of course they were both shaken. Wallace tried to carve it up best he could to salvage what he could, worked in silence. But it was a mess and he was wet, cold.

That night it was even colder than it had been before and the wind whistled through the cracks of the cabin and the window Wallace had broken to get in. The wind howled and moaned and they tried to stretch those blankets to cover themselves. But there just wasn't any getting enough blanket over them both.

It was the first night Jesse cried all night and couldn't stop. Sometimes Wallace would find him standing and staring like he was thinking of something far away, just in the middle of whatever they were doing, Jesse would stop. Sometimes at night Wallace would wake up and hear Jesse whimpering real quiet, but he never wanted to embarrass him. But that night Jesse sobbed with abandon. Wallace lay awake the whole night listening to him and the wind. Awake in a dream, Wallace dreamt he was on a frozen iceberg far off in a dark sea, couldn't see a thing. He was alone, hunted by a fierce raccoon-demon howling with laughter hidden in the clouds.

Next morning, both puffy-eyed and silent, they packed up the car quickly and without a word or a plan, no destination in mind, headed East. Next to the cabin, on the small patio with the drain, the raccoon's carcass, same size as Jesse, half-skinned, its hide hanging like a loose cape, hung spreadeagle, shoulder height on some stakes that were meant to be used for torches.

Wallace and Jesse stopped in Stone Claw Grove when Wallace ran out of cash. Saw a big factory on the outside of town, went in to apply for a job, but nothing there. Applied at the convenience store, didn't know at the time they were always hiring because they were always getting stuck up. Last guy to work there, the guy whose place he would be taking, had just been arrested for beating a kid. So they hired Wallace on the spot, didn't look at him too closely. Good for the store to have someone new up front, someone who had never even met the old guy when all the locals came asking questions, demanding justice. Wallace sure didn't appreciate the extra attention it brought, customers lingering a minute after he gave them their change. But the papers had given up on coming around by the time he came on.

This kid had come in with his pointed finger in his pocket and Will, the guy working there, he played along with his hands up in the air until he caught the kid not looking, grabbed him over the counter and put the kid in a coma banging his head against the counter. Kid wasn't even sixteen yet. Witnesses said that gangly olive-skinned blond kid was out and it was clear he didn't really have a gun, but that guy Will kept slamming and bashing his head. That was the controversy. Wallace heard the guy had some kind of temper, quiet, but quite a temper. When the kid died after lingering in a coma for four years, the guy, Will, got some kind of deal to leave town, disappear. That was the second controversy. Wallace feared renewed attention to the convenience store, but it ended up just a minor news story.

So there Wallace was in Stone Claw Grove, nowhere he knew anyone, with a kid he didn't hardly know. He'd been building up his various identities for awhile, not sure what he was planning, but always knowing he'd be prepared if he ever needed it. Funny that way, how people can be planning on things they don't even know themselves they're planning on. It was just a hobby to him, these identities on paper, a way to know, to confirm he existed at all in his quiet years in northern California, those identities he liked to imagine. Once he figured out one other self, much work as that was and careful as he had to be, he always had fun tempting trouble. Making the second and third and fourth selves on paper was simple.

This one was a youth pastor at the local church, used to have some trouble, but found God to clear all that trouble up. It became a fun puzzle without the big picture in mind before he started, a puzzle whose big picture revealed itself to Wallace as he put it together. This one's a high school football coach, divorced, always bleary and hungover.

But he sure didn't think any of those guys he made up on paper were ever going to kidnap a kid. He had never been attracted to kids, never even thought about them, really. He saw Jesse among all those other kids and, in a way, it hit him—kids! Damn, it'd never really hit him before. A kid, what's a kid know? Look at him, beautiful. He doesn't know a thing. And Wallace would see him struggle. Then, no explanation, he just grabbed that kid.

Once Wallace got to know Jesse, he wasn't even a kid anymore. Suddenly, there before his eyes, he wasn't a kid. He was just a person. And it was even more beautiful. A person who just didn't know anything yet. Wallace wasn't some kind of creep. He didn't like kids before or something. He just liked Jesse and Jesse was a kid.

It was all very simple and natural as it happened. He was himself, Wallace, and he was Terrence Wolfe, divorced high school football coach alcoholic. Sometimes he'd be more himself. Driving and Jesse's in a good mood and whatever, he's himself without thinking. Then sometimes he'd be no-nonsense, practical Terrence Wolfe getting it all figured out. And then sometimes he'd be himself again, and he would find out what Terrence Wolfe was thinking and think, Oh boy Wallace, shit. You've gotten yourself into some shit now.

But it was all simple and beautiful, really. And making love, that was Jesse's idea, really, Jesse, the way he'd look at him and move. Wallace didn't see that coming until it was happening. Once it had happened once, sure there was that moment of "Is this happening?" There was a moment of "Hit the brakes there, Wallace."

But it happened. Then once something happened once, not much for it to happen again. Everything's more tricky once something's happened once. You start looking out for it. After having time to realize what had happened, then you start thinking about it and feeling, knowing, "This is all wrong, I can't do this." But then you start justifying to yourself, "Well it's already happened once, what's the difference something happens twice or once, three times or two?"

That's when Wallace started imagining maybe he was going a little nuts. He and Terrence Wolfe were suddenly having some intense debates. In that little room, that space justification opened up, Terrence stepped in and made himself at home.

Terrence got that job at the convenient store. Terrence got the one-bedroom apartment they'd been in ever since. Terrence just made himself right at home there in Wallace's life. Except it wasn't even his life anymore, Wallace. He was off, way off across the country, closer to home in Louisville than he'd been in a long time, but not that close and home wasn't home anymore any more than anywhere else was. That one bedroom apartment, Wallace didn't know this place. He had to make himself at home in Terrence Wolfe's life.

And Terrence Wolfe, he had these ideas the only way Wallace could save himself, from him, Terrence, and all the trouble that might come looking for him, was, he thought Wallace had to kill Jesse. Terrence would tell him he'd already made love with the boy. Terrence told him he was in so much trouble already. Wallace kept looking back over his shoulder best he could. Wasn't any internet then and it wasn't like the Stone Claw Grove library got *The Sacramento Bee* or the *Arcada Eye*. So he was just waiting, imagining "National Man Hunt," seeing himself on the news.

But nothing ever happened. Turns out it's pretty simple to grab a kid and run away with him, as long as you run fast and as long as the kid likes you well enough, believes your version of the world as you tell it. He didn't like lying to Jesse about his parents and the accident, but he needed to buy some time.

First few days were awful confusing, figuring out baby sitting, figuring out how to work those first few shifts with the kid in the car. His shifts would start so late Jesse would usually be asleep. Wallace kept the car messy. It was natural for him to do so, didn't take much effort. But it became useful too. Jesse would stay asleep in the backseat under blankets. He knew he had to pee in the jar Wallace left there. Wallace could see the car easily through the window, parked alongside the building.

First few nights he stared at that car all night, glancing back every couple seconds between obligations. He felt suspicious. He knew he couldn't keep staring like that. Draw attention to himself and the car. He'd usually buy them both a loaf of bread and some peanut butter, heat up a can of soup in the microwave at work when the shift was over.

Jesse and him spent the days then driving around. Turned out, Jesse told him he was so afraid of the parking lot overnight and being outside of the car, that Wallace had nothing to worry about at all, Jesse running away. Jesse even wanted to stay hidden in the car. Wallace kept Jesse groggy on benzos while he chugged coffee all day and night, and he did not have the nerves for so much caffeine.

This same policeman would come in every night, McRaskin. Slow overnight, took McRaskin a couple visits to get through his long-winded laments about Will and the beating before moving on to make any other conversation. "New in town? Where you from, where you live?" Wallace had to study that town real good during the day. Said staying with an aunt. McRaskin would ask, leaning on the counter with a coffee and donut, "Oh yeah, where's that? What's her name? Oh yeah, don't think I know her. Where exactly is that?"

So Wallace was sure this guy was on to him. He imagined the whole SWAT team was about to descend on him and carry Jesse out of the car, and that would be it. His brother and his sweet sister-in-law would have to see him on the TV news and they'd be shocked, but his brother would say actually he wasn't that surprised at all. And his brother's poor wife, it'd break her heart, all the mending she tried to do between Wallace's brother and him through the years.

This cop, Wallace thought, that's it. If I make it through this shift we're off in the morning. The cop repeats, "Now where exactly is that? What's the address?" And Wallace had to say, "Well, I don't really even recall the address Officer, just been there a few days. Yep, just me and my old aunt. Oh, no reason really, just looking for a start somewhere new and always really liked my old aunt."

His mind was made up, that's it. No way he was waiting until morning. He'd be walking right out of here and leaving the store open and empty, soon as the cop left. Wallace couldn't glance to the car. He meant, if this guy leaves, please.

But that small-town pig, he just settled in and made himself right at home that night until sunrise. Wallace had practiced all his Terrence Wolfe storytelling so long, he had all the answers. Got to be that this small town fool just liked conversation so much, so pleased to have someone new to tell all about himself, well, Wallace started daring McRaskin. Wallace started putting holes in his stories of Terrence Wolfe just to see if this bumpkin was gonna catch it or was even listening.

Mostly McRaskin just wanted to tell Wallace his story about Will. Told him that convenience store was a dangerous place when he wasn't around, and that was fine, because he preferred passing his nights there more than the diner anyway. Wallace didn't know then at that time that McRaskin would be keeping him company every night, sometimes with long winding tales like what's her name in the *One Thousand and One Nights*, sometimes happy to just to look at magazines in quiet, occasionally breaking the silence to lament the disastrous lives of the rich and famous. Wallace didn't know then McRaskin would become the closest thing he'd ever have to a friend in that town.

Soon before the sun came up, the rush hour crowd started coming in, getting their Dr.Peppers and cigarettes. When it began to really pick up, McRaskin figured it was time for him to scoot off. He told Wallace his brother-in-law had a building, just a one bedroom in this big building and if Wallace was really looking to move out of his aunt's, well he could put a word in for him with his brother-in-law to waive the security deposit. Wallace could move in any time he pleased. He gave Wallace the number, told him he'd call soon as his brother-in-law woke up, he'd be expecting Wallace's call.

Wallace had gotten pretty good at this lying, good at looking around at his options and quickly surveying what was worst from what was bad. When McRaskin said, "Well, alright then, Terrence, I'll be seeing you later tonight," then Wallace knew running off too quickly was gonna just draw attention to himself. And he knew not moving into that cop's brother-in-law's building meant McRaskin asking him about his old aunt and her neighborhood and neighbors and how did he like it and his details needed limiting. Turned out he'd be best off hiding out right where this cop wanted to set him down.

Things were tough before they got a TV. For a while there at the beginning, Wallace was so nervous about Jesse poking his head out he had to really up his dosage, keep him tucked in under blankets in the backseat. The landlord was a big guy, loud and nosy, asking lots of questions about why he didn't have more stuff to move in. Terrence was divorced, left it all behind, Who wants to be reminded? The landlord stressed over and over that he wasn't gonna let him slide on that security deposit just because his brother-in-law insisted he let him take the place immediately. Took a while to save some money to get any furniture, had to eat extra bad for a while.

Wallace brought Jesse magazines home from work. He'd look at them bundled in blankets on the living room floor. TV had to be the first thing they got. Being out on the highways and then in the cabin, Jesse was kept occupied by the world. But once they were in the apartment it got hard to pass the time, or even tell time, without a TV.

As they settled in and slowly Wallace got to relax into his new life, he had come to peace with the idea that he had no option but to continue. He wasn't gonna make any decisions or take any more actions except to continue. Jesse seemed happy enough, honestly. Wallace let up on the dosages some.

Soon, they had a day-to-day familiar enough, they could stick with it. But Wallace, it was important to him to have a talk with Jesse about their relationship and about where things were going between them. He couldn't really tell if it made any sort of difference to Jesse, but it helped him to get these things off his chest. They were able to relax around each other more then, the expectations were simplified.

He told Jesse that he liked him a lot. He told him that they were always gonna be the best of friends. Jesse could depend on him for anything, and Wallace would always be there for him. But things would have to be like that. It was an intense time for both of them, everything changing and if they were gonna get through all that, and if they were gonna get through all of that together, well, Wallace just thought they had no choice but to just be best friends and leave things like that.

They had no end in sight. They were gonna have to learn to cooperate. Wallace had never been so good at relationships. People meant a lot to him, but he was never able to really commit or get too close to any one person and have it work out. He really never in his life went on more than a few dates with any one person. He had a girlfriend once, a long, long time ago for a couple months and though she made him feel special, she made him feel like he was so special he didn't even need her. He regretted that, but he learned a lot from it. He didn't want to make that kind of mistake ever again.

He always thought maybe he was just a little bit too much like a monkey and people relationships just weren't something he could understand. He read in *National Geographic* a long time ago about pheromones and how they faded between people who spent too much time around each other. It was just nature. He explained to Jesse that he would never harm him and he would only want what was best for him, what was best for both of them. But it would take some work on Wallace's part. He still had some growing up to do in that way, but Jesse meant enough to him that he wanted to do that for Jesse, for his sake. He really did mean that much to Wallace. Wallace wanted to be a better himself for Jesse. That was the promise he made to Jesse. Jesse didn't say much.

He nodded like he understood. And things really were simpler between them after that. He was a real strong kid that way.

Before they were together like they were, before they were a family, Wallace and Jesse, back in northern California, before they knew each other, every morning Wallace would get off work at the gas station as the kids were walking to school and he'd notice Jesse among the other boys, every morning.

He was smaller, gentle. He would struggle with this big backpack that made him look even smaller, he'd be working so hard to carry it. Wallace knew when he saw him he wanted to help this kid. He could take care of him. That first day he wondered about what that kid could be carrying around that was so big. But when he saw him every day and it was always so heavy, well, then he really wondered about it. But Jesse was always smiling while he struggled with it. He still smiled like that sometimes, even weak as he was.

When Wallace was a boy he had his older brother with his serious older brother tone. And he had Pa. Always with a lit cigarette in hand and mumbling through backwards nails he held in the side of his mouth—with a hammer dangling from his belt loop, and his shirt off, sunburned in cutoffs— he'd tell Wallace, "Don't listen to a word your brother says, that goddamn fool." Sorting between those two, figuring out when to trust which of them, that was the principal lesson Wallace ever learned.

But he couldn't offer that lesson to Jesse on his own. He knew that.

Coming home on Jesse's birthday, shit, he figured Jesse was in the john. He set the big box of gooey ribs down on the counter, the new used Nintendo games he bought Jesse down on the coffee table: a make-your-own-maze game and some modern joust. He set down the microphone he'd rented that plugs into the Nintendo, a CD of TV show theme songs. He called out, "Jesse."

Wallace heard this bump from his room in return, the door to his room open. There Jesse was, standing in the sunlight, dressed up in Wallace's clothes. Jesse's standing there, looking at Wallace like Wallace had walked in on a prowler. The thick green pants were cuffed so high the cuffs came almost all the way back up to Jesse's knees. He had Wallace's nice wingtips on. They fit him like shoeboxes. Wallace's nice pinstriped shirt with the canvas feel to it hung to Jesse's knees. Wallace could see Jesse's hands flipping about, lost just below the sleeves' elbows.

Part 5

1

Camped out in the hall, dazed from staying up all night in the Laundromat, Sarah Ann bunched her coat up into a pillow and tilted over. The radiator clicked and whirred, but the open window above it released its heat. The failure of the heat and chill to resolve in a temperate balance, co-existing instead in their extremes, made her have to pee. Half asleep, middle of the afternoon, hands the size of buildings popped up from within and behind the industrial skyline, the factory-church.

A man carrying a steaming bag of food with loose video games and a microphone pressed to his chest turned at the top of the flight of stairs. He came toward her, down the hall. Glancing up at her and away, he stopped one door short of her, set the bag down to get his keys from his pocket.

Sneaking every opportunity to sniff at his hands between jingles of his keys, he unlocked the lock. He peeked at her again. He had seemingly practiced masking this desire to sniff at his hands to such a degree that it had become integrated completely into his constant, stilted movements. Sarah Ann remained still, aware she was fully conscious, aware she couldn't not pee.

"Excuse me," she called out, cleared her throat and repeated with increased volume, "Excuse me." He spun to her with severe eyebrows, his finger to his lips, "Shhh."

"Excuse me," she said again, in a stage whisper, standing up. He clicked another lock open quick, balancing the videogames and microphone under his arm. She stepped toward him and turning, panicked, he dropped the videogames, the dangling microphone draped across his bent elbow.

"Sir?" she said. "Please."

He bent quick to pick up his videogames and steaming bag, dropping the microphone while doing so. Balancing everything across his arms awkwardly, he turned to her again as he stood. "Shhh," he said, "the neighbors."

"I know sir. I'm sorry, but—"

Shaking his head, he gave her a severe stare as he unlocked another four locks.

"That's what I want to ask you about, the neighbors."

"Look, I don't know who you are or what you want, but shhh."

"I just need... I'm waiting for your neighbors."

"Well, what would I know about their comings and goings?" he asked. He turned the doorknob, but didn't crack the door. His shoulders dropped and with a sigh he turned to her.

"Leviticus says," he said, "'You shall not oppress thy neighbor or rob him,' and I do not oppress my neighbors by robbing them of their privacy." He nodded, satisfied.

"Please," she pleaded, uncertain how to proceed in her appeal if he insisted on an ancient and holy standard of reason. "Can I please use your restroom while I wait?"

His voice cracked at the top of his chesty chuckle. "If they don't answer the door," he said, shaking his head, "I'm sure they're probably at work, so you have no reason to wait around."

He popped into his apartment quick. She could hear the television loud.

With slow steps she returned to her bundle. Early, she'd imagine, for either of them to have to get to The Shhh... It was past the time she'd told Norman she'd come by for the interview. Maybe he wouldn't be around.

YEARS AGO

Sitting alone overnight in a parked car, her deliberate flow and swirls tearing and bunching, Sarah Ann began, on a stack of napkins with a ballpoint pen, what would become her first journal.

Gramma's huffing in her bed increased in volume and its cadence took on an oblong bump. Gramma had fallen on ice, broke her hip. Laid up in the hospital, she got pneumonia. Laid up with pneumonia, she had a heart attack. Laid up with the heart attack, she was fed by a tube and while fed by a tube she developed a string of sores along her trachea. She came home, went back in, came home.

Mom had vertigo. Shuttling Gramma back and forth took its toll. In slippers in the snow, 2 AM, she talked about dropping a box of toothpicks under her car, had to pick them all up while thinking of it or else she might forget leaving for work in the morning and get a flat. Sarah Ann pleaded, come in. A tire's rubber will survive a box of toothpicks spread flat on the snow.

One afternoon Mom fell asleep with an ear candle burning. Woke up hours after it should've been removed. It had drawn so much wax out she suffered a high-pitched squeal for weeks, air rushing in burning, vertigo, couldn't walk.

Sarah Ann had taught herself how to drive that year, eighth grade. First, only around the block, late at night, empty streets with friends at a sleepover. But with Mom's vertigo, it became Sarah Ann's job to get Gramma back and forth to the doctors. No one ever mentioned her age, thirteen. No one asked how she knew how to drove.

She drove Gramma to the emergency room, pulled up to the entrance, a doctor and a cop smoking together in silence, continued through the circle driveway without stopping. Couldn't let the cop see her driving. She parked down the block, left the car running, Gramma huffing. Ran to a side door of the hospital, found a wheelchair that had lost its corral. Back to the car she pushed, the wheelchair's front wheel spinning sideways against her path, loud in the empty streets, piled Gramma into the wheelchair, careful to tilt her from the door. Back to the emergency room entrance, the doctor and the cop still engrossed in late night thoughtful silence together.

Behind the glass doors, a man pushed two wheelchairs at once, one empty, the other a pile of blankets and some flesh, side by side down a wide hall. Sarah Ann wheeled Gramma up to the doctor's toe before either he or the cop noticed her. Turning to bolt, she sprinted a zigzag, hopped a bush and ran straight through a tall row of hedges.

Blocks later, she accepted no one was chasing her, cut through a backyard, approached a car parked far off down one street. Realized it wasn't Mom's car. Another twist, another yard, turned around, the car across the street, still running, passenger side door left open. Walking past, she started to close the door, caught it right before it slammed, noticing the driver's side door locked. She slipped in, slid across the bench to the driver's seat. School in three hours, too wound up to sleep. Hoped Gramma had some ID on her, in her nightgown. Someone would recognize her by that point.

Lighting a cigarette, the orange spiral of the car lighter, left the car running. She had not yet learned to enjoy smoking, but recognized its potential as a dramatic gesture when in need of stress relief. In the dark car, smoking, windows left rolled up. The car's steel body held cold in a feedback loop of environment and shelter.

She doodled on dirty napkins from the floor, ballpoint pen on crinkle. As a little kid, Sarah Ann didn't know she could read. Her dad took her to movies, weekday matinees in empty theaters. That's all she remembered about him. His friend, a young guy that took the tickets, let them slip in. They always arrived after the movies started, sat through the end credits and waited for the next screening to watch the beginnings. They saw each movie a few times before considering if they liked it. Never checked show times, walked into what was playing, however far along it was. Her dad always left after a few minutes, went with his friend, the young man. In the dark, the movies babysat her.

Eventually, anyone she met wondered about her silence. Teachers worried she must have been somehow sick, unable to understand. Uneasy with her stare, neighbors, parents of classmates pulled their kids away. Her dad failed to recognize how determined, how deep and constant her commitment to her silence. She liked movies, he thought. She watches, concentrates, doesn't talk much. She likes to watch.

He never realized the movies themselves meant little to her, it was the next step of the ritual, the drawings when they got home. She drew whatever characters in whatever scenes, so moved, unable to help it, impulse. She couldn't be thrown off course. Some slightest nudge tilted drawing into language. The words only more complex pictures to her, she couldn't determine a tipping point at which picture became word. She couldn't distinguish the degrees of any fade through which one became the other.

Her parents matched her preschool teacher's surprise when the teacher told them she could read.

"How did you teach her so young?"

"I don't know. We didn't."

That night, alone in the car, doodling, free from guide or intention, geometry, shapes and angles, hospital room geometry, shapes and shadings of a hospital room seen from the floor emerged. Uncertain until the shapes came into focus, she wrote associative captions—bleach, choke, germs. She had figured out how to think through things in that way. Worked best exhausted but too wound up to sleep, like dreaming on paper. From hospital room geometry, its bleach smell and shell of false clean evoked, the figure of her father returned in flickers.

It was some aunt of her dad's she'd never seen before, bulges of flesh tied down in tubes, without will, silhouetted by the window behind her at dusk. In a hospital or an old folks' home, the room shades of peach, orange in concentrated flares, white tile and bedding. The chill sharp, sudden over and over, sudden painful tickling, and the stench, sour, inextinguishable.

In a chair pulled bedside, head down, her dad worked his temples with his knuckles. He stared straight down and through Sarah Ann. She pulled at and half-climbed steel piping in pinching angles, tucked up into the underside of the bed's hidden gears. Beeping machinery and the bedded person-pile murmured and whined in harmony.

With her tug at her dad's cuffs, a cracking open of his voice, guttural. Backlit by the window, a single throb of sobbing and a howl. With the contortion of his face and its return to stasis, a spontaneous understanding of sickness, decay, hit Sarah Ann at three, four years old. Intuitive repulsion. Her dad's face shades of shadows. Beeping machinery grounded sustained silence.

With laughter like a flock of gulls taking flight, two teens entered with a radio shrieking a tinny Bing Crosby Christmas favorite. The young man done up in a glittery vest, the young woman, taller, deformed or struggling to project joy. Galloping to the bed arm in arm, the young man took the aunt's arm.

"Merry Christmas! Let's dance!"

"Oh," and "Sorry."

In the cafeteria, Sarah Ann on her dad's knee and he uncertain how to hold her, a different holiday volunteer took the only photo of Sarah Ann and her dad together that she still had.

It occurred to her, drawing in the car that night, perhaps for the first time, that she'd ever even had a dad. His form found through drawing, she let it happen, began to write him—Dear wherever.

Absorbing as her habit of journaling became, she never figured out how to write without addressing someone particular, the pages a long string of letters to this man she couldn't remember but for his shape in that one photo together, backlit in the hospital cafeteria, and wouldn't know how to find.

2

WHEN MEL ATTEMPTED TO RETURN TO DANCING

"I can't believe I slept through the doctor appointment," Mel said.

Norman smoothed back his hair, running his palms flat back on his head.

"Well, here I am now," Mel said. "I'm here now." About to dance for the first time in some months, it didn't seem so bad. She had come to be attracted to men who she couldn't determine for sure were handsome or not. Attraction meant having to look and look again, unsure, with a definite aspect of repulsion. Returning to dancing felt not entirely unlike this, maybe.

Norman got up. "Well, alright. Just hurry up."

Changing positions released a sour sweat stench from him and it hit her in a puff. She didn't want to, but it happened, bad manners that couldn't be helped. She scrunched her nose and recoiled.

"What?" Norman asked, standing above her.

"What? Nothing, what?" She lit a cigarette.

"You made a face?"

"I did?"

"Yeah, what?"

"No, I didn't. I don't know. Did I?"

Norman got up. "Alright, well. Just please hurry up."

Flapping his jacket closed over his open shirt, Norman stepped out.

"Hurry up," he muttered. "Stupid bimbo."

Mel nodded. Alone in the room with the vent, an open paper on her dressing table, Guantanamo photos, she did not feel sexy. Stone Claw Grove, thirty-seven, Ronnie had three kids by the time she was Mel's age, The Shhh..., Jesus.

Nap disorientation, shouldn't wake up more than once a day.

"I gotta call my modeling agency," the girl with the pin-up style had said.

"Modeling agency," always Mel's favorite term, became a trigger, cracking a moment open at a strange angle any time she heard it. One time, not really paying attention, in the dressing room years earlier, one of the girls said it, "modeling agency." Mel didn't know the context, but for whatever reason, hearing it, "agency," in the active sense of the word, taking action, and "modeling," a verb in that instant, to exemplify, to model. It cracked her up, the room in degrees of make-up and undress, an accidental feminist manifesto. Here they all were, together, modeling agency.

A term she heard often, always welcomed. Snapped her to. Mel daughter, Mel sister, wife, legally even still, ha! Mel mother, Sabina dancer, and did these names collapse her meaning, the meaning of her, Mel, or multiply it?

"Agency" noun could be the setting for "agency" verb. That's a different trick of speech. Mel mother, sister, wife wasn't as simple. But she'd never be a mother. Probably, that had just been decided, probably.

She read once that clairvoyants might mistake themsleves for schizophrenics if not open to the unlikely idea that they might indeed be clairvoyant. And that, protection from ever having to consider herself potentially paranoid schizophrenic, had proven sustained reason enough for Mel to believe in at least the possible existence of clairvoyants.

Gus, when she sometimes pressed him on a new poem of his that he read her, would talk about speech imitating thought, never in a way that made much sense. Exactly in the act of attempting to replicate some primal immediate pre-language, Gus stopped communicating. She thought his revolution a devolution.

Wasn't it just her pure Virgo to think so, but Norman's chatter and constant commentary came closer to achieving this. But couldn't tell Gus that.

So she wanted to explain to Gus about "modeling agency." She wanted to understand why what the sister and the wife had in common drew neither toward the other, but instead made them each denounce their own attitudes in common. One seeing the other offered an occasion for both to reconsider some things, self-consciously, with purpose. She wanted Gus to understand this, modeling agency.

She always put make-up on before changing into costume, so that she never had to accidentally see herself in costume without make-up. Pulled her sweatshirt off over her head, slipped into a teddy, the vent and goosebumps. Wrapped her sweatshirt over her face enough to cover her face, but left a small gap open to peek through. This was how she looked in her teddy with her face covered. Could I strap up my boots like this? Bet I could do the whole dance blind if I know where the pole is.

Stone Claw Grove, thirty-seven, Nana would've been a grandmother by next year. What complete impracticality, all of it. Mel ruffled the paper flat, packed up the make-up case the fair-skinned serious girl who couldn't make eye contact and had a boy at home had left open. Total impracticality, picking up and accompanying each other's rhythms, anxious and vulnerable, performing for each other more than the losers, the audience, all of it.

She pinned her hair back in a couple terse motions. All that black, how much would be gray if she stopped dying it? Started dying it, first sighting of a stray gray. Only a couple confident pins held it all down. What was her natural shade of black? Everything on the dressing table must be arranged at perfect angles, hand-mirror and tweezers perpendicular.

Norman pounded in. "You wanna switch with one of the other girls? I can grab one of them, tell her to get up there first."

"No, no. I'm fine."

Cocking his head and leaning heavy on one foot, Norman inhaled a long, slow drag of his cigar.

"She probably can't dance with those floppy cartoon tits anyway," Mel said.

"Yeah, well," Norman said, locking his eyes into hers. "Not much time," he said, walking back out. "It's the classic

Shhh... tonight! Sabina's big comeback!"

His steps heavy down the hall. Coffee pot empty, no one made a new pot. How much more practical, nothing. She set her wig on straight—long, straight red hair. The music downstairs, down the hall, reached the room only as rhythm. But the wooden doors and distance compressed it. A faster song had rhythm dense enough to flatten percussion into a tone. Line up the aerosols tallest to shortest between the wider, identical powders. Here's scissors.

Small units stack and repeat, dances, days, flatten into a tone. A hair stuck on her tongue, between her teeth, she took off her wig. Stretched it straight. Cut it by ¾, why not red butch?

Being late, running late and being late, waking up weird that was part of it, a big part of it. But getting dressed alone, the performance seeped backwards into the setup. Getting ready, talking, laughing, even annoyed or half-paying attention, whatever, one blanked on the task at hand. Freed one to make it from here to there, private to public as a continuum, not a switch flipped. The red wig looked good short. She lit another cigarette.

Stand up and perform. Go now from not performing to performing. This was why she usually got out on the floor early, took the long hall while distracted by conversation.

Wonder what something, carved from nothing, an accidental nap—however many ways there are to sleep, must be at least that many ways to wake up.

Norman told Mel he wasn't sure he could give her any more shifts. Mel danced. Mel got pregnant. Mel danced while pregnant until she couldn't hide it anymore. Mel bartended while pregnant, then no longer pregnant, she tried dancing again, better money. Lasted one time, something had gone away, whatever it was that had allowed her to dance for so many years. She settled on being a bartender. Then Norman told her times were tough, business down, no extra shifts to pick up.

"You want to make some money, Mel, you should work for me, my new business," he said.

Cutting small limes with a dull knife, Mel couldn't look up. "But I already work for you, Norman. I've been working for you since you were in high school."

Norman shook his head and leaning forward, heavy on his elbows, lit a cigar.

"Look, you can't dance anymore, right? What's a girl like you supposed to do?"

Mel paused and looked up. She pushed her sore ankle sideways against the ground for the rush of a twinge.

"Really, what?" he asked. "I'm serious."

She returned to cutting the fruit, remained silent.

"Well, you can't dance, but I'm starting a website. You should be a model on it."

She looked up at him, lit a cigarette. He smirked, slurped from his bourbon.

"Seriously," he said.

"Okay, Norman, what's your website?"

"Well, obviously you'd need to fuck," he said. "The website would be you getting fucked, fucking and being fucked, blowing guys while looking up at the camera. That sort of thing."

She sighed, cut fruit.

"Really, you aren't too old. You could be a MILF."

"Well, now that's ironic, isn't it?"

"What?"

She put down the knife and set her shoulders back, stretched her neck.

"Oh, right," Norman said, "sorry."

Mel picked up the knife, set its dull blade to the lime's thick skin, but didn't press. Taking a long drag from her cigarette, smelling the lime on her fingers, she sighed and looked back up at him.

"What?" he said. "I'm trying to help. I figure you can't dance. What can you do?"

"I can do plenty," she said, picking the knife back up,

pointing at him with it.

"Don't point that knife at me," Norman said.

"Sorry." She set the knife down and knocked her knuckles lightly against the bar a few times, head tilted.

"You can understand I'm trying to help," Norman said. "You always took your clothes off for work before."

She looked up at him. She had never really thought about if she wanted to be a mother, but she had always had the option ahead of her before. Not really anymore.

"So," he continued, spreading his arms wide, "this is the way people take their clothes off to work now."

Mel shook her head, lit a cigarette before realizing she already had one lit, balanced on the edge of the bar. She looked at him. He leaned low to take a swallow from his drink without lifting it.

"You don't see the difference?" she asked.

He shrugged, shook his head.

"Really, you don't?" she pressed him.

He sat up straight in his seat. "No, Mel, I guess I don't," he sighed. "Why don't you explain it to me?"

Pressing her palms flat to the bar, she leaned. "You don't see the difference," she began, "between dancing naked in a room, in a room in which I am present with the other people, in control of the room, and releasing videos of myself having sex online?"

Norman shook his head.

"You really don't?" she said.

He shook his head again. "No. I'm sorry. I guess I'm missing something."

Mel felt good about her contribution to the room. Seen from far above, or on this paper they asked her to fill out when she entered, the room would no longer be only for couples. She had come out for the opera itself, and while the room swelled to capacity, no one else at all, it seemed, could say they were there so much for the sake of the opera itself that they would have come on their own. She enjoyed even the shaking quiet train into Detroit, wished it had taken longer.

Mel liked being alone. It had been too goddamn long since she'd taken herself out for a date, all the activity for a while and then all the quiet, the parasite woven into her through her fluids, until she couldn't take it anymore. A grown woman knows when an operation is the right choice. Or what, expel him like a jellyfish washed up on the beach? Her son, all her own, the new jellyfish on the sunset beach of her. Maybe years ago, maybe, but now, all on her own, the energy. And she could return to dancing again. That's fine.

With a white wine alone among the hum and murmur of the dating public, regal airs intoned this is not loneliness you all see before you. This is confidence. This is a choice, and this is a self-determined act. Yes, she did get dressed up to go out alone. Yes, she will meet your gaze and no, she did not need anyone.

But, actually, she did get bored enough to fill out the Opera House's survey, approached it from the same blank aloof angle with which she confronted the thronging duos. She wasn't above sitting with the survey a few minutes.

1. Yes, been here before.
2. Well in the last year zero times, but many times before this past year. I had very little opportunity to be myself this last year.
3. I would very likely come here more often if I had more time. I would somewhat likely come here more often if there were more operas I wanted to see. I would somewhat likely come here if it were easier to get to. It's very unlikely I'd come here more often if it were less expensive to drive downtown, because I take the train. It is somewhat more likely I would come here more often if friends suggested it more often. It is very unlikely I'd come here more often if I heard more about the operas being shown, because I know about all of them.
4. I am not a member of the museum, but I used to be, so I will say yes.

I am aware I am a type, the type who at every opportunity has rejected any decision that would make one more of a type. In the end I have become that type, a rejecter. I could've coupled, plenty of opportunities, but it never would've made me happy. Always that whispering hidden within my biases, a judgment, some judge whispering, "What type rejects such opportunities? Who do you think you are?"

5. I did not attend any of the festivals this year. I wish I could explain why, explain to these boxes with more than a checkmark.

6. In the past month I have not been here, any of the other theaters, the movies, downloaded a movie on-line, or watched pay-per-view. I did rent 1-5 movies from the video store.

Who do I think I am? The big question, isn't it? And so what is it, this thing with clichés I've been dealing with, so aware of sidestepping? I've grown up to be the type that prefers quiet, prefers red wine and Nina Simone ballads. So what? I am not unaware that this makes me a type.

7. I do read the newsletter every month, check.

8. I listen to NPR, the oldies, and classic rock, check, check, check. The classical show on the college station, check.

9. I don't watch any of those TV shows at any times because I don't watch TV much. Try not to.

10. I don't have cable.

11. I meant to go to a poetry reading and an outdoor concert. I'll check yes this time for my own sake, it's to myself I can't admit I haven't done any of these in a year.

12. I did browse a craft fair and passed through the amusement park last summer. Is it an amusement park if they just set it up for a weekend? It felt like an amusement park. I went to the art museum one

> afternoon. Must've been right before I found out, but
> I must've known already somehow. I was living so
> quietly.

All the things I used to do, activity has faded. My paints have long crusted over the ends of their tubes. I turned down a freelance job to illustrate a series of flyers, no interest in any Prince Charming.

13. The paper's recommendations, the radio, word-of-mouth.

14. I don't know. I don't have five. The paper online. Blogs?

15. I do have a cell phone. Most people have all these things?

16. I receive many text messages by phone each day and I send many text messages by phone each day. I visit a few websites each day and send a few emails each day. I instant message a few times a week.

17. iPod? I wish.

18. I have both MySpace and Friendster pages rotting away. Do these things expire or sit frozen forever?

19. 48508

20. Female

21. 31-40

22. Prefer not to say.

It's all so stupid, ending up unable to recognize oneself in any way except in relation to the type—a middle-aged woman who will never be a mother, a stripper with a heart of gold, a single woman not interested.

23. Currently single

24. Caucasian / White / European-American

I'd hate to die mostly because then I'd no longer have the endless and constant joy of imagining all the possible ways I might die. But really, I am mostly just not interested.

25. $20,000-$34,999. That's really the least anyone makes?

Where's the box: fundamentally uninterested?

Gus had come by the house with Mel after the cemetery, treading along in a collective daze with a few of Nana's slow and quiet old neighbors. With what was on hand, he improvised a bacon and egg spaghetti, explaining each step to Kent. "The trick is to cut the bacon up into small pieces before cooking it, then add a smidge of vinegar. This turns the milk into cheese."

Mixing it all up in a pot, messing his arms halfway up to his elbows, he realized in the little time it had taken him to prepare the dish, he had been left alone with Mel and her brothers. He quickly did the dishes, nodding goodbye to Will, taking Kent's hand in his own wet hand firmly. He insisted he didn't mind walking to the bus, it was only a few blocks and it'd been so long since he'd taken the bus across town. He'd enjoy the quiet.

Stunned as they were by the feat of the bacon and egg spaghetti, after trying one bite Kent dialed D'Arpino's Pizza by memory. Without asking Will or Mel their preferences, he ordered sausage and mushrooms, told them they each owed him six dollars and seventy cents. Giving Nana's address on the phone, he raised an eyebrow to Will and Mel, politely responding, "Thank you. Yes, we're all doing fine."

D'Arpino's had staged the birthdays, retirements, test-cramming and heartbreak decompressions, serious talks, and first dates for the entire town. Red-checkered tablecloths and dim lights were enough. Any night could feel special.

But the family, the D'Arpinos themselves, never let on they recognized anyone. Generations of D'Arpinos warped their ethnic identity according to fetishistic television shows and movies, opening their circle briefly once per generation to absorb a romantic mark into the tribe, a new speech pattern, velour track suits.

And neither Will, Kent, nor Mel could remember ever having actually spoken to any D'Arpino before. When the driver arrived, Kent heard the bell, called him over to the side gate. Exchanging the pizza and the cash carefully over the fence, Kent looked the driver over in the harsh blast of the neighbor's security light. He did not appear in on the condolences, stared at Will over Kent's shoulder. The lighting increased the severity of Will's appearance, giving shadows to lumps, highlighting scars.

The first bite, the flavor returned them each to their youth— coked-up Kent stops by and scares Mel, babysitting and too stoned to watch a slasher movie. Will's anxiety stunted his appetite. He wished he'd just gone home. Mel remained offended on principle, her entire sense of self-determination apparently depending on this right to name her own toppings. Even a simple piece of pizza, Will ate disgustingly, dismantling it into a soup. Mel wondered if it hadn't maybe been so long since Will had eaten in the company of anyone else, years of eating alone, if he would even know how to not make a mess, how to behave. After only a couple bites, Kent set his slice down on the chalky concrete with a sneer, popped a Nicorette in his mouth.

Looking Kent over in silence, Mel snorted, laughing with her mouth full. Will and Kent both looked to her. They looked to each other and shrugged.

"What?" Kent asked.

She shook her head, laughing hard, chewed food up in her nose.

"Are you okay?" he asked, standing up.

She nodded her head, spat her chewed pizza out into her hand and dropped it in the dirt to the side of porch. Kent looked to Will. Will shook his head.

"What the fuck is so funny?" Kent asked.

She shook her head. The brothers remained quiet, watching her as she struggled to catch her breath. Will thought maybe things would get silly after all and he smiled, tried to laugh a little like he knew what was so funny, smiled to Kent. But Kent sneered and rolled his eyes at him. Will had to admit he had no idea what cracked Mel up.

Mel calmed down. Kent asked again, "What?"

Starting to laugh again, she kept herself calm with a deep breath.

"It's just," she began, had to swallow laughter. "It's just, I wonder how you decided to wear that shirt to Nana's funeral?"

She looked to Will. He looked down to his plain button-down shirt tucked in under his sport coat. She shook her head in tight turns and signaled with her eyes to Kent. Stunned, an unprovoked attack, Kent unzipped his leather jacket a little, pinched at his silk shirt covered entirely by the continuous dragon print.

"Me?" He asked.

Mel laughed. Will looked away.

"What's wrong with this?" Kent said.

Mel shrugged, feigning innocence.

Kent waved her off. "I think it's a nice shirt."

He looked to Will and Will nodded. Should've just headed home.

"It is a nice shirt," Kent repeated.

Will lit a cigarette. Chuckling, Mel reached over with her index and middle fingers split into a "V" and Will offered her the cigarette for a drag.

"You two," Kent stood. "Get up, Will."

"What?"

"Come on. I just got this." Kent swung a digital camera toward them.

Will and Mel looked confused.

"It's a camera," Kent said. "One of those new little digital cameras, cheap."

"Such an asshole," Mel groaned. "You jerk, you waited for me to change into my pajamas on purpose."

Kent ignored her. Balancing her beer, the swing jutted out in a lurch as Mel threw her legs out in front of her. She planted her feet, her ankle sore, to steady the swing.

Standing, Will scooted behind the swing. With arms to full extension, Kent deciphered the camera's menu, punching buttons with his fingertip and cursing. "I'm not exactly sure, give me a second."

Will shifted his weight, patted at his hair with a flat palm. Lost in the camera's menus, Kent looked over his shoulder, took a step back to fit them both on the screen.

"Can we just forget it?" Will pleaded, stepping back into a shadow to pop a pill.

"No, no, no, what's the big deal?" Kent had backed up off the porch into the dusty lawn. "It'll just take a second."

Inspecting his framing, he stepped back up to where he stood before. "Come on Will, lean over so I can get you both in the picture."

"This is stupid," Will protested.

6. He was entirely ready to have God remove all these defects of character.

Mel spun in place in the swing. Will leaned forward a little to help her throw her arm around his neck, but held his breath upon contact.

"No big deal, just one second," Kent said. He moved the camera closer and further from his face, unsure. "Smile."

Mel smiled. Will struggled to feign a smile.

7. Humbly asked Him to remove his shortcomings.

"Jesus Will, come on. What's the big deal? Just give me a smile okay?"

"I am."

"For real, smile."

Will held a smile, balanced the swing, thrown-off balance against his thigh. The edge of its weight pulling downward cut into his leg.

"Alright then," Will said without moving his lips. "Take the fucking picture, please."

"Hold on, just... one... just... hold on... one... second." Kent again moved his gaze from the camera's frame to its inner workings. "I just gotta, the flash or the porch light, shit."

"Let go," Will said. Bolting upright, he pulled up against Mel's arm over his shoulder. Careful to tilt her beer, the swing dropped forward and rolled back.

"We need weed," Mel sang out. Both her brothers paused and looked to her. Kent smiling, Will curious.

"Really?"

"Why not?" Mel said. "We can hang this photo up in the guest room."

Kent looked back to the camera's menus. "Okay then, Will," he said, "now I need you to smile with your mouth closed tight."

Will tilted his head. Kent looked up, flashed a strained, closed-mouth smile. Veins popped from his neck. Mel gushed a bubbling sob of laughter. Will was confused.

On the guest room wall, the family museum, Mel found each of Kent's sneers, framed and frozen, amplified each of his other sneers. The hazard in Will's eyes at sixteen, seventeen in a suit riding up high on his wrists, on the front steps of the home of a girl he might not recall as any more than a sweet scent and a sexual daringness, Mel had to choose: confirm or deny the compressed past? The Will she last really knew, a ten-, eleven-year-old kid, conceded to her piercing his ear with a diamond stud on that very bed. Mel had buried it all under her poise and rouge.

"You know," Kent explained, looking back to the menu. "Smile as if your mouth is torn up. You just took your own braces off."

"What are you talking about?" Will said, annoyed.

"You know," Kent said. "That photo in the guest room."

Will shook his head, no idea what Kent was talking about. There was no photo like that.

Kent had always found the curl of Will's smile at twelve, thirteen to betray a gaping, repulsive ignorance, a premonition of Will's susceptibility to paid programming. The simplicity, the posed photos, maybe the family needed the continuity. Kent would've preferred broken plates, ignored cat puke blooming fuzz, handfuls of each other's hair.

Excited, Mel began to stand, "My old ten-speed is hanging in the garage."

Will spun and stepped away. "Forget it."

Will had always thought each of them gave too much away at twelve or fourteen, but by fifteen, seventeen years old they'd all adopted a good mug-shot blankness. Three ghouls suspended two decades through the school system, the park district, the neighborhood. Kent with a green tint to his black and white starkness, the look of having had thumbs pressed into one's eyes. Mel's cultivated gaze was the ecstatic vengeance within her means. In fifth or sixth grade, bleached hair and caked-on make-up. By ninth or tenth grade she looked as much like she did in her mid-thirties as she in her mid-thirties looked eighteen. Even at twelve, thirteen years old, her skin in continuity with the pelts of her handbags had the weathering of a lifelong smoker.

Mel clapped, "Historical recreation! We can collapse different photos on the wall all into one photo."

The interesting issue to Mel, implied by the limitations the wall of photos imposed on her memory, became seeing photos of oneself one had no memory of; in a dress one didn't remember owning, dancing wildly and smiling in a tiki bar with a friend's father one doesn't remember ever meeting.

And how had it become so that no one could know whether or not they had seen something, had been somewhere, until seeing it removed from themselves, framed and frozen? Had Kent been to the Coliseum or Las Vegas?

Will looked at his feet, circled in place, shaking his head. He couldn't believe he hadn't gone straight to the bus station.

Kent smiled. "What? Come on, Will. You still got the same haircut."

Will's careful flattop had always offset the floating little dots of his features with an authority the meander of his face begged for. Even then, his eyes, one lower than the other and too far apart, his nose off-center. His cheeks cut tall. The shadows fell well. But with his little round eyes and his little round nose and his tiny round mouth, he appeared to himself drawn out, a round rubber stamp dropped without care. A sloppy puppet of himself keeping the lopsided sum of his face together best he could. Muscles helped err the distortion of his looks toward his favor, until the slow process of disfigurement, of course, and being disfigured, a monster.

Will rolled his eyes, planted his feet. Kent smirked, "Alright, stand still. I got it."

"No, forget it. Let's go," Will said.

"Look excited," Kent said.

"We are," Will said flatly.

"No, no," Kent directed. "You know, make this face." He held his hands up to his cheeks like a blossoming flower and opened his mouth, widened his eyes.

Mel chuckled. "That's the look of surprise."

"No," Kent said. "That's just the excited look people make in pictures."

"No," Mel said. "That's the look people make when surprised and we're not surprised."

Kent shook his head. Keeping the swing balanced with one toe, its weight heavy on her ankle, Mel waved Will back over, "Come on, Will."

Will stepped back behind the swing in a few slow, heavy steps, circling his precise destination instead of stepping straight to it. Holding his frame steady, the shake of the camera exaggerated through its viewer, the camera's weight intensified in the struggle to keep it perfectly still, Kent held his breath waiting for Will to step into the frame. Will leaned down and Mel released the swing's balance from her toe to set its weight once again back onto Will's thigh.

Back in position and again holding poses, Mel knew if she could only tell Will a few of the details quickly, her circumstances at work, the money Rich had promised her and Norman withheld, Will would stick up for her.

Kent, unable to get the camera to actually take the picture, shouted, "I don't know, just got this piece of shit. It was cheap, but not sure how it's supposed to be so much easier than dropping film off at the drug store."

Mel began to stand, "Let me see."

But before she was up, Kent turned his back to them. "Oh, no, no, I got it."

Still bent, Will relaxed his posed smile. Mel looked to Will.

He would have the strength of character to resist the impulse to begin fighting again beyond just this one time, standing up to Norman. She knew ex-drinkers who could occasionally have a glass of wine or a beer, now and then. Will could fight just this one time and not fall back into it.

"The kids plug it into the TV," Kent said. "The quality is fantastic."

"If you can get the picture taken, maybe," Mel said.

A minute feels like a long time when a few people are together and no one says anything. They each sighed. They each shifted their weight, but there were long pauses of stillness in between any of them doing anything.

Finally Kent was truly ruffled. "Well, I don't know. Is this a new event? Am I supposed to create an album? Why can't I just click it, take the fucking picture?"

"You can," Mel said.

"Slideshow or book?" Kent huffed.

"Forget about that. Ignore that stuff," Mel explained. "It'll organize itself as an event. Don't worry about that."

"An album?"

"Don't worry about that. The album is something bigger, you sort that out later if you want, when you're looking at it, not when you're shooting."

Mel looked to Will, his eyes lowered. She could ask Kent's advice. He'd know if that was unfair to ask of Will. Kent might try to get tough himself, though.

Mel bumped Will with a light headbutt, "Willow."

There was the one time, the karaoke night, Will on Norman.

Will looked up and smiled, shook his head. She settled back into the swing, took a long pull from her beer. Dropping his forehead to the back of the swing, Will studied the angles of the cracks in the patio. The flash went off.

"Here! Got it!" Kent back in position held them in the frame. "Look up, Will."

Will looked up, slouched in a more natural way. Mel shifted to throw her arm back around his neck, but didn't bother stretching to do so. "What's that picture you took? Me drinking and Will with his head down?"

"I'll get rid of it. Say cheese."

Though she was the only one that still lived in town, Mel claimed the guest room, already in pajamas, been there anyway to sort through Nana's stuff and felt a twinge of entitlement to the grief. Neither Kent nor Will wanted the bed Nana died in. Ronnie and Joe had buried the couch under Nana's plate sets and snowglobes, pulling everything from the shelves and cabinets without a strategy.

The pizza, little as they had each eaten, soaked up the will for conversation. Posing, each hoped to give the impression his or her dullness was some variation of thoughtfulness. They all agreed, "long day." Will wished he'd just gone home, stayed home, could be at home.

In the dining room, in the spot where the table had always been until that day, Kent bumped his head on the chandelier.

Will wanted to be silly. Despising it in others, it was still sometimes all he ever wanted, silliness. But it was impossible, always. Nothing could mean more to him than if they could all have been silly together, if the three of them with their separate lives, if the ideal simplicity of their ideal bond could have ushered playfulness, somehow, in any way, into their grown-up lives. But Will never felt okay being silly, not even for a second. The photo an opportunity for silliness, but it wasn't realized. Self-consciousness, some unnamable sense of manners or false fun squashed it.

They lived on display. That was how it was, had to be. They lived their lives on display, expecting Dell to crash in on them at any moment and one could never let one's guard down in case that moment, any time, that could be it, the moment he came back laughing, taunting, sneering, sickening, slapping, brooding, diminishing all within sight of his judgment, devastating, negating, as if his hunched saunter was a swoop on galloping horseback with a flaming pumpkin, Dell.

Being together, instead of giving them the collective courage to drop their guard, instead re-enforced this defensiveness in each of them. A single moment could in fact—a loss or rejection might—define an entire life, each moment in the day-to-day of that life.

When Nana died, she just didn't show up for a brunch date, didn't answer the phone. Some calls determined she hadn't been seen in a couple days. The paramedics showed up, broke down the door as Mel showed up with keys.

When Dell disappeared it was never even mentioned, let alone talked about. Everyone knew it was a given and the day had come. But even once the day had come, no one could know it was The Day until days later. Not coming home one day surprised no one. So continuing to not come home was never a shock, just a sustained suspense, building and eventually settled into, but without a rupture of relief.

Will gathered his plastic bags. He and Kent agreed to head over to The Carroll Motel, split a room, $26.50 each. Kent said thirty dollars was cool to cover gas money, the funeral home to the cemetery, Nana's to the motel. They made a plan to all have breakfast together tomorrow before heading their separate ways, each of them knowing it wouldn't happen. It was simply to divert having to say any sort of goodbye, that night or the next morning.

At the OTB that morning before the funeral—Mel was surprised and proud of Joe that he made it back in time to pick up Ronnie—Joe sat in the back, slouched in his molded plastic chair. The races flashed on screens before him. He struggled to keep track of which ticket in his hand corresponded to which screen, talked out loud to no one in particular.

"You know what she's? You know what she's? I'll tell you what she's. Hate to say it. I do hate say it. She's Ronnie's girl, but can't help it. Gotta call it like see it. She's a mm-hmm. She's a stuck-up mm-hmm. She thinks she's too good for me. She thinks she's too good for own mother. She thinks too smart for everyone and too good.

"Well I'd say it her face. I would. I would say it her face, 'You know what you're?' And I'd say it. Right her face I'd say it. 'You're stuck-up mm-hmm.' I'd point my finger right up to her, I'd jab it right into her goddamned turned-up nose. I'd say right to her face.

"But I don't even have to. She looks at me like stink, like I offend her senses. With her goddamn turned-up nose, look down on me? I don't even have to tell her what I think of her. She knows. She knows. She knows what I think her because she knows I call them like I see it. I'm the kind of guy who's not pull any punches. I'm not gonna tell you something you wanna hear just because you wanna hear it whether or not it's true or not, but I'm not gonna say it anyway just because I think it's what you wanna hear but it's not true. Uh-uh. Not me. That's not kind of guy I'm.

"Mel, pfft. I don't even need tell her. She knows what I think of her and besides Ronnie always wants it so I be nice to her and I can. I'm above that. I can be civil. While she looks at me down her goddamn nose like I stink, like I'm offend her senses, I don't care. I love Ronnie and I can be civil.

"We saw her, oh, don't know. She came round about a year ago? It was spring, muddy. Remember muddy shoes in pancake house. Ronnie gets all nervous before we're gonna to meet her. She'd been calling and she left messages round and Ronnie won't call her back. I don't know. Messages were simple, 'Mom, I'm wanna see you. Please call me.' She left one on tape at my mom's house I heard. She's very formal, polite and sophisticated. She doesn't say anything more than, 'Mom, please call me. It's Mel and I'm wanna see you.' But she sounds like such bitch-Nazi when she says it. Can't blame Ronnie doesn't want call her back, bitch-daughter. Need a lime.

"But finally I had to say, I said, 'Jesus, Ronnie, shit.' I said, 'Goddamn it, I hear her nose turned up to the goddamn phone, even the way she leaves message.' She says it, 'I'm need to see you,' like not even like serious like some serious situation, but like command she says it. She commands it. I said, 'Jesus, Ronnie, your daughter is a bitch-daughter.' And Ronnie, shit, ten years she's been hearing me. She knows I'm a gonna call things like I see it.

"I'm with Ronnie every day. I know Ronnie. I love Ronnie. I love Ronnie and I protect Ronnie and Ronnie loves me. And we're good together. I know. I know her goddamn bitch-daughter, stuck-up mm-hmm. She doesn't need this shit. She doesn't. She doesn't need it.

"But Mel keeps to leave messages, 'I'm wanna see you, Mom,' everywhere we might be, so finally I said, I said, 'Ronnie, shit. I'll call the goddamn bitch-daughter back, shit.' And Ronnie says, she goes, 'No, no.' But I know nervous she gets. Ronnie, she's real sensitive and especially her kids, especially the older two ones, Kent and Mel. Kent and Mel, those two really to scare her.

"So I said, 'Shit, Ronnie, give me the phone and I'll call her. I'll tell it to her like is and get her to stop leaving these messages of her nose turned up all over wherever we go. I'll call her.' But Ronnie says, 'No. I'm go meet her.'

"Well shit, Ronnie how sensitive she is. Everyone bothers her. Her nerves, she just thinks, she really thinks everyone is going out to get her. She calls her and we're gonna go both meet her at the pancake house. We're gonna meet her in the pancake house parking lot, 10 AM We told her, we're smart. This was my idea. We told her 'Meet us at this pancake house,' and it's just off interstate and there's one hundred motels right there by that pancake house. So when she meets us there she'll thinks we're in one those motels. But we're not. We're in a different motel. We're not at one of those motels by the pancake house. We've been a few exits away from there at the same motel we've been at.

"That time it was a nothing time. How we should do know it was this time Ronnie's mom died? Stick up her nose to me. I used to go in, watch Sabina dance."

Earlier, back at Nana's, walking off to get him and Mel coffees, Joe peeked in on Ronnie as he passed the bedroom.

Flat on her back on the bed, shoes on, the folded rag masked her eyes. She scratched her side.

In the kitchen Joe poured two cups of coffee, a lot of sugar in his own and a little cream in Mel's. Picking up the cups, he paused. He creaked the cabinet open, quiet as he could and poured a generous splash of rum into his cup. Leaning closely over Mel's, he spat a thick loogie, plunked his finger in to stir the bubbles into the surface.

Returning to the living room with a smile, Joe found Mel inspecting two snowglobes closely, attempting to determine their differences. Joe held her coffee out to her.

3

Will crossed Nana's brittle yellow front lawn in the moonlight, a step behind Kent, heavy plastic bags bouncing. The night blew through the wide, silent street in low moans.

Kent slipped in his car, leaned over to unlock Will's door. Unable to find the lever to lean the seat forward, Will piled his bags clumsily into the backseat. The crimson interior was pristine except for a couple conspicuous clumps of mud on the floor by the passenger side, the shapes of cleats, and a wide smear of pale mud on the seat. Will paused, put a finger to the smear.

"What?" Kent asked.

"Making sure this wasn't wet," Will replied, turning to sit down.

"What?" Kent sounded alarmed.

"Nothing, it's fine," Will said.

"What's fine? What's not wet?"

"Nothing," Will spun back up out of the car and pointed to the mud smear. "Just this."

Nostrils flared and lips pinched, Kent took a deep breath, put a fingernail to the mud to scratch a smidge. "I can get a towel from inside to put over it."

Will shook his head. "Let's just go," he said.

"My goddamn kid." Kent said.

"Really, it's fine," Will insisted, sitting back down in the car.

"You sure? I don't want you to get dirty," Kent said.

"It's nothing. See? Let's go."

Kent got back in the car and leaned over to look at Will's back against the mud on the passenger seat.

"It's fine. It's dry," Will said. "I'll lean forward."

Kent shrugged, popped a Nicorette. Turning the ignition, the song picked up loudly somewhere in the middle of a verse. Kent reflexively reached to turn it down. But with a deep sigh by the end of the first block, he rewound the tape in a clicking whirl to start the song over at the top. Pausing at the stop sign to make a left, no cars passed. He waited for the brief drum machine intro to start, turned it up loud enough to squelch any possibility of conversation, then stepped on the gas.

Since the first time he'd ever gotten into a car with him, Will knew Kent drove at one speed and one speed only, whether through open country roads, the sparsely trafficked and irregularly concentrated streets of downtown Stone Claw Grove or the neighborhoods of children potentially chasing balls from every driveway. In certain conditions that speed was chillingly quick, and in others it was a panic-attack dawdle. Though it depended on the environment to set its rate, only one criteria mattered to Kent. The streetlights had to strobe in sync to the beats per minute of "Eminence Front" by The Who. Will had never heard another song in Kent's car, and he never stepped into Kent's car without hearing it.

As a teenager, seventeen, eighteen years old, Kent picked Will up for an afternoon together, about once a month. Usually they had every other week planned, and Kent cancelled half the time. Though neither of the two particularly enjoyed the time together or ever got the impression the other one was enjoying himself, they still felt accountable to the ritual for a couple years. By then Dell had been gone five years already. Kent had lessened his pot intake in favor of greater quantities of cocaine, motivating him to occasionally strike out in clumsy earnest gestures at what he saw as his responsibilities. "That boy needs a male role model," as if batting cages and miniature golf were somehow necessities.

"Eminence Front" transported Will back without failure to feeling like the coolest six-, seven-year-old in the world. His brief flirtation with sunglasses humongous on his face, the flashiest manifestation of adulthood's magnetic draw on him, came entirely from soaking and marinating in the song.

Interlocking synthesizers panned hard, curled along. Keith Moon's tidal waves of fills replaced on that record by a straight ahead post-disco groove, the patient structure giving Townshend time to build his solo at the top into a series of climaxes, each impossibly furthering the promise of the preceding crescendo, while Entwistle and the studio drummer kept it all locked down cool. This was Will's idea of adulthood. Adulthood was the freedom to snort powder off the thumb-side of your closed fist at stop signs. Adulthood was pushing your Firebird to its premium resonant rattling point against all better judgment if that's what it took to make the streetlights fall in rhythm with the long suspense and slow decay of each gigantic bass throb.

Will could not recall ever actually being anywhere with Kent. The meaning was in the transport between faded destinations, driving ranges and matinees, stations. Stepping into Kent's car, like returning to the eye of a swirling depression or back into the familiarity of a retired liquor or the heat of fighting, returned Will to a continuous space uninterrupted by the years and miles between each seating. Life in Kent's car was a life set apart, aside, running parallel to their own lives, the land of "Eminence Front."

What a surprise as a teenager, hearing the song at a party in Beau's basement once. Not only could the song exist independently from Kent's car, but within a group. Will's worlds collapsed on each other in a small way.

That afternoon, driving from the funeral home to the cemetery, Will had attempted to ask Kent about the song. Hypothetically, what if Daltrey had sung it? Even mixed as low as they were, could the song have been written without Townshend's synthesizer fixation?

But Kent never acknowledged being spoken to when driving, when the song played. Occasionally, if a stoplight happened to fall on the third guitar solo, he might quickly blurt, "You know, kiddo, most people don't have what it takes to keep it all together under the power of this magic powder." But driving, he'd ignore being directly addressed, even if in response to his own statements.

With his regal airs hung in suspension by the song's pulse, Kent had somehow, even after all these years of listening to it, missed the song's critical dimension, its simple calling out of arrogance and hypocrisy, instead mistaking its glacial façade as an endorsement of what it mocked. Such a basic misunderstanding stripped the song of all tension.

Will knew Kent would not condescend to discussing it. Will was thinking about it too much. It was just a song, he'd say.

Will leaned to the cold glass of his window, closed his eyes. The dim light of the moon splintering through branches striped his vision pale orange. The song halted with comic punctuation and Kent promptly clicked the rewind button. The sideways bounce of the car gripped Will's gut, twisted it. They sat quietly with the harmonies of the rush of the road and the tape rewinding.

Kent was not an aggressive driver. He was only unaware of other cars. This resulted in him driving aggressively. But that was not his intention. His driving did not reflect the imposing of his will out into the world of traffic, only the drift of his entitlement.

From his baby-puke hatchback Chevette to his cherished black Firebird, to his box, boat-white Grenada with the crimson interior which he loved to demonstrate was plush enough to leave a fossilized handprint in, to his current family dumpster, the song played on endless loop to justify his detached recklessness. The song unified his reflexes, smoothing out sudden brakes and lunges.

The lights along the inside of the tunnel glimmered in double time with the synthesizers. Neon beer signs and the expansive canvases of blank billboards through the local industrial corridor flashed along with the palm-chug of the guitar. Downtown, the distance between streetlights increased. Kent slowed down through the mostly empty streets to sustain the rhythmic beaming streaks in half time. Will was turned around, the city's layout cut up and re-arranged compared to his memory.

"Fuck it. Let's stop," Kent said.

Will, alarmed said, "Huh?"

"Fuck. It. I'm. Stopping."

"No, man. Really." Will. said. "I'm tired."

Will riffled through the plastic bag in his lap, dug to the bottom, no marshmallow bars left.

"Let's just have a look," Kent said.

Kent braked quick, turned hard into the far end of The Cave's parking lot with a roller coaster's swoop. Will's stomach headed on straight ahead of them. Tall streetlights lined the lot, tight. Kent slowed to a crawl without noticing he did so, making the steady strut of the song quicken, the drunken tilts and farewells of the closing-time crowd frantic.

"Relapse, man?" Will said.

"What?" Kent turned to him, surprised. "What did you say?"

"Really, man?" Will sank low in his seat. "I said, 'Really, man.'"

7. Humbly asked Him to remove his shortcomings.

8. Shit, what was 8?

Kent smiled, lips tight and nostrils flared, shook his head.

9. Hadn't made direct amends to such people wherever possible, but he will, sure will.

10. Continued to take personal inventory and when he was wrong, promptly admitted it.

"What? You don't want to see who we know?" Kent asked.

Kent stuck to the perimeter, a shark's taunting circle. "You were straining your neck, turning around in your seat."

Will crossed his arms across his chest. Three years working nights at the home, the mentally disabled stronger than any rivals in his previous circuits. He couldn't hit them back. That was part of it. Steer their own momentum away from himself, pin them until they calmed down. That was it. His own strength ethically limited in this way strengthened his rivals, adults with special needs, by comparison. Will assumed the strength of the hooting and smiling, blank-faced and bonered giants he wrestled into peace depended entirely on their inability to conceptualize. He envied their governance by impulse, perfect as robots.

With nothing more than a Fuck it, let's stop, Kent returned him to the scene of the championship he once held and walked away from. Will, confused, almost thought Kent was looking for someone in particular. Felt like Kent maybe wanted something to happen.

Finally finding The Shhh... after getting turned around, Will didn't go in, but instead sat with his plastic bags on a parking block at the far end of the lot. A brisk night, he was pleased to stare at the building, its shape shadowed in the thrown moonlight and neon, bask in the passive blurred drift of countless specific nights spent there. The cute skinhead girl with buckteeth's ex on a jealous tirade, one busy Sunday night before a bank holiday, throwing a salad into the ceiling fan, Scrabble in the afternoon once, betting quarters on *Antique Roadshow*, blood.

The spin of a parked police light threw his shadow up on a tall brick wall in cycles. His hunched silhouette remained solid in the twists of red and blue. Few places in town truly drew him, the fried Okra and limeade at Dan's Drive-In, cheap smokes at the drive-thru tobacco shop near the casino, but they won't let you walk through the drive-thru. Thirty-six hours in town might be just long enough. A day expanded could be enough, make apparent home no longer home.

With a metal bang, Norman backed out the door, muttered, "Asshole-cock-shits."

The police light dropped away, pulled off. The lot was dark. Stretching his back, cracking his knuckles, Will stood. Bent to stack his plastic bags close to the fence, double-checked their balance. With a shallow bounce of his back against the wire fence, Will shuffled in the dust across the lot to the open door. Unlit cigar dangling, Norman didn't notice the gravel crunch, steps approaching. He spun sideways in the door, fussed to get his lighter from his pocket stretched tight to his leg, muttered, "The fuck they think I'll do? Sons of asshole-mother-fuckers."

He flipped at his lighter a few times—flint, flint—but it failed to spark.

Will stopped a step behind him, blocking him in the

door. Giving up on his lighter, Norman turned and stepped, startled into Will, dropped the cigar and hooted, "Whoo!"

Will smirked, nodded. Hand on his pepper spray, collecting himself with a tug at his lapels and a dusting of his front, Norman stood up straight with widened eyes, "Jesus Christ, Will. Will?"

"Norman," Will said, stepping into the light of the door thrown open.

Norman looked Will over. "Jesus Christ, Will. Jesus," he said.

He shook his head, grimaced, studying the seams and folds of Will's face, said, "Long time, Will. Jesus."

Will agreed, "Yep, Norman, long time."

Norman attempted to step past him. Will planted his feet.

Will's agreement to never return to Stone Claw Grove had always pleased Norman. Rich's condition for getting Will's manslaughter charge buried: just leave. Just leave and never come back. Security no longer had to fight off this dancing clown covered in blood, his ghost dance frightening off business from the parking lot. The whole town liberated from Will's self-important and warped sense of vigilante justice turned against himself.

Norman pulled his keys from his pocket and clicked the button to unlock his car, "ee-oo."

"Sorry to hear about your gramma," Norman said.

Will thanked him.

Norman took a deep breath, pinched his cigar down at his waist. "Heard no one was exactly sure where to find you," he said. "Didn't know if you found out, but never expected to see you here."

Will dropped his head and nodded.

"But, well, here you are."

Will smiled Yeah, here I am.

When Will had been too dumb to take the deal that Norman, through Rich, had arranged for him with the city, get out of town and the charges will be buried, Norman used Mel as leverage and Will reconsidered. Norman could accept Will breaking the deal, this one time, what with his gramma and all, this once.

"Real long time, huh?" Norman stepped again, this time Will giving in allowed Norman's girth to pass with a light shoulder bump.

Will agreed. "Real long time."

The door swung closed behind Norman. The parking lot was dark and except for the traffic, far off like a marble spinning in a metal bowl, the night was empty of sounds.

The problem, as Norman saw it, was simple. No one in this entire fucking city had any fucking taste, seriously. You have an opportunity. You do your best. You realize your vision, this vision you'd been detailing. Refining every fucking detail for fucking he didn't know how many years, a life's work, the bank always waiting in the background. And what? You realize your vision and what? You think any of these asshole-morons care? Seriously, that city, wasn't there anyone that had a goddamn clue?

He should've moved. He should've known. But no, I'm so fucking stupid, naïve and generous. That's what I am, he thought. That's how I'm stupid. I hang around here.

He had his shot. The club was his. He should've sold it. Someone would've bought it, the bank or the city. Some asshole would've kept it as it always had been, a museum, that's what people wanted. It's immature, he thought. That's what it is. People could not, just would not accept change.

Now he couldn't go anywhere. Sunk everything into this place, his vision, shit. Even his pathetic "Classic Shhh..." idea bombed. Interior architects, interior designers, mixologist training, the ingredients. The doormen got paid and the girls got paid and the bartenders got paid and the DJ got paid, the fucking shit he fucking played, shit. Everyone got a piece. Everyone got paid but Norman.

His vision, his work, his blood and sweat and tears, he liked to say, for that, for Stone Claw Grove? I'm so fucking stupid, he thought. My god, am I stupid?

He thought those Gomer Pyles would appreciate a little taste. He thought he could introduce them all to a little touch, just a little bit of class. A little sophistication—why should that be only for the big cities? He should've known. He should've known he was thinking ahead of his time. A place like that might not ever be ready for it. He was just way too ahead of his time, that was it.

He got exactly what he wanted. Built it exactly as it looked in his mind, as he envisioned it. If there was some error, some distortion, any kind of compromise, okay. But no, everything came together exactly as he planned. Until he ran out of money, had to leave it half-done, half-done exactly as he envisioned it.

But these people, this fucking city—no sense of loyalty. Years The Shhh... delivered them a reliable product, a refuge from their lives, refuge from their pathetic, miserable, sorry little lives. A fantasy they could walk into, sit down in.

But someone gets too comfortable in a fantasy, what happens? You make yourself at home in a fantasy, get cozy and then what? It's no longer a fantasy. It's just home. You feel at home in it and it's comfortable. So all of them, they had all stopped coming around.

A couple old regulars had stopped by once or twice since the grand reopening. And all they could say was, "Geez, Norman, a little steep for a beer, isn't it?" Or "I just want a Four Roses. What's wrong with that, Norman? Something wrong with Four Roses?" Losers, all of them, no goddamn taste between them.

Gus sat around reading. He should've been in the kitchen. Norman kept the girls dancing now, every minute that the club was open. Even they complained. "Well, Norman, I feel dumb dancing if there's no one here." But how would it look someone walked in and saw them all sitting around, Gus reading his poems to the girls, the girls in costume doing crossword puzzles together. How would that look?

A couple of the real losers, the totally soaked-brain bums, buying their schnapps with dimes, they still came around smelling like piss and cigarettes. Those dopes, Norman didn't know if they realized things had changed around there, didn't know if they even knew they were still in the same place.

His dad, Rich, the son of a bitch, set him up. For that he was thankful. Oh, he set him up. Everyone's best friend, the guy anyone could go to in a time of need, confusion. Just ask Rich. But Norman never met that guy. He knew Rich, the absent guy, the mean old motherfucker, the cocksucker enumerating what he did and he did it only for his son, Norman. Tough and cool, tough as nails and cool, would hardly condescend to Norman, the one he was doing it all for, the one he was setting up. That was his big fucking fat laugh at Norman from the grave, son of a bitch. Norman inherited a sinking ship just in time, so that by the time he took the wheel it was already sunk and looked like he sank it and his dad got to laugh again, his ashes over there behind the bar and scattered in the yard—Ha!

Norman used to watch Gus putting together his "manuscript," his precious manuscript. Couldn't believe Rich would even use that word, "manuscript," with a straight face.

"Oh, Gus, how's the manuscript coming?" as if that were a word that he used every day. Sure, weren't all the guys suffering over their manuscripts, of course. But Norman, fuck it, you know. Rich never liked Norman, okay? Norman never did anything good enough for him. He could never please Rich. Norman should've written a goddamn manuscript of all his poems. That, Rich could have appreciated. His own flesh and blood with opinions and ideas, wanting to help him? No. That was nothing compared to the cook's goddamn poetry.

Gus would even read the poems to Rich sometimes. Gobbledy-gook, meaningless shit, but Rich would listen closely and nod when Gus was done, like he was really thinking hard about it. He'd always say, "Gus, I can't believe that's what you're thinking about. I can't believe you're just walking around or sitting there and that's what's on your mind." And he'd say that like he meant it, like he liked it.

Norman got his dream all done, built. Twenty-eight years

old and the dream all assembled, the plans half-executed of course, but the course set. The distractions of twenty-eight years had all been settled. And now, so, that was it. Everything he counted on, was so fucking sure would make everything just perfect, what had it improved? At least before he had the dream as a dream, all that he needed to do and his perfect life would all come together. Now it was all together, dream built, wasted on those fucking yahoos, credit maxed, and now, now he didn't even have the dream of building it, just the headache of finishing it. Seemed like his life before, his dream of building the dream, wasn't so bad, all potential. Once the potential had been spent, the inherited debts, he was eating pasta, drinking Four Roses. He never thought of a Plan-B dream.

Business on paper, maybe it was even the same. He lost the old regulars, but picked up a little bit of a new clientele. But even same amount of money coming in, things were more expensive now. Seemed empty now. They needed less people in there with their higher prices, but they had higher expenses. The profit was less.

Aren't I fucking genius? He thought, Aren't I a little pencil-shrimp-dicked, fatass, sweaty fucking loud mouth asshole fucking genius? The laughing stock fucking genius that built his dream, built his dream in this shithole town.

Norman struggled with digging into the tight pocket of his pants. "Here, I think I got a, uh…"

Will lifted his hand to scratch at the back of his neck and Norman flinched, stood still. Breathing deep, he continued, "Can't find it. Thought I had a VIP card."

Will shrugged. "But you know what?" Norman said with a big smile, "Wish I could stick around and catch up, you know, I really do. But I got plans, a young hottie, lamb steaks with mint sauce. But you know those guys in there, right? Your sister's working, dancing. Tell you what, tell the guys you saw me and I said to buy you a drink. Okay?"

Will dropped his eyes, sighed.

8. Make a list of all persons he had harmed, and become willing to make amends to them all.

"Everyone's just gonna be so glad to see you, Will. You just tell them I said tonight you're drinking on me, okay? Whatever you want, we got a big, new menu. Get yourself something nice, okay?"

Surprised by a porchlight coming on across the street, they both stood still, quiet, surprised to find themselves standing so close to one another.

"Jesus," Norman said. Inspecting Will again with a concentrated sneer, he shook his head. Will stood straight and still. Norman absentmindedly lifted a finger to Will's cheek and, catching himself before contact, pulled away.

"You look," Norman paused to search for the word, "good."

Will chuckled, turned away. "Yeah? Well, hey, look at you."

Norman waved him off. "Just a good-looking suit."

"Special occasion?"

"Nope, no." Norman popped his cigar into his mouth. "I just found the right suit for me and so, I got a few identical ones."

Will nodded. Norman pivoted. Will dug in the gravel with his heel.

THE LAST OF MEL'S KARAOKE BIRTHDAYS

The room had filled up a little. Bottles held overhead in suspense, the entire wound-up assembly hooted through the dramatic intro, which, extended in the pulse of a speedboat skipping across moonlit curling waves and dock espionage atmosphere, stretched itself into becoming almost the entire song. The man on stage faked his own echo effect. Sounded good to Will. He really could feel it coming in the air tonight.

Mel, lite beer to waist, thumbs through belt loops, tilted forward and back. She felt it coming in the air tonight. When do those big tom fills come in? Norman downed his bourbon in a gulp, slid through the room, a light touch prompted by the hanging mystery of the song's mood to excuse himself past backs turned to him, made his way to the stage. Here? The drums come in now? That guy really did a great fake echo. Gus, eyes bleary and shoulders aching with the joy of depressants, felt it coming in the air tonight, felt real and real happy.

Blinking her expression into a consciously blank grin, Mel looked from Norman, poised to pounce, Oh no, Norman was feeling it coming in the air tonight, to Will, standing back in a shadow, gaze fixed on Norman. Will shifted his weight. Norman wouldn't really crash the stage again, she thought. Would he? Maybe he just wanted to feel part of the throng in suspense, waiting for those big toms to drop.

Mel smiled to Will, hoping she might squelch his irritation with Norman, laugh it off, but failed to catch Will's eye. She understood, couldn't blame him, but still, he had promised. She waved and the drums, of course, when those big drums finally came in, tom-tom—tom-tom—tomtom-tom-tom--tomtomtom—the whole room swung cool, and through every arm in the room flailing air-drums, Norman made his move for the stage. Will lifted a beer from the bar, stepped up behind him.

Waving to Will through the swinging of arms, his nostrils flared and eyes widened, one eye irritated still from Norman's poke, Mel dropped the smile, hopped through the crowd. The man on stage didn't sing but stood at the foot of the stage, arms forward holding Norman back, "No," giving Will an extra instant to knock through the crowd, catch up to Norman.

Norman didn't push, but one foot on stage, shrugged, "What? Geez, I'm just standing here."

Mel, stern and panicked, leapt in front of Norman, a hand to Will's chest as he lifted the beer and tilted it. She bumped her butt hard against Norman's butt behind her to scoot him, his weight too much to really move, but the impact enough for her to receive the balking spill of Will's hoppy baptism.

Eyes burning, Mel wiped her wet hair pressed flat from her face. Over her shoulder, Will glanced at Norman. The man on stage hadn't yet picked up singing again where he had left off, but instead only stared Norman down. Norman puffed up his chest. Rolling his eyes and reading the words from the screen with a glimpse, the man on stage placed the melody on the wrong phrase, started again.

The audience, arms everywhere waving wide, sang, collectively missing the subtle variations of phrasing in the few repetitive lines. All that suspense, the drums finally propelling the song forward, the man on stage could only sing it through to the end, eyes fixed on Norman, defensive of his stage territory. Muttering, Norman shuffled to the bar, passing drenched Mel and fuming Will without noticing, ordered a drink.

Could be the relief, the drums having finally come in. What's left after a puncture? But the singer's distracted defensiveness undid any reserve of tension that had built up in the room. The song, its kernel of a solid body after such an epic build, the fizzle of a leaky air mattress, the entire song ended up being about a single drum fill. People applauded, but the singer knew he should've done better, channeled and focused the energy, carried it beyond the fill. Head down, he started to sneak off the stage, but people stopped him.

"Oh yeah, right," he said. "Uh, 1351, um... Mel."

"Real sorry again, about your Gramma," Norman said.

Standing shoulder to shoulder with Will, he said in a hushed tone, "Real good to see you, Will." Looking Will in the eye, he said, "Now go get yourself a drink on me, alright?"

Will nodded.

10. Number ten. Continue to take personal inventory and when wrong, promptly admit it.

Turning his back to Will slowly, Norman began to walk off. He lifted his feet tall in the parking lot to keep dust from his cuffs. Never turning around, but listening closely, step, step, step, he called out as he crossed the lot to his car, "And you take care, Will. Really is good to see you, man. Good talking to you." Only a few steps from his car, keys in hand, "You take care, Will, take care."

His car between he and Will, Norman stopped before getting in, threw his arms across its roof and leaned.

"Oh, Will," he called out. He unlocked the car, cracked the door.

"Yep," Will responded.

"So, uh, how long exactly do you think you're staying in town for?" Norman asked.

"Oh, I'll leave tomorrow after the service," Will said.

Norman, his elbows on the roof of his car, nodded with his chin in his cupped hand. "And," he continued, "you just stopped by here tonight to say hello? Find me, let me know you were around?"

Will nodded. "See if I could sleep at my sister's."

"Right," Norman said. "Your sister, of course. Like I said, she's dancing tonight, in there right now all dolled up, up on stage."

Will put his hands to his hips, looked away.

"But that's all?" Norman said. "That's all you came by here for tonight?"

Will nodded.

"That's it, all that's going to happen?" Norman said.

Will inhaled deeply, continued nodding. "Yeah, Norman," he called out, awkward, loud. "That's all I stopped by for."

Norman tapped a knuckle lightly on the roof of his car before getting in.

"Well, if you're still around later, my buddies The Russians might be coming by later," he said. "You know those guys, don't you?"

"No," Will said. "I don't know if I do."

"Oh," Norman said. "Well, they're fun, always a good time."

Will shrugged.

10. Continue to take personal inventory and when wrong, promptly admit it.

Without looking back to Will again, Norman got in his car. Revving his engine before shifting into drive, gave Will a fingerpoint goodbye.

Will didn't move until Norman pulled off, kicking up gravel as he sped off, full throttle all at once. Will dragged his feet back across the lot, toed the parking block a moment before throwing his head back and sighing deeply. The factory-church was lined with stories of boarded up windows like blocks of broken teeth. The moon reflected in the single window that still had glass in it.

Piling his plastic bags up into his arms, Will walked off, running his finger along the fence to its end, moved to the middle of the street where the streetlights fell. Among the rows of wood on the factory-church, splotchy with stained edges, like teeth after coffee, the window reflecting the moon looked like a shining gold tooth.

He'd hoped to find Mel, crash on her couch, but didn't want to walk in on her dancing, didn't want to wait around, watch her all dolled up, cooing for creeps. The bus station would be fine, plenty of practice sleeping sitting up. And if he saw Norman, goddamn it, he really had meant to apologize, was supposed to. Just couldn't name why, remember exactly what for.

Kent continued, carved slowly through the parking lot of The Cave and back out, a survey of the scene seemingly enough.

"No one special you were looking for?" Will asked. Kent shrugged.

On the main road, a detour to avoid driving past Ronnie's old place, overgrown, would only have given the abandoned house more power. Each of them sensed the other hold his breath as they passed the house, Castle Grayskull under twenty years of weeds. Will was surprised, how boring, continued to stand exactly as it always had, smaller than he remembered it.

"Fuck it. Let's stop," Kent said, smiling a block later, a sharp turn on to the next street. No longer under streetlights, but in darkness, he slowed almost to a stop for a moment before creeping along. Moved slow up the street. Will checked the plastic bag on his lap again, but found only the torn up wrappers of marshmallow bars.

Will imagined a family of raccoons might have made themselves at home there in Ronnie's old place. This raccoon family probably picked up Ronnie and Dell's life from the moment before Dell split, the Mama-raccoon happily handing the children sack lunches as they headed off to school together, while the Daddy-raccoon finished the morning paper over a coffee, before heading off for the office park. How silly.

Kent let the car idle a moment at the stop sign at the end of the block. Couldn't see the neighborhood beyond the beams.

THE LAST OF MEL'S KARAOKE BIRTHDAYS

Gus, smiling, scrambled over to Mel, pushed her from Will to the stage as her song began, surprised and confused by her wet, sticky arms but too excited to halt his mission.

"Gus, no, no," she said. "I don't want to, not now."

"Don't be shy," he smiled, tugging at her as he bounced. "Why you wet, anyway?"

She shook her head. "I prefer to just watch," she said. "You do it. You sing."

"No, no, no," he said, pressing the microphone into her hand, Depeche Mode's "Enjoy the Silence."

"Here you go," he said, smiling big, pointing to the bouncing ball on the screen. "It's you, go."

Missing her cue, she stood, smelling the beer on her hair, aware of her shirt suctioning to her breasts. Norman returned to the front of the stage. Her eyes floated along one wall to the back of the room, clusters of people standing, talking like the cliquey girls at the club. Mumbling to catch up, she picked up the lyrics mid-melody, plodding along in her throaty speaking voice. If it's easier to sing it in the wrong key, fuck it. It's easier. The faces in the room, individuals within clusters, with a transmission of nerves, a charge passed, watching her so nervous made everyone else nervous to watch her. Her fingers fussed with her blouse's buttons, peeled her shirt from her skin with a tug. She looked down, continued to mumble along. Unbutton?

She had really wanted to sing "Knockin' on Heaven's Door," the simplicity of the *oohs* inviting the whole room into participation, but felt somehow bashful about it. Party animal types often basically lip-synched an anthemic song, "Pour Some Sugar on Me" or something, the audience sings the whole thing and all the singer has to do is be a hype-man of sorts. She thought she could've done her version of this with "Knockin' on Heaven's Door," hype a dirge, but chickened out. Even if singing was really about the physical guttural sensation of tuneful breath, the words, the pretense of the words' presence had to be retained. She wished she'd sung it. Goddamn "Enjoy the Silence" hardly had more words and lacked the sing-a-long to hide behind.

Will had to watch her reflection, couldn't look at her directly, she was so nervous. In the mirrored wall, bounced, she was half-hidden behind the crowd. He heard her, *Words are very unnecessary, can only do harm*. This, her annual party she insisted on. Six months out she would begin to consider what song she'd sing that year. And that was what she wanted, to publicly mumble off-key, wanted quiet.

She shrank, withered. Dancing is different, voiceless. Couldn't do this, and the room, no one had come out to see this. Everyone's supposed to demonstrate his or her ability to stand tall and fail, the ritual. She looked at herself in the mirror, even worse clothed. Saw how they all saw her, what value clothed? The ritual was about proud amateurism, not shame. Had to be. The more she heard her own voice, the deeper her listening, the more stilted she sang. Her arm hairs stuck flat to her forearm. Decaying before them all, my god, she had stood up to decay. Sang through gritted teeth.

Top of the second verse, after the first chorus, feeling faint, hot under stage lights and the audience, each a performer in waiting, all talking. They were all talking about her. She knew it, popped her top button open.

Norman grabbed her by the wrist, her whole arm a

microphone stand, overtook the song with his celebratory moan. Liberated from singing, Mel rolled her eyes, spun and gestured to him, presenting him, "Ladies and gentlemen..." The crowd detonated to attention with roaring boos.

She could not un-sing her song, but she had been shielded. No one would remember her nerves, standing up on stage sticky with beer for a mumbling display, compared to booing this guy, his projection of shame he mistook for a projection of cool.

And by offering himself up like that to save Mel, like he knew all along, knew how he was, how people saw him. At the end of the song, cutting across the room to the bar through booing and jeers, Norman, like a hammy pro-wrestling villain, took it in stride with a snide smile and waves.

After rinsing herself off in the ladies room Mel wanted to get out of there, but Gus insisted they wait. He was signed up for one more song, then he was ready. Not long to wait before chatter silenced, no one ordered or served. The dart game suspended. No one moved. A hand in his pocket, Gus stunned the room, a flutter in the public veil, "If You Could Read My Mind," by Gordon Lightfoot.

People sometimes sing a song about vulnerability with a pride that undoes the song's impact. They hit all the notes or whatever, but Gus, his performance went beyond pride or shame. A transferral of loss, all the same dull gut ache, a shadow, which passed over whatever walls, might recede, linger even for extended periods, but never diminished. Gus himself, did he know? He, the vessel, the song, the charge, but did he even know this, what he could do, simply allowing it to pass through him, did he know? Presenting absence. The doorman sniffled.

Gordon Lightfoot must've been older when he wrote that song, older than most songwriters in the karaoke book. *What a story his thoughts would tell*, but he was singing his thoughts. How would the story have been different if he didn't have to translate his thoughts into the act of singing? Wasn't it the act of representing his thoughts, their expression, that was affecting, more so than the thoughts themselves?

The song's protagonist, he's *a ghost*, and *a hero*, but *heroes often fail*. His situation, *like a paperback novel*, the recognition of the cliché of his own experience, felt real to him from inside the experience. Not only real, but devastating, the most real, and the recognition of it as a cliché only added to the devastation. He walked away like *a movie star*, cool and collected, needed only *a movie queen to play the scene*. The singer asked the listener, came right out and sang it, *read between the lines*. The self-reflexivity wasn't a stretch. *He never thought he could feel that way.* He admitted it, the alienation from himself, the experience set next to his expectations.

Let's get real. I never thought I could act this way and I have to say that I just don't get it. Reality was being witness to one's self, surprised by one's own actions. Facing reality, getting real, meant the risk of not recognizing one's self.

The song ended. There was a moment of silence before applause. Mel looked to Norman watching Gus. Will leaned against the wall, hidden in the shadow left by the unplugged jukebox, toeing the light thrown from the pinball machine. Norman chomped down on an ice cube, looked to Mel. The applause tepid after such attentiveness, the room as confused in its appreciation as it was as witness.

Gus returned to Mel and Norman through the silent crowd.

"Okay," Gus said. "Let's go?"

"Was that that Whitney Houston song?" Norman asked so loudly that the whole room could hear him.

"What?"

"*I decided long ago never to walk in anyone's shadow.*"

"It was Gordon Lightfoot."

"Huh? Sounded just like that Whitney Houston song, but I knew it wasn't it. Sounded just like it, though."

"Gordon Lightfoot, the Canadian James Taylor?"

Gus lit a cigarette from Mel's cigarette.

In the kitchen at the Shhh... it hit Sarah Ann, what didn't expand in every direction? She'd maybe never before been so aware of the pulse and charge of her skin. But, what couldn't expand in every direction at once when it had to?

She recalled the double-parked Coca-Cola truck making a delivery at the hospital.

She saw herself as Gus must have seen her. This man a stranger, not quite sixty, not quite not dumpy, hardly taller than her. His hair like a single layer of feathers stuck to his lacquering of sweat. Sweat on sweat on grease on sweat on grease, the layers of his make-up, his kindness and how easily it came to him. He made it effortlessly and immediately apparent how simply able to be kind he was.

The walls of the kitchen beat and beaded, the outermost layers of his own skin and she and any and all else that entered there, entered into a realm of him. Entering this kitchen, systems of knives stacked according to his reach, color-coded towels, each for a specific use, who could help but see him- or herself as he must have seen them? His bicycle stood flipped upside down on its seat and handlebars in the corner, its front wheel bent, folded.

Shuffling pans over eight flames, he picked this one up then that one and gave them each a gentle shake. Tater tots in the deep fryer smelled only of the oil they fried in. A baking tuna steak, frying pierogis, and a pulled pork barbecue couldn't mingle scents and only the deep fryer's oil claimed the space and hung. Gus leaned heavy on the prep table for a blink and breath as if allowing himself to do so only after staving off the necessity as long as possible. The weight of his sudden gesture surprised her, but just as suddenly he was up again, hands on his lower back and stretching. He looked her over closely.

The judgment all came from within her. Yes, eighteen. Yes, needed a shower and needed a night's sleep somewhere humane or at least a change of clothes. Yes, carrying everything in this overstuffed backpack. Yes, a fool in the grossest of lashings out. Yes, threw a tantrum all over her own life and struck out against it like some kind of wild jackal basking in tearing it all apart, whatever struck her comfortable, anything familiar. Yes, she may as well have blood running down her chin and a mad puppet's laugh. No, it wasn't really her. She wasn't really like this. But no, she couldn't say who it was, what overtook her.

" 'Sarah Ann,' you said?"

She nodded a shallow nod. Tell him her old name?

Gus said, "Didn't expect to... after last night, you scared us leaving, when we came out of the grocery store."

"Sorry," Sarah Ann said. A tangle of hair stuck to the grease on the bottom lip of the steel stove.

"It's fine, fine," he responded. "Just made us a little nervous."

She nodded.

He rubbed his hands together and took a deep breath. "So, why would you want to work here?"

"Norman said you were a poet."

Gus recognized she'd said "poet" without the usual mocking tone everyone else there said it with.

"Norman? That's his name, right? Out there?"

Gus nodded, "Yeah, that's Norman, but how—"

"He showed me how to dance sexy," she said with a big smile.

Gus squinted, picturing this, and sighed. "Yeah, he's manic when he's not lugubrious."

"Yeah, he quite sincerely danced sexy for me, asked me to dance like he was."

Gus smiled and shook his head. "I thought that was you sitting out there with him."

"Yeah," Sarah Ann continued, "he put on some Fleetwood Mac, but I told him I wouldn't dance to that Clinton music."

Gus nodded.

"The stupid neoliberal conception of freedom, the self-absorbed, unchecked ego, that's what opened the door for this corporate fascism. It allowed everyone to assume it's their right to have opinions about everything, when there are, in fact, facts in the world," she went on. "Facts that are not disputable."

Gus rubbed the back of his neck. "I kind of like Fleetwood

Mac," he said quietly.

She felt a little embarrassed about getting excited. "And well, finally he said, 'Go talk to the poet' and pointed back here."

"Yeah," Gus's voice a creaky moan. "I mean," he croaked, "I write, they laugh at me some," waving his arms to the club beyond the kitchen. "It's okay, they give me a hard time."

Sarah Ann thought maybe this was the sweetest little man she'd ever seen. And even with so little said between them, seeing herself as he must have seen her redeemed her in some way. This sweet, sweet little man with his constant squirming wouldn't judge her so harshly. Cooking must have kept him still.

"I've just always done it, you know, helps me think through things, figure stuff out," he said.

She tilted her head.

"Writing, I mean," he said.

"Yeah," she blurted. "I mean, I understand. I hate *The DaVinci Code* and its stupid exclamatory big-string swells every thousand words."

He nodded.

She repeated herself, "Yeah."

Freedom, she believed, was only potential, the potential to change one's circumstances. And if one had the privilege to change one's circumstances, one had the responsibility to do so, for the sake of all those who didn't have the privilege. She'd go back to that bus station, submit to the time warp of a four-day bus ride to L.A. She knew she wouldn't be saying goodbye to anyone, so sentimental. Maybe it would've been simpler to not even say hello.

"You know, I have nothing to do with hiring the girls. I only run the kitchen." Gus figured it must have been some kind of set-up by Norman, to see if he would talk her out of dancing. He could see Norman's angle. He wouldn't say a word. The kid wanted to dance, fine, who was he to talk her out of anything?

Gus's shape was exactly as she remembered it from the one photo together, backlit in the hospital cafeteria. She wouldn't mention it, wouldn't say goodbye. Hello was weird enough.

4

Stumbling to the car together, Norman admired the gang's shared shadow thrown across the gravel by harsh yellow lighting. "We need a picture taken," he said. "Don't we all look like Fleetwood Mac together?"

Mel would always regret that night, the last of her karaoke birthdays. Will at his barbaric peak form, made sense then. Her campaigning, his rehabilitation, all the effort to contain his rage, she couldn't ask him to undo that. Once unleashed, she'd quit smoking twice, four months each time, and both times started again in the same way. She'd think, Well, I've gone four months, obviously I can do it, so what's the big deal if I smoke this one time? And then it started again, no decision made. It was just happening.

Asking Will to fight, even passively, could she ask him passively? She could imply permission. Maybe that'd be enough and she could get what she wanted, a few of Norman's fingers broken or a rib. And then she could still scold Will. No. Would've made sense then though, that one night was her chance. That night was her one chance. An inflated raft blew bumping end over end through the parking lot.

Synthesizers, the beginning of The Who's "Eminence Front" began. No one took the stage. The band kicked in with a brisk disco strut, louder than the synth-squiggles. No one took the stage through Townshend's series of solos, each building and deepening the crescendo of the previous solo. Someone wanted to make a dramatic entrance.

A minute in or so, the vocals should come, but no one took the stage.

The man who had sang that he had felt it coming in the air tonight realized that the man that last sang, the guy that sang the Gordon Lightfoot song, he left without setting up the next song. He grabbed the microphone.

"Will?" he called out. "Will, you're up."

People looked around, but no one came to the stage. Mumbling that he didn't know the song, the man shrugged and set the microphone down with a twirl of feedback.

The song played through. The room began to hoot a collective phantom vocal. Instrumental, without a central distraction, the production values of the karaoke re-recording presented themselves as obvious, square approximations of the original song. A great pleasure through the whole room, a song playing like a runaway dog or ghost ship, familiar, but not itself, no one singing it into completion.

After Kent and Will left, Mel couldn't sleep. She'd never, that she could remember, ever spent a night alone in Nana's house before. Sour dip, a fruitcake in the fridge, but Nana's concept of the lifespan of a fruitcake assumed all the fruit of Eden would remain to this day if it had not yet been eaten. Mel wouldn't touch that. Looking over her old paintings didn't interest her. Baby would've been due this week.

Fast-forwarding through a stack of videotapes, the mechanical click into place and fluttering delay of tape winding up suppressed her tempo. Tempted to box them all unwatched, put the box in a closet or box them all unwatched and bury the box in the yard, tempted to crack open the plastic exoskeletons with a butterknife, unwind them all into a giant nest, the swept-up aftermath of a parade, Mel couldn't leave the tapes in a pile at the curb. Curious, maybe she'd have to stuff some of the tapes through a paper shredder, she fast-forwarded through the whole stack.

One videotape, masking tape label disintegrated in digital sweat, thick marker strokes beaded on its glossy surface, hyper-pink or orange, the first Christmas with the camcorder, the camcorder plugged into the television. No Ronnie, just Nana and the kids passing the camcorder between them. Each operator experimented with fast zooms and dizzy pans immediately after the shake of the handoff.

When the shot settled, they all looked to the television, spoke to each other only to point at the television. The Christmas sweaters and the feathered haircuts, the fake wood paneling, sure, but the event itself, their collective actions didn't even look familiar to Mel. Each of them turned quick, looked into the camera, back to the television and back when seeing one's own profile framed.

With a dense wire brush through his blowdried hair, over and over, Kent, sixteen, seventeen at the time, jumped in front of the camera and brushed his hair continuously while looking straight into the camera. He'd glance aside to the television screen without interrupting his strokes. Though playful at the time, Kent failed to recognize the set-up as a set-up—the camera plugged into the TV not only a complex mirror, the camera made evidence, specifically to be watched later. Later, when the wit of the hair-brushing joke had diffused, it instead became nothing but more proof, Kent once again, on record as an asshole.

Exhausted and wound up in equal measures, Mel considered maybe moving in to Nana's place might be simpler than selling it. Gus could have his own room. She could accept Gus as a partner of sorts and no longer a guest who had over-stayed his welcome. A new start back at the most familiar place, preserve the guest room and Will and Kent might even visit.

Kent didn't feel he had to talk to Ronnie. He didn't have to make peace or pretend to be friendly or even say hi, and her stupid fucking shell-shocked drunk-ass boyfriend, forget it. She deserved him. Kent didn't care if her feelings were hurt. Weren't his feelings hurt, his kids would ask how come they'd never met white-Gramma?

Kent layered on the ChapStick. He wondered if Will would even know his kids if he saw them. His boy was eleven, his daughter eight. They were beautiful, genius fucking beautiful fucking miracle little gremlins. He stayed at the goddamn toothpaste factory to get them their clothes and their books and his boy was playing football now, wide receiver and safety, the kid was quick and she'd started jazz dancing. That shit cost money. But he didn't mind because he saw them happy and he knew he would do anything for them, anything. They were getting to an age, they didn't even appreciate the trips to Florida, but he didn't mind.

So, where the fuck was Ronnie? He was supposed to feel bad for her? She was the poor victim of her own bad decisions, locking up her house and leaving it to rot for twenty years, with that huffing maniac, he couldn't even sit still without rattling, all those weird sounds Joe made, the wheezing even when he was at rest. And Kent was supposed to feel bad for her? Her chatter and scratching, she couldn't help it. She was the Mommy. You know what Kent couldn't help? Getting beaten, getting pissed on, did Will even know Dell did that?

Dell would say, "Take out the garbage," and Kent said "Gee, Dad, it's really coming down out there, I dunno, can't it wait until morning?" and Dell was like "No, it can't wait until morning. Take out the trash, I said. You questioning me?"

And so of course Kent was like, "Of course not, Dad, I'm not questioning you," and he went and got the trash and it was, like, half-full at most. Kent knew Dell was setting him up for something but it didn't matter how careful he was because he could never know what angle Dell was coming at him from. Dell maybe didn't even know himself. Just knew he was getting something started.

So Kent took out the garbage and it was really coming down and the whole yard was just mud, always was, soon as a single drop of water hit it the whole dust-spread of it all transformed at once. Kent was buried in fucking mud of course, and he took out the trash and he knew Okay, this is the set-up, can't track mud in the house.

He was soaked and he took his shoes off outside. But Dell, all quiet and sinister, "Your shoes are muddy." And Kent's shivering and Dell said "You're gonna get the flu, get undressed and get in the tub."

So what can he do? Ronnie was at work. It was night and he was always left alone with Dell at night. He just didn't want to get in the tub. He wanted to do anything else in the world, but fucking Dell. Kent was ten years old, eight years old—fucking didn't remember—seven years old?

So he got in the tub and sat down. Dell stood over him and said, "You like to play in the rain, do you?" and Kent's sitting there and Dell spreads his feet and clears his throat and looking Kent directly in the eye, a twinge of a smile to one side of Dell's mouth before he draws it back into his usual unreadable deadpan, and his eyes are all big under his glasses and his brow furrows, and he tugs at the waist of his jeans and clears his throat again and says, "My boy likes to play in the rain," and he unzips his fly and draws it out, digging in there and scratching and Kent turns over onto his knees and Dell gives him a look that freezes him and Kent remains there kneeling, his knees hard against the dry tub and with a sigh Dell whips out his cock and it just hangs there over Kent's head a minute and Kent's not sure why he doesn't move, but doesn't or can't, his knees pressed to the tub and Dell closes his eyes and inhales and that's it. He pissed on him.

He pissed all over Kent's goddamn head. That was it. He just pissed on his head and Kent tried to lower his head and Dell said, "No, no, you look up at me," and he just fucking took it. Kent closed his eyes and put his face up into the stream and it was hot and it stung, but he just took it. He just kept breathing. Just keep breathing.

Dell drank a lot. A twenty-four pack of Hamm's takes a hell of a long time to piss out. At least there was so much piss it was pretty watered down.

Kent looked at his own boy. He was just a boy, a little kid. He didn't know anything. He didn't know shit. He saw him and his friends, they strut some. He saw them puff out their chests. They wore the top buttons of their shirts undone. Kent didn't know where they picked that up. They were just kids. They were older than he was by the time Dell split, but they were still just little kids and Kent just wanted to protect his boy's strut. His boy didn't know yet that someone somewhere would knock that strut out of him at some point. Whether it was some young beauty, or the toothpaste factory, or whatever it would be. Someday that strut of his was going to fade if it wasn't sent crashing somehow first. But he saw it and it was precious. How could he not protect it? It was like an egg or a baby bird. Kent watched him tumbling out there, going full speed and tackling, running in the sunshine, coming up with grass clots stuck in his helmet. And he knew he had to let him go, but it was hard for him. It was something he had to figure out with his boy, with his wife, with himself. He'd carry the kid around on a pillow if he could.

So, where the fuck was Ronnie? Ronnie had never even met his wife. Twelve years they'd been together.

He'd visit Nana and sometimes give in to asking, "Alright, you heard from Ronnie?" Nana would hem and haw then say "It's been some months, but she came through. Found me with the girls one Friday morning eating pie like we do and Ronnie pops in scratching and doesn't she just make all the old gals feel special" and what a riot Ronnie's working them all up to, before she drops it.

"Seems Joe and her have got a line on some kind of sure thing. It's a can't-lose situation, they just need some startup funds and soon as six weeks she'll be back around with everyone's investments paid back in double." That's right. She'd double all their money.

And Nana was squirming, "Oh, Ronnie honey, now you just leave the old gals alone now, won't you, honey?" But Ronnie it seemed just couldn't help herself, all that festering away in some rotten little motel room somewhere, she'd just been charging up. Her charm had been recharging and she'd have story after story and line after line. She had a whole routine worked out. She'd have the rhythm and the pacing just perfect and there was Nana sitting with her cream cheese crumble cake and hazelnut coffee, so pleased just to show off her new cakepan when Ronnie had to barge in with some kind of strong-arm robbery all the golden gals didn't even recognize was happening.

So Nana told Kent, "Yeah, I saw your mother some months ago, but I can't say where she is now. And I can't say when we'll see her again."

Nana always felt so bad for Ronnie, always said Ronnie just never did have an easy time with anything. Now she didn't need her own children giving her a hard time. And Kent didn't know if it was him she couldn't admit all this to or herself. But they had to feel ashamed for her, Ronnie, because she didn't have the decency to be ashamed of herself. What was she, two-hundred and fifty pounds? Three hundred? Hardly any teeth and half-bald and she thought her greasy tangles covered it up somehow, those stupid rhinestone sweatshirts and disgusting tights, the constant scratching.

Kent thought Will just wasn't realistic about her, about her and Kent. Will tried every couple years, to get through to her in some way. He was friendly to Joe, that was nice. Will wanted to be a bigger man than all that. She was his mom and he thought he could somehow help her, even if that meant just being there for her in some way, some way he could never ask her to be.

Will was always her favorite. He was too young to remember. He didn't know what it was like. He knew how things had turned out, but he didn't know. He didn't remember Dell.

Will considered maybe there was a long moment in every life, a lapse of awareness one made one's self at home in, a long moment that only later could be recognized as a suspended fiction. Years maybe, the better part of a life even, but it couldn't last forever. Not only childhood, though it might often happen to adults for the sake of their children, and it was for this reason that throughout most childhoods it happened, a fiction held to. A fiction which could not be seen through without stepping away from, and which could not be stepped away from without being seen through. The piercing of this governing fictive tissue was freedom. That's what people meant, Will figured, by freedom. The need to seek new grounding had to take priority over understanding that need.

Pulling up under the streetlights, Kent paused, back at the main street. He drove past Ronnie's house again, "Fuck it. Let's not stop."

Will recognized no one gathered outside Sluggo's.

"Shit, the motel?" Kent said.

"Yeah, back that way."

"Shit."

Security dribbled a man's head against the wall outside The Cave. Returning to catch glimpses of downtown's same rituals and familiar goings on without him, it was as if Will had returned to find his own life some years ago being played out now by actors.

Out front of The Carroll Motel a French-Canadian couple choked on constant sobs of laughter in the light of the Coke machine. The man sang "You Can't Always Get What You Want" with the wrong inflection and the woman sang it back to him correctly, only to have him sing it back to her wrong again. In shorts and slippers, underdressed for the night air, they fluttered about the small front area in their hilarity, like birds trapped in a chimney. The automatic sliding doors were locked and the couple never noticed their pacing kept triggering the doors, attempting to pull open, to bang and fail.

Kent crashed through between them. He rang the doorbell at the night window, immediately clicked a quarter against the glass shouting, "Hello, hello."

A young man approached with a dignified scamper. Will couldn't see him too well behind the thick glass, but instead saw his own smeared reflection hunching behind Kent. From what he could make out, the new man working the front desk had taken on the exact affectations of the guy who used to work the desk. The man, visibly annoyed by the drunk couple, quickly realized Kent was not with them, but remained curt. Were these guys trained in the subtleties of this attitude, the tightened stance and sneer of a stink only they were prone to catch waft of, or did this attitude blossom somehow from circumstances specific to the job? He never looked up at Will while Kent quickly filled out the form for the room. Neither Kent nor the clerk said anything specifically rude, but Kent's clipped tone with the man embarrassed Will.

The man gestured for them to come inside. Kent nodded a moment but didn't move, decided he'd prefer the night air, thanks. Long hallways always made him nervous. The man shrugged, pointed the way around the building.

As Kent turned from the window with a key, the French-Canadian man, carefully handling its bladed edges, tried handing Kent a beer can ship as a gift, insisted it wouldn't fit in his luggage. After a couple curt waves, Kent accepted the ship and throwing his head back, knocking a hip to one side, he forced the ship through the small opening at the top of the plastic trashcan. He turned and walked off toward their room. Will, a few steps behind him balancing his plastic bags, took the brunt of the couples' groaning and shrugged an apology. The man surfed it out of the trash, shouting behind them that Kent had twisted it and he'd cut himself on its edges.

"Trash!" the man called out behind Will. "Look at the monster-faced trash, even his nice dress up clothes he gets muddy across his back! Trash!"

Will didn't acknowledge that he heard him, kept walking, never turning around. The brothers walked a long lap around to the back of the building. Kent never turned back to the shouts behind him. They entered and walked down a long hall. Will had walked it before, that last night before leaving town, almost the entire way back up to the front of the building.

Kent opened their door and held it open for Will with his knee. Kent's deep sigh wrote up a quick contract for silence. Will nodded his signature approval as he passed. Kent followed behind him closely. He let the door fade closed before Will found the light-switch. They stood in complete, blind darkness.

Will froze. Kent traced the walls with open palms. A cold tickle ran up his spine at the feel of the wallpaper ribbed in slim stripes of mellow fuzz and a tacky grip. Will, feet planted, lifted an arm slowly to shoulder height, to dot a mirror or a picture frame's surface with a single fingerprint. Kent knocked on ahead, bumping past Will.

Will had a flashing vision of the rest of each of their lives spent stumbling in this unfamiliar dark room together, unable to find the light-switch, unable to stop looking for it. Giving up and turning back they'd be unable to find the doorknob. They'd topple every object. Their eyes would never adjust to the darkness. Nudging over and over into the definitions of the corners, they'd each eventually crash their own inner-circuitry one crushed toe at a time.

If one of them did end up with the cool brass of a lamp in his grip, following it to its base, running its cord to the fangs at its end, he'd realize it wasn't plugged in. That would begin the search for the outlet, same as the search for the light switch had begun, but bringing them both down to their knees. They'd run their palms along the walls just above the floor, reaching back into tight turns behind beds, dressers, desks, and nightstands, the shapes and locations of each, they would both have to retain by memory.

Goddamn it. Unbelievable, Gus thought to himself, scooting his hips across the corner booth and slunking down against the far wall. Sometimes it's hardest to believe the things that have happened the most often, Gus thought to himself, and quickly made a point to repeat that to himself. Maybe a poem would grow out of it later.

He expected Mel would probably stay at Nana's for a while. It'd be a couple days before she started calling maybe, before she realized he'd left. Maybe she wouldn't call. He had never claimed to not be a coward.

The parking lot through window grime, shades of gray and densities of dirt, another parking lot through another window. Another blistering steel grill, another flat field of heat. Another asshole pig in command, another half dozen dead-ends waiting on him.

Goddamn it. But the girl had found him. Another application.

APPLICATION FOR EMPLOYMENT

APPLICANTS MAY BE TESTED FOR ILLEGAL DRUGS

DATE HIRED

PLEASE COMPLETE PAGES 1-5 and attachments

DATE 9/18/08

Name Shelley   Gus   Joseph   Maiden
     Last   First   Middle

Present address 2878 Westnedge Ave #2C   Stone Claw Grove   MI   48508
     Number   Street   City   State   Zip

How long   **Social Security No.** 318 – 28 – 7241

Telephone (___) none

Position applied for (1) line cook
and salary desired (2)
(Be specific)

How many hours can you work weekly? 40

Employment desired ☐ FULL-TIME ONLY   ☐ PART-TIME ONLY   ☒ FULL- OR PART-TIME

TYPE OF SCHOOL	NAME OF SCHOOL	LOCATION (Complete mailing address)	NUMBER OF YEARS COMPLETED	MAJOR & DEGREE
High School	St. Patrick's Academy	5900 W Belmont, Chicago	4	diploma
College	Northern Illinois University	DeKalb, IL	1	none
Bus. or Trade School				
Professional School				

HAVE YOU EVER BEEN CONVICTED OF ANY CRIME?   ☒ No   ☐ Yes

If yes, explain number of conviction(s), nature of offense(s) leading to conviction(s), how recently such offense(s) was/were committed, sentence(s) imposed, and type(s) of rehabilitation.

PLEASE PRINT ALL
INFORMATION REQUESTED
EXCEPT SIGNATURE

APPLICATION FOR EMPLOYMENT

DO YOU HAVE A DRIVER'S LICENSE? ☐ Yes ☒ No

What is your means of transportation to work? Bicycle

Driver's license
number S103-9279-1262 State of issue MI
Expiration date 6/11/10

☐ Operator ☐ Commercial (CDL) ☐ Chauffeur

Have you had any accidents during the past three years? How many?
Have you had any moving violations during the past three years? How many?

OFFICE ONLY

Typing	☐ Yes ☐ No	_____ WPM
Personal Computer	☐ Yes ☐ No	PC ☐ Mac ☐
10-key	☐ Yes ☐ No	
Word Processing	☐ Yes ☐ No	_____ WPM
Other Skills		

Please list two references other than relatives or previous employers.

Position Graphic Designer

Company Self-employed

Address 2878 Westnedge Ave #2C

Stone Claw Grove MI 48508

Telephone (616) 576-1999

Position Sales Rep

Company Micor Media Group

Address 3343 N Pulaski

Chicago IL 60618

Telephone (773) 255-5582

EMERGENCY CONTACTS:

NAME_____ PHONE_____ NAME_____ PHONE_____

ADDRESS_____ ADDRESS_____

CITY/STATE_____ CITY/STATE_____

An application form sometimes makes it difficult for an individual to adequately summarize a complete background. Use the space below to summarize any additional information necessary to describe your full qualifications for the specific position for which you are applying.

I first cooked for the army when I was 18 years old. The army promised to teach me lots of things and it did, but cooking has

probably proved the most useful. I've cooked in every conceivable situation and setting. I can make anything work.

I am confident in my abilities, but I am not cocky and understand my place here. I will execute your vision as directed

to its greatest potential. I've been doing this a long time. You won't have any problems with me.

PLEASE PRINT ALL
INFORMATION REQUESTED
EXCEPT SIGNATURE

APPLICATION FOR EMPLOYMENT

MILITARY

HAVE YOU EVER BEEN IN THE ARMED FORCES? ☒ Yes ☐ No

ARE YOU NOW A MEMBER OF THE NATIONAL GUARD? ☐ Yes ☒ No

Specialty Infantry   Date Entered June 66   Discharge Date Nov 69

Work
Experience

Please list your work experience for the past five years beginning with your most recent job held.
If you were self-employed, give firm name. Attach additional sheets if necessary.

	Name of last supervisor	Employment dates	Pay or salary
Name of employer The Shhh... Club Address 1336 Ravine Rd. City, State, Zip Code Stone Claw Grove MI 48508 Phone number (616) 654-2119	Norman Okalani	From Jan 02 To July 08	Start $6.50/hr Final $11/hr
	Your last job title Kitchen Manager		

Reason for leaving (be specific) New management made big changes

List the jobs you held, duties performed, skills used or learned, advancements or promotions while you worked at this company

List the jobs you held, duties performed, skills used or learned, advancements or promotions while you worked at this company.

I ran the kitchen, developed the menu, invented the recipes, handled all the ordering of food and scheduling of kitchen staff. I was hired as a cook, but soon had many more responsibilities put on me.

I enjoyed it very much, felt very much at home there, worked hard and cared very much for the place until the owner, who had become a good friend of mine, passed away suddenly and his son decided to change the business greatly.

Name of employer Address City, State, Zip Code Phone number	Name of last supervisor	Employment dates	Pay or salary
		From	Start
		To	Final
	Your Last Job Title		

Reason for leaving (be specific)

List the jobs you held, duties performed, skills used or learned, advancements or promotions while you worked at this company.

May we contact your present employer?	☒ Yes ☐ No	
Did you complete this application yourself	☒ Yes ☐ No	
If not, who did?		

HAPPY HOUR AT THE LEGENDARY SHHH...

Norman had to reach into the toilet to grab the drowned mouse. Wallace crumpled his starched work shirt on the bar, checked his wristwatch against the bar clock. The clock set twelve minutes fast, he arrived at The Shhh... earlier than he'd left the forest preserve.

The past was the past and Wallace could remember it all well enough, and he had it mastered. All up to him how he chose to understand the past, make sense of the future. But the future, it was the future that was just killing him. It was just fucking killing him. He couldn't for a second remember what he ever thought his future would be.

The dark room swelled into focus. A wide mirror propped up against the far wall, its top coming up waist high, doubled the bottom rungs of a steel ladder set on a plastic throw leaning against it. The room's dimensions difficult to gauge, assorted purples over black, Wallace momentarily mistook the thin-coils-of-glue swirling bare-wood board above the mirror as a window looking out over a sand-blown parking lot.

Wiping his hands dry on his suit pants, Norman stepped behind the bar, sighed, nodded hello. He leaned his substantial girth forward, nodded again. Wallace ordered just a ginger ale, please. The piece of pink paper left sitting on the bar, Norman picked it up and folded it, stuck it in his coat pocket. He set the ginger ale down in front of Wallace.

Goddamn fish-stinking Russians would come around for vengeance. He knew it, just couldn't anticipate what their angle would be. Should've asked Will for protection, his sister started it. Norman reached for his cigar.

Wallace took a sip of his ginger ale, reached for his wallet. Some kind of dirty dance club, don't touch anything. All the dirty pictures he ever had in his mind, sprawling flesh, a smorgasbord or buffet he would gorge on, at times. But fantasy couldn't really work like that, flipping across things, sampling. He resented those desires. Figured without focusing on a specific, a fantasy became just a fantasy of whatever all the dirty sprawling pictures all had in common, a lowest common denominator of filthy beauty. And that's no kind of beauty or fantasy. That might, by definition, be an exact contradiction of fantasy. Fantasy needs to be specific in some way, not diluted, to overwhelm you and if it didn't overwhelm you, it wasn't a fantasy at all. He dropped a dollar on the bar, hoisted a leg outward to scoot up onto a stool.

At the bend at the end of the bar, Norman sat perpendicular to Wallace, lit his cigar.

With some effort, Wallace managed a pained squint-into-the-sun sort of grin. Silent, he bobbed his head back and forth, rolled his eyes. Could really only accept his situation as it was. Little had been his choice, but he couldn't continue to play dumb. He cleared his throat. Mostly, really the hardest things he'd ever had to do had been continuing some stuff that had already been started.

Norman shook his head, stood up, took a few steps and poured himself a bourbon while standing. He lifted the bottle to Wallace to offer a drink. Wallace shook his head. "I don't really party," he said.

Norman nodded, spun back around the bar to his stool. He took a sip from his bourbon. It was all pretty simple really. The sustained experience of being a stunned orphan, tasks and administrative chores, paperwork mazes to navigate, in a daze most of the time, a kick in the gut occasionally wakes you, simple, like a dumb animal.

Attempting to hide it, Wallace sniffed both of his hands with a quick gesture. Had some time before work and didn't know where to go, but his neighbor, he didn't exactly tell him what kind of club The Shhh... really was. He thought it was some kind of supper club, thought he'd eat some supper. He'd left those good ribs on the counter.

The two men, who had never seen each other before, sat together, alone, said nothing.

I do feel, Norman sighed, I do feel like a dumb animal. Death the abstract, death the concept was no preparation for the drawn out dumb confusion of death the specific. Really a wonder any living ever gets done, all this death in waiting everyone has to clean up after, account for within themselves, all the bureaucracy and social existence.

Wallace stood up, moved around the perimeter of the room in straight-legged, purposefully loping steps. Decorative steel moldings, sculpted sperms chasing eggs, sat stacked, un-hung next to a pile of large bolts. "Why?" was no real question, but still maybe helped to moan it. Jesse kept saying that: "Why?" Everything all so unnecessary and wrong, unreal and reckless, why?

Norman watched Wallace as long as he could without turning his head, sipped from his bourbon. Right after his dad died, Norman had started wearing this old coat of his around, a coat Rich hadn't worn in years.

Wallace sauntered over to the stage. Hand on hip, sipping his ginger ale, he admired the karaoke machine left set up from the night before. He nodded, *Yeah darling go and make it happen. Take the world in a love embrace. Fire all of your guns at once and explode into space.* He grinned and snorted, dropped his head.

Norman spun his stool, did not hide watching him. Vague as death must be, so too life. At least death carried some charge, an urgency for meaning, meaning in the immediate, the perpetual seemingly meaningless immediate.

Wallace smirked and waved, embarrassed to have drawn attention to himself. Everyone always all had the best of intentions. He cleared his throat.

"Your machine over there?" Wallace said.

"Yep," Norman said. "Yep."

Head down, without a word, the girl Wallace had met in his hallway earlier that afternoon walked quick across the far wall of the bar and straight out the front door. Surprised, Wallace looked to Norman.

"I must say," Norman continued, nodding with satisfaction, "it truly is the best karaoke machine I have ever heard, hands down."

"Yeah?" Wallace said.

"Oh yeah," Norman nodded. "Yep. And I have sang through a few of those in my time. But no other machine I've come across sounds like that one."

Wallace nodded, took a sip from his ginger ale. "And what," he asked, "makes one karaoke machine better than another?"

Norman chuckled. Right after his dad died, he started wearing that old coat of his around. He remembered it from when he was a kid and they first moved to Stone Claw Grove from Hawaii and it was cold. Norman wore it for those first couple weeks right after Rich died.

"Well, I'm sorry to ask," Wallace smiled. "I'm embarrassed to be so naïve as to have to ask, but I, well, I guess I never really thought about it before, that one karaoke machine might be any better or worse than any other one."

Norman stretched, cracked his neck. "My friends," he began, "they don't know why they sound so much better on my machine than on any other. They figure it's just if they're here, they've been drinking a lot. They're comfortable."

Wallace nodded. "Context," he said.

"Right," Norman said. "That's what they think, context."

"Makes sense," Wallace said. "It's just an illusion, a matter of confidence, they all just think they sound better singing."

"That's what they all think," Norman said.

Wallace took a sip from his ginger ale. Who could say really that most people didn't always all have the best of intentions? Wallace had emptied the pantry with food, filled two garbage bags for Jesse.

Norman took a sip from his bourbon. He didn't believe in an afterlife or not. The distinction was too simplistic, not really even interesting and hardly offered any comfort regarding a man, Rich, who lived totally indifferent to such concerns. Rich had quiet humility and quiet pride, his withdrawn demeanor and regard for order, but then these outbreaks, bursts or flights of goofiness and abandon, that mystery man that seeded that egg that became him.

"What is it, then?" Wallace said. "Makes the world's greatest karaoke machine?"

"Well," Norman said, "context, that's not it."

He looked Wallace in the eye and Wallace held his gaze a

moment, nodding casual. Wallace really just could not, for the life of him, remember his future. He had walked Jesse to the car. Jesse complained he was cold.

"The secret is pretty simple," Norman said. "It's just a matter of time and a little bit of discipline, knowing the gear."

"Oh yeah?" Wallace said.

"Reverb," Norman said.

"Reverb?"

Norman nodded. "Reverb," he said.

Wallace looked around the room. "Well, okay."

"You know what reverb is?" Norman asked.

Wallace shook his head, shrugged. "Reverb, it's like an echo? Makes it so you sound like you're in a big hall?"

Norman nodded. "That's right," he said.

"And," Wallace asked, "that makes it so someone sings better?"

"The DJ here set it up for me. What it does is, that short echo effect, makes it sound like you're in a big room."

"Uh-huh," Wallace said, nodding. Norman looked at him. Wallace sipped from his ginger ale and cleared his throat. Never seeing someone again, never touching them or smelling them or hearing their laugh again, meaningless really, compared to having ever known them.

"Well, what that does is, it covers the mistakes a little bit. Gives the singer a little bit of wiggle room," Norman said.

"And this is the best karaoke machine in the world because it has some of that reverb?" Wallace asked. He had driven to the forest preserve outside of town, stopped the car.

"Not only that," Norman said.

"The DJ also helped me," Norman continued. "Marked two knobs on the sound mixer, one for the microphone level, how loud the singing is, and the other for the level of the backing tracks."

"Oh yeah?" Wallace said.

"So," Norman continued, "what that does is, there's these little lines he drew there on the sound mixer and of course some people are going to sing quieter or louder than some other people, but mostly people sing quieter if the song is quieter and louder if the song is louder. So it's by no means a perfect system. You have to be there and work it to really make it perfect. But, think about it."

Wallace nodded. "Okay," he said.

"If that mix isn't right, and a lot of places they don't take the time to do this, but it doesn't matter, if that mix isn't right, you might hit every note perfect like Judy fucking Garland perfect, right? But it won't sound good. Still doesn't sound good if the music is too loud and you can't hear the singing or if the music isn't loud enough and the voice sounds weird and loud or the person might become self-conscious and not sing with the full force of their voice to correct it and that sounds weird too, holding back."

Wallace smoothed out his work shirt crumpled on the bar, nodded. Don't say goodbye to anyone. Jesse was confused getting out of the car. Said he wanted to go back home, needed to know how his stories ended.

"But," Norman said, "the right mix, some reverb, the reverb gives the singer a little wiggle room, a little room for error, voila."

Norman pinched his fingers in front of his lips and blew a kiss in the air. So one day he wore that coat of his dad's that his dad hadn't worn in years out in the rain.

Wallace shifted his weight. "Well," he said, "I see you're really into this."

Norman shrugged. "I don't know," he said.

"I really thought," Wallace said with a chuckle, "that's all real simple stuff you're talking about to make it better. Just setting it up right."

Norman sipped from his bourbon and nodded. So one day he wore that coat out in the rain and didn't think anything of it, and then later, only after having come in from the rain and his clothes began to dry, did the scent of his dad's old cologne from when he was a kid hit him.

"I really thought," Wallace continued, "I really thought you were about to tell me about some clever tricks you had."

"No, not at all," Norman said. "Not at all."

"Really very simple, isn't it?" Wallace said with a wide

grin. He had hugged Jesse, then pulled away quick when a sob broke the surface. He didn't look back at Jesse when he walked around to his side of the car and got in. It's all really very simple.

"It really is," Norman agreed, smiling. "Just set the levels right, the right amount of each thing. Give yourself a little wiggle room. It really is all very simple."

Wallace thought he'd sure like to sing "Gimme Shelter" if not "Sympathy for the Devil."

Norman lit a cigar. He hadn't smelled it in years, his dad's old cologne from when he was still a kid. Most of his life had passed and then all at once there it was from that old jacket he'd worn out in the rain. His own new sweater, underneath the coat, had absorbed the smell.

Wallace looked to the bar clock. Jesse had kept pulling on the door trying to get back into the car, calling his name, "Wallace!" Wallace watched him in the rear view mirror as he pulled off, standing in the mud, two garbage bags of food in his hands. Wallace looked to his wristwatch. Had to get to work, eat first.

"The real money, though," Norman said, "I'll tell you. The real racket what I want to get into, you know what it is?"

Wallace shook his head. "No, what?" he asked.

"Producing the karaoke backing tracks, man. You can get a little home studio on your personal computer now. Just make it sound just like the original. Think of all those karaoke machines, right? What's the one thing they all need?"

Wallace nodded. He had been fine out in the woods as a kid. Just about that same age Jesse was now. Jesse would figure out how to play with himself.

Acknowledgments

Special Thanks to Mairead Case for the close reading and thoughtful notes, Zach Dodson for the sweat and hours that made this possible, and Donna Kinsella for the keys to the hideout.

Thanks also to Kristin Aardsma, Sam Axelrod, Megan Baker, Devendra Banhart, Edgar Bryan, Jennifer Buffett, Matt Clark, Jim Garbe, JDK Goodman, Mark Maxwell, Caroline Picard, Joe Proulx, Robert Ryan, Chris Strong, Dee Taira, Mayo Thompson, and Jonathan Van Herik.

And thanks to the SAIC Writing Department, especially Jesse Ball, Mark Booth, Ann Calcagno, Liz Cross, Mary Cross, Janet DeSaulniers, Matthew Goulish, Michael Meyers, and Beth Nugent.

And Yo to my enablers: Bobby, Theo, Mike, Nate, Paul, Todd, Victor, Naomi, and Sam.

About the Author

Tim Kinsella (born 1974) Libra / Chicago / Joan of Arc band